I0780982

Their War
INVI WRIGHT

Editing by: Amy McNulty

COMPLETED WORKS
by Invi Wright

***

<u>STANDALONE</u>
The Nanny

Aine

Lord of Dread

<u>THE FEMALE SERIES</u>
The Female

Her Males

Their War

Chev's Mate

Queens (coming 2025)

<u>THE CURSED KINGDOMS SERIES</u>
The Cursed Kingdom

The Shattered Kingdom (coming 2025)

TRIGGER WARNINGS CAN BE FOUND ON:
inviwright.com

THANK YOU

***

The largest thank you possible to my husband. You gave me the confidence and support to pursue writing, and none of this would be possible without you.

Also, to my Patreon subscribers: Inesha Thompson, Ashleigh Drew, Bhavini, Emily Anne, Leilani S., Melissa Childs, Marlo Burto, Jack Lewis Landsmen, Dakota Lane, Gigielle, Lone Hornbech Bünger, Maria Anderson, Artemis Howl Landsmen, Lora Beth Farmer, Vanessa Turpin. Your support is the sole reason I'm able to do this, and I can't properly convey in words just how much you mean to me. I hope you enjoy this story!

Chapter One

CHARLOTTE

A STRAND OF Aziel's black hair falls into his eye as I step into his office, and he mindlessly pushes it away before rubbing at the stubble covering his jaw. He didn't shave this morning as usual, and he took just enough time to yank on a black shirt and pants before heading downstairs to meet with the Wrath war generals.

Aziel's black eyes flash to me before he turns to the general standing on his left.

There are three in total surrounding Aziel's desk, two with their backs to me. I eye their matching brown uniforms and dark, cropped hair as they lean forward and peer at the large map covering most of Aziel's desk.

The war generals are intimidating, and I wrinkle my nose as a wave of their power hits me. It doesn't affect me as it once did—thanks to Aziel's bond—but I can still sense it.

I've been around these men before, but this is the first time they've ever been inside our home. Aziel summoned them after Rock's announcement, and they've been working on a plan to dismantle Mammon for hours now.

As the Queen of Greed, Mammon holds a lot of power, and

Aziel believes that if she steps back, Valentine and the ogres will follow.

"These mountains are too wide for most demons to teleport across. Mammon's soldiers will have to climb or go around, and it should slow their journey," the Wrath general on Aziel's left says. I think his name is Raum, but I'm not positive. All of Aziel's generals have traditional demonic names, and I struggle to remember them.

Raum's arms are covered in black tattoos, and they shift on his skin as he leans forward and taps on an area on the map. I can't see it from here, but I assume he's pointing to the mountains he just spoke about.

The other generals bend their necks to get a better look, the men tall even for demons. It makes sense that Aziel would have large men as his generals, the Wraths placing significant value on physical strength.

The general directly across from Aziel shakes his head.

"Unless they cut through the lava fields," he says.

I raise a brow at the mention of the lava fields. Silas took me there on a date once, and I couldn't imagine anybody, let alone an army, trying to navigate them. The area Silas took me to stretched as far as the eye could see, and the heat was unbearable. We were a good distance from any of the actual lava, too.

Aziel purses his lips, his eyes darting along the map before he picks up a red marker and circles two spots.

"This is where I want your units stationed," he says, capping his marker.

I take a second step inside the room.

Another wave of thick power fills my lungs, the scent intense. Aziel and his generals exert more than necessary, which I assume is a stress response.

It would've brought me to my knees before, and I'm glad for

the immunity Aziel's bond provides.

"That leaves the valley unprotected," Raum points out.

I shift my weight from foot to foot, waiting for Aziel's inevitable anger over having a weakness in his plan so publicly acknowledged. Instead, to my complete surprise, Aziel uncaps his marker and redraws the second circle.

"This better?" he asks.

Raum grunts, and I take that as a *yes*.

I didn't realize Aziel could be so collaborative. He was always so commanding in his meetings with Levia, the King of Envy.

Aziel runs a hand through his hair before waving over Rock. The shadow enters the room and slides past me, his dark robes swishing around his hazy form, before slotting himself between the Wrath generals standing across from Aziel.

"Remind me what areas you overheard Valentine discussing," Aziel says.

Rock clears his throat and takes the red marker from Aziel's hand, and I lean forward to try and peek at what he's doing. I want to know what's going on.

My movement seems to draw Aziel's attention, and I freeze as he frowns and turns in my direction.

"Charlie, why don't you go see if Silas needs help?" he suggests.

The hidden meaning behind his question isn't hard to discern. He wants me to leave. A small part of me wants to argue and insist I be allowed to listen, but instead, I give a slight nod and exit the room.

I can feel Aziel's stress through the bond, and I'm sure my lingering is distracting.

Silas's office door is cracked open, and I peek inside to see him sitting behind his desk on his laptop. He looks stressed, and he pushes the sleeves of his brown sweater up his forearms as his black eyes dart over his computer screen.

I'm sure he's aware I'm here, but he doesn't look up as I push open the door the rest of the way and take a few steps into the room. We haven't discussed where things stand between us after our night together, but now's not the time to approach that conversation.

My palms feel clammy as I reach his desk and tap on the surface, quietly asking for his attention. Silas purses his lips and finishes typing something on his laptop before turning to me. His gaze is intense, and the muscles under his sweater shift as he waits for me to speak up.

"Yes?" he eventually asks.

I square my shoulders in an attempt to look larger. Confidence is key. That's what the shifters always say.

"Is there anything I can do to help?" I ask.

Silas sinks his teeth into his full bottom lip, the man probably thinking hard about how best to shut me down. After a moment of tense silence, he shakes his head. His computer pings, and immediately, his attention on me is lost.

"One second," he says, his eyes darting over the screen.

My males are frantic to prepare before Mammon strikes, the unknown putting them on high alert, and I don't take offense when he turns away from me entirely and begins to type out a response.

"Fuck," he mumbles, pinching the bridge of his nose when another message comes through.

Silas looks borderline panicked, and I peer around the computer to try to peek at whom he's messaging. The demons typically prefer to conduct business in person, finding it easiest to teleport to whomever they need to speak to and get the conversation over with quickly, but I think everybody's hesitant to leave me here alone.

Especially after everything that happened with Shay.

"What's going on?" Gray asks, stepping into the room.

He's dressed casually in a white, boxy T-shirt and loose-fitting jeans, and he tucks a strand of his wavy, black hair behind his ear before wedging his phone between his shoulder and cheek so he can use both hands.

Gray exudes sex, even when he's not trying to, and blood rushes to my cheeks as he ducks and kisses my temple. He quickly straightens back up and continues forward, and I try to hold back my frustration as he walks around Silas's desk to peer at the screen.

Why didn't I do that?

Silas leans to the side so Gray can better see, and I hope I look like I know what I'm doing as I follow Gray's actions and walk around Silas's desk.

Gray moves to the side as I come up behind him, and he lifts his arm so I can squeeze underneath and fit between him and the back of Silas's chair. My pulse races, and a sense of accomplishment flows through me until I look at the screen and realize everything is in the demonic language I still can't read.

Gray's jaw clenches as his eyes dart over the words. He's visibly pissed, and he pulls his phone away from his ear and hangs up on whoever's on the other end of the line.

"Is Valentine still refusing to meet with us?" Gray asks, wrapping his arm around my waist and resting his hand on my belly. "Should I pay her a visit?"

Silas shakes his head, rejecting the idea without consideration.

"Valentine wouldn't take sides in a war without protection," Silas says, shutting his laptop lid. "I'm sure Mammon's got soldiers stationed throughout Lust. We're not getting in without a fight, and we don't have the Wraths to spare right now."

I clear my throat, drawing their attention.

"Why is Valentine's involvement such a problem? Aren't the

sex demons notoriously weak?" I grimace and glance up at Gray. "No offense."

He only shrugs, his lips twitching before he bends and presses another kiss to my cheek. The affection is making me flush, as I'm unused to it after so long of Gray ignoring and avoiding me.

I'm not sure where his sudden change in attitude is coming from, but I hope it's here to stay.

"Weak, yes, but also filthy rich," Silas explains. "Mammon doesn't need Wrath to support her plan if she has the kingdom of Lust on her side, and this provides her the perfect opportunity to take ownership of the females and take down Wrath at the same time."

Silas's computer pings again, and he opens it up before sighing and slamming it shut. He's going to break it if he keeps doing that.

"Why does she hate Aziel so much?" I ask, struggling to wrap my brain around this. "And why is Mammon fighting so hard to lead the female project?"

I'm glad so many people want to help, but Mammon's desire to start a war over the females seems extreme. Especially when she and Aziel are working toward the same goal. All they're doing is prolonging getting help to the females, which directly contradicts her claims of wanting to do something as quickly as possible.

Silas groans. "*Fuck!*" The word is a favorite of his today. "Whoever takes control of the Seekers and oversees the rehabilitation facilities will have eyes in every realm. With the blessed breeds backing it, there's not much anybody can do. It's an advantage, and Mammon would rather risk everything than let Aziel have it. He killed her oldest son a while back, and she's been harboring a grudge ever since."

Gray begins to pace the room, his long legs carrying him

smoothly from the door to the desk before spinning and repeating the action. I shove my knotty, brown hair behind my ears and glance between the two men, unsure where I fit.

I want to help, but I don't know where to start.

"What about the shifters?" I ask. "They might help."

Gray shakes his head, shutting down my idea, before grabbing his phone to make another call.

"They've made it clear our alliance is for the females only," Silas says. "Shifters aren't ones for politics. They have a goal and will support whoever will get it done with the least hiccups."

"It doesn't hurt to try to talk to Kato, though," I argue. The shifter alpha has proved helpful many times already. "He might be willing to supply some men to help us take over Lust."

Silas shakes his head, copying Gray's earlier rejection.

I clench my fists, struggling to remain calm.

It doesn't hurt to ask, and Kato values loyalty more than they give him credit for. He's obviously going to put his people and the females first, but he knows we're in it for the right reasons.

Or I am, at least.

I'm sure Aziel's excited with the possibility of getting eyes in the other realms, the man always a good three steps ahead of me, but at least he's ensuring things are getting done the right way.

Mammon was doing the bare minimum, but Aziel is spending his own money and resources on this. That's got to count for something in the eyes of the shifters.

I jolt, alarmed as Aziel comes storming into the room, his generals in tow. Gray hangs up his phone as he waits to see what Aziel has to say, and I take a step closer to Silas to put some space between me and the intimidating Wraths.

Aziel turns to me, his eyes cold as he approaches. I know it's not me he's angry at, and I wipe my sweaty palms against my pants as I step forward and meet him halfway. He gently grabs my cheeks with a quiet sigh, holding them in his large palms before kissing me.

The kiss is urgent, and it's over sooner than I'd like.

"We need to leave," Aziel says, cutting straight to the point. "Rock is staying behind to look after you. Do not leave this house," he adds, giving me another kiss before turning to Silas and Gray.

Both men scramble to collect their things.

"What do you mean you're leaving?" I ask.

Why can't they work from here? My males have never had to leave at once like this, and the sudden change has a sense of panic rising within me. I grab Aziel's hand before he vanishes, wanting more explanation.

How long are they going to be gone? Are they leaving Wrath? What if the ogres get them? Or Mammon? My breaths turn shallow, and I squeeze Aziel's hand to keep him here. I just got all three of them back. What if they get killed?

Questions swirl in my mind as I stare wide-eyed between my three males.

The generals along the far wall are watching, but I don't care. I know they already think lowly of me.

Aziel crouches to my level, and our bond squeezes. The heightened emotions between us make it feel like a stress ball.

"We won't be gone long—a few hours at most," Aziel explains, curling his fingers around mine and removing my hand from his wrist. "We don't know where Mammon's planning to strike, and we need to be alert. My generals and their troops are splitting up to protect some of our weaker points, and Gray, Silas, and I need to ensure the other units are secure."

His breath tickles my ear as he leans in closer, and he pushes my hair out of my face with a gentle smile.

"Do you feel that tightness in your chest? Our bond?" Aziel

waits for me to give a jerky nod before continuing. "As long as that's there, I'm alive and healthy. And if I'm okay, so are Gray and Silas."

Gray and Silas come up alongside me, caging me between them. I can practically see their hesitation as they shift their weight between their feet, exchanging looks over my head before Gray bends his knees and joins Aziel at my level.

"I love you, Charlie, and I'll be back soon," Gray promises.

I choke back a gasp. I didn't think I'd ever hear him say those words again.

"I love you, too," I hurry to say.

Gray beams, his eyes darting toward Silas. The fate remains silent, but he smooths his hand down my spine in a comforting gesture.

Aziel steps back and grabs Gray and Silas. He waits for them to release me before teleporting, and the generals disappear the moment my males are gone.

"They'll be fine. They've prepared for this," Rock says, stepping into the room.

He's still covered in blood, the red splattered all over his dark robes. I eye him as he approaches, trying and failing to see through the haze that covers his tall frame. I hope it's not his blood I'm looking at.

There's a lot of it.

I still haven't determined if it's his or not when he pulls me into a tight hug. My face is pressed against a surprisingly muscular chest, and I don't hesitate to wrap my arms around Rock's midsection and squeeze.

I missed him.

"I'm sorry you're stuck being my babysitter again," I mumble into his robes.

Rock shrugs and pulls back, his hands squeezing my biceps

before he spins and leaves the room.

"Come on," he urges, waving for me to follow. "We're going to get Asmod's body back from the shifters."

I shiver. I haven't seen the King of Lust since I stabbed him, and I prefer it that way. I'm aware Aziel brought Asmod's body back to the shifter lands after rescuing me, but the shifters hid him away and have been secretive about it ever since.

Rock slows and peers back at me, and I shake my head with a quiet sigh before rushing after him. Aziel explicitly told us to remain here, but I should've known better than to think Rock would follow those orders.

He's proven time and time again that he's willing to ignore the wishes of my males.

My lips pull into a wide grin as Rock turns the portal on, the man able to do so surprisingly fast. This must be a standard mode of transportation for the shadows.

Rock has it ready in seconds, but he turns to me before stepping through. He eyes me head to toe, his lips curled down at the corners.

"You know you're pregnant, right?" he asks.

I run a hand through my hair. I figured as much.

All three of my males have been sniffing me, and Aziel is always grabbing at my belly. Even Gray's taken it upon himself to continually tell me about all the baby things he's good at doing.

"They haven't told me yet," I admit.

Rock shrugs, unapologetic. "Oh, sorry." He gestures for me to step through the portal. "Don't tell them I told you, then."

I snort and step into the blue haze.

We've got a body to find.

Chapter Two

CHARLOTTE

ROCK WRAPS AN arm around my waist as I lead him toward Kato's cabin, the shadow silently helping to keep me from stumbling over any tree stumps as I walk at a breakneck speed.

"I doubt Kato's going to hand Asmod over without a fight," he says.

He cranes his neck to peer around me and take everything in. Unlike Aziel, he respected the rules the shifters put in place during his stay here, and he never traveled farther than a few steps outside of our cabin.

A shifter, Turk, appears on the trail. He's a hulking, bearded man with long, dark brown hair and leathers at least two sizes too small. He has an axe thrown over his shoulder, and he raises a brow as I lift an arm and wave.

He once panicked and ran over to teach me how to chop wood when he saw me almost cut my toe off trying to do it myself. It was the only interaction I've ever had with him, but it was friendly.

"Morning!" I greet him, hoping he doesn't say anything about the shadow on my left.

Turk's eyes dart between Rock and me. He looks to be contemplating his next move, and after a second, he shakes his head and looks away.

"I didn't see anything," he says.

I chirp. "Thank you!"

Rock chuckles as I grab his wrist and tug him forward. We're almost to Kato's, and I don't want to risk being seen by a shifter who will force us back to the cabin. Most of the bear shifters treat Kato's word as law, and he's made it well known that Rock isn't allowed to wander around the lands.

He can be here, but he needs to stick to our cabin.

Kato said the same thing about Aziel, but nobody was particularly keen on enforcing that decree. I have a feeling they knew it wouldn't go over well, and since Aziel wasn't hurting anybody, they chose to let it go.

"Why do you think Kato's keeping Asmod's body?" I ask. "And why does Gray need it, anyway?"

Rock pauses, his arm tightening around my waist before he catches himself and continues forward as if nothing happened. The action immediately puts me on edge, and I slow to a stop before spinning and planting myself in Rock's path.

"Tell me," I order.

He grimaces, his eyes darting around.

"Not now, Charlie. I'll tell you later."

I press my lips together, debating, before turning back around. Now's not the time to push for answers, but I expect them soon. The second we have a moment to breathe, I'm going to be dragging him into my office and demanding he gives me the information I want.

I refuse to be kept in the dark any longer.

The bond in my chest aches, Aziel yanking on it every other minute. I have a feeling he knew the second I left Wrath, and I'm banking on him being too busy to come and get me. I'm sure he intends to drag me back home the moment he's free, though, and I pick up the pace with that thought in mind.

He's going to kill me, but I'm hoping he'll be more lenient if I return with Asmod.

I'm not going to be some trophy wife who sits around looking pretty while they do all the work. Being physically weak doesn't mean I'm incapable of helping, and I trust Rock to keep me out of harm's way.

My males need Asmod's body for reasons I'm still unaware of, and if there's an opportunity for me to get it back, I intend to take it.

My speed-walking shifts into a slight jog when Kato's cabin enters my line of sight. He's not usually home in the middle of the day, but his mate, Emily, almost always knows where to find him.

Rock follows me up the steps of their cabin, but he positions himself in front of me before I reach the door. My males will be pissed when they discover I've come here, but I hope the fact that Rock is with me and it's for business keeps their anger at bay.

I'm doing this for Gray.

I wring my hands together before raising a fist and knocking on the door.

"Emily?" I shout through the wood. "Kato?"

On the odd chance he's home, I want him to know it's me. Sometimes he likes to ignore visitors, the shifter grumpy when interrupted while spending alone time with Emily.

There's a loud crash from inside, and I step back as the door is pulled open.

Emily stands on the other side, her black hair pulled into a tight ponytail and her leathers wrapped tightly around her body. A wide smile spreads across her lips as her eyes land on me. I straighten my spine, the memories of our last time together flashing through my mind. Regret settles deep in my chest, and I glance at the ground when it grows too intense.

I can't believe I allowed myself to go as far with her and Kato as I did. The memory of her kissing me while she pleasured Kato makes me wince, and I fight the urge to frown as I look into Emily's black eyes.

She spreads her arms, looking like she wants to hug me, but I shake my head and shut it down. My males would be devastated to know I touched her, and I intend to keep our contact to a minimum.

Her smile falls, but she quickly recovers.

"Charlie!" Emily clears her throat when my name comes out rough. "Are you okay? I've wanted to speak with you so badly, and I can't apologize enough for what happened. I never intended to cause you or Kato any pain, and you have no idea—"

Rock interrupts her.

"Where is Kato?" he asks.

He sounds pissed, but I don't blame him. Rock's probably worked for Aziel longer than I've been alive, and I'm sure he wasn't pleased to learn what happened between Emily and me.

I clear my throat, preparing to speak, only to flinch when Aziel yanks our bond again. He's getting more aggressive with it, and it's growing painful.

You'd think he'd be gentle with me, considering I'm carrying his child, but that's not his style.

"There's no need to apologize," I say to Emily. "We don't mean to be rude, but we're in a hurry. Do you know where Kato is?"

Emily grimaces and shakes her head.

"He's with Chev and his brother, Vont, on a hunt. They'll be gone for another day or two. What's wrong? I'm sure I can help," she says.

I turn toward Rock before shifting my attention back to Emily. That's not ideal.

"We need Asmod's body," I admit.

Emily stills. It's not the response I'm hoping for.

"Kato's very protective of it," she says. "He doesn't believe the power should be absorbed, and he plans to obtain a witch to destroy it."

Okay, so I most definitely should've taken the time to demand Rock tell me why we need Asmod's body. Absorbing power? I've never heard a damn thing about that, and I turn to Rock for answers.

He shrugs.

"A royal demon's power can be absorbed through bloodline," Emily explains, seeing my silent confusion. "Asmod's got dozens of children, and the one who claims his power has the best claim to the throne. Many are looking for it."

I blink and suck in my cheeks as I take in that information.

"So, Gray wants to absorb his dad's power? How's that even work?" I ask.

Emily recoils, and I cringe. Maybe I shouldn't have said that in front of her, but I figure it's pretty obvious why we'd want the body.

Rock shoots me a sharp glance as Emily adjusts her hair tie. Her scent doesn't affect me as it did before my bond with Aziel, and I find myself staring at her in a new light.

She's beautiful, as all succubi are, but I'm no longer drawn to her. I feel gross for having been intimate with her and Kato.

Aziel yanks on the bond, and I gasp and double over. Rock darts toward me, curling his arm around my waist to keep me on my feet until Aziel lets go. I feel Aziel's panic as he does so, the demon probably not realizing his strength until he felt my pain in response to it.

"Please, Emily. It's an emergency," I plead. "We don't have time to wait for Kato to return."

Emily purses her lips, her head rocking back and forth as she takes in my request.

"Valentine's taken over Lust," I say, hoping that sways her.

Emily lived in Lust long before she met Kato, and given how she's feeding almost exclusively on him, I'm assuming she's considered broken just as Gray is. Valentine's not known to be kind to the sex demons who are different, and I'm willing to bet Emily's had more than a few not-so-pleasant run-ins with the other succubi.

Emily's nose crinkles, and she lowers her chin to her chest with a quiet sigh.

"Kato's going to kill me." She shakes her head as she mumbles to herself. "Come on."

I grin, happy with the win, as Emily spins and shuts her front door. Her movements are jerky as she looks around to ensure nobody's following, and she seems nervous as she leads us down the porch and to the right.

Kato won't be pleased about this when he gets home.

We slowly make our way to the part of the pack lands even I'm banned from venturing into. The trees are thinner here, making it hard to hide as we weave around buildings and avoid running into other shifters.

Eventually, we come upon a hatch in the ground. I'd never have noticed it if Emily hadn't pointed it out, and I kick at the leaves and vines growing over the top of it until I spot a wooden handle.

"It's going to smell," Emily warns.

Rock and I exchange glances as Emily bends and rips open the latch. The stench hits me even as I breathe through my mouth, and I'm thankful Aziel's stopped yanking on the bond as I step away and heave.

What the fuck?

The putrid scent is sickening, and I put some needed distance between me and the hatch while Rock drops to his knees and peers inside. How is this not affecting him? I know dead bodies smell, but this is horrific. I take a few moments to settle myself before lifting my shirt to my nose and approaching the hole.

It's too dark for me to see inside. Naturally.

"What's in there?" I ask, my words muffled through the fabric of my shirt.

Rock and Emily pointedly ignore my question.

"Stay here," Rock instructs, dropping inside.

Emily's quick to follow, and, for once, I listen. I have no interest in getting anywhere near the hole, where I'm pretty sure more than a few rotting bodies are being kept.

I don't want to know why the shifters have a hole filled with dead people.

I keep guard as Emily and Rock argue. Their voices are muffled, making it impossible to know precisely what they're saying, but they seem to figure it out as they eventually emerge. Rock comes up first, quiet grunts slipping from his lips as he drags Asmod's body behind him.

Emily climbs out afterward, and she seals the hatch with a loud huff.

I stare at Asmod's naked corpse.

He looks exactly as he did the day I killed him, not so much as one piece of him decomposing. He should be a puddle of soup by now. How is that possible?

"He won't decompose until his power's been extracted." Rock grunts as he and Emily work together to pick up the body. "The only way to destroy it is through a witch."

Asmod's a large guy, and I'm sure he isn't easy to lug around.

Rock takes the head and shoulders while Emily grabs his feet. They make brief eye contact before lifting at the same time.

"Let's go," Emily says.

My cabin's on the opposite end of Kato's land, and Emily takes us the long way around so we aren't seen. We keep an eye out for any nearby shifters, desperate to avoid them. I don't know what they'd do if they caught us trying to sneak Asmod's body into Wrath, but I have a feeling they wouldn't be pleased.

I'm surprised Emily even agreed to help us, especially knowing what we intend to do with Asmod. I wonder if this is her form of an apology, but I don't ask.

We can probably expect a visit from an angry Kato when he returns and discovers Asmod's gone, but hopefully, he'll understand why I had to do it. He'd do anything to protect his pack, and my males are mine.

Wanting to make myself useful, I rush ahead of Emily and Rock to ensure our path is clear. Thankfully, it's empty, but I just about shit myself when a male shifter approaches the trail and begins heading toward me.

"Hello!" I shout.

The man pauses and gives me a curious side-eye. We haven't spoken before, and he glances behind himself to ensure I'm not greeting somebody else before clearing his throat and turning back to me.

"Hello, Charlotte," he says, greeting me.

"Where you headed?" I keep my voice loud, hoping Emily and Rock hear and step off the path.

The shifter male points behind me with a frown.

"Home. You aren't welcome to join me."

I recoil, shocked he'd say that, before awkwardly glancing at my feet. He and his mate probably heard about what happened between Kato, Emily, and me. It's nothing short of humiliating, and I have no idea how to respond.

The shifter shuffles past me, keeping a noticeably wide berth before he hurries down the path. I spin and watch him disappear, and I wait two minutes before making my way down it.

"He's gone," I whisper-shout into the woods.

Rock and Emily emerge a second later, and we continue forward.

Thankfully, we don't run into any more shifters, and poor Emily is panting when we finally make it to my cabin. I grimace as I watch her, worried I should've offered to help carry Asmod.

It's not like Emily and Rock would've let me, my physical strength sad compared to theirs, but the offer would've probably been appreciated.

Asmod's skull bounces off the floor as Rock drops him and hurries to turn the portal on.

"It's gone idle," he explains.

A second later, the blue haze has returned.

"You go first, Charlie," Rock says. "If your males have returned, I imagine they're lingering near the portal, and I'd like not to be beheaded today."

I grimace, already knowing Aziel's waiting for me. He coaxes our bond, urging me to return. A small part of me is complimented that he chose to remain in Wrath instead of coming here and dragging me back himself, but my panic outweighs that emotion as I stare at the blue haze.

He's going to be pissed. I clench my fists and square my shoulders, working up fake courage before stepping through the portal.

My eyes land on three angry males the second I'm on the other side.

Gray paces the hallway, his hair and clothing a complete mess, while Silas stands a few steps away with a pinched expression.

Aziel stands directly in front of the portal, his body so close that I have to come to a hard halt to avoid running into him.

"Is everything okay?" I squeak.

Aziel doesn't respond, instead grabbing my arms and pulling me into his chest. "You're an infuriating fucking woman."

He spins, seemingly preparing to carry me away, and I dig my heels into the ground to try to stop him.

"Wait!" I shout. "We have Asmod."

Aziel stills, but only briefly, before he hands me off to Silas. What the fuck?

Rock and Emily come stumbling through the portal with the body, but Silas wraps an arm around my stomach and lifts me into the air before I can explain what happened. I screech, trying and failing to break free as he carries me down the hallway. My anger reaches levels I didn't even know was possible as Silas takes me to the library and sets me on the floor.

"Silas!" I snap.

He blinks and steps in front of the door, blocking my escape.

Chapter Three

GRAY

CHARLIE FIGHTS AGAINST Silas as he carries her to the library, her gangly limbs flailing as she attempts to wiggle out of his arms. It's an action I'd typically find myself obsessed with, but it hardly registers as I spin toward Rock and Emily.

They step through the portal with my father, their arms full as they carry him through and drop him haphazardly on the floor by Aziel's feet.

Aziel stands only inches in front of the portal, refusing to let either of them enter our home beyond that.

Charlie lets out a loud shout, and I turn just as Silas rounds the corner of the hallway and disappears. I'm surprised by his quickness to leave. Silas is the nosiest of the three of us, and I assumed he'd be most eager to see what comes of this.

"Leave," Aziel hisses.

He's practically vibrating with anger, his body stiff as Rock and Emily stare at him. My eyes track their movement, the tightness in my chest growing at the sight of my dead father.

We were never close, but seeing his body isn't exactly fun.

Rock has the decency to look guilty, his hazy figure hunched forward in an attempt to appear small. He's the same height as Aziel, but you'd never be able to tell.

Emily doesn't carry the same timid position, the succubus appearing entirely unafraid in Aziel's presence.

I lick my lips, my mouth dry as Aziel senses my anxiety through the bond and rubs at his sternum. He steps to the side, attempting to block my view of Asmod, but I grab his arm and hold him in place.

I'm not some child in need of protection.

"I'll be taking my leave," Emily says.

Her eyes dart quickly between Aziel and me before she escapes back through the portal.

I've never really liked her, especially after what she and her mate did with Charlie, and I wonder if Charlie knows just how well Emily and I are acquainted. I've never been directly intimate with the succubus, but I've taken enjoyment in seeing her be passed around the den.

I'm sure she's seen similar of me.

"We got Asmod," Rock blurts out, pointing to the body on the floor.

Aziel sucks in a slow breath, his shoulders rolling back as he does one of his breathing exercises in an apparent attempt to remain calm.

I tighten my grip on his arm and pull him into me, hoping the touch helps him settle. Charlie's pregnancy is making him more possessive than usual, and Rock taking her on side missions to the shifter lands isn't helping.

My attempt to calm Aziel doesn't seem to do much, so I bury my face in his neck instead. He shivers as my lips graze the mark I left on him, and I kiss the scar before scraping it with my teeth.

Charlie cares for Rock, and Aziel can't hurt him. The shadow's made it clear his loyalty lies with her, and we can't punish him for putting her desires above our own. He's good to her, and he keeps her safe.

"Go," I warn Rock, jerking my head to the side.

He hesitates before nodding and leaving. He doesn't bother using the ring he stole from me to teleport as he shuffles past Aziel and disappears down the hallway, the action showing just how confident he is in his position within our household.

He's got Charlie's protection, and he knows it.

With the hallway now empty, I let my lungs deflate and bring my attention to Asmod. He's been stripped of his clothing, and I scan the stab wounds all along his neck and upper body.

What?

Aziel wouldn't have killed my father like this, the work too uncoordinated. It looks like the shifters have cut up and torn off large strips of his skin over some of the sloppiest stab wounds, the sight even more confusing.

I turn to Aziel just in time to see him grimace and give a subtle shake of his head. It doesn't take an expert to understand what's happened, and I appreciate the care he and the shifters have taken to cover Charlie's actions.

After seeing Asmod's body, it's obvious what happened, and I won't acknowledge the lie I've been told.

"Gray," Aziel says.

I feel disconnected from my body, and with a grunt, Aziel pries his fingers underneath mine to try to loosen my grip on his wrist. I struggle to do so, my brain slow to respond.

"Let's get this over with," he urges, nudging me toward Asmod's body.

I gulp, ignoring the shouting from Charlie that travels down the hall.

It sounds like Silas has taken her to the library, and I listen to her lecture Silas as I drop to my knees beside my father's body.

I'm glad she's not here to see this, even if I know she's frustrated by the secrecy.

I'm more than happy to face her wrath if it means she doesn't have to watch me steal the power from my father.

Aziel kneels beside me, offering his silent support as I place my open palm on Asmod's cold chest. I can feel the power swirling inside him, and I squeeze my eyes shut as I reach for it. I've always feared I'm not truly his son, and I'm slightly relieved when his power responds and begins trailing up my arm.

It burns, flames licking my skin and settling in my chest. Lust demons may not be known for their strength, but being of royal lineage made him stronger than most.

I adjust, the pain growing as my father's skin begins to lose its color. The pain moves to my torso before trailing down my legs, and it takes everything in me not to cry out. I clench my jaw shut to stay silent, breathing loudly through my nose.

"Gray?" Aziel asks, worry lacing his tone.

I can't respond, the fire burning my throat and clamping the muscles shut.

Aziel opens our bond without another word, giving me an outlet for when it becomes too much. I can feel his power within it, and I faintly recall the last time he offered himself like this.

It was when I went to the human realm to bring Charlie's belongings here, and I was furious to accept Aziel's handout.

A small part of me appreciates it and wants to take him up on the offer, but I hold back. I want to do this independently, and I hate to admit my body's too weak to take and hold all my father has to give. I'm still considered young for a demon, and I'm willing to admit I'm not particularly strong.

Absorbing all my father's power will kill me, overstuffing my body until it explodes out of me.

Still, I try.

My entire body burns, and I drop my chin to my chest when it becomes too much. I can't focus on anything beyond it, but I continue fighting Aziel's help as I curl my fingers into Asmod's cold skin. I can barely hear my shallow breaths over the sound of my blood rushing through my ears, and with a pained grunt, I begin funneling everything into Aziel.

It's too much, and a low cry slips from my throat as I admit defeat.

Aziel's lips meet my temple, his skin soft as he curls his body around mine and takes what I can't.

I'll take it back as my body adjusts, but that doesn't stop the crushing embarrassment from warming my cheeks. I'm not strong enough to take my father's position as the King of Lust, and this alone proves it.

Valentine could probably take his power with no problem, the succubus older and stronger than I am.

"Does it hurt?" I ask.

Aziel nods.

I'm not surprised. This power is different from what I get from feeding, pure and permanent. It's meant to be passed through bloodline only, and using the bond to let Aziel hold my father's power goes against fate.

We'll have to keep this from Silas.

I don't release Asmod until his skin's gone gray and his body's empty. Aziel continues to hold me as I stare into the unmoving eyes of the man who created me.

I'm barely listening as Aziel summons two shadows.

"Burn the body," he orders.

They turn to me, waiting for my confirmation before following through. I appreciate the respect, and I nod.

It's best that way.

The shadows quickly remove Asmod from the room, their

movements hasty. I'm sure Aziel isn't giving off the friendliest energy right now, the burning inside him probably irritating.

"The attack from Mammon was just a test," I say, eager to change the subject before Aziel gets it in his head that we should talk about my feelings.

Aziel takes a moment to respond, his body twitching as he struggles to adjust to the fire inside him. I also feel the heat, but the pain lessens with each minute. Asmod's power will eventually feel like an extension of myself, but Aziel will never find comfort with it.

It'll burn until it's returned to the bloodline.

My guilt grows when Aziel lets out a low grunt. I move to take the power back, not wanting to cause him pain, but Aziel closes the bond before I'm able to retrieve any.

We both know I can't, my body stuffed. I can barely contain what's currently inside me, the power unsteady as it searches for a place to live. One wrong move and it'll come exploding out of me in a dramatic display of death I'd rather not encounter.

"It's okay," Aziel promises, clearing his throat when his voice cracks. "We don't need you overextending yourself, especially not now."

I nod, grudgingly agreeing.

Mammon sent almost two hundred ogres to a small village on the outskirts of Wrath. They would've decimated the entire area if it weren't for Rock's warning, the shadow giving us just enough time to move troops into the lands.

She was probably hoping to distract Aziel and draw his attention away from a deadlier second attack, but the readiness of the Wraths had the ogres retreating almost immediately. We were too prepared for her to follow through, and I'm sure the woman is re-calculating her plan as we speak.

It won't be long before we see a real battle, though, and I'm dreading the deaths we're sure to have.

"We can't support both a war and the females," Aziel admits.

I hum, distracted as his arousal fills the room.

My father's lust has him aching in more than one way, a side effect of taking what doesn't belong to him. We'll have to keep this from Silas, too. He's too attentive not to notice Aziel's heightened arousal, and even if he tries to ignore it, the fates will know. Silas is rarely able to keep things from them, and the pain it causes him to try is nothing compared to the burn of my father's misplaced power.

Aziel clenches his jaw and throws his head back, his eyes darting down the hallway, where Charlie is still fighting with Silas.

"Do you enjoy being with me?" I ask.

Aziel's eyebrows furrow.

"Of course."

"You're not attracted to men," I say, shrugging.

Aziel snorts, finding humor in my statement. "I'm attracted to *you*, Gray. I like touching *your* skin and feeling *your* body on mine," he promises, grimacing as he pulls his erection into the waistband of his pants. "You're my incubus, and I love feeding you."

I smile. *Good.*

Aziel chuckles, clearly at my expense, before bringing his lips to my throat.

"Now, stop being so insecure," he whispers. "It's unbecoming for an incubus and the future King of Lust."

I shut my eyes, debating whether or not it would be inappropriate to remove my clothes and put him inside me. I lied when I told Aziel how long it's been since I last took a man. In truth, I haven't been fucked since before we bonded, and I'm desperate for it.

I'll die before I admit just how much I was holding out for Aziel, though.

He'd think me a lousy incubus.

"Your touch helps the burn," Aziel says, pressing himself against me. "Fuck," he continues, burying his head in my neck. "You smell so good."

His lust is thick in the air, and I hold my breath as I fight the instinctual urge to feed. I can't take any more right now. The fire in my lungs grows when I try, the pain amplifying until I'm convinced they're bleeding inside my chest.

I glance down the hallway one last time before getting onto my hands and knees and lifting Aziel's shirt. The tip of his cock is peeking out of the waistband of his pants, and I look up and meet his eye before sucking it into my mouth. Asmod's power already has him on the edge, and it only takes Aziel a few seconds to cum.

I swallow every drop he spills down my throat.

"I'm sorry," I say, wiping my lips as I pull back. "I tried to take all of it."

Aziel's eyebrows crinkle until he realizes I'm talking about Asmod's power, not his dick.

"Don't apologize," he orders, squeezing my hips so hard that the skin's sure to bruise. "You took so much, and when you get adjusted, you'll take the rest. You're going to be so strong, Gray. My strong, powerful incubus."

He licks up the side of my neck, tasting me.

"You're going to be the King of Lust."

I crane my neck, silently begging him to bite me, and I'm pleased when his teeth sink into my neck a second later. All I've ever wanted was his physical claim, and I preen as he pulls away and admires his mark.

"We should go calm Charlie," I say.

She's still yelling at Silas.

Aziel grimaces, and I stand up and wait as he readjusts his clothing. I can't help but smile, pleased with this side of him. My little virgin is finally experiencing intimacy.

I should buy him a memento to help him remember this year.

I wipe at my mouth to ensure all traces of Aziel are gone as I make my way to the library. Charlie sounds like she's on the verge of tears, but I don't blame her. I'd be hurt if I were in her position, but I don't regret it.

I didn't want to see her absorb my father's power.

She spins to glare at Aziel and me the moment we step into the room, her lips curled into an angry snarl as she plants her hands on her hips.

"We need to talk," she says, stealing the words straight from my lips.

She's angry, but I can tell it's nothing compared to Aziel's fury as he nudges me aside and walks into the center of the room. He's beyond pissed she left Wrath, and I'm sure he's got his entire lecture already planned out.

"Yes, we do," he agrees.

He glances at me, a nervous glint in his eye before he levels his expression. I cross my arms over my chest, struggling to ignore the burn in my veins as I step to the side and sit on the arm of the nearest chair.

I hate when Aziel stresses over me.

"What'd you do to Rock and Emily?" Charlie asks.

I don't like her worrying about the female she was intimate with, and I purse my lips before glancing at Silas. He seems to be feeling the same way, the muscles on the side of his jaw tensing.

"Well?" Charlie urges when nobody jumps in to explain.

She wipes her palms against the sides of her pants, her face reddening as she glances between the three of us. Silas moves toward me, his nostrils flaring when he's only a step away. I pretend I don't notice as I stare at Charlie and Aziel.

"Where are Rock and Emily? And what happened with Mammon?" she asks. "I understand you guys are protective, but I have a right to know what's going on. You can't forcibly remove me from every situation you don't like."

Aziel runs a hand through his hair, and the bond between us squeezes as he begins to pace the room. His legs carry him down an aisle of messy books before he pauses at the end and turns back around.

Charlie glares at him every step of the way.

"Emily went back home, and I imagine Rock has done something similar," I say.

Aziel storms back toward us.

"Do you have any fucking idea how dangerous it was to leave?" he asks. "We need to protect our people and keep clear heads now more than ever, and it's impossible to do that when you're off frolicking with Rock every time we turn our backs."

Charlie winces, and I intervene before Aziel says something he regrets.

"We want you to have your freedom," I say, approaching and cupping her cheeks, "but you need to understand you're a weakness for us, one everybody knows about, and now's not a good time to leave unannounced. Mammon attacked a small village today—one full of quiet farmers and large families."

Her lips smoosh together, and I enjoy the sight as I tilt her face toward mine.

"The ogres would've slaughtered every man in the village before taking turns raping and murdering the women and children," I continue. "That's nothing compared to what they'd do if they got their hands on you."

Silas clears his throat and joins me by Charlie's side. Aziel continues to linger near the bookshelves.

"We will make a better effort to loop you into our plans and include you in decisions, but we expect the same from you," Silas says. "No more running off."

Charlie gnaws at her bottom lip before nodding.

"Would you have stopped me from going to the shifter lands and getting Asmod if I'd told you about it beforehand?" she asks.

Aziel scoffs. "Yes."

He stalks forward, and I release Charlie's cheeks as he comes to a halt in front of her. She clears her throat, refusing to back down. I enjoy seeing her stand up to him, and I step back to let her.

A piece of me wants to fight her battles for her, arguing with Aziel on her behalf, but I know that's not my place. Charlie has her own voice, and I need to let her use it.

"And that's why I don't tell you things," Charlie says. "You don't respect my opinions." Her gaze travels toward Silas and me. "None of you do."

I don't like being lumped in with Aziel and Silas, and it takes everything in me to remain quiet.

Aziel narrows his eyes. "What opinions have you provided?"

"I can ask Kato if he'd be willing to help you take Lust back from Valentine," she says.

I faintly remember her bringing up that idea in Silas's office, and she's correct that we shut her down. Silas shifts his weight from foot to foot, probably also remembering.

"Kato's a good man," she says, "and I think he'll understand where we're coming from. He won't be happy when he discovers we've stolen Asmod's body, but I don't think it will affect his decision. He knows we're trying to protect the females for the right reasons."

Aziel sucks in a deep breath, practicing one of his breathing exercises. Silas's lips twitch as he recognizes the action, and I fight back a smile as I subtly nudge him in the side.

"Very well," Aziel says through clenched teeth. "I'm meeting with my generals tomorrow to discuss Mammon. You're welcome to join, and I'll take you to see Kato after."

Charlie beams, and her gaze darts toward Silas and me before she lifts on her toes and kisses Aziel. I'm pleased, and I cock my head to the side as I watch Aziel wrap her in his arms and deepen their kiss.

The scent of his arousal fills the room, but he's smart and pulls away before it grows too intense.

This will be a problem until I can take all my father's power, but I trust Aziel to be smart and keep himself under control.

He's sure got a lot of practice.

"What'd you do with Asmod?" Charlie asks.

Aziel sticks his face into Charlie's head and inhales, probably smelling our baby.

I glance at Silas. After seeing the body, I understand why he's so weird about the situation with Asmod. Killing a demon royal upsets the balance, and the fates will react. He's pointedly trying to remain in the dark.

"Gray absorbed his power, and we burned the body," Aziel says.

The bond in my chest tightens to an uncomfortable level, but it's nothing compared to the burn. Charlie glances between Aziel and me, an odd glint in her eye before her attention shifts toward Silas.

It seems I'm not the only one concerned about the fate.

I don't like keeping secrets from Silas, from any of my mates, but it must be done.

"Absorbing my father's power helps strengthen my claim to Lust," I say, moving the topic along. "We need to find a way to get in and overthrow Valentine, and the sooner, the better. My father implemented a council several hundred years ago, and we'll need to win them over."

Aziel paces the room, lost in thought, before he returns to Charlie and touches her belly. I don't think he even realizes what he's doing, and I wince as Charlie cocks a brow. He's being too obvious.

"What happens once you overthrow Valentine?" Charlie asks.

Aziel slips his hand underneath her shirt and palms her bare stomach, and Silas seems to lose interest in the conversation as he turns and gets to work organizing his books.

"Once Gray takes over, he'll pull support from Mammon," Aziel explains. "We can't financially support both a war and the females, and Gray taking over Lust should give us the money we need to protect our people and continue with our plan."

Silas perks up at the mention of Wrath's finances.

"Don't promise her that," he says. "We don't know enough about Lust's wealth to guarantee anything. It's just speculation."

Charlie runs her hands through her hair, looking stressed.

If Lust doesn't have the money we think it does, Aziel will choose to protect his people over helping the females. The blessed breeds will shift support to Mammon, so it's not like the females will be entirely abandoned.

Still, it's not ideal.

"And you'll wait for me to talk to Kato before you try overthrowing Valentine?" Charlie asks.

Silas sucks his cheeks into his mouth as Aziel nods.

"I'm coming, too," Silas decides. "I want to be there when you speak to Kato."

Charlie nods, looking nervous, but she visibly perks up when Silas steps forward and pulls her into his arms. He's been distant with her, at least emotionally, but I'm pleased he's warming up.

Silas seems to notice how giddy Charlie gets, and a timid smile spreads across his lips before he ducks and kisses her.

"Don't worry about me, Charlie," he says. "I can control myself."

Aziel mutters something about returning to work before leaving, but I linger behind. I want to watch Silas and Charlie.

"I'm sorry for yelling at you," Charlie whispers to Silas.

He holds her shoulders before sliding his hands down her waist.

"I'm sorry I forced you into the library," he apologizes. "Even if it was dangerous, I'm glad you were able to secure Asmod's body for Gray."

Charlie squeezes him, and Silas snorts before squeezing her back. The pressure on her lungs makes her squeak, but she seems pleased.

I am, too.

"I love you," she blurts out.

Silas releases Charlie, a tight-lipped smile spreading across his face.

"Will you help me finish organizing my books?" he asks, ignoring her words.

Even I cringe hearing that, but Charlie smoothly brushes it off as she nods and makes her way to the nearest pile of books.

Chapter Four

AZIEL

CHARLIE TUGS ON my arm, and I slow my pace.

The burning from Asmod's power courses through me, making it hard to focus on Charlie as much as I typically do. I've had to partially close our bond so she doesn't feel my pain, but I can tell by her occasional glances that she can tell something is wrong.

I smile down at her, hoping to soothe her worries.

Gray is strong, and adjusting to his father's power won't take long. He'll be able to take what I'm storing soon enough, and hopefully, my incessant arousal will leave with it.

Is this what it's like to be an incubus? Every touch from my mates sends me into overdrive, and all I can think about is burying myself inside them. It's distracting.

"What time will your generals be here?" Charlie asks.

It's obvious she's nervous about joining our meeting. Sometimes, I forget how new she is to all of this. While Silas and Gray take it upon themselves to join any of my meetings they find interesting, Charlie doesn't have that same level of confidence.

She doesn't think she belongs, but she does.

She's my bonded mate, and she's correct in saying she deserves to know what's going on. We can't keep her in the dark forever, and she's already proven to be an asset.

My males and I have become hardened over the years, and we struggle to empathize with others, but Charlie doesn't. She's been instrumental in helping us pull in the shifters, and I believe she'll continue to do so with the elves.

The blessed breeds have always been led by emotion, and they have a soft spot for Charlie.

With time, the Wraths will grow to care for her, too.

My people anticipated me picking a strong female, and I can tell resentment is brewing among them. I've been distracted since we acquired Charlie, first by hiding myself in the pits and now with Mammon and the females.

Many are angry with my decision to weaken Wrath by sharing our information about the female decline, but I'm confident they'll accept it with time. Wrath females are tired of being trapped within our borders, and they'll enjoy the freedom that comes with our new widespread regulations.

"Aziel?" Charlie says, drawing my attention. "What time is your meeting?" she repeats.

I shake my head as we round the corner to the dining room.

"Thirty minutes," I answer.

Gray is sitting at the table eating breakfast, and he looks up to watch as we enter the room. He looks pitiful at the large table alone, but I know he doesn't mind. He eats twice as much as we do, a habit he's picked up on after being forced to sustain himself through food instead of lust.

He beams at me before directing his attention to Charlie.

"Morning," he chirps.

We decided to sleep together last night, but Gray and Silas were gone by the time Charlie and I woke up. It seems Gray got hungry and came down to eat, and I can hear Silas puttering around in his library, the man desperate to get a few hours of organization in before our meeting.

I'm beginning to worry about him.

Gray looks giddy as Charlie approaches, and I lean against the doorframe to watch. He's dropped his anger toward her infidelity rather abruptly, but it seems genuine. I know he's been fighting with himself since I brought her home and she declared her promise to earn his trust again, and it seems he finally gave in after our intimate moment the other night.

Now that I'm feeling the burn and the arousal, I understand why.

Charlie could stab me in the chest and gouge out my eyes, and I have a feeling all I'd want to do is hold her. Incubi are desperate to please and soothe, and Gray is no exception. He craves peace, and I'm happy he seems to be finding it.

I absentmindedly rub my chest, feeling our bond.

Gray scoops up a forkful of his food, a traditional demonic meat dish, and holds it out for Charlie. She plants a hand on his shoulder as she leans over the table to accept it, but I can only focus on how her lips close around the fork and the way her throat bobs as she swallows.

I gulp, and Gray shoots me a cocky smirk.

Any guilt he seems to have harbored over the burn I feel from containing Asmod's power is gone, now replaced with glee at the near-constant arousal it forces from my body.

I'm not surprised.

It's not the first time I've been forced to live in pain, and I'm sure it won't be the last. My mates are always getting themselves in trouble, and it's only a matter of time before they do something stupid and my body pays the price.

"It's good," Charlie says, taking another bite of Gray's food before returning to me.

I like the way he makes her eat.

Charlie's prone to getting distracted and pushing her necessity for food aside whenever she's busy, but Gray keeps an eye on her intake. I should make an effort to pay more attention to how much food she's consuming, too.

It's embarrassing being the only male of hers who doesn't understand what her body needs to survive.

"You can stay and eat if you'd like," I offer, not wanting Charlie to be hungry because she feels she needs to remain by my side. "I can send a shadow to get you when my generals arrive."

I love Charlie, but I've lived thousands of years without a female. I can handle being alone for thirty minutes. She's safe in our home, especially with the additional shadows I've employed to monitor the grounds.

Charlie doesn't seem to have noticed she's being watched, and I fully intend for it to stay that way.

Silas wanders into the room and plops into the seat at the head of the table. Gray hurries to fix him a plate, and my bond with Charlie pulls as she finds enjoyment in seeing the two men interact.

I feel the same way, and I step farther into the room so I can rest my head on hers. My hands find their way to her waist, holding the skin while subtly sliding my fingertips over her belly. The scent of my child grows stronger inside her each day, and I'm obsessed.

Charlie laughs and places her hands over mine. "When are you planning on telling me I'm pregnant?"

The room freezes.

Silas glares daggers at me as I hum and move my hands entirely over Charlie's stomach. He doesn't want her to know until he's deemed it safe, but I can't stop myself from grinning as I press against her.

"After the twelve-week mark," Silas says.

Charlie snorts. "You think I wouldn't notice I haven't gotten my period for three months?"

Silas shrugs, still frowning.

"Silas is being dramatic," I say. "We can smell it almost immediately, but there's no guarantee it'll take. We read that most humans don't know until about five weeks in, so we figured we'd tell you then."

Gray sets a plate full of food in front of Silas.

"How do *you* know, Charlie?" he asks.

Silas and I agreed Gray could be the one to tell her, our incubus threatening our lives—and manhood—if we stole that moment from him. He hides his disappointment well, but I can still see it in the slight dip of his lips and tightening of his grip on his fork.

He can tell her next time.

"All three of you are always sniffing and touching my stomach," Charlie says. "Not to mention Aziel went from constantly talking about how he wanted to get me pregnant to suddenly refusing to utter the words. You've made it pretty obvious."

Gray scrambles out of his chair to get closer, Silas and his food long forgotten.

"I want to name it Gray," he says, shoving my hand out of the way so he can take a turn feeling her. "I know humans sometimes name their children after themselves."

There's not much to touch yet, the fetus too small to protrude from her skin, but it's comforting nonetheless. I like knowing my child is in there, growing.

"It's not even your baby," I tease Gray. "If anything, it should be Aziel."

I immediately realize it was the wrong thing to say, my bond with Gray yanking as he pulls his hand from Charlie's stomach. He refuses to look at me as he turns away, and I open my mouth to apologize, only to be cut off by an angry Charlie.

"That's a fucked-up thing to say," she snaps, spinning in my arms.

I didn't mean it like that, and I lick my lips as I try to find the words to fix the situation. Silas stands and moves to Gray's side, his anger reflected in how he places a hand on the incubus' back for comfort.

"It was a bad joke," I admit. "I'm sorry, Gray."

Gray refuses to look in my direction as he grabs Charlie by the hand and storms away. Silas isn't far behind, but he takes a detour in my direction so he can punch me in the arm. It hurts, and I flinch as his knuckles bury into my muscles.

I suppose I deserved that.

Having mates is more challenging than I thought it would be. I huff before following them out of the room, eager to proclaim my innocence. It's not good for Charlie to get so worked up, and Gray is prone to lashing out when he feels I've wronged him.

Gray and Silas turn left, heading into the library, and Charlie heads in the opposite direction toward our offices. I hesitate, debating which to go to first, before making my way to Charlie. My generals will be here any minute now, and I don't want her alone when they arrive.

They'd never dare harm her, but she's not their favorite person and I don't want her to pick up on any subtle hostility.

"Charlie," I call out as I round the corner leading to our offices.

Gray and Silas are moderately loud as they bicker, but it goes in one ear and out the other as I notice the blinking of the portal. A blue haze flickers before coming to life, and I realize in an instant that we forgot to shut it off after Rock and Emily returned with Asmod's body.

"Charlie!" I shout.

Panic laces my tone as I disappear and rematerialize by the portal, and Silas and Gray emerge just as Kato comes barreling through the blue haze.

The shifter towers over Charlie and fills the portal doorway, and my lip curls as he shakes out his brown hair and turns his bright green eyes toward my female. I don't hesitate to wrap my arm around Charlie's waist and yank her behind me.

Kato looks pissed, and my wrath pushes at me the second we lock eyes.

"Where is Asmod?" he spits.

Silas materializes behind me and grabs Charlie, pulling her farther away. My wrath continues to push at me, urging me to lash out in response to Charlie and Gray's danger.

Objectively, I know Kato won't hurt Charlie, but it's hard to see that right now. The shifter's children are the only ones I tolerate, and Kato knows better than to come to our home uninvited and angry.

"Emily gave him to us," Gray says, purring the woman's name.

He cocks his head to the side as he scans Kato, lingering at the shifter's waist. I know what he's doing, and Kato also seems to understand as he shakes his head and turns to me. The man's obsessed with his mate, and Gray's unspoken words aren't going to change his opinion of her.

"Give him back." Kato stalks toward me just as Chev comes storming through the portal, the man a spitting image of his father.

Chev pulls his leathers down his thighs as he glances between Kato and me, his eyebrows furrowing with annoyance. He doesn't look pleased, but he doesn't seem nearly as irate as his father.

He'll be a better leader than Kato, and I look forward to the day he takes over.

My eyes narrow as Kato continues his approach, and I shove the calm I'm receiving from my bonds aside as I face the two aggressive males standing in my home.

The two aggressive males who are only feet away from my pregnant female.

"You had no right to hoard Asmod," I say, struggling not to exasperate this situation further. We need the shifters on our side.

I stalk toward Kato, eager to move him back toward the portal. He's too close to Charlie, and it's making it hard to contain myself.

Breathe, Aziel. Breathe.

Another enters through the portal, this shifter moving fast, and without looking, I swing my arm to the side. I aim to break their trachea with my forearm, and I feel it crack as I make contact. My head moves slower than my limb, and by the time I lock eyes with the new intruder, I'm being knocked off my feet.

It's Echo. *Fuck.*

Kato tackles me to the ground, already in his animal form. I pry his snapping jaws away from my face as the room erupts into chaos, my focus on Chev as he shifts and lunges for Gray.

My incubus is the weakest of the three of us, and Chev's attack narrowly misses Charlie.

The sight of Charlie stumbling away has me seeing red, and I grab hold of Kato's fuzzy ears and use them for grip as I flip us around and smash his face into the ground. His nose gushes a thick stream of blood, and it spreads across the floor as I connect my fist with his temple. He immediately falls limp, but I don't care.

He should have known better than to come here in his agitated state, and Echo should have known better than to run through the portal during an argument.

Charlie screams as I land another hit on Kato, her shrill shout accompanied by a painful tightening of our bond as she rams her tiny body into mine. I move with her impact, allowing my body to tumble to the side so she doesn't bounce off me and get hurt.

I wrap my arms around her as we fall, one arm holding her head while the other covers her belly. She flails, but she quickly regains her footing before trying to pin me to the ground.

The lack of movement from Kato tells me he's out cold, but I doubt I killed him.

Still, I hope I cracked his fucking skull.

Silas rips Chev off Gray.

Blood seeps out of a deep wound in Gray's chest and pools onto the floor below him, and Silas casually throws Chev aside as Gray pushes his torn skin back together to speed up the healing process.

Charlie flattens her body against mine, her salty tears spreading across my neck as she cries incoherent words into my skin.

I run a bloody hand down her back, holding her to me as I sit up in search of Echo. The shifter female seems fine, thankfully, as she drops to her knees beside her unconscious father. He's shifted back to his skin form, the sight causing an uncomfortable tightness in my chest.

Shifters typically remain in the form they were injured in, and I must have hurt him more than I realized if he unconsciously returned to his skin.

Chev finally settles as he realizes we're not trying to fight, and he shifts mid-run so he can wrap an arm around his sister and throw her through the portal. She stumbles through it, and I watch silently as Chev grabs his unconscious father's ankles and pulls him through as well.

His eyes dart between the three of us, untrusting as he brings his family back to safety.

This has been a fucking morning.

Gray continues to pinch together his sliced skin as Silas shuts off the portal, his hand smacking roughly against the screen. When the blue haze is gone, signaling it's been turned off, I direct my attention to Gray.

He was wise not to fight back, his current predicament making him unpredictable. The last thing we need is for him to lose control of the power he's trying to keep held inside, and he shouldn't be exerting any energy until it's settled.

Silas ignores his torn knuckles as he drops to his knees next to Gray, but his eyes dart toward Charlie and me to ensure we're okay.

If this had happened before Charlie, I would've had to go to the pits, my anger impossible to control when I get too worked up. The bonds in my chest help calm me, though, weighing me down until it's impossible to stay enraged.

"Are you aroused right now?" Charlie asks, breaking me from my thoughts.

I grimace.

I like the violence, and Asmod's power makes my excitement hard to control. Charlie scampers off my lap with a disgusted grunt, her thigh pressing into my bulge as she moves. I shut my eyes and suck in a deep breath, trying and failing to keep my hips from jerking upward.

Fuck, that felt good.

Gray watches silently as Charlie stands and moves away from me, her face wet.

There's a sizable pool of blood where I fought Kato, the crimson liquid smeared from the center of the hallway to the portal from when Chev dragged him away.

"I suppose that means the shifters aren't going to be much

help with Valentine," Gray mutters.

Silas shakes his head, wordlessly silencing him. Now's probably not the best time to bring that up.

"Not after Aziel hit Echo," Charlie says, kicking my foot. "What's wrong with you?"

I run a hand down my face, not wanting to deal with this.

"I didn't know who it was," I argue. "She should've known better than to storm in here like that."

Charlie doesn't seem to care much for my explanation, and she roughly wipes her cheeks with the back of her hand before shoving past me and storming into her office. I move to follow, pissed with her dismissal of me, but Silas places a hand on the center of my chest before I make it far.

"Give her space," he says.

I frown, unsure what to do, before turning to Gray. He refuses to make eye contact with me, clearly still angry over my comment about Charlie's baby not being his, and I ensure his chest is healing properly before walking away.

My office is quiet, and I slam my door before changing my mind and cracking it open. Charlie or Gray might decide to come and visit me, and I don't want them to think they aren't welcome.

I sit in my chair and drop my forehead onto my desk.

What the fuck has happened to me?

Chapter Five

CHARLOTTE

I SHOOT AZIEL the frostiest glare I can muster as I step into his office. I'm a few minutes late to his meeting, thanks to Gray insisting I accompany him upstairs so he can change.

"We've got six units of men spread along the coast of the lava fields, and two near Black River," Aziel's war general, Raum, says.

He's the one with the tattoos who openly critiqued Aziel's plan yesterday.

Silas stands on Aziel's right, staring down at a map of Wrath spread across the desk. Four generals also stand around the desk, the three from yesterday and one I've never met before.

"We need more men at Black River," the general next to Silas says.

Gray places a hand on the small of my back and guides me forward.

I didn't dare approach yesterday, too nervous about being sent away to insert myself, but Gray silently urges me to walk around Aziel's desk and plant myself on Aziel's left. Gray nudges the general on the other side of me away before sliding in next to me.

There's not enough room for all of us to stand around the desk, and Aziel smoothly grabs my hips and moves me in front of Silas.

I do everything in my power not to show any sign of being anything less than completely in control as Silas takes a step away from the table and makes room for me. His front is pressed into my back a second later, and his breath hits my head as he peers at the map over top of it.

"We don't have more men to place at Black River," Aziel says, grabbing Gray next.

Gray beams as he's moved in front of Aziel, seemingly no longer upset about the rude comment about our baby not truly being Gray's. I'm pleased, and even Aziel smiles as he peers over Gray's shoulder.

The two generals Gray not-so-politely nudged aside return to their original positions.

"We can relocate a unit from the lower mountains," Raum says. "The ogres can't teleport, and Mammon won't exhaust her soldiers by making them climb them."

Aziel reaches around Gray to grab a red marker. His lips purse as he erases one of the roughly drawn red dots on the map and redraws it near what I assume is Black River.

I've never seen an accurate map of Wrath before. Plenty of speculated ones are floating around, but Aziel's done an excellent job of keeping the geography of his kingdom out of the public eye. My pulse races as I stare at what I know is a secret.

Aziel's kingdom is large, the shape somewhere between a rectangle and an inverted triangle with a tapered bottom and a flared top. A long mountain range runs down almost the entire righthand side, and a river runs straight up the center. It branches out about a third of the way through Aziel's kingdom, and Aziel has placed three red dots, which he's using to symbolize units of soldiers, along the very base of it.

At the top of the river and slightly to the left is a blue X.

Seven more are scattered throughout, but most are near the flared top. It's clear these symbolize the major Wrath cities.

Lava fields span the bottom left-hand corner of the map, and they curve up the side of Aziel's kingdom before tapering out about a quarter of the way up.

Silas curls his hand around my waist and gestures to the blank area below Aziel's kingdom.

"This is Mammon's land," he explains. "We're pretty closed off from her, thanks to the lava fields and lower mountains. The easiest way to travel from her land to ours is through the Black River and the lava field."

I nod, pleased he's taking the time to explain this to me.

Raum clears his throat, drawing Aziel's attention. I turn, surprised to see Aziel staring at me, a slight smile toying at the corners of his lips. My face warms, and I look back at the map as Aziel shifts his focus to his generals.

"We need at least two units in Hell," Raum says. "It's the closest city to Lust's borders, and if Mammon's going to funnel in troops through there, that will be the first city they attack."

I raise a brow, my lips twitching despite the seriousness of the moment.

"You have a city named Hell?" I whisper.

Silas chuckles, his chest vibrating against my back. "It's a nickname it was given a few hundred years ago. Several research facilities are there, and humans would often visit on missions before the female decline. They coined it Hell, and the name stuck."

Good to know.

Silas points to the flared top half of Wrath, where most major cities are located. "The Lust borders are here, but we aren't worried about an attack from them. Valentine may support

Mammon's fight, but the Lust council would never allow a war to be fought near or on their land."

"Silas is right," Aziel interjects. "The council would never agree to it."

Raum huffs but doesn't argue.

I continue to scan the map, happy to listen and be included.

I hope someday I'll get to travel through Wrath and visit all the cities. Aziel's been hiding me in his home, which is understandable for now, but someday, I'd like to explore. I've only ever been to the lava fields with Silas and the one pool bar with Gray, and I'm eager to see more.

"Where are we?" I ask.

Silas drops a finger onto the lowest city marker, the one closest to the river.

"We're just west of here," he says.

It's close to the lava fields, and I wonder if that's why it's so damn hot here.

Aziel, Silas, and the Wrath generals continue going back and forth, debating where best to allocate their troops. It's an intense conversation, and tensions rise the longer they discuss. Neither Gray nor I have anything to say, both of us silently listening.

With Mammon and the ogres working together, they outnumber Aziel three to one.

Aziel doesn't sound too concerned about the odds, claiming the Wraths are trained for this, and the tricky part is making sure the Wraths are in the right place at the right time. There are hundreds of small towns and independent family farms on the southern border of Wrath, and Aziel doesn't want Mammon targeting them.

Which is something he's convinced she would do.

She knows she wouldn't beat Aziel in a fair fight, and she intends to slaughter enough innocent Wraths that Aziel's people turn on him. They're already angry by his decision to take me as a mate, and she intends to use that to her benefit.

"Do you really think Gray taking over Lust will make a difference?" I ask as the generals take their final orders and leave.

Silas steps away, his warmth and comfort immediately missed. Gray takes that as an opportunity to wrap himself around me, his limbs pinning mine into place as he lifts me a few inches off the ground and carries me to Aziel's couch.

"Yes," Aziel says. "Gray will be able to pull financial support from Mammon, and she doesn't have the funds to start a war without it."

I sink my teeth into my bottom lip, absorbing that information as Gray sits down and pulls me on top of him.

"But we don't have enough men to spare to get into Lust," I point out.

Aziel nods. "That's our current predicament, yes."

There was a possible solution to that problem before Aziel punched Echo in the throat. My blood still boils as I think about his rash, violent decisions. We knew the shifters would be angry we took Asmod's body, but I'm confident we could have talked it out.

Kato's a reasonable man, and his mate was the one who helped us, after all.

"We should apologize to the shifters," I say.

Aziel hardly looks pleased with my decision. He purses his lips and turns back to his map, studying it while Silas silently does the same. The two are clearly in their element here, and Gray watches them as he shifts so he's lying on the couch with me tucked up against his side.

It feels good to cuddle with him again.

"At the very least, we should reach out to ensure Kato is okay," I continue.

Echo seemed to heal before the fight ended, but Kato was unconscious as Chev dragged him through the portal.

"What if he's dead?" My voice cracks, and Silas sneers.

"One can only wish."

I stiffen, and Gray ignores us as he trails a finger down my neck. He presses into the spot where he always said he wanted to mark me, and I can't help but shiver. I bonded with Aziel through sex alone, so I still don't have any physical marks.

"Shifters are hard to kill, and they're extremely protective. Chev wouldn't have left so easily, or of his own will, if Kato was dead," Gray says before clearing his throat and continuing. "I don't like how much you're stressing over the man you cheated on us with."

Guilt renders me momentarily silent, and the entire room grows quiet as I clear my throat and curl my fingers around Gray's shoulder.

"You have no idea how much I regret what I did," I admit. "And I promise you I only care for him as a friend."

Aziel's quick to interject. "He's a slimy man who allowed his mate to manipulate you so they could live out their dirty fantasies."

"He should've known better than to be aggressive around our pregnant mate," Silas chimes in. "Aziel's attack wasn't unprovoked, and I'm sure they'll realize it soon enough. They would've done the same thing if they were in our position."

Gray brings his mouth to my neck, his teeth scraping the spot he was stroking with his fingers only moments ago. "You're mine," he mumbles into my skin. "I won't let anybody take you away from me, and I'll kill anybody who tries."

I lick my lips, struggling to concentrate on the conversation at hand. I love Gray's possessiveness, even when it occasionally borders on obsessiveness. Silas and Aziel turn to face us entirely, the map long forgotten as they watch Gray playfully bite at my neck.

Right over the spot where he's always said he wants to mark me.

"You smell like Aziel, but I'm tired of you walking around without any physical signs that you're ours," Gray whispers. "I want to see my bite on your neck."

He sucks on my skin, and I gasp as I reach up and cup the back of his neck. I continually glance between Aziel and Silas, nervous Gray's doing this in front of them after everything we've gone through these past few weeks, but thankfully, neither looks upset.

Aziel looks like he's holding back laughter, and Silas watches with his head cocked to the side.

"You're touching my mark," Aziel says.

I release Gray's neck as I realize my fingers are resting on the mark Aziel put on Gray. Gray once told me a mark is sacred, only to be touched by the person who placed it. Still, Gray makes an odd noise in the back of his throat, grabs my wrist, and drags my fingers back to Aziel's spot.

Aziel chuckles, hardly looking upset. "I didn't say to stop."

I shiver, prodding more aggressively at Aziel's mark.

"What does it feel like?" I ask. I'm desperate to know.

"It feels good," Gray admits, still kissing my neck. "I've wanted it for a long time."

I lean forward and lick Aziel's mark, enjoying the way Gray's voice grows shaky. He lets out a quiet moan before pulling away and turning to Silas.

"I want to mark her," he says, asking permission.

Silas sinks his teeth into his bottom lip, glancing between Gray and me before nodding.

My heart fucking soars. Silas isn't ready to forgive me, at least not completely, but the fact that he's allowing Gray to mark me speaks volumes.

Gray pulls me onto him, encouraging me to straddle his hips. He's already hard, and I curl my fingers into the fabric of his shirt as he presses between my thighs.

Leaning forward, I sink my teeth into his neck. It's not hard enough to break the skin, but hopefully, it's just enough to hurt. Gray moans, and before I know it, my shirt's been pulled over my head and I'm on my back with Gray hovering above me.

Silas takes a seat on the edge of Aziel's desk.

Gray grins, his hair falling into his face as he peers down at me. He looks good, and I'm pleased Aziel and Silas have kept him well-fed. That's what he's always wanted, and I'm sure he's ecstatic to finally have them for himself.

"I want to fuck you," he whispers.

I gasp, wanting nothing more. I love Gray, love all my males, and I'm tired of the fighting and distance. I want things to go back to how they used to be.

Gray rolls his hips into mine, his eyelids fluttering shut as he feeds. Almost immediately, he winces, his nose scrunching before he subtly shakes his head and reopens his eyes. It's an odd reaction, but he's pulling down my pants before I can question it.

I lift my hips, my pulse racing and my chest heaving as Gray removes the remainder of my clothes and does the same to himself.

He's so fucking beautiful, with long, muscular limbs and smooth skin. His abs flex as he sits back and peers down at me, his gaze heavy.

I'm faintly aware both Aziel and Silas are watching as I reach for Gray, my hand shaking as I place the flat of my palm against his chest. His skin is warm, and he licks his lips as I trail it down his torso until I reach the trimmed hairs at the base of his shaft.

I've touched Gray plenty of times, but it feels different when

I know where it's going to lead.

"You shaved?" Gray asks, spreading my thighs so he can slot himself between them.

I shrug, my cheeks warm. "I thought I'd change it up."

Gray slides his fingers over my newly smooth skin with an appreciative hum. I've never had any complaints about my body hair, but I thought it'd be a fun change.

Aziel chuckles. "I suppose this explains why you were in the shower for so long last night."

His words are followed up with the sound of skin smacking skin, and I peer over at him just in time to see Aziel frown, rub his arm, and step away from Silas.

"Do you want me to shave, too?" Gray asks, glancing down at himself. "I don't know the human traditions for body hair."

I shake my head, resisting the urge to laugh. None of my males are hairless, but they keep themselves trimmed. "I like the way you keep it," I admit.

Instead of responding, Gray crawls down my torso.

My heart pounds as he settles his chest between my thighs and brings his mouth to my sex. The first touch of his tongue has my jaw going slack, and I weave my fingers through his hair as he moans and licks my clit.

Oh.

Gray pins my hips down, refusing to let me wiggle as he runs the flat of his tongue up the length of my slit. I bite the inside of my cheek, holding back a moan as I instinctively shut my thighs around his head.

Gray grabs the insides of my thighs and smoothly pulls them back apart.

He licks me until I'm shaking, on the very edge of release, before pulling away with a cocky smile. I pant, sneaking a glance at Aziel and Silas, and I just about choke on my spit as I take in their positioning.

Silas is on his knees in front of Aziel, and even though I can't see exactly what the fate is doing, I can put two and two together.

"Fuck." Aziel moans, cupping the back of Silas's head.

Silas only manages a muffled response, his head bobbing as Aziel pushes him further down.

"Do you like watching them?" Gray asks, capturing my attention.

There's a dangerous glint in his eye as he slides back up my body. He plants his hands against the couch on either side of my head as he slots his hips between mine. His cock presses against me, but he makes no attempt to slip inside.

I roll my hips, eager for it, but he tuts and pulls back with a quiet laugh.

Aziel chuckles, too, but his noise is cut off by a choked gasp. Silas gags, and Aziel tightens his grip on Silas's head before guiding him back down.

Gray presses the tip of himself against my entrance, and I bite back a moan.

"I love you," I whisper.

Gray brings his lips to mine. "I love you too, baby."

He's pushing inside a second later, and I shift underneath him until he places a hand on my hip to hold me still.

"Slow down, sweets," he says. "There's no rush."

Gray pulls back as if to prove his point, the few inches of him inside me sliding out until only the tip remains. He curses as he peers between us and watches me stretch around him, and I squeeze his waist with my thighs.

"Gray," I whine.

He's taking too much enjoyment in this, and his smile grows as he finally sinks the entirety of himself inside me. It feels so good, and tears fill my eyes as Gray's hips meet mine. He grunts when he bottoms out, giving me a moment to adjust before thrusting.

"I love you so fucking much," I cry, grabbing his shoulders to hold him close.

Gray buries his face in my neck, his mouth quickly finding the spot he intends to claim. His shoulders shift with every roll of his hips, and I slide my hands down his muscular back before finding his butt and pulling him in harder.

He understands my silent plea and picks up his pace, his hips snapping against mine as he reaches between us and finds my clit.

Gray applies the perfect amount of pressure before rubbing in quick circles, the man knowing exactly how I like to be touched. My back arches as my nails dig into his skin, probably leaving small indents that I'm sure will heal within seconds of me letting go.

"You're mine," Gray hisses in my ear. "This pussy is mine, and soon everybody will know it."

He brings his teeth to my neck to make his intentions clear, and I tilt my head back so he has more room. I want this, want his mark, and I'm ready for it.

"Please, Gray," I beg. "I want you to mark me."

Aziel curses, and I watch him grow rougher with Silas out of the corner of my eye. He fucks the fate's throat, and after a few seconds, he stills. Silas whines, a low, high-pitched noise, as Aziel cums, and it's not until now that I notice the movement of Silas's arm. He's touching himself while pleasuring Aziel.

Silas's back curls, and Aziel makes eye contact with me just as Gray grabs my chin and angles my face upward.

"I want my mark to be pretty," he mumbles.

A heavy amount of lust pours out of him as he sinks his teeth into me, the scent a good distraction from the pain. His smell doesn't affect me nearly as much as it once did, Aziel's bond ensuring that, but it still warms me if I let it.

My skin splits open as Gray buries his teeth in, but I can tell he's holding back.

He went in deep with Aziel, their bonding aggressive after years of neglect, but I'm glad that won't be our experience.

It still fucking hurts, though, and I grab Gray's shoulders as a bond forms. It's uncomfortable, and Aziel's bond pulsates as the two learn to work around one another. It feels more like they're fighting, though, trying to outweigh the other.

I hiss through my teeth, the burn spreading from my neck to my chest, before wiggling my face into Gray's neck. He tilts his head back, offering himself, and I don't hesitate to bite down. I have to apply a lot of pressure, my teeth not made to bite through the skin like this, but Gray shows no inclinations that it hurts.

He softly rolls his hips, the drag of his cock a sharp reminder that he's still inside me.

I release Gray, eager to see my mark, but I freeze when I realize it slightly overlaps Aziel's. My jaw drops, frantic apologies preparing to pour from my mouth, but Gray smashes his lips to mine to stop them.

"I fucking love it," he says. "Don't you dare apologize."

My eyes flash to Aziel, but he hardly seems to care. He's still watching us, his head cocked slightly to the side and a smile toying at the corners of his lips.

He's not exactly sentimental.

Gray pulls back and thrusts into me, his rhythm quickly steadying despite the distraction of our bonding. It doesn't take him long to get me on edge, and I grab his forearms and roll my hips to meet each of his movements.

"My pretty female and her pretty pussy." He chuckles, looking wild as he stares at where his cock slips into me.

Aziel appears out of nowhere, standing behind Gray. He pulls

Gray's head to the side, exposing his neck before licking up the blood I left after marking.

"Fuck." Gray gasps, his eyes screwing shut as he spreads my thighs farther apart. "Fucking take me."

My face warms as my orgasm nears, and my hands frantically slide from his shoulders to his biceps to his chest. It feels so good, too good, and I clench around him as I tumble over the edge.

Gray fucks me through it, his noises growing louder before he stills and cums.

I scream, another orgasm tearing through me.

It's more than I've ever felt before, and I yank my knees to my chest as Gray pins me to the couch. My eyes roll back, and a choked sob falls from my throat as my every nerve ending fires.

It takes me a long time to catch my breath, and my body convulses every few seconds before I slump back into the couch, my muscles weak.

I've always wondered how it felt to make an incubus cum, and I understand why Gray was hesitant. Before my bond with Aziel, that probably would have been too intense.

I see how people get addicted to the Lust demons so easily.

"Sorry about that." Gray chuckles, sounding anything but sorry.

Aziel steps away, wiping at his mouth as he vanishes. Silas is still at Aziel's desk, a black marker in his hand as his eyes dart continually between Gray and me.

I'm nervous to see his reaction, and my pulse races until he offers me a quick wink.

Gray flops on top of me, stealing all my attention.

"Gray!" I shout, his weight crushing.

I can't help but laugh as I try to push him off, but he doesn't budge. His cock slips out with my movements, and I choke on my spit as he smoothly reaches between us and shoves it back in.

Aziel did the same thing the first time we had sex, and I chuckle at the similarities between the two.

Aziel returns with a washcloth, and Gray finally climbs off me so Aziel can clean us. He focuses on me first, wiping all the cum away before doing the same to Gray. He drops to his knees as he cleans the incubus, and I stifle a gasp.

"I'm sorry I said the baby isn't yours, Gray," Aziel says, his voice soft. "I didn't mean it, and I'm excited for us to raise our children together. I'd be honored to name our baby Gray."

I'm pleased, but Gray doesn't seem to share the same emotion. He flicks Aziel's hand off his leg with a frown.

"I'll name my own baby Gray. I don't give a fuck about yours."

I stiffen, my muscles growing taut before I shove my elbow into Gray's ribs. He grunts, and I shoot him a sharp glare.

"I'm sorry, Charlie," he mumbles before turning to Aziel. "I'll consider your offer."

Aziel raises a brow, but he's smart and doesn't push the topic as he shakes his head and stands back up. Gray takes that opportunity to throw himself back on top of me, forcing cuddles while Silas and Aziel return to work.

Chapter Six

CHARLOTTE

ROCK FLIPS THROUGH his book as I finish the last few sentences of my apology letter.

It's been three long days of sun-up to sun-down meetings with Aziel's generals, and we're nowhere closer to solving the issue of Valentine.

Mammon hasn't launched another attack, although my males believe one is coming shortly, and I can tell they're beyond stressed.

Aziel and Silas have been having not-so-secret, secret meetings trying to figure out a way to move forward with the females without putting Wrath at risk, but I can tell by Aziel's angry glaring and Silas's quiet brooding that they haven't come to a conclusion.

Silas even finished reorganizing his library yesterday. Every book now has a home on the shelves again, but that hasn't been enough to calm him down.

Everybody is on edge, and there's a simple solution.

One that my males are too proud to go after.

They should feel lucky I don't have the same ego.

We need the shifters, and we're running out of time. Mammon is known to be ruthless in her goals, and we need to take over Lust and pull Valentine's support before she launches a full-scale war.

Pulling Wrath warriors from the posts is too risky, especially when we know we're outnumbered. The second Mammon hears word we're in Lust, she'll attack.

I tap my pen against the paper, reading over my apology letter one last time.

It's the sixth one I've written, and I think I've found a good mixture of groveling and promises. Aziel won't be happy about it, but he should've thought of that before he punched Echo in the throat.

"When are you going to start showing?" Rock asks, breaking the silence.

I shrug, not exactly sure. There hasn't been much time for pregnancy research with everything going on.

"Probably not for a few months," I say.

Rock's obviously concerned about me after my loud meltdown the other day. It seems the entire manor heard how I screamed at Aziel after his fight with Kato. Things are better between us, and while I'm willing to grudgingly admit that I understand where Aziel's anger stemmed from, I still don't think violence was the correct answer.

We're going to bring children into our home, and he can't go around punching everything and everyone he doesn't like.

Rock straightens his spine to peer at my stomach over my desk. There isn't anything for him to see, and I raise a brow as he cocks his head to the side with a quiet hum. I don't take him for much of a family man, his interest seeming to lie with the baby-making activities more than the actual parenting ones.

To be fair, though, I would've said the same of Gray when I first met him.

I was terrified of my incubus, convinced he would force himself on me. Looking back on it, I can't help but laugh. Gray was so eager to have a family, and he couldn't stop himself from coming on way too strong.

"And you'll get quite round, yes?" Rock asks.

I set my pen on my desk with more force than necessary. Rock knows I'm worried about the changes my body will go through, and he's having too much fun teasing me about it.

"Yes. I'll get so round that you just might have to carry me around like the little bitch you are," I snap.

I faintly hear howling from Gray's office, and I take pride in knowing my dig was heard. I'm not usually able to come up with good retorts off the top of my head, and I'm glad this one is getting some recognition.

I stare at Rock, trying and failing to see his reaction. I know he'll begin to solidify as he grows older, but it's been months and there hasn't been a change in his hazy figure.

"How long until you're solid?" I ask.

The haze around his head moves, which I take to mean he's shifted to look at me. I may not see the detail, but it's relatively easy to understand where his head is facing.

"Unless it's sped up, probably not for another twenty or so years."

I blink. "What?"

I didn't know it could be *sped up*. What does that even mean?

Rock snorts, apparently finding my lack of knowledge funny. I'm not sure why, considering he's my tutor. My lack of understanding is a direct result of his teaching ability.

Or, at least, that's what I'll say the next time he laughs at me.

"If I bonded with somebody stronger than me, it would quicken my solidifying," he explains. "I can also speed it up by putting myself in power-saturated areas. My body naturally takes what it needs, which isn't a lot, but sometimes during big events, the air gets saturated and my body is forced to take in more. That helps speed it up, too."

Oh. That's interesting.

"Most Wraths born into shadow bodies choose to go to the pits and fight until they've got a physical form, but I'm not a big fighter," he continues, laughing.

I chew at my bottom lip, absorbing that information before returning to my letter. I don't think Rock would last very long in the pits.

"What're the odds you think this works?" I ask, gesturing to the paper in question.

Rock shrugs.

"Low, but it's worth a shot."

That it is. The worst the shifters can say is *no*, and I genuinely believe they'll at least consider it. I'd have said I believe they'll say *yes* before Aziel punched Echo in the throat, but his dramatic actions really hurt the relationship.

I pick up my pen and read over my letter one last time, wanting to ensure it's perfect.

Kato has a big ego, one almost as big as my males, and I think he'll have a hard time turning down the opportunity to hear Aziel apologize. I've begged him to let us meet him at the meeting cave for a *friendly* discussion, and I've promised Aziel will apologize in front of all the shifter leaders.

Stupid fucking Wrath.

"It's as good as it's going to get," I say, turning to Rock.

He stands and takes the note from me, a loud laugh slipping from his throat as he reads it over. It's a long shot, but thankfully, Rock doesn't comment on my promises as he makes his way to my office door and peers around.

I follow.

The hallway is empty, and Rock and I sneak toward the portal before one of my males comes over to check on us.

I don't want to risk Rock teleporting to the shifter realm and getting too tired to return. He struggles even with the ring he stole from Gray, but if he used the portal to get there, he should have enough juice to teleport back should things go bad.

"If you take one more step toward that portal, I will drag you away kicking and screaming."

I spin, plastering an innocent smile on my face as I turn toward Aziel. He crosses his arms over his chest, his eyes darting rapidly between Rock and me.

"Rock's delivering apology letters," I say. "I'm not going."

Rock turns on the portal and disappears into the blue haze.

"No, you're not," Aziel confirms.

I frown, not appreciating that tone. Aziel hardly seems to care, though, as he makes his way down the hallway and shuts the portal off. Our bond pulls, his anger stressing it out.

"You can't keep me trapped here, Aziel," I say. "You wouldn't stop Silas or Gray from going to the shifter lands."

He brings his teeth together with a quiet click.

"If they were as weak as you, I would," he admits.

I recoil, and Aziel runs a hand down his face with a low groan.

"I don't mean it like that…" He sighs. "You don't have the means to protect yourself as they do, and I won't apologize for wanting to keep you safe. I love you, Charlie, and I want you to have freedom, but that doesn't mean I will sit back and let you put yourself in dangerous situations."

I open my mouth, but he lifts a hand to stop me.

"I understand you trust the shifters," he says, "but at the end of the day, I hurt one of their females. They're angry, and you're my greatest weakness."

Aziel steps into my personal space and cups my cheeks, but I brush him away.

"I get that, Aziel, but I need you to trust me. You didn't even ask me what I was doing near the portal before threatening to drag me away," I point out.

Aziel's nose crinkles. "I suppose I did do that, didn't I?"

I nod, and Aziel bends and brings his forehead to mine. "I'm sorry, Charlie," he whispers. "I won't do it again."

My lips curl into a soft smile. He will, we both know that, but I'll keep reminding him until he remembers. Aziel's as old as dirt, and I know it will take time for him to shift his mindset. Besides, there's already so much going on, and I don't wish to start an argument.

We need to keep a united front, and he and Gray argue enough for the four of us.

Aziel kisses my cheek before returning to his office, and I rock back on my heels before approaching Silas's. Things are still awkward between us, but they're improving.

He no longer avoids me, and I often catch him staring at me.

Silas is behind his desk, and he looks up as I push open his office door and step inside. He scoots back his chair before gesturing for me to sit on his lap, but there's a slight hitch to his movements that signal they aren't entirely natural. He's consciously trying to act the way he did before everything went to shit.

My heart cracks every time he does it, but I pretend not to notice so he doesn't feel bad. He's trying, and that's all I can really ask for.

It's my actions that led us to this.

My pulse races as I lower myself onto his thigh, and he wraps a loose arm around my waist as I turn toward his computer.

"What're you working on?" I ask.

There's a complex-looking spreadsheet open, the screen full

of numbers and figures I don't understand.

"I'm looking at options should we not be able to take back Lust," he explains, flipping between pages. "Wrath is wealthy, but it's safe to assume it's a drop in the hat to what Lust has. They've got intense revenue streams through their brothels, and it's been that way for hundreds of years."

Silas presses a kiss to my shoulder before continuing.

"Depending on how much Valentine convinces the Lust council to approve, we may have to dip into our personal savings. Gray has no money—" Silas is cut off by a loud shout from Gray's office, but the words are muffled and I can't make out what's said. Still, Silas rolls his eyes before continuing. "Gray has a *little bit* of money, but Aziel and I have a significant amount saved. It should be enough to support the war efforts."

It's clear he's avoiding addressing the topic of the females, and I know why. They can't fight Mammon and save the females without completely draining their resources.

Aziel knocks on the open doorway, subtly announcing his entrance.

"We're not giving up on the females, Charlie. We'll find a way," he promises.

I nod, but I'm not sure how confident I am that they'll be able to figure something out.

Aziel enters the room and rounds Silas's desk to see what we're looking at. He leans over us to click between the tabs, his eyes flickering around the screen. I'm sure he's seen this before, and he clicks into a few cells to check the formulas.

Silas huffs, clearly displeased with having his work fact-checked.

I place a hand over my mouth to hide a smile.

Sometimes I forget how long Aziel and Silas have known one another, the two working side by side for a length of time I'll never truly be able to conceptualize. I wonder if they feel weird being intimate after so long of being nothing more than friends.

"Do you two ever kiss?" I ask. "Like, when it's just you two?"

Both men go silent. I flush, immediately regretting asking. This should've been one of those thoughts that remained in my head.

Aziel smirks, but Silas is the one to answer.

"No," he says, trailing his hands down my arms.

I frown.

"You should."

Silas laughs, his mouth pressing against my temple before he turns toward Aziel. I fail to keep my excitement at bay as Aziel grabs Silas's chin and tilts his face upward. Silas doesn't fight it, and his eyes flutter shut as Aziel leans in.

The kiss is soft at first, the two pressing their lips together in a basic gesture, but then Aziel tightens his grip on Silas's jaw and opens the fate's mouth wider.

Aziel doesn't hesitate to slip his tongue into Silas's mouth, the sight making me squirm. I like this.

A hand lands on my thigh, the fingers digging into the muscle as Silas tilts his head to the side with a low moan. They keep an angle that gives me the best view, and I'm more than happy to watch. They look good together.

I squirm on Silas's lap, and Aziel pulls away with a sinister smile. I can feel that Silas is aroused, and a quick glance at Aziel's hips confirms he's feeling something similar.

"Did you like that, Charlie?" Aziel teases, wiping his thumb against Silas's lip to dry it off.

I nod. "You two should do that more often."

Silas grins, his swollen lips capturing my attention. He licks them as he notices my gaze, and without thinking, I lean in to take a turn. Aziel's hand slides up my thigh as he watches me kiss Silas.

Silas seems genuinely into our touch for once, his thumbs rubbing soft circles into my hips. Despite the fact that we've been sharing a bed every night, he hasn't gone out of his way to touch me. He only does it when Gray or Aziel tell him to, but we haven't addressed it.

I'm sure we're both painfully aware of it, though.

When Silas pulls away, I whine. His black eyes stare into mine before sliding to the door, his grip on me tightening. I frown and turn to see what he's looking at, and I straighten my spine when a shadowy hand rounds the corner of the doorway and knocks against the open door.

Is Rock back already?

I sit up straighter, practically bouncing in excitement.

"Yes?" Silas asks.

Rock storms inside a second later, his hazy figure zooming into the room. I'm unsure why, but I expected it would take him longer to return. He halts in the center of the office, and I scan him for blood or injury.

Thankfully, he looks fine.

"Well?" I ask.

My toes wiggle, and I hope the way Rock cocks his head to the side is a good sign. He wouldn't be teasing me like this if it were bad news.

Nobody builds suspense for bad news.

"The shifters have agreed to meet with you tomorrow," Rock announces.

Silas stiffens below me, and Rock is quick to correct himself.

"Meet with all of you," he clarifies.

Fuck yeah. I beam and shoot Aziel my best 'I told you so' look. The Wrath takes it in stride, his lips twitching before he dips his head in silent acknowledgment.

"They said to arrive at dawn in their meeting cave," Rock

explains.

Aziel shakes his head, immediately shutting it down. I resist the urge to scream.

"They're delusional if they think we're going to bring Charlie to their lands before we have anything sorted between us," he says.

I grimace, exchanging an awkward glance with Rock.

"It was my idea to meet at their caves," I admit. "It's a sign of trust. We mean no harm, and we're willing to put ourselves in a vulnerable position to prove it."

Silas rests his chin on my shoulder, his arms tightening around me. Aziel shows zero emotion, his face growing entirely calm, but his anger swirls through our bond. I can tell it's taking everything in him not to lash out, and he runs his hands through his hair before sucking in a deep breath.

His chest expands, and he holds it for a few seconds before slowly exhaling.

I'm so happy Silas decided to teach him those breathing exercises, and I'm sad I wasn't around to see it.

"Please, Aziel," I plead.

I won't fault him for not being excited about my decision, but I want him to trust me. I've seen how the shifters treat their families and females firsthand, and I know they'd never hurt me.

They're good people.

A bit brutish, but good people nonetheless.

"I'll remain by her side," Silas says, his voice growing soft. "I won't let anything happen to her or the baby."

He curls his hands around my stomach for good measure, and he and Aziel exchange a silent look before Aziel purses his lips and turns back to Rock.

"Very well," he decides.

I scamper off Silas's lap, too excited to remain sitting.

"Wonderful!" I say, bringing my hands together in a loud clap.

"You and Silas can begin working on your apologies now, and I'll let Gray know."

I rush toward the door before my words sink in. I don't want to be here when my males realize precisely what I signed them up for. Aziel makes an odd noise in the back of his throat, and I grab Rock's arm to drag him out with me.

"Excuse me?"

It's Silas who speaks, and I burst out into loud giggles as Rock and I make our escape.

Aziel doesn't bother hiding his annoyance as he pulls back the shower curtain.

The cold air hits my naked body, and I frown as Aziel not-so-kindly nudges me aside so he can step inside. Scoffing, I shuffle closer to Gray, fully aware the incubus isn't going to share his showerhead.

There's a reason he had one built solely for himself.

"An 'excuse me' would be nice," I say as Aziel inserts his oversized body right where I was just seconds ago.

He's made it clear he's pissed with my promise he, Silas, and Gray would apologize to the shifters today, but I don't feel bad about it. Even if Aziel had his reasons, he still punched Echo in the throat and needs to make things right with her and the other shifters.

Aziel tilts his head into the water, hogging the spray. Shower time is my favorite, and I don't appreciate him ruining it just to be petty.

"Aren't you supposed to be concerned with keeping your pregnant mate comfortable?" I ask. "Not cold and wet."

Aziel turns, his eyes scanning my naked frame before he

wraps an arm around my waist and pulls me under the water. The spray hits my face, and I splutter before getting myself situated.

I ignore his laughter and reach for my shampoo. It's not that funny.

Aziel takes the shampoo from my hand with a quiet, "Let me."

My heart thumps, and I fight back a cheesy smile as he gestures for me to spin around. I happily do so, and my eyes fall on Silas as Aziel begins to wash me.

The fate is standing by himself in the corner of the shower, silent as a mouse as he cleans himself. He joins us in bed every night and in the shower each morning, and he eats every meal with us, but there's still distance. It kills me, and I let my tears mix in with the shower water as he cleans the suds off his body and turns away.

"I've been thinking," Gray says as Aziel has me tilt my head back for a rinse.

I hum, letting my eyes slip shut as all three men turn toward me. They'll know I've been crying if they see my eyes, and that's the last thing I want.

"I'd like to name the baby Ephraim," Gray continues, thankfully not noticing.

My nose scrunches before I shake my head.

"I don't like that name," I admit. "It sounds too much like an old person's medicine."

I'm met with silence, and I peek open my left eye to see what I'm missing. Silas sucks in his cheeks, holding back laughter while Gray scowls. I glance between the two, confused by their reactions. It's an ugly name, and I can't be the only one who thinks that.

Our poor child will be bullied if he walks around with a name like that, probably by his peers and most definitely by Rock.

Maybe even by me, too.

"That's Gray's real name, my little warrior," Aziel says.

He forcibly tilts my head back before I can react, and he aims the shower spray at my forehead to clean the last of the shampoo from my roots. I push against his hands with a grunt, horrified as I turn toward Gray.

I would've never said that if I'd known, and I honestly forgot Gray's real name isn't Gray.

He's always refused to tell me what it is, and with everything going on, it slipped my mind. Guilt and regret course through me as I reach for Gray, my fingers curling around his biceps.

"I'm so sorry. I'd be happy to give our baby that name," I say, lying between my teeth.

We can always give them a nickname.

"It's okay, my love." Gray chuckles. "I know it's not the most stylish."

Aziel begins washing my back, and Silas continues to watch from the corner like this is the most entertaining thing he's ever seen.

Gray bends and presses tons of tiny kisses to my belly. I can't wait until it's big enough that there's something to feel, and I can already sense how excited Gray will be when our child begins to kick and move around.

He will make a great father, and I love how thrilled he is.

Aziel and Silas seem excited, too, but it's nothing compared to Gray.

He continues to kiss my stomach while Aziel kicks my legs open so he can wash between them. There's no teasing or inappropriate touching, the Wrath still angry over my promised apology to the shifters.

Silas steps closer to give his routine morning butt pat and chaste kiss. I want more, but I refuse to rush him.

Our kiss is short, and Silas pulls away before smirking and

pointedly taking his time kissing Aziel and Gray. I'm sure they can smell my arousal as I watch them touch, their naked, wet bodies tentatively pressing against one another.

I like it when they press themselves against me, and I can't imagine how it must feel when doing so to one another—especially when they're as hard as they are right now.

Gray almost immediately gets carried away, but Silas urges everybody to hurry up with soft commands and physical readjustments. They continue until we're in the bedroom getting dressed, and I roll my eyes as he grabs Gray's shoulders and forcibly leads him out of our closet.

"We're going to be late," Silas huffs.

I frown as I make my way downstairs, feeling awfully a lot like cattle.

Silas is too effective in keeping all four of us moving along, and he looks like he's about to cry when Gray detours into the kitchen to grab food.

"We should eat before we go," Gray insists.

Aziel stands stiffly by the door, his hands clasped tightly behind his back as he waits.

I'm pulled into his arms the moment I finish my food, his intent to be the one to teleport me made clear when Silas and Gray lift their hands in surrender and step away. Aziel's arguably the best when it comes to traveling with me, the man able to do it with minimal discomfort.

Still, I feel dizzy when the world vanishes and solidifies around me.

Gray was full of shit when he told me it would grow easier with time.

Aziel rubs the base of my spine as I recover, our bond pulled tight. Gray's tugs, too, their nerves inadvertently making me feel worse. I can only imagine how intense it will be when my pregnancy progresses, and I dread how much they'll be tugging when I go into labor.

"I'm okay," I say, clearing my throat as I straighten back up.

Gray and Aziel turn toward the cave entrance, but Silas continues to look at me. I grin as I watch the concern play out on his face, selfishly enjoying it.

"Let's go," Aziel says, stepping into the cave.

Gray wraps an arm around my shoulder and pulls us between Aziel and Silas. I'm sure having the two weakest links walk in the middle isn't nearly as coincidental as they want me to think it is. I can tell Gray's not necessarily happy about it, either, his footfalls rougher than they need to be.

So dramatic.

My eyes have adjusted to the darkness by the time we make it to the cave opening, and Gray releases me just seconds before we walk inside. I spare a glance at Aziel, hoping he chooses to do the right thing as I walk past him and step into the meeting room.

Kato and Chev stand near the large wooden table, and Echo is behind them with a shifter I've never seen before. He looks like a classic bear shifter with giant muscles and shaggy brown hair. His green eyes bore holes into mine, but I don't have a chance to get a good read on him as Aziel storms in front of me.

Silas grabs my biceps and pulls me to his chest.

"What's Vont doing here?" Aziel asks. He sounds pissed.

I've heard the name Vont before, but I have no recollection of when or in what context.

"I'm protecting my niece," the man with Echo says.

His niece?

I faintly remember Kato mentioning that his brother was mated to Mammon, and that she frequently used him to sire her children before sending him away. Is that Vont? This means that Aziel killed this shifter's son, the one who was messing around with Gray. That's not ideal.

Kato interrupts. "Once you have apologized to my daughter, they will leave."

He crosses his arms over his chest, and Gray snorts before shoving past Silas, me, and Aziel.

"I'm sorry I was unlucky enough to be in the vicinity of you three when Chev decided to go bear shit and tear open my chest," he says.

Kato raises a brow before giving a jerky nod, and Gray pulls out a chair and sits at the table.

"I'm not apologizing," Silas says, pulling me toward Gray. We stand behind Gray's chair, and Silas places his hand on Gray's shoulder. He's probably preparing to teleport us away should something go wrong with Vont. The shifter is glaring at us now, his attention rapidly darting between me and Silas.

"I'm sorry Echo got hit when she came storming through the portal unannounced and without invitation," Aziel starts. I drop my head onto Gray's. For fuck's sake. "I'm also sorry you got hurt after you almost knocked over my pregnant mate in your attempt to attack me," Aziel continues.

He's purposefully being an asshole, and he's going to ruin this entire fucking thing.

Echo raises a brow, and Kato's hands clench into tight fists as Chev steps forward. My palms grow clammy, anxiety coursing through me as I wait to see what's about to happen.

Aziel doesn't move even as Chev comes to a halt in front of him.

They're so close that their toes are practically touching. I mentally plead for Aziel to behave, hoping for once that he's inside my head. I don't know how much access our bond gives him to my brain, but it doesn't hurt to try.

Chev gives no warning before swinging, his fist sailing

smoothly through the air before connecting with Aziel's jaw.

Aziel's body remains still as his head swivels to the side, a few droplets of blood spraying from his mouth at the impact. I jolt, battling tears as Aziel shuts his eyes and clenches his jaw. His hands are still clasped tightly behind his back, which I'm going to take as a good sign.

"I'm sorry you got hit when you came walking into our meeting cave," Chev says.

The two men stare at one another in tense silence, and after a few seconds, Aziel unclasps his hands and clenches his fists.

God fucking dammit.

The shifters are the only hope we have, and he knows that.

Aziel brings his fist to Chev's head, and all oxygen escapes my lungs when he lightly taps his knuckles against the shifter's temple. Even Chev looks shocked, his eyes wide as his muscles relax.

It looks like he was anticipating getting punched as well.

Chev's frown spreads into a wide grin, and with a slight nod, he knocks his knuckles against Aziel's forehead.

Kato doesn't look satisfied as he glares daggers at Aziel and Chev.

Chev turns toward the table, his corny smile remaining as he sits at the head. I blink, surprised. That's usually where Kato sits, and I hide my shock as Silas finally releases his possessive hold on me. Gray notices and quickly pulls me onto his lap, stealing me from the fate.

"Are you serious?" Kato asks, turning toward Chev. "He hit your sister, Chev."

Chev sighs. "I'm Alpha now, Dad. You don't need to approve my decisions, but you *will* respect them."

What? That's new.

There were talks of Kato getting ready to hand his title to

Chev, but I didn't realize they'd do it so suddenly. There was no buildup, no announcement. I'm selfishly happy about it, though. Chev has a soft spot for Aziel, the two forming a friendship despite how much Aziel likes to pretend it doesn't exist.

Echo clears her throat, drawing our attention. She's looking at me, and her right eye drops into a quick wink before she steps forward and clasps her hands behind her back.

"I'm satisfied with this," she decides.

Kato doesn't look pleased, but Chev sure does. He smirks, clearly delighted his sister's on his side. They've always been close.

"Thank you for apologizing, Aziel," she pointedly says.

Aziel cuts me a sideways glance before huffing and lowering his shoulders.

"I'm sorry."

He says the words like they're acid on his tongue, but I'm still pleased.

Vont interrupts. "This is not enough."

He steps forward, but his movements slow when Aziel's power permeates the room. I didn't realize he was holding his power back for this meeting, but I sure notice as it quickly saturates the air.

"I wouldn't if I were you," Aziel threatens.

Vont's lips curl before he places a hand on the back of Echo's shoulder and gently nudges her forward. The tension in the room is unbearable, and my underarms begin sweating as Vont and Echo leave the cave.

Silence fills the room, and after a long moment, Kato joins us at the table. He still looks pissed, and I'm sure he'll give Chev a mouthful when they're alone. Shifters are all about respect, and it probably doesn't look good to try to undermine the new Alpha's decisions in public.

Even if they are father and son.

"I believe you wish to discuss Valentine," Chev says.

I nod, and Chev cracks a crooked smile before reaching over the table and bumping his pointer finger knuckle against my forehead. Silas brushes his hand aside.

"You're making it a habit to ask us for favors, Charlie," Chev continues.

I cringe. I know I am.

Chev clears his throat. "Well, what is it you need?"

My mind races as I think over all the different ways to begin this conversation. I doubt the shifters will show much interest if I come right out and say we need men to help take over Lust, but if I angle it to highlight how their assistance will help the females long term, they might bite.

I can do this.

Chapter Seven

CHARLOTTE

MY PALMS ARE sweaty, and I subtly wipe them on my pants as I shift in Gray's lap.

He wraps his arms around my waist, holding me tightly as I face Chev. The shifter wears an encouraging smile, and it helps. I'm not sure why Chev likes us so much, but I'm not complaining.

I like him, too.

"I'm sure you've been made aware that Valentine has taken over Lust," I start.

Chev nods.

"Well…" I continue. "She's convinced the council to funnel money into Mammon's war efforts. Mammon is working with the ogres, and they've already launched an attack on Wrath's borders."

I take a short break to collect my thoughts.

"We're already outnumbered, and we don't have the means to defend our borders and infiltrate Lust," I say. Gray runs a soothing hand down my arm. "To be blunt, we need more men, and we're hoping you can help."

Chev crosses his arms over his chest and leans back in his

chair. About half of me was convinced he would shut down the idea immediately, and I tap my fingers against the outside of my thigh while I wait.

"What do you plan to do once you've infiltrated Lust?" he asks me.

Is that not obvious?

"Gray intends to displace Valentine as the ruler of Lust," I answer.

Kato chimes in. "Which you'll be able to do because you stole Asmod's body."

I clear my throat. "That's correct."

"He was *my* father, and it was Aziel's kill," Gray says. "The shifters had no claim over him."

The room grows quiet, and Chev and Kato lock eyes before glancing at Silas. We all know Aziel wasn't the one who killed Asmod, and I'm glad we're all in silent agreement not to acknowledge the blatant lie.

I gnaw at my bottom lip, wishing I had a glass of water to hydrate my throat. It feels so dry.

"Taking over Lust will allow us to pull funds from Mammon and reshift our focus onto the females," I say. "Mammon is standing in the way of our shared goals, and taking over Lust will eliminate that problem."

Chev and Kato exchange another glance.

"We have our own problems with Lust," Chev quietly admits. "The incubi and succubi have found our lands, and they're tormenting our young adults. We kill them when we can, but…" He pauses and shoots Gray a sharp look. "Your kind spawns like wild animals. There are too many."

Does Chev not consider himself a wild animal? He very literally turns into a bear.

"We'll see to it that the shifter lands are off-limits," Gray assures him. "And we'll take care of the ones who don't listen."

Chev sighs, running a hand through his hair. "We can supply you with fifty men, but I don't want them going into battle. You may swap them out with your soldiers, and they will help defend the Wrath/Greed border until you have returned. I expect new policies on shifter lands to be implemented within a timely manner, and you may consider this the last favor we'll entertain."

Chev leans over the table and clasps my hand within his. It's one of the few times he's ever touched me, and I know it means he's about to say something important.

"We like you, Charlie, and Echo privately pushed us to forgive your mates' actions and continue to support you, but we can't continue to justify the cost your alliance is having on us." He releases my hand and shifts his attention to my males. "You need to figure your shit out."

I peek at Aziel, already knowing he won't like hearing that.

He raises a brow, holding Chev's stare.

"Do we need to have a contract or agreement drawn up?" I ask before Aziel says something rude.

Chev snorts. "There's no need for that. If you don't hold up your end of the deal, we will crush you."

He's out of his seat a moment later, his leathers riding up his thighs as he makes his way out of the cave.

What an exit.

Kato stands, too, beaming as he watches his son leave.

"Your traps are full, Charlie," he says, turning to me. "I've had to fight off many impatient bears who wish to steal your kill."

Silas makes an odd noise in the back of his throat. Neither he nor Gray has had a chance to see my traps, and I've been too busy to check them these past few days.

"We'll check them now," I promise.

Kato nods, confirming he heard me, before leaving.

I jump out of Gray's lap and spin around the moment the shifter is gone.

"That went so much better than I thought it would," I say, ecstatic.

None of my males look particularly happy, at least not as much as I think they should be, but I'm willing to overlook it for now. I shove my chin into the air and make my way out of the room, my steps slowing considerably as my eyes struggle to adjust to the dark cave.

My males follow me, their footfalls quiet as they form a line behind me. I feel like a mother duck leading her ducklings, and I chuckle as I step out of the cave and begin the short journey to my traps. I've never gone there from the caves before, and I have to tromp through weeds more than once.

"I can't wait to see these traps I've heard so much about," Gray admits after a few minutes.

Aziel chuckles. "Our little warrior is quite the huntress."

My cheeks are a thousand shades of red, and I dip my chin in embarrassment. I love when he calls me his "little warrior," and I have a feeling he knows that.

There's quiet whispering behind me, and I spin around to see who's speaking. Silas and Aziel are a few steps behind Gray, and Aziel looks pissed as he talks with Silas. My steps slow, and Silas shakes his head before turning to me.

He quickens his pace until he's by my side.

"I need to head back to get some work done, but I'll see you at home," he says, bending to press a quick kiss to my cheek.

Oh.

My heart drops, and immediately, I feel my throat close.

"You can't stick around to see my traps?" I ask.

I don't know why I'm so desperate for him to see, but I am. I'm proud of everything I learned here, and I want to show him.

"Not today," Silas says. "You can show me another time."

He's gone a second later, his body vanishing.

I face forward and roll my shoulders back, refusing to let myself cry. I messed up, and Silas needs time. Still, that doesn't mean his silent rejection doesn't hurt. Gray steps forward and wraps an arm around my waist, stopping me from walking.

"I love you so, so, so much, baby, and I'm so excited to see your traps, but I need to be there for Silas right now," he says.

I smash my teeth together and dig my fingernails into my palms. Gray looks genuinely apologetic as he crouches to my level, and he cups my cheeks before leaning in and bringing his lips to mine. His kiss is soft, and he slides his thumbs over my cheekbones as he pulls away and looks into my eyes.

"Be patient with him. He's trying, but seeing Kato and being in these lands is hard for him," he continues.

Gray's eyebrows furrow as he takes in my watery eyes, and I force a weak smile onto my face so he doesn't feel guilty for choosing Silas.

"I understand," I promise. "I really do."

Gray's lips flatten into a straight line, and he releases my cheeks before vanishing just as Silas did.

Aziel steps forward, the man quiet until now. "I'm sorry, Charlie."

I shrug. "You have nothing to apologize for."

We walk the remainder of the way to my traps in silence, my movements robotic as we check them. Two are full, and I squeeze my eyes shut before reaching into the cages and snapping each animal's neck. They crack with a sickening pop, and Aziel wordlessly takes them from me before grabbing my hand and bringing me home.

Gray and Silas are locked away in the library, and Aziel and I bring my catches to the shadows in the kitchen before I excuse myself to the bedroom. I can tell Aziel is reluctant to let me go, but he seems to sense my need for space and orders three shadows to stand outside our bedroom wing and guard me.

They're quiet as they follow me upstairs, and they linger outside the bedroom as I shut the door and strip out of my clothes.

I hate killing animals, and I want to wash the remnants of their deaths off me.

Aziel loves it, but I'm not a fan.

I mindlessly shower before making my way downstairs to meet with Rock. He's insisting I resume my studies of the demonic language, and it's not going well. I've forgotten everything I learned, so we have to start from scratch.

We work for several hours before Gray pops his head in with food, and Rock and I spend the remainder of the afternoon hiding away in my office. I'm sure he's aware I'm trying to avoid running into Silas. I don't know what to say to the fate, and I fear I'll cry the next time we're face to face.

I need time to settle my emotions.

Rock's snoring on the couch when a knock on my office door draws my attention, and he jerks up with a gasp as Silas pushes open my door and peeks inside.

"It's time for dinner, Charlie," he says.

I glance at the clock, surprised. It's gotten late.

Rock leaves, and I fiddle with the papers on my desk before standing and following Silas to the dining room. Gray and Aziel are already here, Gray at the head and Aziel to his left. The incubus fills our bowls with tonight's stew as Silas and I sit, me on the right of Gray and Silas on the other side of Aziel.

"The shadows cooked your catches and made a stew," Gray tells me.

I try to make an excited chirp, but it comes out as a choked cough.

"Awesome," I say, my pseudo-happy tone falling flat.

Aziel clears his throat. "Silas, Gray, and I spent most of the afternoon drawing up plans for taking over Lust. We can walk you through them tomorrow if you'd like."

I nod, eager to hear their plans, before reaching underneath the table to scratch my leg. It's been bothering me for a few hours now, an unbearable itch spreading up my calves, and my eyes roll back as I roughly drag the material of my jeans over them.

That feels so good.

A low moan slips out of my throat as I scratch myself, the noise capturing the entire table's attention. I can't bring myself to care, and I dig my fingernails in harder.

"Charlie?" Gray asks.

I grudgingly release my jeans and straighten back up.

"Sorry. I had an itch," I admit.

All three men stare, their expressions a mixture of confusion, worry, and amusement. I pretend not to notice as I grab my spoon and eat. It takes them a few seconds to do the same, but eventually, they begin chatting and eating like normal.

I bounce my knees, painfully aware the itch is back. What's going on?

The itch is all I can focus on, and the table conversation goes in one ear and out the other as I count down the minutes until I can escape to a hidden corner of the manor and get wild with my legs. I'm going to tear my skin off, shredding it with my fingernails until there's nothing but bone left.

And I'm going to enjoy every second of it.

I make it two more minutes before pushing back my chair and jumping to my feet.

"I need to use the bathroom," I say, my voice breathy.

Heavy footfalls follow me as I run upstairs, and I try and fail to slam the bedroom door shut on the three males who have taken it upon themselves to follow me.

"I need privacy!" I shout, reaching for the bathroom door.

Aziel presses his hand against the wood, refusing to let me move it.

"What's going on with you?" he asks.

I grimace, shifting my weight from foot to foot before giving in with a pained groan and tugging down my pants. Gray and Silas appear in the doorway as I plant my butt on the bathtub's edge and kick my pants off my legs.

Oh.

My shins are covered in a nasty, red rash, and I flinch before reaching for it. I don't care how gross it is. I'm going to itch it.

Silas lunges. "Nope." He grabs my hands, refusing to let me touch the rash.

I cry and tug at my arms, desperate for him to release me.

"Please," I beg.

Silas drops to his knees to get a better look at my shins, and I silently pray he gives me a little scratch while he's down there. He doesn't—because he's a fucking monster—and instead, he cups the back of my calf and twists my leg side to side.

"It looks like you stepped through some poison ivy this afternoon," he says.

I scowl. "What do you know about poison ivy?"

I've never had a rash from it, but my dad used to get them all the time. The human realm has been overgrown with plants and weeds, and poison ivy is everywhere.

Silas smiles, a real, genuine smile, as he meets my gaze.

"I've done a lot of research on humans, Charlie," he admits. "And, luckily for you, I had our medicine cabinet stocked with just about everything you might ever need."

My heart lurches as Silas turns and lists off a series of items for Gray to grab. Gray nods like he's being given the most important task known to man, and a moment later, he appears with his arm full of products. Silas finally releases me, and I curl my fingers around the tub's edge as I fight the urge to itch.

Aziel remains by the door, but I can tell by the pulling of our bond that he's worried. Gray feels relaxed, our bond humming contentedly inside my chest.

I wiggle my toes, thoroughly uncomfortable as Silas slathers a pink liquid all over the rash. The worst is on my shins, but there's some on my ankles and a bit on my calf.

I reach down, my hand freezing in midair as Silas tuts.

"The more you mess with it, the longer it will take to heal," he says.

I pout. "I thought bonding with you guys would make me stronger."

"It does, and hopefully, you'll burn through this in a few days instead of a few weeks."

A few *days*? Absolutely not.

I stare at the mittens on my hands, hating the mere sight of them.

Aziel wrapped my wrists with thick tape when he realized I was sneaking my mittens off every moment I had alone, desperate to scratch.

Chev stands in the hallway with us, his back straight as he stares at the portal. He arrived about an hour ago to sign off on our plans with his men, and now we wait for them to make their way through the portal. It's been three days of non-stop planning, and my anxiety is at an all-time high now that we're finally making moves.

Mammon's been getting aggressive with her attacks. Last night, she found a weakness in Aziel's border, and an entire hoard of ogres slipped into Wrath undetected. They razed a small village, committing acts my males refuse to tell me about, and Aziel has been forced to evacuate the remaining border villages for the time being.

It makes him look weak, like he can't adequately protect his people, but it's the right move.

Especially considering they're going to be entering Lust tomorrow.

They fear Mammon will attack the moment word gets out that Wrath soldiers are taking over Lust, and we can't risk any more innocent Wraths getting hurt.

I calmly reach down to smack my shin with my mittened hand. It itches so fucking bad, and I resist the urge to scream when Silas smoothly snatches up my wrist.

I rub my legs together and shoot Silas the nastiest glare I can muster.

They're making a big deal out of nothing. A little poison ivy never killed anybody, and I don't care about getting a scar or two if it means I can bury my fingernails deep into the damned boils.

I don't care if it spreads. I don't care if it oozes. I just want to stop fucking itching.

"Please, please, please," I cry. "Just let me do one pat."

Chev spins around. "You sound pathetic."

I gasp, offended. "You have no idea what I'm going through right now."

Chev eyes my mittens before raising a brow and turning back around, his silence speaking volumes. Aziel bites back a laugh, and even Silas lets out a tiny chuckle.

They're supposed to be on my side.

Shifters begin to step through the portal, their eyes wide as they look around Aziel's home. A few shadows slide into the hallway, directing the shifters into the grand foyer, where temporary beds have been set up. My males aren't happy with Chev's warriors being here, but the portal is the best way to get them into Wrath undetected.

The fewer people who know they're here, the better.

I was disappointed when Chev said he could only spare fifty men, but I suppose that's a decent amount for the stronger species. They don't have the same population numbers I'm used to hearing about in the human realm.

The shifters will stay here for the night before being transported into Wrath. They're being spread out along the border, replacing the strongest of Aziel's men who can safely manage long-distance teleportation.

Once the last shifter is in place, the demons will teleport to Lust.

Silas is staying with me, but Aziel and Gray plan to leave with the Wraths.

I know why, even when they try to deny it. They want to ensure somebody is around to lead and make decisions should the other two be attacked or killed. They don't want to leave Wrath without a leader.

The backup plan tells me this mission is more dangerous than they let on.

Lust is likely swarming with Mammon's soldiers and ogres, and fighting through them won't be easy.

Aziel says a few words to Chev before excusing himself, and Chev moves forward to guide his soldiers as Aziel approaches Gray, Silas, and me.

"Come on, Charlie. Let's go to bed," he says.

It's well past the time we usually go to sleep, but I doubt any of us will get a good rest when our home is full of strangers. Still, my males pretend everything is normal as they lead me upstairs.

"What about the shifters?" I ask.

Aziel shuts our bedroom door before approaching me and reaching for the bottom of my dress.

"The shadows have it handled, and Chev's staying the night to ensure everything goes smoothly." His lips curl as he whispers in my ear. "Stop stressing, baby."

I'm still nervous as Aziel kneels and gestures for me to lift my leg. He scans my rash before moving to the side to let Gray put more ointment on it.

Both men roll their eyes when I try to rub against Gray's finger, the itch unbearable.

Gray gives in and gives it a little scratch when I whine, his smile large even as Silas and Aziel yell at him. It feels so fucking good.

That's all I've been asking for.

Silas pushes our decorative pillows off the bed, his movements more than a little hostile, before he pulls back the covers. He hates the pillows, his constant aggression toward them giving away his true feelings despite what he says.

None of my males had them on their beds before I came along, choosing only to use the pillows they rest their heads on at night, and it warms my heart to know they took the time to pick out and purchase these extra ones for me.

They make the bed look cozier.

Silas and Aziel are tucked under the covers by the time Gray finishes wrapping my leg and removes the mittens from my hands. They whisper to themselves as I slip on comfortable black underwear and join them. I'm sure it wasn't an accident that Aziel removed my clothing and didn't put anything back on.

Gray takes his spot on the edge of the bed next to Aziel, and I flick off the bedroom light before slipping next to Silas.

Despite how much they deny it, Silas and Aziel are the cuddlers, so it only makes sense they take the middle.

I reach for Aziel and Gray through my bonds, desperate to feel them.

What if they die tomorrow?

The thought steals my breath, and I place a hand over my chest as Aziel props himself up on his elbow and peers at me over Silas's shoulder.

"Come here," he orders.

I don't need to be told twice, and I practically launch myself over Silas in my attempt to get to Aziel. Silas groans as I knee and elbow him, before moving to the side to make room for me.

Silas curls his arm around my waist and pulls me against his chest, and I sink into his embrace with a contented sigh. It feels incredible, and Aziel smirks as he watches the two of us. I'm sure he's eager for the tension between Silas and me to smooth over, and we're all just taking it one day at a time.

"Everything's going to be okay, Charlie," Aziel promises, cupping the back of my head and running his fingers through my hair.

Still so scared, I let my eyes slip shut. Things are just finally starting to go right for us, and I'm afraid to lose them.

"I love you," I say.

I reach up and grab Silas's arm, eager for him to understand those words are spoken to him, too. He gently squeezes me and nestles his face in my hair before breathing in and smelling me.

"Which one of you would like to volunteer yourself to me tonight?" Gray asks, his head popping up over Aziel. "I'm getting hungry."

His question is met with silence.

He huffs. "Don't all fight over me now."

Aziel laughs and rolls onto his back. "I suppose I wouldn't mind a visit from a certain incubus."

Gray beams and kisses Aziel's chest before dropping his head onto it. We lock eyes, and I hold back a snort as he shoots me a quick wink. I can only imagine how pleased he is to have permission to venture into Aziel's dreams, especially after so long of having to fight his way in.

I let my body sink into the mattress, trying not to think about what tomorrow will bring.

This could very well be the last night we spend together.

Silas presses kisses to the top of my head, his lips remaining until well after I've fallen asleep.

Chapter Eight

AZIEL

GRAY LOOKS NERVOUS, his hands clenching and unclenching at his sides while we await the announcement that the last of the shifters have been stationed.

I glance at Gray's hands before taking them with my own. We're surrounded by Wrath warriors, and it doesn't look good when the man they're meant to follow is fidgeting. We need the Wraths and Lusts to respect and view Gray as a strong leader, and standing around like a nervous little boy isn't going to do that.

I regret not taking the time to teach him how to command a room, and I give his hand a firm squeeze before attempting to release it. I'm unsurprised when he refuses to let me, his fingers clinging tightly around mine.

Silas and I had been leading together for hundreds of years before we met Gray, and by the time he came around, we were already in the thick of it and didn't bother taking the time to guide him. It didn't seem necessary. Asmod didn't groom him to be a king, and he'd never be able to lead Wrath if I died.

Gray's more intelligent than we give him credit for, and he's been able to pick up on a lot, but there's still so much he needs to learn.

Starting with not broadcasting his inner emotions to my top warriors.

Our bond warms as I run my thumb along the back of his hand, hoping the gesture is enough to calm him. Gray loves physical contact—all Lust demons do—and after a moment, his heart rate slows to an acceptable speed.

My body still burns as Asmod's power courses through my veins, but Gray secretly takes a bit from me every night. His body is adjusting quickly, and the power flowing from him is stronger than ever.

A quick scan of the room tells me we're about ready to go. The shifters left hours ago, and the last of the Wraths they switched places with have arrived. Chev stands in the center of the room, and I have a feeling he will remain in my home until his people have been returned to him. I'm not too shocked or upset about it.

He has my trust, and a small part of me I'll never admit to almost likes that he'll be here while Gray and I are gone. Silas is more than capable of keeping Charlie safe, but it never hurts to have another strong being around.

My eyes slide to Rock as he begins to scold one of my men, the shadow taking it upon himself to ensure everybody's adequately prepared. He's upset we aren't allowing him to come, but he hides it well. His parents were Wrath nobility, but I suspect he'll choose to be a demon of Lust once he solidifies.

He's not a born incubus, but many who live in Lust aren't.

I won't ask it of Rock until he's decided, but I'd like him to be our proxy. The council won't like it, but Gray won't be participating in the sex parties or annual games as Asmod so enjoyed doing.

Rock can handle those responsibilities for us.

I clear my throat, drawing the room's attention.

Gray squeezes my hand, his palm sweaty. I tuck him under my arm before pressing a kiss to the side of his head, silently answering the question inside all the lingering looks we've been getting from my men. He's my mate, and I recognize him as such.

"Is there anybody here who hasn't been briefed?" I ask.

Nobody speaks up, and I give a pleased nod before continuing.

"This mission needs to be efficient. We suspect the Lust castle will be swarming with Mammon's soldiers and ogres, but we aim to clear a path to the council chambers as quickly as possible. We aren't deviating off the path, and we're remaining focused."

The ogres will try to anger us and trigger a frenzy before running away, urging us to follow and break formation.

I glance at Charlie, eager to see her one last time before we leave.

She's standing with Silas in the foyer doorway, her hand clasped around his so tightly that I'm surprised his knuckles haven't turned white. Chev stands next to her, his arms crossed over his chest as he stares at each of my men.

They avoid meeting his gaze.

Shifters are probably one of the only species comparable to demons in strength, and they're not eager to set the giant bear off.

My bond with Charlie pulls, and I shoot her what I hope looks like a comforting smile before turning back to my men. Silas will take good care of her while Gray and I are gone, and I hope they use this time to talk. They've been teetering around one another for weeks, and I'm growing impatient.

"There will be no killing of Lust demons," Gray says, speaking up.

We've rehearsed this, and I'm proud of how assured his voice comes out. I know he doesn't like speaking to my men, but he'll need to get used to it. I want them to respect him as a leader, but unfortunately, I can't force them to.

He needs to earn their respect himself.

"If they attack you, you're to disarm and brush them aside," Gray continues.

His order is met with quiet grumbles, but I'm pleased nobody outwardly questions him. Wraths aren't afraid to speak their minds. I wait a few more seconds, giving them the opportunity to speak up, before giving the order to leave.

The Wraths disappear as it slips from my lips, and Gray and I aren't far behind.

Charlie pulls our bond again, this time in panic, and I give it a playful tug before teleporting Gray and me to Lust. We're meeting in the lands just outside the castle, the closest we can get with so many men.

Charlie's brief distraction has Gray and me arriving mere seconds after everybody, and I take only a moment to scan the chaos before releasing Gray and letting my wrath take over. My reflexes are better when I let myself fall victim to my inner nature, and I watch through unfocused eyes as I spin toward an attacking Greed.

An ogre runs up to me from the side, and I smoothly dodge him while I focus on the Greed first. The demons are harder to kill, especially when they can teleport, and I shove my hand into his chest cavity while Gray brings down the ogre.

Mammon was prepared for us, as expected, and her soldiers are unified in their fighting.

We're easily outnumbered three to one, but given that a Wrath's strength lies in fighting, those odds aren't too daunting.

My hands quickly grow wet, blood coating almost every inch of my exposed skin as I work alongside my men to take down the demons and ogres who lunge at our throats. I position myself to always have an eye on Gray, and I'm proud of how he fights despite his lack of experience.

He spent years learning in an attempt to earn my affection, and it's paying off.

I mindlessly slam my fist into the temple of an ogre before using my free hand to grab the knife he aims for my throat. He's an easy opponent, and he falls to the floor in a heap as I throw his blade into the lung of a Greed heading toward Gray's back.

"We need to move," I grunt, reaching for Gray.

We don't have much time before news of our attack spreads.

There are no Lusts to be seen, and I assume they've been avoiding the Greeds and the ogres. They knew an attack was coming, and they didn't want to be caught in the middle of it.

My men swarm around Gray and push back Mammon's troops, clearing a path into the Lust castle. We file inside, making quick work of the demons waiting for us. These ones are significantly less prepared, and their actions grow more frantic as we make our way to the throne room.

Lust demons are notorious for sex, and it seems they've got Greed's soldiers in their clutches. The farther into the castle we get, the less clothed they are. It's a best-case scenario, and I curl my hand around Gray's bicep and pull him into my side when an ogre gets too close.

Gray stumbles over his feet, panicked as he realizes he was only seconds away from having his throat ripped out.

I throw myself onto the ogre, tackling him to the floor before sinking a knife I grabbed earlier into the side of his neck. Blood pours down my arm and onto the ground below us, and I toss his body into the arms of a Wrath while I turn back to Gray.

They'll finish him off.

Gray glues himself to my side, his arm brushing against mine as I quickly bury my face deep into his mess of curls. His scent helps calm me, keeping my bloodlust at bay so I don't accidentally lose control. I can feel myself on the verge of it, but my bonds with Charlie and Gray help to keep me settled.

Barely.

We make our way farther toward the throne room doors. They'll lead to the council chambers, and Mammon's men grow scarce the closer we arrive.

Lust demons appear around us, quiet screams and cries slipping from their throats as they see my bloodied men. I'm sure we reek of death, a scent the Lusts detest.

They scamper away from us, and when one Wrath steps out of line and attacks an incubus, I release Gray to handle it. Our bond pulls, my mate uncomfortable before he steps forward and grabs the Wrath around the neck.

A sharp twist and a loud snap later, the man goes limp.

Gray drops him to the floor and returns to me.

I smooth my hand down his back before shoving the throne room doors open.

The room is empty, and I hope my intel was correct and Valentine's in the middle of a private, closed-door meeting in the council chambers. If I'm lucky, word of our attack hasn't reached them yet.

A handful of Wraths surge to fight the Greeds who try to take down Gray and me.

They've likely been instructed to keep us out of here at all costs, and my eyes flicker back and forth as I follow Gray toward the long corridor that leads to the council rooms.

I disembowel two Greeds and one ogre along the way.

Gray pauses before making his way down the hallway, and he cups my cheeks and pulls my face toward his. It takes him a few tugs to get me to comply, my wrath making me argumentative.

"Breathe, Aziel," he whispers, cleaning the blood splatter off my lips before kissing me.

I fight it, my eyes continuing to flicker around the bloodshed surrounding us.

"Aziel," Gray repeats.

He yanks on our bond, but it's the hard slap to my cheek that finally draws my attention. My eyes narrow on my grinning incubus, and lust surges within me as I take in his bloodied state. He's covered in it, none of it his, and I want more.

I want *him*.

He pulls away as I reach for him, a satisfied hum slipping from his lips before he turns back toward the long corridor. I place a palm between his shoulder blades, silently ordering him to straighten his spine before we continue.

He needs to put his best foot forward.

A few Lust guards nod slightly as we storm through the hallway, the demons subtly showing their support. Gray's long been favored among the common people, their general dislike for his lifestyle made up by the fact that he's bonded to me.

I'm sure Valentine's immediate participation in this war has only furthered their silent preference toward Gray. Lust demons don't like to fight, and they know we'd never ask them to. The Wraths are strong enough to protect both kingdoms, and we'd leave the Lusts to spend their days fucking and feeding as they love to do.

Gray speeds up as we round the corner leading to the council's meeting chambers. Given the calm atmosphere, it's safe to assume news of our arrival hasn't made it this far.

The doors leading to the chambers are guarded by four men, all Lusts who take one look at us and step to the side. Valentine isn't well prepared, her faulty arrogance biting her in the ass as Gray pushes open the doors.

Immediately, the room falls silent, all eyes shifting to us.

Ten council members sit at a large table in the center of the room, the dark wood covered in a flashy red velvet runner and large serving platters of food. A few demons lay on daybeds in the corners of the room, their bodies writhing as they pleasure themselves and fill the space with lust.

I cock my head to the side as I spot a succubus between two men. They fuck her at the same time, one in her pussy and the other in her ass. Would Charlie like that? Would she let us try? I'd quite like to be inside her at the same time as one of my males.

The woman's breasts bounce as the demons on either side of her thrust into her, the sight captivating. Her eyes lock with mine just as she begins to cum, and my jaw drops.

I'd most definitely enjoy taking Charlie like this.

Now that I'm having sex, I should make a point to come here and learn. I've never paid too much attention to Lust, not wanting to grow eager for something I couldn't have, but now I want to know everything.

My jaw clenches as I turn to another corner and watch a different succubus shove her fist inside herself. She seems to enjoy it, but I don't want to see Charlie do that. She's small, and it would cause her too much pain.

Although maybe it'll be beneficial to get her stretched before the baby. I'll have to discuss it with Silas.

He's the expert when it comes to her health.

I stand by the door and let Gray take charge, but I change my mind and join him when I spot the telltale signs of him getting ready to fiddle with his hands again. We need to work on that.

"Hello, Valentine." Gray nods toward his sister before turning to the rest of the room. "Council members."

Valentine's sharp laugh cuts through the room, and I take Gray's hand as I level my gaze with her. I fucking hate that woman.

"I genuinely hope you're not here to try to claim the throne," she says before pausing to sip her wine. The council doesn't join her in laughter.

Gray clears his throat.

"Actually, I am," Gray says, ignoring his sister as he makes eye contact with each council member. "The people have been urging for me to be named heir for years now, and with Aziel as my mate, there's nobody better suited. And… I have absorbed Asmod's power."

I shift, but I don't move to cover myself as Gray releases the full extent of his power. The ever-present fire in my veins pulses to life as it recognizes its other half, forcing borderline painful arousal to spread through my body.

A few council members visibly relax, and the moaning from the daybeds grows as the Lust demons feed off Gray's scent.

Valentine looks around, disbelief briefly flashing across her face before it shifts into indifference.

"This is pathetic," she says.

The council members don't respond, and her face grows red as she sees the adoration in their expressions. There's nothing they love more than lust, and Gray is the most substantial source of it right now. Valentine's the only unaffected, her body recognizing kin and rejecting the temptation.

"It's incredibly convenient how you two show up with marks pretending to be a strong unit after years of neglecting your bond," Valentine says, her heels clicking against the floor as she stands and rounds the large table. "It's a miracle you could even take our father's power, Gray, but even with it, I am better fit to rule."

Gray's hand tightens around mine. I remain silent. This is his battle to fight.

The Lusts already respect me, but I'm not the one claiming the throne.

"I've spent more time than you've been alive being groomed

for this position, and I honor the true Lust lifestyle. How long have you and Aziel been bonded? How many times have you taken him?" Valentine asks, her lips curling into a cruel smile as Gray visibly stiffens. "And you want to pretend you're fit to lead?"

A few council members nod, silently agreeing. They value sex above all else, and Valentine's argument is strong. Gray doesn't live a traditional lifestyle, and our lack of intimacy over the past years isn't helping his case.

"Then I'll fuck him, and you'll see how fit I am to lead Lust."

Gray doesn't bother waiting for a response before he grabs the back of my neck and forces my head down.

It takes everything in me not to fight it, and I suck in a deep breath as I let him bend me over the table. I knew this was a possibility, and I squeeze my eyes shut as he wraps his arm around my waist and begins to undo my pants.

Submitting to Gray isn't something I've ever imagined myself doing, let alone in front of an audience, and I take solace in the fact that he'll at least make it pleasurable. He's good at that.

One of the councilwomen lifts her hand to stop us.

"No, not here," she says.

I sigh, but my relief is short-lived as she continues.

"If you want to lead us, you will honor our traditions—a feeding ceremony. If you can do it until we're sated, we'll concede," she says.

Two council members at the far end of the table complain. They're saturated in Valentine's scent, though, so it's not much of a shock they're defending her rule.

Valentine smirks. "I think that's a wonderful idea."

I clench my jaw, wishing Gray would just fuck me here and we could be done with this.

A feeding ceremony will be painful and daunting, and as much as I love Gray, I don't know if he can do it. Asmod would take dozens of partners when he hosted one of his ceremonies, and even then, it would take him hours to push enough arousal from their bodies to sate the council members.

Gray only has the three of us, really just two. Charlie's both pregnant and a human, and I'll give up Lust before I willingly put her and my baby in harm's way. We could always take Lust by force, but that won't be setting up Gray for a good rule.

"I'm happy to," Gray accepts. He has no other choice.

His grip on my neck loosens, and with a slow inhale, I straighten up and roll my shoulders. The council members stare at me with wide eyes, probably having never imagined they'd see a day when I willingly submitted to the incubus who trapped me in a bond all those years ago.

"Wonderful," Valentine says, her voice sickly sweet. "We'll set everything up while you alert and prepare your offerings."

News of this will cause uproar within my kingdom, even more than I'm already dealing with, but that's a bridge I'll cross when I come to it. Bending for another man doesn't make me any less of a strong leader, and if somebody wants to doubt that, they're welcome to challenge me for my position.

Chapter Nine

SILAS

I FIGHT BACK a frown as Charlie's head bobs. She didn't get any sleep last night, and it's showing in the deep bags underneath her eyes and her complete inability to stay awake for longer than twenty minutes at a time.

It's a sight I'd find endearing if it weren't eleven in the morning.

"Let's go upstairs and rest," I say.

Gray will kill me if he comes home and sees her like this. He seems to think I don't care for Charlie properly, and I'm getting tired of his near-constant corrections of my behavior.

He's proclaimed himself the Charlie whisperer, and he takes great pleasure in telling me how to make her happy.

I already fucking know how. I've been around her just as long as he has.

Charlie blinks, her movements slow. I know she wants to argue, but I don't give her the opportunity to do so as I push back my chair and approach the couch she lies on. She watches, caution thick in her brown eyes as I kneel and pull her into my arms.

I'm glad she doesn't fight me.

"I can't feel Gray and Aziel through the bond," she whispers.

I chuckle, knowing they warned her about this. They need to focus, and they can't do that when the bonds are pulling and sharing the stress and worry from both ends. It's common for demons to block off their bonds when they're in battle.

"I'm sure they're fine," I promise.

Charlie wraps her arms around my shoulders, her breath tickling my neck.

"You don't know that," she says.

Has she always been this full of worry? My lips curl as I recall her excessive fear that Aziel would kill Gray when they disappeared after their big fight all those months ago. Charlie is a big ball of worry, and it's quite endearing.

"Aziel knows what he's doing," I say, tightening my grip. "They dulled the bonds so they don't get distracted. It's a common thing to do, and I'm sure they'll open them back up when they return."

Most mated pairs choose to live with the bonds muted, but I have a feeling Charlie would be incredibly offended if Gray or Aziel ever tried to separate themselves from her for any extended period of time. She's made it known she likes being able to sense their emotions, the female always giggling when she feels Aziel's frustration or Gray's arousal.

Charlie sighs, and I hold her tighter to my chest.

I enjoy having her in my arms, and I give her a tight squeeze as I grab my computer and carry her out of the library. She can pretend she's not tired all she wants, but I know she'll be asleep the moment I set her in bed.

Her fingers dig into my shoulder as I carry her through our home, the tight hold nice.

Chev paces the length of our dining room, the shifter deep in conversation with Rock.

They both pause as I step into the room, and Chev stares as if I'm the one intruding when I walk through it. I don't care much for the shifter, his father putting a bad taste in my mouth, and I hate that Aziel permitted him to remain here in their absence.

If Chev weren't providing us with his men, I'd kick him out.

His eyes slide to Charlie as I run my hand down her back, and I adjust so he can't see her as clearly.

"Keep your eyes to yourself," I snap.

Aziel's never had a friend outside of Gray and me, the man taking solace in his lonely life, and I don't understand why he chose the son of the man Charlie was intimate with.

There are many better options.

Chev frowns and averts his gaze before resuming his conversation with Rock. I want to eavesdrop, but when Charlie presses her cheek against my shoulder, I decide against it.

Rock will tell me about it later, or, at the very least, he'll tell Charlie. She's not known for her secret-keeping abilities, our human much too happy to share all the gossip she learned while we lie in bed each night.

We already know most of it, but Gray does a good job pretending to be shocked.

Aziel tries his best.

"Chev hasn't done anything wrong," Charlie mumbles, her breath warming my skin.

I don't respond.

Objectively, I know she's right, but that doesn't change my dislike for the shifter. I'm ashamed every time I see him, and it worsens with every encounter. Chev stuck around to save Charlie when I abandoned her, risking his life because I let myself be overruled by pesky emotions.

It's a big pill to swallow and seeing him doesn't help alleviate my guilt.

I continue carrying Charlie to our bedroom, not wanting to think about this anymore. I should be pleased to have Charlie in my arms, not obsessing over the past.

Charlie doesn't usually like to be carried around, and I take deep enjoyment out of her letting me do it now. Aziel claimed getting to bring her to bed at night, the one time she allows us to do it without complaint, and I don't think I'll be able to convince him to give that up.

Gray's tried a few times already, and all that's gotten him is an angry Wrath and hurt feelings.

Charlie clings to me as I push open our bedroom door and set her on our bed, her fingers burying into my arms so I can't leave.

"I'm not going anywhere," I promise, kissing her forehead.

She nods and cracks a smile for the first time today. It's weak and full of anxiety, but I have a feeling it's the best one I will get. I don't blame her for being nervous, even if it's unnecessary. She's never seen Aziel fight before, and while I know he's more than capable of protecting Gray and himself, she doesn't have the same faith I do.

She'll learn with time.

I use my thumbs to smooth the wrinkles on her forehead before pulling away to grab my computer. A lot of work needs to be done, and assuming all goes well with Aziel and Gray, I'm about to have heaps more.

It's doubtful the Lust council is doing a good job of managing finances, and I put Gray under strict orders to have them send me everything as soon as possible so I can get to work without delay.

My head aches at the mere thought of how long it will take to sort through everything, and I settle on the bed next to Charlie as I open my laptop and try to remember what I was doing last.

Maybe Aziel's right in saying I need to delegate some of my work.

I doubt anybody will be able to do it as well as I can, but it wouldn't hurt to get some of the more straightforward, time-consuming tasks off my plate.

"Do you think you'll ever love me again?"

My fingers freeze where they rest on the trackpad, and I hover them in the air before shutting my computer lid and turning toward Charlie.

"What?" I ask.

Her cheeks grow red as I give her my attention. Does she think I don't love her? I'm hurt, so fucking hurt, but I've never stopped loving her.

"You're distant, and you have been since I returned," she says, clearing her throat when her voice cracks. "I know you're doing your best, and I'm not trying to rush you. I just want to know if you see yourself ever being able to truly love me again."

I blink, at a complete loss for words.

"Charlie, I…" I start, pausing before I continue.

I do love her, that's never changed, but that's not all she's asking about. She wants things to return to how they were before she left, and I don't have an answer.

At least, not one she'll like.

A small voice in my head whispers that Charlie's cheating whenever she's not in my direct line of sight, and I don't know if I'll ever be able to get rid of it. I want to believe her when she says she loves us and we're the males she wants, but I believed her the first time she said that, and it didn't work out so well.

The trust is gone, and I hate that she's picked up on it despite my attempts to hide my doubt.

Charlie sniffles and sits up. I still don't know what to say.

"You're physically here, but not mentally," she says.

I nod, understanding why she feels that way. I want to move past the cheating as Aziel and Gray have, and I feel overwhelming guilt that I can't.

My expression must give away my feelings, and Charlie's face falls. The hope in her expression fades, my female giving up on me before my very eyes.

This isn't what I want.

I set my computer aside and pull Charlie onto my lap. I'm tired of this friction, too, and I don't know how to make it disappear.

I've searched through all my books and purchased more relationship and self-improvement ones than I'd care to admit, but none have fixed the issue. They all give some generic nonsense about needing to find the strength within myself to trust her again, but if I could do that, I wouldn't have gone to the fucking books in the first place.

"I'm sorry," I say. "I want you, Charlie, I really do, but I can't get rid of the voice in my head that says you don't want the same." The truth is painful to admit, but I force myself to give it anyway. We can't get through this if I'm not honest. "The thought of you betraying us kills me, and I'm scared to open myself up to being hurt again."

I'm not a fan of sharing my emotions, especially after I've already been made a fool of, and my cheeks warm as I admit these things out loud.

Charlie isn't crying, but her eyes are wet. She curls her fingers into the fabric of my shirt, twisting and squeezing as she absorbs my words.

I brush my fingers through her hair, enjoying the feel of the silky strands before bringing a few to my nose to smell them. Her scent's almost entirely soaked with Aziel, the baby inside her overpowering her weaker human pheromones.

Our baby will undoubtedly be strong despite being half-human, and I fear it will carry many of the Wrath attributes we spent years struggling to teach Aziel to control.

I do hope the human genes prevent the fates from giving them a curse, though.

It was tiring trying to keep Aziel's sexual urges under control when we were teenagers. He was always horny, and often, he was willing to take the risk of bonding if it meant he could get his dick touched. My lips twitch as I recall the few times I had to physically drag him out of Lust when he had too much to drink.

He'd get so mad at me, convinced I was trying to ruin his happiness. It got so bad, I went abstinent for several years so he wouldn't feel left out.

It made the both of us miserable.

I don't regret it, though, and I'm glad he saved himself entirely for Charlie.

Charlie places her fingers underneath my chin, her lips curling as I release my hold on her hair. She adjusts on my lap before trailing her fingers down my neck. The skin there is smooth and free of marks, and she frowns as she feels it.

"Mark me," she says, bundling her hair into a loose bun at the base of her neck. "I want you to mark me and feel exactly how much I love you."

I pause before responding, my eyes narrowing. I don't want Charlie to do this because she feels she has to. I'd know where she is at every moment of every day, and she'd never be able to run away from me again.

"If I mark you, you can't change your mind about me. I won't let you leave," I warn, eyeing her neck.

It's thin and pretty, and I trace the visible vein running down the column of her throat before moving to Gray's mark. She relaxes as I touch his scar, and I smirk, knowing how pissed he'd be if he saw me doing this.

He's possessive of his claim on her, his mark included.

Charlie lets out a shaky breath, her throat bobbing as I move to the unblemished area on the opposite side of her neck. I press my thumb into the spot where her throat meets her shoulder, letting myself feel the area I decided to claim long ago.

It's still my favorite spot on her, and she shivers as I admire it.

Gray and Aziel are always talking about how much they love being able to feel Charlie whenever they want, and I've been growing jealous of the connection they have with her.

"I'm yours, Silas."

Charlie would look good with my mark, and everybody would know she's mine. Her scent would mix with mine, and nobody would dare touch her. No male would ever bat an eye at a female who smells of a fate. They're scared of what I know, and they're afraid of what I can do with that information.

My mark would ruin her for any other man.

"I'm yours," Charlie repeats.

Her heart pounds as she grabs the back of my head and guides me forward. I let her, and I can't stop myself from leaning in and licking her neck. Charlie always tastes so good, and I let my eyes slip shut as I slide my mouth to my spot.

My spot. My mark. My female.

Mine.

I open my mouth and let my teeth graze her skin, beyond tempted.

Gray and Aziel warned me that bonding hurts Charlie, her body reacting differently than a demon's. Humans aren't made for bonds, and there's a short adjustment period that's hard on her. I saw it when Gray bit her, the grimace and pain that spread over her face as his teeth sunk into her skin.

I pause to give Charlie time to back out. She doesn't, and a quiet moan slips from my mouth as I bite down.

Charlie flinches, but she makes no attempts to push me away as I sink in as deep as I can safely go. I want my scar to be big, and I want everybody who meets her to see it and know she's mine.

Pleasure as I've never felt before courses through me as the bond between us forges. It's more intense than I ever imagined, and I instinctively cup the back of her head to hold her in place as my teeth dig in further.

I would've marked her long ago if I'd known this was what I was missing out on.

Charlie lets out a quiet hiss when I pull away, but she refuses to let me go far as she rests her forehead against mine and squeezes my biceps.

The bond feels foreign as it grows, but I can immediately sense the connection. It's like a small tunnel leading from my body to hers. I can feel her heart beating and the dull ache in her neck within the bond, the tunnel pulsating as it relays information between us.

Fuck.

I know I shouldn't, but I pry.

Charlie's end of the bond is open wide, and she holds nothing back as I let myself feel her current emotions. There's a slight annoyance toward the rash on her leg, and I can't help but laugh as I dig further and find her love.

It's intense, and I hold my breath as I soak it in.

This is how she feels for me? It's so strong that it almost hurts, and I pant into the air between us as I bring her mouth to my neck.

"Mark me back," I order.

I want it. I want to wear her mark.

A bond only needs my bite to be created, but I still want her scar. It's symbolic, and I want every female to know I'm spoken for. I want Charlie to touch it in front of them, claiming me as hers for the whole world to see.

Her bite scarred Gray and Aziel after the bond was created, and I hope it does the same to me as I curl my fingers around the back of her head and scratch her scalp.

"Do it," I plead.

I need it.

Charlie sinks her teeth into me, their flat surface painful as they break through my skin.

It's nothing I can't handle, and I play with the ends of her hair as she forces her teeth in deep. Her tongue presses against my wound as she pulls away, tasting blood I'm sure isn't enjoyable, and I reach up to ensure there's a scar as I heal.

There is, and I grin as I trace it with my fingers. It's big.

I push Charlie's hair back to admire my mark on her. It's hard to see through the blood, but I'm hesitant to wipe it away until her neck is healed. Still, the outline is visible.

Hopefully, it won't take too long to heal. I don't like the idea of her having an open wound on such a sensitive part of her body.

"I love you," Charlie whispers, but I already know that.

I can feel it.

She wiggles on my lap before reaching for my hand. I let her take it, holding my breath as she drags my fingers down her belly. My free hand slides to the hem of her dress and pulls it up. Aziel knew precisely what he was doing by not letting her put on any underwear this morning, and her recent decision to shave gives me a clear view of her slick entrance.

My body reacts, and I suck my bottom lip into my mouth as she leads my hand down her mound. I play with her clit, assuming that's what she wants, but to my complete surprise, she leads me farther back.

This female's going to be my death.

I press my fingers against her ass. Is this what she wants? For me to play with her ass?

She doesn't have to tell me twice.

Her lips part in a quiet moan as I feel her, her arousal filling the air around us. I may not feed on lust like Gray, but I still take pride in drawing it from her.

"I've never been touched here before," she admits. "I want you to have it, and I won't ever let Gray or Aziel touch me here without your permission."

I gulp, struggling to believe her words even as our bond promises them to be true. Would she really save a piece of her body just for me? I know Aziel and Gray would like to take her ass, and Gray's whispered that he looks forward to sharing Charlie with us at once. They're going to be jealous to learn her ass is all mine.

My cock aches at the mere thought, and I drop my forehead against Charlie's with a low groan.

"You're trying to kill me," I say.

Charlie giggles and reaches between our bodies to rub my covered length. She's not ready for anal play right now, her hole clenched tight despite the confidence she tries to portray. I doubt I could even get a finger in without hurting her.

I'll need to be careful, getting her accustomed to small toys and fingers before I even dream about slipping my dick in.

That's fine, though. I'm patient.

"Take off your clothes and lie on your back," Charlie orders.

She squeezes my cock to make her point known, and I can't help but grin as I strip. I'm already hard and leaking, and my thickness smacks against my belly as I lie back on the bed. A bead of precum smears against my skin, and I mindlessly wipe it away while she watches.

Charlie's satisfaction is thick within our bond, my female finding pleasure in telling me what to do.

"I want you to hold my hips and help me ride you," she says, stripping off her dress and straddling me.

Seeing her soaked pussy only inches from my cock is pure heaven.

I'm the only male who hasn't been inside her, and I've patiently waited for my turn. I want to know how she feels wrapped around my length and how hard her muscles will clench when she cums with me deep inside her.

Charlie feels at my abs before tracing the V-line that leads to my cock, my female having no idea what that does to me. I struggle to keep from rolling my hips when she finally settles her fingers at the base of my shaft.

"Silas, I—" she starts, clearing her throat as her cheeks tint red.

My sweet human doesn't know what to do.

I offer a small smile as I grab my length and point it upward, letting my cockhead slip through her folds before pressing against her entrance.

Gray and I shouldn't have teased her so much about being on top. She really thinks she's going to hurt me.

I open my mouth to assure her it's okay, but the words are lost in my throat as she sinks onto the tip of my cock. I don't think I've ever felt anything as amazing as this, and Charlie looks so pretty hovering over me, her eyebrows furrowed in concentration as she wiggles her hips.

She's so fucking tight, and she clenches around me as she gets used to the feeling.

I'm a bit bigger than Aziel and Gray, and I selfishly enjoy how her nose crinkles as I stretch her more than they ever have.

Mine.

Grabbing her hips, I guide Charlie up and down as she told me to. I only pull her halfway up before urging her back down, still a bit afraid of being bent if I fall out and she tries to drop on me to get it back in.

I love my female, but she can be sporadic.

Maybe we were right to tease her.

Charlie plants her hands on my chest as she finds a rhythm, and I'm immediately captivated by how her breasts bounce. I lean up to put my mouth on them, but Charlie pushes me down before I make contact.

I frown before returning to my back. So bossy.

"Does it feel good?" She pants.

I let out a low moan. "You feel amazing, but you already know that."

She beams, and I can't help but squeeze her hips. Charlie's so fucking adorable, and I want to squeeze her until she pops. I would if it weren't so bad for the baby.

I reach around her, desperate to feel the ass that's been promised to me. I know Gray once touched her there in her dream, but I never got any details.

I'll have to ask him how she reacted.

"I'm yours, Silas. Nobody but you and our males will ever feel me like this. Nobody but you will ever feel my ass." Charlie moans, rocking faster on me.

I bring my other hand to her clit, desperate to get her off. I want her to cum around me as she does for Gray and Aziel. Touching all of her feels incredible, my hands on her ass and clit while my cock fills her. She seems to enjoy it, too, if her loud cries are anything to go by.

I feel eerily like Aziel as my orgasm builds sooner than I'd like it to. Gray's always touching me, but his hands and mouth feel worlds different than Charlie's wet pussy. I clench my jaw, desperate to last longer, but Charlie squeezes around me when she notices my effort.

She's trying to make a fool of me.

"Can I cum?" I ask.

My eyes screw shut as I struggle to hold back.

"Please," I beg when Charlie doesn't immediately respond. "Please, baby, I'm so close."

I could cry when she shakes her head, and instead, I move my hips in tandem with her thrusts. Her chest is red and splotchy, and I stare down at where my cock disappears into her.

I could die happily inside this woman.

"I love you. *Fuck.* You told me to wait to say it until I'm inside you, and I did. I love you," I cry, my muscles tense as I rub her clit in firm circles.

Please cum for me.

Charlie whines, rolling her hips before a dirty smirk spreads over her face. Her lips touch my ear as our bond hums, my female excited about whatever she's about to do or say.

"Good. I love when my whore listens like the little pet he is."

"Fuck."

I lose what little control I have.

Noises I don't recognize slip from my lips as I cum deep inside my mate for the first time. Charlie takes it with pride, her motions steady even as she yanks our bond in punishment. It only takes her a few more seconds to cum, her body shivering.

Charlie collapses on my chest, and I wrap my arms around her waist with a contented sigh. For the first time in a long time, there's no hesitation, the bond between us buzzing and preventing me from feeling my usual fear.

She's mine, and I can feel that as clear as day now.

"'Your little pet'?" I joke, running my fingers down her spine.

Charlie nods and sits up. "Yes. I might have to get you a collar, too."

I pull out and drop my head against the pillow with a low

moan. And to think I once lived with so much shame regarding my sexual desires, fully convinced no woman would ever be happy having a mate who doesn't enjoy dominating her.

It's uncommon for demon men to submit, let alone ones of my status.

"I meant what I said earlier. It's obvious there's a lot we need to work through, but I do love you," I say, wanting to reaffirm my feelings. "I've always loved you. That's never changed, and it never will."

Charlie's eyes grow wet, and I wipe the tears away when they spill onto her cheeks. She's always crying.

I don't mind.

It's a nice change from the stoic household we've always managed. Gray would probably be the second most emotional, but he's more prone to anger and, before Charlie, he rarely found himself angry. He and Aziel were best buds, and other than the occasional fights when Gray would sneak into the Wrath's dreams, things were calm.

My lips curl at the memories of Gray and Aziel fighting.

I'd be forced to spend all night listening to Aziel moaning in his dreams, the man loving whatever Gray was doing, but he was storming into the incubus's room to fight the second he woke up.

Gray was usually good at avoiding the Wrath for a few days afterward, and I accidentally let out a small laugh as I recall the time I had to physically tear Aziel's hands off Gray's throat.

Charlie touches my lips with a small smile, seemingly happy to watch my face change as I relive some of my favorite memories. I hope someday I'll get to watch her remembering our memories as we lie together in bed.

I wonder what she thinks of now when she looks back on her life. Most of her memories are probably with her parents.

"I found your mother," I admit. I've been putting off saying anything until I had more information, but now feels like a good time to share. "She was put in a human facility in what used to be called Colorado, but I pulled some strings and had her moved to one of the more favorable ones in Montreal."

Charlie gasps, urging me to continue.

"With everything going on, it's best to leave her there until our issues with Mammon are over," I explain. "Your mom's not on anybody's radar right now, but the second we bring her here, she becomes a target."

We can keep her relatively safe within the manor, but I don't see a reason to take the risk if we don't need to. The facility she's in now has some of the most stringent regulations, and she's not at risk of being sold or hurt.

I run my thumb along Charlie's lower lip, pulling the skin out from between her teeth just as she nods.

"When do you—" she starts, pausing as my phone begins to go off on the other side of the room.

I frown, debating whether or not to ignore it before rolling out of bed. We've largely stopped using our devices after Charlie stole Gray's to call Shay, but Gray told me they'd call if anything came up. I walk across the room and grab it.

Aziel's name flashes on the screen, and I accept the call and bring the phone to my ear. "What?" I grab my discarded clothing.

"Come to Lust. Bring Charlie," Aziel orders.

The line cuts off a second later.

"What is it?" Charlie asks.

I shrug and gesture for her to get dressed. "I'm not sure. Aziel wants us in Lust."

It wouldn't kill Aziel to explain why we're needed in Lust, but I know he won't pick up his phone if I try calling back.

"Is everything okay?" Charlie asks.

It better be.

Chapter Ten

CHARLOTTE

SILAS'S GRIP IS borderline painful as he leads me through the Lust castle.

I didn't get a good look the last time I was here, and I try not to appear too overwhelmed in front of all the Wrath warriors.

I also pointedly ignore the bodies littered on the floor.

Three ogres are kneeling along the far wall, their faces cast downward as they stare at the feet of the Wraths standing in front of them. Everybody is covered in a thick layer of blood, and an uncomfortably strong scent of shit is lingering in the halls.

I suppose I've always known that people defecated themselves when they died, but I never realized the scent would be so strong. It's potent, and I wrinkle my nose as I walk alongside Silas.

Whatever fighting happened here has ended, but the Wraths still stand on guard, their eyes flickering rapidly around the room. I suppose Mammon's heard word of the attack by now, and I'm surprised she hasn't sent more warriors here.

Does this mean she's attacking the Wrath borders?

Aziel is convinced that'll be her next move.

I press myself against Silas's side, trying my best not to think about the itch on my legs and the ache between my thighs. Gray and Aziel are large, but Silas puts even them to shame.

"The council's temporarily shut down the Lust borders."

I spin, a relieved exhale slipping from my lips as I lock eyes with Aziel. Our bond pulls, and I bounce on my toes as Silas leads me toward him. He refuses to loosen his grip on my waist until Aziel's only a step away, but even then, he keeps a hand on me.

Aziel chuckles as I fling myself at him, wrapping my arms around him and squeezing. He gives me a dramatic groan, pretending it hurts, before kissing my forehead and turning to Silas.

"The council wants Gray to host a feeding ceremony," he explains.

A what?

I move to pull back, but Aziel doesn't give me the opportunity. He not-so-gently urges me to turn and walk down the hallway from which he just arrived. Silas lets out a string of curses, his footfalls loud as he follows behind us.

My bonds with both men tighten, the reaction only worsening my nerves.

"What's a feeding ceremony?" I ask.

Gray often refers to sex as *feeding*, a word choice I've never loved, and I hope that doesn't mean they're asking him to participate in a sex ceremony. The Lust demons don't view intimacy the same way I do, and I'll be damned if these people expect me to sit back and watch Gray fuck somebody other than our males.

I don't think I can stomach it.

"When?" Silas asks.

Aziel runs a hand through his hair, looking thoroughly stressed.

"Now. The room is being prepared as we speak," he says.

I frown, slightly annoyed they're ignoring me.

We continue down the hallway, our paces fast. Wrath warriors stare at us as we pass—well, they stare at me—and I keep my head high, as Aziel taught me. I may not have the physical strength they wanted in Aziel's bonded female, but I refuse to look meek next to my males.

I want to be seen as an equal.

"Where's Gray?" Silas asks, taking the words straight out of my mouth.

Aziel makes a sharp right. "In Asmod's old office."

I barely avoid tripping over my feet as I rush after Aziel, struggling to keep up with everything. I was under the impression Gray and Aziel would come here, kill some people, and take Lust back with words and slight intimidation.

There was no discussion of any ceremony.

"You should have spoken to us before agreeing to anything," Silas says.

I nod, wholeheartedly agreeing.

"There wasn't time," Aziel argues. "Nor was it my decision to make."

Aziel glances at Silas and me over his shoulder, his steps faltering as he takes notice of the marks on both our necks. I can't help but smile as he spins around to face us entirely.

"What's this?" he asks, approaching me.

I tilt my head to the side, eagerly showing him my still-healing mark. It stings a bit, but it's well worth it.

Aziel locks eyes with Silas as he reaches out and touches my neck, pointedly sliding his hand over Silas's mark. It tingles, and my bond with Silas hums under the attention.

A part of me was terrified Silas's end of the bond would be full of contempt and anger, but so far, I haven't found any. If anything, he seems as giddy as I am.

He masks it well, at least externally, but he can't hide it from the bond.

Aziel brushes my hair out of my face before turning to Silas, and he feels the already-healed scar on the fate's neck with a grin.

"That didn't take long," he says.

Silas shrugs, letting Aziel prod at his scar.

Marks are supposed to be sacred, but Aziel enjoys touching the ones that don't belong to him. It's probably because he seems to think he owns all of us. Therefore, using his logic, he also owns our marks.

Men.

I clear my throat, glancing at the Wrath warriors still staring at us.

"If they have a problem, they're welcome to speak up," Aziel says, not sparing them a glance.

He continues to mess with Silas, entirely unbothered by the eyes on him. I suppose when you're the King of Wrath, and have been for hundreds of years, you get used to people looking at you. It comes with the job.

Silas's lips curl before he grabs Aziel's hand and pulls him away.

"Gray," he reminds Aziel.

Aziel nods, snapping out of his daze as he turns back around and continues leading us down corridor after corridor. This place is a maze, but my palms grow sweaty as we come up on a pair of large double doors I recognize. This is where the incubus who stole me from the shifter lands brought me, and I find myself holding my breath as we step into the room.

It's virtually unchanged from the last time I was here, excluding the bodies of Greeds and ogres littering the floor. I try to keep my eyes above the ground as I follow Aziel to a corridor near the left of the room. It's where Asmod took me, and my palms grow sweaty as we make our way down it.

Silas clears his throat, and an intense feeling of anguish travels down our bond before he grabs my hand and squeezes it tightly.

"I'm so ashamed, Charlie," he says.

I want to tell him it's all right and I've moved past it, but I'm afraid I'll begin to cry if I speak. Instead, I slightly bob my head and continue forward, focusing my eyes on Aziel's back.

His muscles are taut, bulging beneath the fabric of his shirt, and I wonder if it's because he can feel my emotions through the bond. I'm sure all my males are feeling them, despite how hard I try to hide them.

We turn right down another corridor and approach a set of gold-plated doors.

Aziel pushes them open, and I let out a relieved sigh as I step inside and realize it's empty.

The room is small, vaguely resembling an office if it weren't for the giant bed in the far right corner. I stare at it, the object looking out of place next to the desk and filing cabinets that line the walls directly across from the door.

"What's a feeding ceremony?" I ask as Aziel shuts the door behind us, wanting answers now that we're alone.

Aziel walks through the room and leans against the desk.

"We weren't anticipating it," he begins to explain. "Asmod used to host them, and it was done whenever he needed to display his strength. He'd have sex before the council members, and they'd feed off the lust he and his partners produced."

What the fuck?

"They want Gray to host a ceremony to prove his strength," Aziel continues.

I lick my lips, struggling to wrap my mind around this.

"They want Gray to have sex?" I ask, needing clarification.

"In front of them, with multiple people?"

I don't want to be here for this.

I refuse to sit around and watch Gray have sex with strangers, and I shake my head before they can try to convince me otherwise. Aziel frowns as he catches my frantic movement, and Silas moves to the desk and begins sorting through the paperwork sitting on top.

"Yes," Aziel says. "But it's just going to be us. Me, you, and Silas. Nobody else."

That makes me feel better, but only slightly.

"Do you think Gray can do it?" Silas asks.

He doesn't look at us as he speaks, his attention captured by the files he flips through. Leave it to Silas to search the room the second he has the opportunity.

Aziel shrugs. "I don't know."

That answer only leads to more questions.

"I'm fairly confident we'll be able to provide enough to feed the council," Aziel says. "But Gray's barely containing the power he got from Asmod, and I'm not sure he'll be able to go that long. He's adamant he can, but he's got a big ego."

I raise a brow, surprised Aziel's talking about somebody else's ego. He's got the biggest one I know, and he turns and shoots me a sharp glare as he feels my humor through the bond.

Silas runs a hand through his hair and mindlessly prods at the mark on his neck.

"Charlie's human," he says, sliding his eyes to my stomach. "And pregnant."

I wouldn't say I like the implication, but I don't argue. It's no secret I'm the weakest of us, and I doubt I have much to provide the council.

"He'll be feeding primarily on you and me," Aziel tells Silas.

I sink my teeth into my bottom lip. "So, what's my role?"

It's clear they don't intend for me to be any help.

"Gray has to be feeding the council continuously," Aziel explains. "We'd never force you to participate, but it's safe to assume there'll be times when Silas and I need a small break." His gaze darts to the door behind me.

I spin just in time to see Gray walk in, and he quickly glances around the room before dropping the bag in his hand and rushing toward me. His eyes linger on my new mark, a smirk toying at the corners of his lips, but he doesn't say anything about it as he folds me against his chest.

"So, I'm the between-meal snack," I deadpan, resuming my conversation with Aziel.

Gray laughs, his fingers digging into the fabric of my shirt before he kisses my cheek.

"The most delicious snack," he teases.

I enjoy his jokes, and his always-happy attitude helps to smooth the tense atmosphere. He's making a pointed attempt not to let his nerves show, his smile infectious as he approaches Silas and pulls him in for a deep kiss. Silas smoothly avoids it, his attention captured by a sheet of paper.

"What's this ceremony going to be like?" I ask.

"There's a special room for it," Gray explains, leaning against the edge of the desk. "There's a large bed built into the center of the room. It's flush with the ground, and circling it are smaller daybeds that the council members will lounge on. They'll be close to us, but I convinced them to push the daybeds ten feet away from the main bed."

Aziel interrupts. "How?"

Gray points to my stomach. "I told them you're protective over the baby, which isn't exactly a lie."

Aziel nods, looking pleased. "Did you talk with them about having a privacy sheet put up around the bed?"

Oh. A privacy sheet would be nice.

Gray grimaces and makes his way to the bag he dropped onto the floor earlier. "I did, but they wouldn't go for it. I convinced them to allow us to wear sheer garments, though," he says, pulling out some shimmery fabric. "Once the doors are sealed, there's no entering and exiting. We'll be stuck inside until either the council is fed or we concede."

The room falls silent as Gray hesitates.

"Should we bring in some incubi and succubi, just in case?" he asks.

My jaw snaps shut with an audible click, and I direct my gaze to the far wall as I wait to hear Aziel's response.

"No."

Aziel and Silas speak simultaneously, and I peer through my eyelashes to see them glaring at Gray. Gray lifts his hands in surrender, but I still hate that he asked.

The room is tense, and after a minute, Gray glances at the clock with a sigh.

"It's about time," he says, gesturing to a subtle door behind the desk. "A private hallway through that door will take us there."

The door blends in with the wall, and if it weren't for him pointing it out, I probably wouldn't have ever noticed it.

Aziel approaches me and pushes my hair to the side. He eyes the marks on either side of my neck before lightly grazing his thumb over my newest one. Silas begins to strip, tugging his shirt over his head before removing his pants.

Without thinking, I reach up and touch the bite he left on me, happy to finally have it. Silas follows my movement, his twitching lips shifting into a full grin. Aziel rolls his eyes, finding amusement with us despite the tension coiling through the room.

I doubt any of us are excited to have sex in front of an audience, but it needs to be done. Gray needs to take over Lust if we want to stop Mammon and continue helping the females.

Gray fucks us for a few hours and gets Lust. It seems like an easy enough trade.

"Let's change before we go in there. I don't want the council watching me struggle to pull off my socks," Aziel says, going to the bag of clothing Gray provided.

I strip.

Aziel pulls out a loose, translucent dress and slips it over my head.

He pauses to trace one of the scars on my shoulder, the thick, white line permanently etched onto my skin. It's where Echo got me good with her stick during our training, and it's one of many scars she left on me.

I like them, though, and I look forward to the day we can resume our training.

"My little warrior's body is for our eyes only," Aziel says, removing his fingers from my scar so he can finish pulling the dress down my body.

It's sheer, but it does an excellent job of blurring. The council will have a rough idea of my figure, but the details will remain hidden.

I like it, and I adjust the hem as Aziel fastens something similar around his waist. I've never considered him to be particularly shy, the man the picture of confidence, and I find the way he leans forward to ensure he's covered incredibly cute.

Gray doesn't seem to have the same concern, stripping himself bare alongside Silas.

"What's stopping Mammon from attacking while we're in there?" I ask.

If I were her, I'd use this as the perfect opportunity to strike. All three males will be exposed and weak, and she could easily teleport inside and take them out while we're distracted. The thought alone has my pulse racing, and I can tell my males feel it in the way they reach up and rub their chests in synchronization.

I grimace, releasing their bonds.

Aziel grabs another sheer fabric and tries to get Silas to put it on while Gray answers me.

"Asmod's first wife was one of the original witches," he explains, running a soothing hand down my spine. "They were together during a time of war. When she got pregnant, she enchanted the nursery room so no intentional harm could be committed inside and no teleporting could occur inside or out. She and the baby died during childbirth, and my father turned the space into his ceremony room."

Leave it to Asmod to turn the room made for his unborn child into one used for sex ceremonies.

Silas and Aziel begin to bicker quietly, Silas refusing to put on the fabric Aziel holds out for him. The fate grimaces as he pushes it away, his words too quiet for me to hear.

"This is the last thing standing in our way, right?" I ask. "After this, we're all set to move forward with our plans to help the females."

We've done all the planning, but we haven't had the opportunity to make any changes. I don't blame my males since I know Mammon isn't making it easy, but I'd love to see some progress once this is over.

Especially if that means I get to see my mom again.

With everything going on, there hasn't been time to process that Silas found her, and I take solace in knowing she's alive and well.

Soon, we'll be able to bring her home. Silas mentioned long ago that he saw her with a male when he looked at her fate, but that's not a thought I'm ready to face. Nor is the fact that my dad's dead.

"This is the last thing, I promise," Gray says.

I lean forward and plant a wet kiss on his cheek. "Will the ceremony be just the council and us?"

Gray curls his fingers around mine. I eye his naked form for a brief second before turning to Silas and Aziel. It seems the Wrath has given up trying to get Silas to put something on, but now they both look tense and frustrated.

"Just us, the council, Chev, and Rock," Gray answers.

What?

Why would Chev and Rock need to be there? I don't like the idea of having sex in front of the council, and I especially don't want to do it in front of Chev and Rock. They're my friends, and I don't think I could ever look either one in the eye if they saw me with my males.

Some things are meant to be private.

"The room is protected, but we want somebody in there as a precaution," Aziel explains, sensing the questions on the tip of my tongue.

"Why wouldn't you just put a few Wrath generals inside?" I ask.

Aziel purses his lips and glances to the side.

"I don't want them to see me being taken. Chev and Rock are the only two I trust enough," he admits after a moment. "My generals will handle everything happening outside."

I suppose I understand that. Aziel's perceived as the leader of us, especially by his people, and I'm not surprised he wants to preserve that image.

A loud knock on the door behind the desk draws our attention, and I follow Gray toward it with a shaky breath.

Here goes nothing.

Chapter Eleven

GRAY

I HOPE MY excitement is hidden. I'm sure Silas is already well aware of my inner emotions, the man too observant not to notice, but he hasn't commented on it.

I don't want Aziel and Charlie to know how much this ceremony intrigues me or how hard my pulse races at the thought of taking them in front of an audience, and I'm going to great lengths to keep it hidden from our bond. I've always enjoyed exhibitionism, my incubus traits strong there, but those feelings aren't shared amongst my mates.

Aziel would probably be into this if he could be himself for it, leading and taking charge of our interactions, but today it has to be me.

This is more than just feeding the council, even if that's what they want to disguise it as. This is me proving I can hold my own against my mates, proving I'm not a doormat. The council wants to see me take charge, which means putting Aziel in a submissive position.

I reach down and cover my hardening length with a grimace.

I'm going to take Aziel first.

He and Silas walk into the ceremony room with their chins high, both refusing to show any signs of weakness as they make their way to the large bed in the center of the room. I asked the council to give us a few moments alone in here, and I release a relieved sigh as I realize they listened.

Charlie gasps as she steps inside, her heart racing as she pauses to look around.

The room has been designed to be sensual, with dim lights and soft fabrics strewn throughout. Large, overflowing trays of food cover nearly every surface, most near the daybeds on which the council members will rest.

Silas and Aziel feel confident in their abilities to feed me, but I'll have to ensure they're eating to keep their energy up. I won't insult them by sharing my worries for their health, and I hope they don't fight me when I try to shove some berries down their throats between uses.

This is going to be more than they're anticipating.

Incubi and succubi of my generation choose to feed off what the body naturally releases during an orgasm, finding the satisfaction it leaves our partners with enjoyable, but the older demons, especially the council, enjoy urging their partners to provide more.

They'll take pleasure in draining my males, using their power to force out more than Silas and Aziel typically release.

I know my males will let them, too, choosing not to fight it because they want to help me.

At least I don't have to worry about that with Charlie. The council knows better than to try to drain her. Aziel would notice immediately, and I doubt he could keep himself from losing control. He'd kill them, somehow finding a way around the wards in here that prevent intentional harm, and there's nothing Silas or I could do to stop it.

I run a hand through my hair and watch Charlie get adjusted on the bed. She looks small as she crawls onto the large mattress, and she glances around before settling where she'll be most hidden from the council. She sits cross-legged and looks about ready to shit herself.

I know this makes her nervous, and I wish I knew what to say to comfort her.

My female is so brave.

"The sheets are soft," Charlie says to Silas.

He smiles and joins her on the bed, and I turn to seal the door we just came in through.

I run my hand along the seam until it sets into the wall and hums with magic. I'm the only person who can open it again, and I'll have Rock seal the other door in case something urgent comes up and he needs to leave.

He better feel honored by the trust we're putting in him.

The door opposite us opens, cutting Silas off mid-sentence.

Rock and Chev enter, and the shadow can hardly contain his excitement as he bounces in his steps.

Chev looks haunted.

He spares one glance at Charlie before gasping and turning away, his face beet red as he hurries toward Aziel. Her dress doesn't leave much to the imagination, and I'm willing to bet she's the first naked female Chev has ever seen.

The shifters are intense about their virtue, but I'm sure he'll get over it. Chev's part incubus, for fuck's sake. It's in his blood.

Although maybe I should be glad he doesn't linger on my female. I don't want him admiring Charlie.

This entire ceremony has my emotions all over the place, and having my father's power coursing through my blood isn't helping. It's making me want things I've historically turned away from. I don't know how to deal with it, and ignoring my desires isn't a suitable long-term plan.

I'll have to confess to my mates eventually, I know that, but I'm putting it off.

The council members file into the room, every one of them staring at my mates. Their eyes flicker over Aziel and Charlie before settling on Silas. They're excited for Aziel, mainly because they're interested in seeing him submit, but almost all Lust demons are obsessed with Silas.

Everybody knows about his preferences, and they're eager to see how we interact.

Plus, the fact that he's a fate doesn't help. The elusiveness and rareness surrounding the fates make Silas especially tantalizing, and this is the only opportunity most of them will ever receive to feed from one.

Rock stands by the door, his outward hostility toward the council members shocking. I'm surprised he doesn't go the extra mile and pat them down, too.

My lips twitch at the thought, but they fall flat when Valentine enters the room.

She's dressed in a red, floor-length ballgown for the occasion, and she smirks as she makes herself comfortable in the lounge chair farthest from us.

Bitch.

I don't like her being here, but I'd rather her be locked in the same room as us than off working with Mammon in our absence. I wouldn't put it past her to try to sneak around the temporary travel ban the council has put into effect.

Rock seals the door after the last person walks in, and I approach to confirm it's entirely shut. I'm faintly aware of Aziel standing and double-checking my work, but I don't take offense.

Feeding the council will make us weak.

"I'll guard the far door," Chev says, moving to the one my

mates and I entered through.

He holds a cloth over his face to protect himself from inhaling too much lust, and he stations himself flat against the wall as far from us as he can get. He's so fucking dramatic.

"Let's begin," the head of the council, Aphrodite, decides.

My bonds with Aziel and Charlie tighten, but both do an excellent job of keeping their inner emotions hidden. The room is silent as we all settle on the bed, and I gesture for Charlie to sit with Silas so I can work on Aziel.

"I'm going to let my power out now. You can play, but don't cum without me," I instruct, letting my fingers graze the inside of Silas's thigh. "My touch will draw out more, and we don't want any of your orgasms going to waste."

Silas nods, and I smile before turning to Charlie.

"You can tell us to stop at any time," I tell her, leveling my stare with hers. I'm confident Silas and Aziel would speak up, but Charlie is the type of person to put herself through something she doesn't want to because she feels obligated to. "You're more important than any throne."

Charlie clears her throat before giving a quiet, "Okay."

Her voice is shaky, but the tight, encouraging squeeze she gives my knee makes up for it.

I love her so fucking much.

I shut my eyes and relax my body, letting my lust pour out. It feels good to release it, and I wait for it to seep into the air before opening my eyes and checking on my mates.

Charlie and Silas are affected, their pupils blown out, but they're still in control. I grab their hands and place them on one another's bodies, silently urging them closer. Neither moves right away, but after a second, Charlie climbs onto Silas's lap.

I turn away as his arms wrap around her waist, eager to get started on Aziel.

My forbidden fruit.

Aziel kneels on the bed, the stupid fucking skirt he insists on wearing pooling around his thighs. I smirk as I crawl toward him, my excitement growing as I place a hand on his chest and push him onto his back.

"How should I take you?" I ask. "On your hands and knees, or on your back?"

Skimming my hands up his thighs, I lift his skirt's fabric until it rests just below his cock. I'll keep him covered, even if I think it's stupid. Aziel bites his bottom lip as I spread his legs and slot myself between them, letting my length press against the inside of his thigh.

"I bet you'd like to ride me. Then you can take back some of the control you're so desperate for," I say, chuckling as he breathes in my lust and shifts.

Aziel's hard, but he was halfway there before I let my scent out. A small part of him is excited about this, and I'll be damned if I disappoint.

I continue to feel him, sliding my palms over his abs and lower belly as he clears his throat and glances around the room.

"How do you want me?" he eventually chokes out.

I know this doesn't come naturally to him, the man unused to submitting, and I appreciate his attempt. This will go a long way in the eyes of the council. I want their respect, and I need it if we're going to rule together. I've always preferred my father's way of governing, even if Aziel and Silas hate it.

It can be dangerous to have one person in ultimate control, and Aziel's father is proof of that.

"Get on your hands and knees," I decide, smacking the outside of his thigh as he rolls over.

Aziel stiffens when I spin him to face Charlie and Silas, but he doesn't question it. He trusts me, and I want them to have the perfect view of his aching cock as he takes me.

His back is rigid, and I push against his spine until he arches.

I like the view, and I lift his skirt until it rests on his lower back. The bond between us pulls as I take my time stroking the back of his legs, not wanting to rush. I'm sure I won't get this opportunity again, and I want to make it as enjoyable as possible.

Aziel is still tense, and I press my lips to his shoulder and pepper his skin with gentle kisses.

I continue until he relaxes beneath me.

"I love you," I whisper.

Aziel sighs and drops to his elbows. "I love you, too."

Silas and Charlie grind against one another, quietly panting into each other's mouths as they kiss. It's relatively tame, and I can tell they're aware of the audience.

"It's just us, Az," I whisper, pressing my chest against his back. "I'm going to take care of you. I promise."

Aziel shivers, arousal beginning to seep from his pores. It smells faintly of Asmod, and I grimace before urging him through the bond to open up. He does, and I slide my hands up his inner thighs as I silently take the rest of my father's power from him.

It hurts, but thankfully, there isn't much left. I've been taking little bits every night, but we can't risk the council smelling Asmod in Aziel and realizing our lie. It would discredit my claim to the throne, and they'd choose Valentine over me in a heartbeat.

Even if that means losing Wrath's protection.

My lungs burn as I fill myself with the remainder of what Aziel's holding, and I take a few moments to settle before pulling back and taking hold of my cock. I'm aching, and I give myself a few quick strokes to ease my arousal out.

Aziel keeps his back arched, and he readjusts his grip on the sheets as I collect my arousal and bring my fingers to his ass. He flinches as I touch his hole, and he clenches as I ease my middle finger inside.

"Relax," I say, plastering myself to his back as I gently rock the digit in and out.

I know my arousal feels good inside him, easing my movements and soothing his pain.

"Touch me," Aziel orders, his voice cracking before he clears his throat and continues. "Please."

I hide my smile into the skin of his shoulder.

I really fucking like it when he begs, and this might be something I argue becomes a yearly tradition. Aziel's been softening since accepting our bond, and I'm willing to bet I could convince him to give me this.

Eager to please, I wrap my free hand around his waist and take hold of his cock. He's hard despite his nerves, and his length twitches as I work another finger inside him.

Slowly, he begins to relax, his ass loosening as I finger him. I rub against his prostate, applying pressure until he's biting back moans and rocking slightly against me.

His motions are subtle, but they're undeniably there.

My little whore likes this.

I continue until I comfortably have three fingers inside before pulling out and wiping my hands on one of the wet towels provided.

"Are you ready?" I ask, covering myself with my arousal.

Aziel nods before dropping from his hands to his elbows. I like this angle, his ass in the air while his chest rests against the mattress, and I drop a hand to his shoulder to keep him there as I line myself up with his entrance.

A quiet moan slips from my lips as I begin to push inside.

He's tight, and I sink inside a few inches before pausing. Aziel clenches around me, and I wait until he relaxes before pushing in some more.

Aziel breathes harshly through his nose, and I slide my hands down his back as I roll my hips and bottom out.

"Fuck." I gasp, dropping my chest onto his back.

Aziel readjusts his position, the movement pulling me out halfway before pushing back in. He's not fooling anybody, and I let out a hoarse laugh when he does it again.

So fucking desperate.

I'm more than happy to oblige, though, and with a wide grin, I grab his hips and begin to fuck him. Charlie and Silas stop what they're doing to watch, their flushed cheeks and constant shifting letting me know just how much they're enjoying seeing this.

"On your knees," I order Aziel, wrapping my hand around the front of his neck and lifting.

He grunts before sitting up, his body jerking forward with each of my thrusts. Arousal continues to pour out of him, the scent confirming how much he loves this. He loves me fucking him.

I resist the urge to smack his ass, knowing that'd be too far. The council wants to see Aziel concede to me, but I'll wait until we're alone to have my fun.

"Show Charlie and Silas your cock," I whisper in his ear. "Show them how much you love being fucked by me."

Aziel's hands twitch where they hold my thighs, squeezing the muscle before he grabs the front of his skirt and lifts it for them.

Charlie's eyes widen as she stares at his cock, and Silas smirks as he brings his mouth to Charlie's neck and licks over his mark. I may not have commented on their bonding earlier, but I'm pleased to see it, and I hope this means things between them will be better.

"Aziel…" Charlie giggles.

I'm sure his cock is bobbing with each thrust, begging to be touched. I like Charlie and Silas seeing just how much Aziel is enjoying this, and I slow my thrusts to see how needy I can get him. I want Aziel to beg me to let him cum.

He groans quietly, his head dropping back against my shoulder. I turn and kiss his cheek, his stubble tickling my bottom lip. Lust pours out of him in thick waves, and when he tries to rock back against me, I grab his hips to hold him still.

"Harder," Aziel grunts after a moment, his skin turning an impossible shade of red as he clenches around my cock. "Please, Gray. Harder."

Hearing those words is even sweeter than I envisioned, and I don't hesitate to give him exactly what he wants. I pull out about halfway before slamming back in, my hips smacking his ass. Aziel jerks forward, a quiet hiss slipping from his mouth as his hands find my thighs.

"You're going to watch Aziel cum without even being touched," I tell Charlie and Silas. "That's how much he loves having me inside him."

Aziel bites back a moan, but low noises still seep out of his throat as his cock leaks into the sheets between his knees. He's trying to fight it, but I can tell he's about to cum. He squeezes my thighs as he jerks, his ass clenching around me as he lets out a choked cry and stills.

I grin, continuing to fuck him as his cock leaks onto the bed. The council members feed as he cums, drawing out his orgasm until he's sagging against me.

"That was so good," I praise, sliding my lips to my mark on his neck. "I'm going to finish in you now, and you're going to cum again."

Aziel nods, gasping as Charlie drops to her hands and knees and licks the cum smeared on his cockhead.

I'm fucking obsessed with her.

She continues to taste him, her tongue darting out with small licks. Silas joins in to help, grabbing Aziel's shaft to hold him still for her. Seeing them working on Aziel is enough to do me in, and I bury myself deep inside him as I cum.

He curses as my actions force another orgasm from him, and Charlie takes it all in her mouth.

Fucking. Obsessed.

I expect her to swallow it, but instead, she turns and kisses Silas. I stare wide-eyed as she opens her mouth and pushes Aziel's cum between his lips.

I rush to clean my cock before turning to Silas.

"Don't swallow," I order, wanting to take him while he has a mouth full of Aziel.

He eagerly nods. Always such a good boy.

Silas grabs my forearms as I push him onto his back, his fingers digging into my skin. He's already so worked up, his cock hard and leaking onto his stomach.

I love the sight of him like this, and I take a moment to enjoy it before shaking one of my arms free and lowering it between his thighs. I've already played with his ass a few times, teasing him with my fingers as I pleasured him with my mouth.

He seems to enjoy it, and he arches his back as I ease a finger in. I'm not surprised he takes it better than Aziel, but I still spend several minutes warming him up before grabbing my cock and lining myself up with his entrance.

I want him to enjoy this.

Aziel's relatively easy to bully into doing the things I want, but Silas can be stubborn.

"I wanted to fuck you with romance for the first time," I whisper in his ear, "so when this is all over and I light a bunch of candles and force you into a bath, I don't want you questioning it. We'll pretend this never happened."

I love Silas, and sometimes, I worry I don't make enough

effort to show it. I spent years pining after Aziel because of our bond, and I want Silas to know I love him just as much. He's my mate, too.

Silas's cheeks flush as he nods, his mouth still full of cum as I push inside him. His jaw clenches with a silent moan, the man not making nearly as many efforts to hide his enjoyment as Aziel did.

He once was ashamed of his desires, but he's come to embrace them over the years.

"You can touch yourself," I say, sinking into him. "And you can swallow when you cum."

He seems eager to do so as he immediately drops a hand to his cock, his fingers curling around it. I'm entranced by how frantically he strokes himself. Charlie got him worked to the edge while I was with Aziel, and as his arousal thickens and pools from his pores, I know he's close.

I loop my hands around the backs of his thighs and push them toward his chest, folding him in half so I can drive in deeper. He seems to like that, choking on the cum he holds in his throat.

He can't speak with a full mouth, but I know what he's asking when he looks at me with wide, frantic eyes.

"You can cum, baby," I say, grinning as his abs tense and he begins to spill on himself.

His throat bobs as he swallows Aziel's cum, and with only the pride he can muster in a situation like this, he opens his mouth afterward to show me just how well he did.

A few council members audibly moan, but I can't blame them. I love it too, and I bring my lips to his to taste Aziel. Silas eagerly opens his mouth for me, and I let out a low cry as I still and find another release.

Silas hisses as my actions force him to orgasm again, and I pause to give him time to recover before turning toward Charlie.

She's already panting, desperate, and I feel bad knowing how hurt she'll be when I refuse to cum in her today.

Aziel hands me a towel, and I give him a quiet thanks as I use it to wipe Silas. My fate flinches as I rub it over his spent cock, but he remains still and lets me clean him the best I can.

I can tell the council is getting impatient as I take my time, and I dare them to say something as I move to a tray of food and grab two sandwiches.

Silas takes his without complaint, and Aziel avoids me before grudgingly opening his mouth and biting when I smush the sandwich against his lips. I know it tastes good, and I urge him to take a few more nibbles before moving to Charlie.

He'll be begging for something to eat later.

"My sweet, sweet human," I say, guiding her to lie on top of Aziel, face to face.

He's still soft from his two orgasms, but I'm sure this will be enough to get him hard.

With a grin, I lift her dress and lay her flat on Aziel's chest.

She buries her face in his neck, finding comfort in him as I slip my hands between her thighs. I'm not shocked to find her already soaked, but I do jolt in surprise when Silas grabs a towel and begins wiping furiously at my cock.

"Can I help you?" I ask, wincing.

Silas swallows his mouthful of food before leveling his stare with mine.

"Humans are prone to infections. You need to clean yourself thoroughly," he explains, lifting my dick so he can wipe my balls.

My cheeks warm, a bit embarrassed for not knowing that.

"Will an infection hurt the baby?" I whisper, my words quiet so she can't hear.

I won't put myself inside her if it could harm Ephraim. Or Raim. Whatever she's decided she wants to call our baby.

Silas hesitates before shaking his head. "There's medicine she can take to clear any infections should one happen."

I don't love that, but I trust him as I grab her hips and line myself up. Charlie feels fantastic, she always does, and she gasps against me as I sink into her.

I could kill Silas for having had sex with her right before this. He didn't know what would happen next, but the man's oversized cock has made her sore. Charlie heals quicker now that she's bonded to us, but it's not immediate and there hasn't been much time for her to rest.

Still, she seems to enjoy me as she moans into Aziel's neck. Her breaths bring him back to life, and his cock rubs against her stomach with each of my thrusts. After a few minutes, he plants his feet into the mattress and rocks with her, his cock slipping between their bellies.

I bet he wishes he was inside her, and I can't help but smile as I bring her to orgasm directly on top of him.

Charlie lets out the prettiest noises as she cums, and it takes everything in me not to do the same as her walls clench around me. I want to finish inside her, but I force myself to pull out and lower to Aziel's ass.

He's still nice and loose, and I slip inside with an appreciative sigh. Charlie remains on him and happily eats the sandwich Silas feeds her, taking a few bites before moving to the marks on Aziel's neck.

He moans as she licks them.

"Do it again," he orders, placing a hand on the back of her head.

Charlie does, and she shifts to rub her pussy along the length of his cock. Aziel leaks onto himself as she teases him, and he rocks back against each of my thrusts.

It takes him a bit longer than usual to finish, the slight pain caused by back-to-back orgasms making it harder for him to enjoy it. I feel his conflicting emotions through our bond, and I push the tip of his cock inside Charlie for added pleasure.

Aziel seems to understand that she's sore, and he keeps his thrusts light and soft so she doesn't feel any pain.

It seems to do the trick, the man's arousal thickening as he rocks the first few inches of his length into Charlie before dropping back down on me. He takes me entirely, his ass swallowing me like the greedy bitch it is.

After only a few seconds of it, he lets out a strangled noise and stills.

I wait until he's finished before cumming myself, guilty as he cries out and shivers, his cock pulsating inside Charlie as he's forced to cum again.

The younger council members lean back in their seats, their eyes half shut as they grow full. I'm happy to see it, even if the older members still look at us like we're their last meal.

We aren't anywhere near finished.

Silas looks wary when I turn to him, seemingly just now realizing what he's gotten himself into. This won't be easy for me, but it will be even more challenging for them. My males were cocky in their assumptions, the fools thinking they would only need to fuck once or twice to feed the council.

We're dealing with ancient incubi and succubi here, though. Their entire lives revolve around feeding, and this is nothing to them.

I swallow past the lump in my throat as Silas rolls over and props himself on his hands and knees. It's the easiest way to do this. He shivers as I push inside him, but he refuses to show any sign of the discomfort I'm sure he's feeling.

I wish I had a bond with him as I do Charlie and Aziel. It's comforting to sense precisely how they're feeling, and I debate sinking my teeth into Silas's neck before deciding against it.

I don't want our marking done in front of the council members.

"Cum for me, baby," I urge him.

He does, his entire body convulsing as I finish seconds later and force another orgasm from him.

I sit up to clean myself after Silas, wiping any remnants of him and Aziel off my dick. I'm concerned about an infection in our female, and I look to Silas for confirmation that I've done a good job before turning toward Charlie.

Aziel nudges her aside and offers himself instead.

One look at Charlie tells me why. Her body wasn't made for this, and her bond screams exhaustion. The baby makes her tired, but with Silas and me and then Aziel fucking her, her poor body needs rest.

I kiss her temple before moving to Aziel.

His body breaks out into a cold sweat when he cums a few minutes later, and I can practically tell his energy is being sucked up faster than his body can reproduce. I want to pause and give them time to rest, but the council will take that as me conceding.

Impatient bastards.

Still, I waste as much time as possible as I grab fruit from the platter and carry them to my mates.

"Eat these," I say, holding out my hands. "Please," I continue, lowering my voice when I sense the argument on Aziel's tongue.

He frowns but takes the food from me without complaint.

While he and Silas snack, I turn to Charlie. She's already waiting for me, and she spreads her legs obediently as I crawl in her direction. I sink my teeth into my bottom lip as I stare down at her, and I adjust the fabric of her loose dress to cover her from the council's eyes.

"Take your time," she says, her eyes darting toward Silas and

Aziel.

I nod, already on the same page, before settling between her thighs. The council will grow angry if I take too long, but I should be able to stall for a little bit.

Anything to give Silas and Aziel time to recover.

Aziel holds Silas protectively as the man enters the fated world to try to feed from the energy there, but I know it won't help much. There's not enough time, and it's risky for him to go there when surrounded by so many people.

It leaves him too unalert and vulnerable.

Only fifteen minutes pass before the council grows impatient with Charlie and me, and with a defeated sigh, I lower my fingers to her clit and rub. She wiggles on my cock as I ease it in and out, going slow so it doesn't hurt.

I can feel the skin inside her swelling, my poor female's body ready to be done with sex.

She finishes with a gasp, and I rush to grab her some food before returning to my males. Silas offers himself up next, and I let him bury his face in the sheets so the council doesn't see his grimace.

"It's okay, baby. You're doing so well," I whisper, desperate to encourage him.

He usually loves praise, but he hardly reacts to it. It's not a good sign.

Even I'm starting to feel the effects. The sex itself isn't painful, but drawing their lust while simultaneously pushing out my scent to keep them going is exhausting.

I go three more rounds with my males before turning to Charlie.

"Stop pushing me aside," she huffs as Aziel tries to pull her behind him.

She shoves at his chest until he gives in and lets me approach her. Her desire to help is endearing, and I happily grab her ankle and drag her in my direction before lowering my mouth to her slit.

She tastes like Silas and Aziel, and I hum quietly as I flick her clit with the tip of my tongue, avoiding her entrance like the plague. The skin is red and swollen, and I fear she might bleed if I try to enter her again. I'm done fucking her, and I don't care how angry that makes her.

When she cums, it's with a frustrated moan, my female disappointed she couldn't fight her orgasm off longer.

Silas is napping when I turn to him, his hair disheveled and lips pulled tight. Aziel doesn't look much better, his eyelids half shut as he tucks Charlie against his chest and prods at her belly.

Her scent hasn't changed, so I know all is well. My Ephraim is strong.

Aziel avoids eye contact as I approach him, and I urge him onto his back so he can rest while I use my mouth. I get more when fucking him, but I can't do that.

Not when he's sitting around looking like the living dead.

He's barely able to get hard, his cock only stiffening halfway as I pleasure him. When it becomes clear it won't work, I kneel above him and touch myself instead. My dick burns as I stroke it, the skin raw, and when I'm close, I grab Aziel's hand and place it on me.

It serves to do the trick, and as I cum on his chest, his cock gives a sad twitch and spills only a dribble of cum.

Fuck.

My eyes grow panicked as I look between my three mates, unable to decide whom to go to next. It's apparent none of them want it, their bodies spent.

"It seems your offerings have been emptied, Gray." Valentine laughs.

I glare at her, hating how right she is. Aziel and Silas were so confident in their abilities, and I should've done a better job warning them of the stress this would put their bodies under.

This isn't sex like they understand it.

"Are you finished?" Aphrodite asks, cocking her head to the side.

I suck my lips into my mouth, not knowing what to say. I could probably roll Silas onto his stomach and take him that way. He wouldn't fight me, but that doesn't feel right.

I can't do that to him.

Chapter Twelve

CHARLOTTE

I'M FAINTLY AWARE I'm being rolled to the side and pressed against a warm, naked body.

The scent tells me it's Silas.

He curls around me, shielding my body from the council members. I appreciate it, and I fight sleep before sinking back against his chest. He's so warm, and my body refuses to cooperate with my mind.

It feels unnatural, and I realize why as the bonds in my chest soothe and comfort the second I try to move. My males are using the bonds to force me to relax and sleep. I didn't even realize that was possible.

I fall back asleep, but I jolt awake as Silas begins to move. He crawls over me, his chest pressing against mine as Gray leans over him. Gray frowns, trailing his hands down Silas's back before leaning down and placing his lips by Silas's ear.

"You're doing so good, baby," Gray whispers.

Silas's brow furrows before he buries his face in my neck. His body jolts as Gray pushes into him, and his muscles tense where they press against me.

"I just need you to cum once for me, and I'll return to Aziel," Gray promises.

The mention of Aziel has me turning, eager to see him. My heart jolts when I spot him less than an arm's distance away, the man lying on his back with his cock out. It seems he's given up on preserving his modesty, and I wiggle underneath Silas until I reach the discarded skirt.

Silas lifts his chest to give me more room, and I ignore the loud complaints from the council members as I cover Aziel. They're rude, and I frown as I turn toward them.

I have to blink a few times to ensure I'm not seeing things, and I straighten up as I realize that most of them are asleep.

I hope that means they're full, and I turn back to Silas just as he grunts and slumps into the mattress. Gray continues fucking him until Silas cries out and shivers a second time. Tears fill my eyes as his pain reaches me through the bond, and Gray grimaces as he feels the worry in mine.

"Use me," I tell Gray, tired of him avoiding me.

Gray hesitates, glancing at the sleeping Aziel before cleaning himself and moving to me.

I grab his chin when he tries to peer between my thighs, refusing to let him see. It hurts, and the last thing I want is for him to get cold feet and reject my help. I don't have much to offer the council members, but I want Aziel and Silas to rest.

"It's okay. I promise," I say.

Gray drops to his elbows, his hair tickling my forehead as he eases himself inside me. It takes everything I have not to wince, the pain of taking him more than I anticipated. I shut my eyes and breathe evenly through my nose as he places his fingers on my clit and begins to rub.

Blood rushes through my ears, and I fight the urge to cry as I let Gray pleasure me.

My orgasm comes quickly, and I stiffen with a quiet gasp as it tears through my body. I've cum enough for a lifetime, and I'd be happy never feeling it again.

"You're bleeding," Gray says, pulling out. "I'm so sorry. I shouldn't have done that."

I shake my head, but Gray isn't listening as he grabs a warm towel. His actions are gentle as he cleans me, and I refuse to show any pain even though every touch burns.

His end of the bond vibrates and soothes, and I huff when Silas begins to do something similar. The fate comes up from behind and wraps his arm around my waist, and I hate when my eyes involuntarily slip shut.

It feels like it's only for a moment, but I have a feeling it's much longer than that.

"No." Aziel's grunt wakes me up.

I open my eyes just as he smacks Gray away.

Gray purses his lips, but it's hard to tell through my blurry vision. I push myself into a sitting position, but Silas tightens his hold on my waist and yanks me back down before I get far.

"I'm sorry," Gray whispers, his voice hoarse. "We're so close. Roll over, and I'll blow you," he says, trying again to get Aziel off his stomach.

Aziel pushes him away again, the rejection loud and clear. Aziel's done.

I don't blame him.

It's been hours, and the few remaining council members show no signs of stopping.

Gray tries one last time before glancing at Silas and me. Silas pants quietly in my ear, the man in no better condition, and Gray shakes his head when I move to get up and offer myself.

"No more from you, Charlie," he says.

Gray doesn't look so hot himself, his face and skin a splotchy shade of red I'm unaccustomed to seeing on demons. Even when he was on the brink of starvation, he maintained his usual, tanned color. The more I scan him, the more I realize how much of a toll this is taking on his body.

His hair's lost its curl, the strands hanging limply at his shoulders, and the bags under his eyes are a deep purple. I knew this would be hard for him, but I never anticipated it being anything like this. I thought he'd fuck us once or twice and be done with it.

Gray moves away from Aziel, his eyebrows pulled tight before he collapses on the bed next to me.

"I'm so sorry, Charlie," he says, clearing his throat when his voice cracks. "I so badly wanted to do this for you and the females."

I offer Gray a watery smile and take his hand. He tried his best, and I don't blame him for not forcing Silas and Aziel to give more. Already, I'm worried about them, their bonds weak in my chest.

It's known that people can die if a Lust demon overworks them. Silas and Aziel are strong enough to resist and overpower anybody who tries with them, but I know they'd let themselves be taken to the brink of death for Gray. They trust him, and I suspect they've given him so much that they couldn't defend themselves right now even if they wanted to.

I try not to think too hard about what that means, and I focus on Gray as one of the council members stands and approaches the bed.

This is probably what Valentine hoped would happen, but we'll find another way. I know we will.

"Are you finished?" the councilwoman asks.

Gray squeezes his eyes shut, and I follow suit.

I'm so tired.

"For fuck's sake!"

I struggle to work up the strength to turn toward the voice. I think it's Rock, but instead of his usual hazy figure, I'm met with leathers.

Chev climbs onto the bed with an exaggerated huff, his body momentarily stiffening when he gets too close and breathes in Gray's lust. The shifter has been careful to keep his distance, and I cock my head to the side as he moves past me and pushes Gray toward the far corner of the bed.

I could reach out and touch them if I tried.

He faces the wall, exposing only his back, and roughly grabs Gray's wrist. I'm sure I'm hallucinating as he drags Gray's hand to the front of his body.

I blink a few times to ensure I'm not imagining this.

I'm surprised it's Chev, not Rock, volunteering himself, but I suppose Rock doesn't have much to provide, given he's a shadow. The council probably wouldn't even let it happen.

Gray's lips twitch, our bond roaring, before he settles himself and turns to us. He wants our permission. Aziel and Silas are too out of it to understand what's happening, and I stroke them through the bond before giving Gray a tentative nod.

We do this for the females.

Gray returns his attention to Chev. His eyes drift down the shifter's body, but he's stopped as Chev grabs his chin and forces his head upward.

"The sight of my erection is for my mate only," he snaps.

Gray's lips spread into a full smile, and his softness hits me through the bond a second later. He likes Chev's loyalty, finding it endearing, and he pointedly turns away as he slips his hand up the bottom of Chev's leathers.

I look away, wanting to respect Chev's privacy.

This is a big deal for him, and I hope his mate will understand.

My arms are sore as I grab Aziel and drag him closer. He's heavier than I expected and doesn't move an inch. Instead, he jolts awake, his gaze flickering around the room before settling on Gray and Chev. He raises a brow, mindlessly watching before turning to me.

He doesn't seem upset, and I'm glad.

I can't see what Gray and Chev are doing, but I hear muffled grunts accompanied by something wet.

I'm still in shock Chev is even doing this, and I press my hands against my ears to stop the noise from reaching them. Chev's saving as much of himself as he can for his mate, and I don't want to hear the sounds reserved solely for her.

Aziel rubs my head, and Silas wakes up and curls around me a second later.

I can feel through the bond that neither Silas nor Aziel enjoys what's happening between Gray and Chev, but I can also tell they aren't angry or hurt.

They understand, and Gray isn't taking pleasure in it. He's not being touched, and he only uses his hand.

As uncomfortable as it is, I'm relieved. I don't even want to think about how painful sex has become for Silas and Aziel.

After a few minutes, a loud grunt reaches my covered ears.

I uncover them as the remaining council members moan, but when I turn to see what's happening, Chev's sweaty palm presses against the side of my head.

"No," he says.

Silas brushes Chev aside and smooths over where the shifter's palm touched me.

"That was Chev's first time having an orgasm that wasn't by masturbation," Silas explains. "He had a lot to feed the council."

I nod, barely comprehending the words.

"Again." Chev clears his throat. "Cover your ears, Charlie."

I sigh, struggling to get my arms to obey the command. Silas comes to the rescue quickly, cupping my ears for me. Averting my gaze, I wiggle between him and Aziel until my face is underneath an armpit and the space around my eyes is dark.

I don't know how long I'm out, but when I wake up, it's to Aziel rolling and burying his face in my neck. His breath is warm, and I let myself enjoy it as a pair of hands slide between our bodies and prop up his hips.

"Just breathe in Charlie's scent," Gray says, his face coming into view as he leans over Aziel's shoulder.

He sinks his teeth into his bottom lip and rolls his hips forward, fucking Aziel slower than usual. Aziel's soft cock rubs against my thigh with each movement, the man putting his trust entirely in Gray as he lets himself be taken for what feels like the hundredth time tonight.

Despite Gray's words, Aziel starts to grow hard as he's used, his body responding positively to the touch. I reach down and take hold of him, my grip feather light as I give him something to thrust into.

The sooner he cums, the sooner he can rest.

"Thank you for letting me fuck you. I love it when you treat me for being good," Gray says, urging Aziel with his words.

It seems to do the trick as Aziel shutters, his length twitching in my hand before he lets out a pained cry and cums. I wouldn't have even known he had an orgasm if it weren't for the satisfied sighs from the council members, Aziel's dick offering nothing.

It twitches a few times before gradually growing soft, no cum emerging.

Gray moves to Silas next, but I don't stay awake long enough to see the fate's orgasm.

I'm being carried the next time I come to. I jolt awake, pushing against the bonds that try to lull me back to sleep. I'm tired of them doing this, and I grab Aziel's shoulder as I realize he's carrying me. He looks exhausted, with dark bags under his eyes and sunken cheeks.

"What's going on?" I ask, peering around.

We're back home.

Silas and Gray are walking right behind us, and they don't look much better than Aziel. If anything, Silas looks even worse.

Gray wraps an arm around the fate's waist for support, the sight shocking. Silas is always the picture of health and control, his confidence in himself and his abilities unwavering. Now he wears the expression of a young boy who stayed up too late past bedtime.

"We did it, my sweets," Gray answers, using his free hand to smooth my hair out of my face. "I still have to sort out things at Lust, but we returned to rest for a few hours before tackling all that."

We did it? I perk up, ignoring the pain radiating from practically every muscle in my body as I wrap my arms around Aziel's head in a tight hug. He chuckles into my chest, the sound hoarse.

"And Valentine?" I ask.

"She killed a guard and tried running to Mammon the moment the doors were unsealed, so she's been locked away for the time being," Gray says, reaching around Aziel to open our bedroom door.

"Mammon's been attacking the Wrath borders, which we anticipated, but Aziel's war generals have it under control. Chev's offered to monitor while we rest, and Aziel will take over *after* he rests." Gray shoots Aziel a pointed glare before continuing. "The council is working on pulling financial support from Mammon now, so hopefully, that will force her to pull back her armies and regroup."

I lick my lips, taking a moment to process that.

"That was nice of Chev," I say.

Gray smiles. "I think he's got a soft spot for me now that I've touched his penis."

Aziel snorts, and even Silas makes a mocking noise in the back of his throat. It clearly makes Gray feel good to think his sexual abilities have earned the affections of the shifter, and I'm not going to be the one to break the news to him.

We step into the bedroom, and Aziel sets me on the bed before crawling onto the mattress to my left. He's silent as he buries his face into the sheets and falls limp, and Silas quickly does the same on my right.

I expect Gray to follow, but instead, he walks into the bathroom and turns on the sink. My eyes slip shut as I listen, curious about what he's doing but too tired to keep them open. Even when my males are on the brink of death, they still use what little energy they have to soothe me through our bond.

It's easy to resist when only one of them is doing it, but when all three are working together, it's impossible to fight.

The sink shuts off seconds before Gray returns from the bathroom. He has a handful of wet washcloths, and he sets them on the edge of the bed before beginning to clean Silas. The fate doesn't move as Gray wipes his back and thighs, but he rolls over with a groan when Gray taps his hip.

His chest rises and falls with each slow breath, and I watch the movement as Gray finishes cleaning all the dried cum and sweat off his skin. I reach for a rag as Gray turns to me, ready to clean myself and save him the work, but he shakes his head and pushes my arm away.

"Let me do it. It's important to me," he says, nudging my legs apart.

I go limp, letting myself be maneuvered around.

Gray cleans Aziel last before finally wiping himself, and only once we're all clean does he climb into bed next to Silas. I grab the demons on either side of me, holding them tightly before letting myself nap.

I'll yell at them for using our bond to manipulate my body into sleep once they're feeling better.

Chapter Thirteen

GRAY

IT'S WEIRD BEING served by the demons who once scorned me, and I work hard to put my grudge aside as a succubus knocks on my office door and peeks inside.

Her black hair is thrown into a loose bun, and her lips have been painted a dark red. It matches the red lining around her eyes, and I gnaw at the inside of my cheek as I wave her inside.

"Good morning, Sax," I greet her.

Silas looks up from his computer and mumbles something similar.

She's a woman I spent ample time with before meeting Charlie, and I do my best to remain formal as she enters my office and sets the two cups of coffee I requested on my desk. She tried to seduce Silas and me earlier today, but it seems she's gotten the hint as she turns and rushes out of the room.

This is my first official day as the King of Lust, and I'm glad Sax has quickly picked up my lack of interest. I'm not my father, and I'm loyal to my mates.

Aziel would kill me if I so much as thought of another, and I'm pretty sure Charlie would rip my nipple off.

Still, I can't blame Sax for her attempts.

After years of being my father's assistant, she probably associates this office with feeding. I hope that image will change as the Lust demons come to think of this room as my space.

Even I can't wrap my head around the fact that I'm the new King of Lust. Asmod made it abundantly clear I'd never hold this position, especially after I left the den. He hated how I claimed my first love, Nicolette, as mine, so much so that he took it upon himself to marry her just to hurt me.

I tap my fingers against the side of my coffee mug as I remember how Aziel killed her during that Lust party all that time ago. I've never seen him so lost to his wrath before, and I'm pleased it was for Charlie. Even back then, he couldn't handle the thought of anybody but us touching her.

He's been obsessed with her since the first moment he saw her.

I know it.

I turn to Silas, knowing he felt something similar. He tried hard to keep his distance and remain only friends with Charlie, but she wormed her way into his heart just like I knew she would. My plans worked out perfectly, and I couldn't be more pleased.

There was only one moment I was worried, when Asmod and Valentine came over for dinner and tried to convince Silas to trade Charlie for Valentine. Asmod was so fucking adamant I could be thrown aside, but now it's I who sits in his office ruling his kingdom.

Me.

And the woman he mocked and called weak; she was the one who killed him.

Silas leans across my desk and grabs one of the coffee mugs Sax brought in.

He doesn't look good, the dark bags under his eyes and his

sunken cheeks just as bad as they were when we left the ceremony, and I wish he would've slept longer.

We're still in the middle of a war with Mammon, and being physically weak isn't safe. He needs rest.

Silas throws back the contents of his mug before reaching for mine. He immensely enjoys the caffeinated human beverage, but we can only drink it when Charlie isn't around. It's addictive to humans, and Aziel banned it from the house the moment he learned that. Now Silas and I have to sneak it in private.

Silas's eyes dart around his laptop screen as he works, and his eyebrows furrow whenever he stumbles upon something interesting. I don't find much interest in reading the Lust financial reports, but Silas has always been into these things.

I'm glad I can provide him with such entertainment.

"Why are you staring at me?" Silas asks, still looking at his computer.

I shrug, debating whether or not to tell him it's because he looks like shit. He should be back home with Aziel and Charlie, not here trying to figure this Lust stuff out with me. I understand his weird love for controlling everybody's money, but it won't kill him to take one day of rest.

Besides, he's admitted the Lust finances aren't nearly as bad as he thought. The demons who handle our accounting are good at their jobs, and they've kept everything tidy.

"Am I rich or not?" I ask, deciding not to inform him of his less-than-attractive appearance.

Silas rolls his eyes and turns away, but not before I catch sight of a sly smile. He likes me, even when he pretends not to.

"Yes, Gray, you're rich," he says, spinning his laptop so I can see the screen. "Asmod began charging for portal entry into Lust several years ago, which sounds ridiculous, but it was effective. People are willing to pay a lot for sex, especially since the female declines, and you guys provide the best."

Interesting. I didn't know anything about that, but that's probably because I don't use the portals.

I'm glad it's working, though. We need the money, and this guarantees we can continue supporting the females. War strains resources, but we've just doubled our reserves.

Silas continues to walk me through the intricacies of Lust's revenue streams, his voice soothing. He loves this stuff, and I listen intently as he explains everything in borderline excruciating detail. Even if he intends to handle most of the day-to-day, it's good for me to have a strong understanding of what's going on.

I don't want to be an incompetent leader.

"What are your thoughts on doing away with the council?" Silas asks, drawing my attention.

I grimace, knowing he's not going to like my answer. Aziel prefers the complete control he has over Wrath, but it comes with consequences. His workload is no joke, and he and Silas are always playing catchup. They can't take a day off without stressing, and they refuse to delegate.

I don't want that for myself, and the council takes much of the pressure off my back.

"I want to keep it," I say.

Silas purses his lips, his fingers tapping aimlessly on his keyboard before he shuts his computer and gives me his undivided attention. "That means you're always going to be playing politics with them. Now that you're King and the people recognize you, we can get Aziel to help you push out the council. You won't have to do it alone."

Wraths love Aziel, but Silas is the one who keeps everything running smoothly behind closed doors.

My hand shakes slightly as I run it through my hair, my body still drained from the ceremony.

"I want to be with our family," I admit. "You and Aziel are always so busy, and I want to spend my mornings making breakfast for our children and my afternoons on my hobbies."

I can't remember the last time I worked on my garden.

If I had my way, I wouldn't choose to be King. I'm taking this role because we need Lust to reach our goals, but I loved my job at the forest service and all the free time I had to spend with Charlie and my males.

I enjoyed being a househusband.

I hope one of my children is interested in ruling Lust, and I'll pass my job off to them the moment they feel they're ready.

"If that's what you want, Gray." Silas pauses to clear his throat, and my worry spikes as he takes a moment to collect his thoughts. Silas never loses his train of thought.

"Why don't you go home and rest?" I suggest.

I already know he won't like the insinuation that he's weak, but he's just going to need to get over that. I can see how drained he is, and the multiple cups of coffee he's drinking aren't helping.

"I'm fine," Silas says.

Liar.

I could kick him out and ban him from Lust until he's rested, but that would only cause more issues. He'd obey me to preserve my reputation, but I could see Aziel banning me from Wrath as punishment.

I want to avoid that as much as possible, considering that's where my growing baby is.

"I'm worried about Charlie," I say, trying a new route.

Maybe I can convince Silas to go home and check on her. She'll bully him into resting, and I know she'll be more successful than I would be.

She took a four-hour nap and woke up as good as new, bouncing around as she showed off her healed poison ivy leg. We told her it would heal quickly, thanks to our bonds, but it seems she got it in her head that the rash would last forever.

Still, Charlie's chipper mood was welcome, and Silas and Aziel used her as a distraction so they could sneak off.

I thought Aziel was going to the bathroom, but instead, he ordered Rock to remain with Charlie before teleporting to the Wrath borders to check on his men and regroup with Chev.

There were several attempted attacks on Wrath during the feeding ceremony, and while we were able to hold Mammon and the ogres back, this is far from over. Mammon lives up to her kingdom's name, the woman full of greed, and I have a feeling she'll risk everything to bring us down.

We're stretched thin despite Chev's help, and I hope Aziel can convince him to continue providing support. The two seem to be developing some sort of friendship, and I think Chev has softened toward me now that I've touched his penis.

Or, potentially, it has done the opposite.

Purity is everything to the shifters, and even though we did what we did for the greater good, that doesn't remove my hand from his cock. I tried to keep it as clinical as possible, not even using my good moves, but I'm sure he'll still struggle.

A pang of intense guilt mixes with excitement at the thought of taking something that doesn't belong to me. I like that I was the first to touch Chev, and I shake my head to get rid of the thoughts before they fester.

My new urges aren't me, and I hope they settle as my body acclimates to Asmod's power.

I'm happy with my family, and I don't need to actively try to ruin others.

If Chev has a shifter mate, or any from a blessed breed with fated mates, she could reject him for this.

I'd like to think Chev wouldn't be paired with a woman so

shallow, but shifters have been known to reject their other halves for much less. They take their promises seriously, and it's incredibly frowned upon when one breaks them.

I grab my nearly empty coffee mug and take a sip, my guilt growing.

Silas watches me, the man much too attentive for his own good, before standing and rounding my desk. He brings his hands onto my shoulders, his fingers burying into the muscle. It feels good, and I groan as I drop my chin to my chest.

I've only been doing this for a day, and already, I'm exhausted.

I miss the days when I had all the time to do whatever I wanted. I'd spend my mornings eating, my afternoons annoying Silas, and my evenings trying to weasel my way into Aziel's good graces.

Things were simple.

If I could do it over, I wouldn't change anything, but having a small break would be nice. Humans enjoy dedicating specific days to relaxation, and I'd like to try that when things settle with Lust and Mammon.

I could get Charlie and my males to do it, too. It would be good for the baby.

My pulse races as I think about our Ephraim, and I knock Silas's hands off me before spinning around.

"Have you checked Charlie for an infection?" I ask.

Silas's lips twitch, the response less than comforting. He's always teasing me about my worries, and it's growing annoying. Charlie's body is so weak compared to ours, and I don't want to take any risks.

I'm unsure if she can still get infections and diseases with our bonds strengthening her, and I'm not trying to find out the hard way. I want her to live forever, which won't happen if Silas continues to slack on her health checkups.

"Yes, Gray, she's perfectly fine," Silas says, patting my arm before grabbing his computer.

I snatch his wrist, stopping him before he returns to work.

"Please rest," I beg. "You can take a nap on the couch."

Silas visibly hesitates. We both know he's tired, and there's no good reason for him to push himself so hard. He needs his strength, and he's aware of that. He's like a thousand years old, and taking one day off is hardly a chore.

Besides, teleporting between Wrath and Lust is draining. Silas needs to keep his physical activity to a minimum.

I let out a quiet sigh and stand when it becomes clear Silas is going to argue.

I'm the only thing keeping this family together, and I grab his wrists before gently tugging him toward the couch. I sit on the edge before lying back and patting my chest.

"We could both use some rest," I say.

Relief as I've never known spreads through me when Silas gives in and lowers himself onto the couch with me. About fucking time. The sofa is too small for us, but I have little interest in going anywhere near the bed in here.

Silas likes to joke that my old bed has seen terrible atrocities, but it's nothing compared to what I'm sure has happened on the mattress in the corner of my new office. When things have calmed and redecorating this space seems less frivolous, I'll have it replaced with a new one.

Preferably one my father hasn't fucked somebody on.

I like the idea of tying Silas and Charlie up while I hold meetings and do my work. Nobody will be allowed to touch them, but I want everybody to see and want what I have.

I want them to lust after my mates.

At some point, I should have a conversation with them about

my new urges, but I'm struggling to find the right time to bring them up. My desire to be with only them hasn't changed, but I'm lying by not telling them how absorbing my father's power has amplified things.

Lust demons value sex and arousal too much not to be upfront about it.

"I'm not touching your penis," Silas says, shifting his leg that rests between my thighs.

I snort and run my hands through his hair.

"I don't expect you to."

If I'm honest, I don't want him to. Despite my body's reactions to my thoughts of tying him up, I'm exhausted. This nap will be good for me, too.

My fingers freeze, and I turn to glare down at Silas. What a sneaky son of a bitch. He did this on purpose, lingering around with his tired expression until I gave in and lay down with him.

Silas tightens his grip on my waist as if reading my thoughts, refusing to let me get up and return to work. He wiggles even further on top of me a second later, seeming to decide his tight hold isn't enough. I wasn't planning to get up, but I appreciate his efforts to keep me here.

He's needy.

"There's something I should tell you," I say, swallowing past the lump in my throat.

Silas hums, his tone signaling he's on the verge of sleep.

"Absorbing Asmod's power has me wanting things. Things that are more common amongst my kind," I admit. "I want to show you three off, and I'm enjoying feeding on all the sex here. I don't want to participate, and I swear I'm happy with what we have, but these things will be hard to avoid when I'm in Lust."

My pulse races, and I do my best not to look too panicked as I wait to hear what Silas says. I trust him with this information more than the others, his calm demeanor making me feel safe. Aziel's too quick to anger, and Charlie's a bit of a wildcard.

I don't want them to think I'm unhappy with our relationship.

I also don't want them growing concerned with me being alone in Lust. I'd never cheat on them, and just because I enjoy seeing the intimacy between my people doesn't mean I want to be part of it.

Silas presses his lips against my collarbone, gently kissing it before moving to the center of my chest. His stubble catches on the fabric of my shirt, and I curl my fingers around his waist with a shaky breath.

"You've always been a kinky motherfucker, Gray," Silas says, chuckling. "As long as you're not trying to touch or bring in anybody else, I don't care."

My tense muscles relax, a weight taken off my shoulders.

"Do you promise?" I ask.

Silas laughs, resting his cheek on my chest. "I promise, Gray."

I slide my hand up his spine before cupping the back of his head, my fingers slipping through his hair. I was afraid he'd be angry or disappointed with me, and I take this as a good sign.

My mates love me, even when I'm feeling a bit kinky.

Chapter Fourteen

SILAS

I HOPE I don't appear too bored as I listen to Gray's council members drone on.

We all sit around a large, wooden table in one of Lust's conference rooms, this one thankfully free of any fucking. It still reeks of sex, though, and I'm sure the red fabric covering the floor is permanently covered in the body fluids of the Lust demons.

I'm not a fan, but Gray doesn't seem to mind.

This is our first official meeting with the council, and I'm glad Gray was able to push it off until today. They wanted to do it yesterday, but Gray insisted we have another day to rest.

I needed it.

Gray convinced me to go home and check on Charlie after the nap I took on his couch yesterday, and my female took one look at me before dragging me to bed and lying on top of me until I fell back asleep. I only meant to rest for an hour or two, but almost twenty-four hours had passed by the time I woke up.

My exhaustion is still bone-deep, but I no longer feel moments away from death.

Gray clears his throat, and I straighten my spine and turn in his direction.

He's taking all of this in stride, and he's adapting quickly to the many changes being thrown his way. It's impressive, and it makes me realize just how much Aziel and I have been underestimating him. Gray's always been so carefree and wild, doing whatever he wants whenever he wants to.

I honestly wasn't sure he could handle such big responsibilities.

He and I make brief eye contact before he clears his throat and begins to speak, and I nod slightly to show my support.

"At the end of the day, Valentine threw Lust into the middle of the war for reasons even she can't identify," Gray says. "Asmod managed to remain neutral for hundreds of years, and Valentine's eagerness for violence only proves she's a liability."

The council members glance amongst themselves, but none speak up. They aren't pleased with Gray's decision to lock Valentine up, but I agree that it needed to be done. She tried running to Mammon the moment we left the ceremony, and we needed time to heal and secure Gray's position here. She'll be let out once things have settled.

The head of the council, Aphrodite, taps her nails against the table.

"Very well," she decides.

I'm surprised they aren't trying to push against Gray's decisions to see how much they can control him, but I figure that will come with time. They're impressed with his performance during the ceremony, but I'm sure their attitude will change once that wears off.

Asmod was a pushover, but Gray won't be.

"We'll make an announcement on her imprisonment," Aphrodite continues. "Before people begin asking where she is."

I lean back in my chair, impatiently waiting for the topic to shift to financials.

I typically don't enjoy sitting in meetings like this, the conversations almost always a waste of my time, but Gray asked me to join this one with him for moral support. It made sense initially, but after seeing how he interacts with the council members, it's clear he doesn't need me.

He's handling it on his own.

I pull up messaging on my computer and ask Aziel for an update.

He doesn't respond.

He only came home to sleep last night, and he was gone before I woke. His body regenerates his power naturally, so he doesn't need the rest as much as I do. I gain strength by going into the fated world, and the safest and easiest time to do that is when I'm sleeping.

The fates have been ignoring me recently, and I'm beginning to grow suspicious. Fate typically guides me toward the moments across the realms they wish for me to see—future, past, and present—but I've been finding myself alone most nights.

It means they're hiding something from me.

The last time they were elusive was when I was searching for Charlie's future.

They weren't pleased when I took it upon myself to search for Charlie's mother, either, but they didn't try too hard to keep it from me. I'm glad, and I can tell it pleases Charlie to know her mom will be okay.

I hope we can bring her to Wrath soon.

"We should discuss how we want to handle the Wrath/Lust borders," Aphrodite says.

I should've waited until the meeting was half over to join.

It would be disrespectful to leave in the middle of Gray's meeting and return later, especially since he's so new. I waited many years before beginning to do those things to Aziel, and even then, my actions were met with hushed whispers by the Wrath generals. They were pissed, and I'm sure they were ready to fight me in defense of Aziel's honor.

They don't even blink an eye now, which is ideal for me.

I hate sitting through these meetings.

"Actually, let's hand it off to Silas," Gray says, gesturing to me.

Finally.

There's a large TV built into the far wall, and I connect my computer to it before sharing my screen. I've put together a proposal for the female effort, and I don't hesitate to launch into an explanation of our plan and the financials we'll need from Lust to back it up.

Things like this would be much easier if Gray agreed to do away with the council, but I won't push him. I know how much he enjoys being home, and I refuse to pressure him to give it up.

If I need to play politics, then that's what I'll do.

The council seems interested in what I have to say, a few of them occasionally asking questions about the social workers we intend to work with the shifters to hire and our plans for mass collection of purchased females. It's a big task, I'm fully aware of that, but with the blessed breeds and Lust's support, I'm confident we'll be able to get it done.

Gray grins as I finish speaking, and he stands next to me as the council begins with their onslaught of questions. Most are expected and easy to answer, but I have to turn to Gray for help when they start getting intricate into the implications this could have for the Lust lifestyle.

I'm not as familiar as he is with Lust culture, and I stand back as he speaks.

"This won't have much of an impact on day-to-day inside

Lust," he says. "There aren't many purchased females here, and we won't put a rehabilitation facility on these lands if you feel it will be too disruptive."

We agreed privately with the blessed breeds that no facilities would be put in Lust, and I like the way Gray frames it so the council members feel it'll be their decision. The females we rescue most likely aren't going to be interested in intimacy, and we don't want to risk any Lust demons trying to break in and take advantage.

It's not worth the risk, and it would undermine our efforts.

The meeting drags on, and it's not for another hour that Gray finally calls for a vote.

I hold my breath, anxious, and release it with a big sigh when the council approves the funds.

Lust is one of the wealthiest kingdoms, second only to the dragons who love to hoard, so it's not like this will have a considerable impact on Lust economy. It's a drop in the hat.

I practically sprint from the room the moment the meeting ends, and I hurry toward Gray's office to shut my eyes and turn off my brain. My head pounds, and being alert for such a long period of time is tiring. The ceremony exhausted me more than I'd care to admit, and it's taking longer than I thought it would to recover.

"Are you okay?" Gray asks, shutting the office door behind him.

I nod, not caring if he can see right through it, and drop down on his couch.

Gray frowns, scanning my figure before climbing onto my lap and straddling me.

"Yes?" I laugh, letting my hands rest on his hips.

He wiggles, getting comfortable before reaching for my neck. I crane my head to the side, letting him see Charlie's mark.

"She got you good," he says, tracing the scar she left behind.

I can't stop a smile from spreading over my lips as I spot the jealousy in his eyes. Her bite is deeper on me than it is on Gray and Aziel, and I proudly let him feel it and realize just how aggressive she was.

My eyes slip shut as I search for her through the bond, enjoying how I can sense her heartbeat and emotions even when we're so far apart. I'll always be able to feel her, and even better, I'll always be able to locate her.

"Can I mark you now?" Gray asks.

I blink, but I'm not surprised. I expected him to ask soon.

Gray's not exactly known for his patience, and he's been eager to sink his teeth into me. I've been holding out because I wanted to honor our female with my first bonding, but now nothing is holding me back from Gray.

His eyes widen as he stares at my neck, his excitement visible as he licks his lips and leans forward. He's made his desire to mark me more than evident these past few weeks, and I can't stop smiling as I tighten my hold on his waist and nod.

Gray grabs my chin and tilts my head back as he decides where to do it.

My pulse races, and I'm eager to see where he goes. Charlie and Aziel chose the right side of his neck, leaving the left open for me.

I will mark him in the center, claiming the entire side as my own. I don't want to leave room for anybody else.

Gray's throat bobs as he gulps, his eyes locking in on the spot he wants. I sigh, relaxing underneath him as he brings his lips to my skin and kisses over his chosen area. It's opposite Charlie's, and it's low enough that Aziel will still have room.

My jaw drops as Gray scrapes his teeth against my throat, and I press myself harder against him with a quiet gasp. He's taking too long, always trying to tease me.

"Fuck." I gasp when he finally bites down.

It stings, but it feels more pleasurable than anything else. My body's made to take a bond, and it welcomes Gray's with open arms. He moans as our souls intertwine, and with a low grunt, I push his hair out of the way and return the gesture.

It occurs to me halfway through that maybe I should've asked him before biting, but when Gray gasps and rocks his hips, I figure he's happy with my decision. His arousal hits me a second later, the intensity of it shocking.

My body responds, but neither of us moves to do anything about it. I'm still sore from the ceremony.

Gray lets me rest my teeth in his neck before pulling away, his movement drawing an instinctual whine from me. My cheeks warm at the noise, a bit embarrassed about the desperate tinge.

"I love you," I blurt out, prodding him through the new bond.

I can feel him doing the same to me, the incubus wasting no time forcing his way into my mind. He's careful not to pry too hard, the man smart enough to know how dangerous that can be. My head isn't normal, and his ability to walk through dreams gives him more access to my mind than I'd like him to have.

"All that's left is Aziel," Gray says.

He jumps to his feet and grabs my hand, always so sporadic. I let him pull me off the couch and into his arms, humoring him. Any weirdness I may have felt with our relationship vanished during the ceremony, the man touching and holding me in enough vulnerable positions that nothing feels uncomfortable anymore.

Gray squeezes hard and sniffs my hair before mumbling that he'll teleport us home.

Instinctively, I move to argue with him, accustomed to always being the one who has to take him, but I shut my mouth as I remember he's more than capable now. Asmod's power has made him stronger, and the little things he used to struggle with are child's play to him now.

I relax into his arms as he takes us back to Wrath and our bedroom materializes around us. It smells like home, and I chuckle as my eyes land on Aziel and Charlie.

It seems I'm not the only one who's fallen victim to Charlie's demands. She lies on top of Aziel, playing on his phone while he snores underneath her. He's still wearing his clothes, and Charlie threw Gray's pillow over his bare feet to keep them warm.

She looks up at us, carefully setting Aziel's phone on his forehead as we enter the room.

Gray slaps a hand over his mouth to stifle his laughter, but the noise is enough to have Aziel jerking awake. He curls his arms protectively around Charlie as he sits up, his phone tumbling down his face as he turns in our direction.

I bite back a laugh. I suppose that explains why he didn't respond to my message earlier.

"Have a good nap?" Gray teases.

Aziel rolls his eyes and falls back onto the bed. "Charlie can be quite persuasive. How'd the meeting with the council go?"

I kick off my shoes and go into the bathroom to clean the blood off my neck while Gray explains everything to Charlie and Aziel. Charlie wanted to come with us today, but we convinced her it would be best to stay out of Lust until everything with Gray was settled.

The Lust demons will test Gray's authority, trying to push his boundaries, and we don't want Charlie getting caught in the crossfire.

Gray's showing off his new mark to Aziel and Charlie when I step back into the bedroom, a wide smile on his lips as he turns his head from side to side so they can see it at every angle. I'm pleased he's so proud of it.

Charlie meets my eye, her lips curling.

Feeling her love and having the absolute certainty from our bond that she's genuine in her apologies and desire for us has me feeling like I can finally breathe. My chest no longer feels tight when I see her, and I no longer fear what she's doing when she's not in the room.

I trust she's faithful to us, and I believe our relationship is genuinely what she wants.

"All that's left is you and Silas," Gray tells Aziel before grabbing my arm.

He pulls me in front of Aziel, the incubus not nearly as subtle as I think he's trying to be. Aziel reaches for me, and Charlie rolls away as I kneel on the bed. The mattress sinks under my weight, and Aziel pulls me onto his lap before cupping the back of my head so he can see my mark.

I shiver when he runs his thumb over it.

"You bonded with Gray," he says.

"Yes."

Aziel grins, and I kiss the unmarked spot on his neck. It's smooth, and I wait patiently for him to give me permission to bite. I don't have to wait for long, and Aziel curls his fingers around my neck to hold me steady.

"Do it," he orders.

His skin is a bit salty, and I lick it clean before claiming him as my own.

Aziel jerks, a quiet hiss slipping from his lips as the bond between us forms. I moan quietly as it grows, and after a few seconds, I pull out and tilt my head back, waiting for the bite in return.

I'm excited for it.

Aziel chuckles and flips us over, putting me on my back with him hovering above. I'm unsure why, and I pant as Aziel crawls down my torso.

What's he doing?

He slips his fingers under my shirt and pulls it up, and I grab the sheets below me as he makes his way to my pants. I thought he'd want to mark me back, and I do my best to hide my disappointment as he unbuttons my bottoms and removes them with my underwear.

He tosses both items aside.

"Spread your legs," he says.

I gulp, a bit confused as I open my legs as instructed. Aziel settles between my thighs before grabbing my cock with his right hand. I'm soft, and he squeezes me tightly before stroking me into hardness.

Gray leans in, the incubus more than a little curious as he walks around us so he can better see. Out of the corner of my eye, I spot Charlie's hand curling around his bicep and yanking him out of view.

"Give them privacy," she hisses.

I laugh, the noise ending in a breathy gasp as Aziel brings his lips to the inside of my thigh.

"I only have one opportunity to mark you, and I want it to be in a spot that's truly mine," he says, grinning as he moves my cock to the right and places his mouth on the side of it.

I pant, shaking my head to ensure I'm not seeing things.

Aziel's never put his mouth on me before, and I sink my teeth into my bottom lip as he slides his lips down the length of my shaft.

Is he going to mark my dick?

Marks are sensitive, and my sex life will be ruined if he does that. I'll be lucky to fuck for even a minute before cumming. That thought has me stiffening even further, my body loving the idea even if I'm still burnt out from the ceremony.

Aziel sucks my tip into his mouth, his cheeks hollowing around me. My eyes screw shut before I force them open, not wanting to miss a second of this.

Did Gray teach him how to do this?

"Is this mine?" Aziel asks, pulling back.

I glance at Charlie and Gray. "Yes," I say. Aziel likes to control us, and I shouldn't be nearly as surprised as I am that he wants to claim ownership of my cock.

Aziel tightens his grip before sinking his teeth into the base of my shaft. A loud curse bubbles out of my throat, and I shut my eyes as my thighs clamp around his head. Aziel pulls them apart with his hands, spreading them so far, they burn.

His bite hurts so fucking bad, and I hold on to Aziel's shoulders. My cock softens, the pain overwhelming, and Aziel's quick to pull back and apply pressure until it heals.

I squeeze my eyes shut as I work to catch my breath.

"Are you okay?" Aziel asks, using his shirt to wipe off the blood.

Our newly formed bond vibrates with concern, and I run a shaky hand through my hair before giving a jerky nod.

"I'm good," I say.

Aziel crawls back up my body and wraps his arms around me. He pulls me against his chest and kisses my head, comforting me.

"You did so well, Silas," he whispers into my hair. "I'm proud of you."

I feel him smirking as my pulse races, the man knowing how much I love the praise. Cocky bastard.

Chapter Fifteen

CHARLOTTE

HOT. I'M HOT.

I kick my comforter away with a low grunt, desperate for fresh air.

Gray breathes loudly on my left, and I roll over and grab him so he can't leave while I'm sleeping. Each of my males has been getting up and leaving early, Gray and Silas to Lust and Aziel to the Wrath borders, and they don't return until well after bedtime.

Not today, though. I'm keeping Gray hostage.

"Come here." Gray chuckles, his voice low as he pulls me over him.

I happily rest my head on his chest.

We aren't usually big cuddlers, but the distance has made me needy. I think it's the bond, the tightness in my chest worsening whenever he's in Lust. Aziel says it will get better with time and it's only this strong because it's fresh, but that doesn't comfort me.

A body rolls into the spot I once occupied, settling next to Gray and me. My face is buried in the incubus's armpit, so I'm not sure who it is, but it's only a matter of time before Gray begins to feel constricted and pushes us away.

My muscles relax as I fall back asleep, but after a second, I rip myself from Gray's arms and rush to the bathroom. Feet stomp behind me, and I slam the door in the person's face before dropping to my knees in front of the toilet.

The door bounces off the wall half a second later, and somebody pulls back my hair as I get sick.

"Are you okay?" Silas asks, tying my hair in a knot at the base of my neck.

I nod, more than a bit embarrassed he's watching me puke. I rest my head against the toilet bowl, so fucking nauseous, before working up the strength to face Silas.

He rubs the back of my neck, his touch comforting as Aziel and Gray step into the room.

"It's the infection," Gray cries.

He's pushing past a concerned-looking Aziel a second later.

I have no idea what infection he's talking about, but I don't have the opportunity to ask as another bout of nausea takes over my body. Silas rubs my back as I get sick, and Aziel hands me a glass of water to swish around my mouth once I finish.

Gray continues to fret, the man anxiously pacing the room.

"I'm okay," I say.

It's the baby, and I've felt this way for days. I've been doing my best to be subtle about it, my males not very good at being calm when it comes to human illnesses. Silas is better than the others, but Gray gets all panicky and Aziel unsuccessfully tries to hide his fear by lurking menacingly in corners.

"There's medicine we can get you for the nausea," Silas says, flushing the toilet for me. "How often is this happening?"

My skin is clammy, and I lie back on the cool tile floor before answering Silas.

"Not often," I lie.

Gray grabs my thighs and pulls them apart.

I only wore Aziel's shirt to bed, and Gray seems to be taking full advantage of that as he examines the lower half of my body. I don't know what he's looking for, but sometimes it's better to let him do what he needs to.

I think it's an incubus trait.

He feels he needs to care for us, and more often than not, it drives him to do odd things like this. Gray's been more intense with it recently, and Silas has whispered to Aziel and me that Gray's been feeling stronger urges after absorbing Asmod's power.

Silas seemed to feel guilty about going against Gray's wishes and telling us, but I'm glad he did. I love Gray, and it's helpful for us to know he's sensitive about his urges.

I suck in a few slow breaths before shooing Gray away and sitting back up. I'm feeling better.

"Stay here," Aziel orders, grabbing my shoulder when I move to stand. "Give yourself another minute."

Eventually, Aziel grabs my arms and helps me stand, his actions slow so he doesn't risk making me nauseous. I appreciate it, and I clasp my hands behind my back as Aziel drops to his knees. He rarely kneels for us, and my cheeks warm as he grabs my waist and kisses the smooth skin just above my belly button.

"Stop making Mom sick," he says, giving me another soft kiss.

My heart flutters, and I place a hand over my mouth as he stands back up. Aziel's not one for romantic gestures, and I never thought I'd have the pleasure of seeing him talk to my belly.

"Do you feel better?" Silas asks, running his hand down my spine.

I shrug.

There's a faint pulling from each of my bonds, which I assume is my males prying to see how I'm feeling. It's weird how they can dig into my mind whenever they want, and even though they can't actively hear my thoughts, they can figure out just about everything else.

These men are too smooth for their own good, and I need to learn how to do the same to them. I'm not as coordinated, and I usually get a sideways glance whenever I attempt to pry on them through the bond.

The good news is I have all the time in the world to learn how to be as sneaky as they are.

"What time is it?" I ask.

Gray pushes his hair out of his face and reaches for me. "It's still early. We can relax in bed for another twenty or so minutes."

The offer's enticing, but I reject it with a shake of my head and go to the sink to brush my teeth.

Aziel and I are meeting with Chev early this morning, and we should prepare. Mammon pulled back a significant number of her troops yesterday, and this is the first time Aziel will be working from home since the feeding ceremony.

Chev agreed to leave his shifters in Wrath for another three days, allowing the Wrath soldiers who fought in Lust to remain there and keep Mammon and the ogres out.

Silas watches as I ready my toothbrush, and I make eye contact with him through the mirror as I shove it in my mouth. I feel guilty for waking him and the others up, but at least he's starting to look more like himself.

All my males are.

The dark bags underneath their eyes are gone, and they're finally starting to get some color back into their skin.

"What're you two doing today?" I ask around my toothbrush, turning to Silas and Gray.

Gray's been busy catching up on what's been happening in

Lust for the past hundred or so years he's been absent, and I can feel his stress through the bond each day he goes there. Silas is no better, both men a bundle of nerves.

"We're meeting with the council to get approval on a few items, and Silas is going to help me sort through paperwork," Gray says, wrapping his arms around Aziel's torso. "I think the council members are in love with me."

I laugh. Gray seems to think everybody's in love with him.

"How are things with Chev?" Silas chimes in, changing the subject.

Aziel shrugs, not at all bothered as Gray hugs him from behind. The Aziel I first met would've never considered letting Gray hug him, let alone so intimately.

"He hasn't brought up the ceremony, if that's what you're asking," Aziel says, crossing his arms over his chest.

He looks calm, but embarrassment floods our bond at the mention of the ceremony. I've tried asking Aziel about it, but it's not a topic he's open to discussing. Still, I step forward and wrap my arms around him and Gray, hoping he can feel my love.

He feels bad about not being strong enough to feed the council, but I'm more than impressed by what he did. He and Silas went for hours, and Gray told me Asmod used to bring in dozens of partners when he hosted.

Aziel stiffens as he's trapped between Gray and me, and he loudly groans when Silas comes up behind me to join. He doesn't pull away, though, which speaks volumes.

"As fun as this is, I should prepare for our meeting with Chev." Aziel grunts, smoothly trying to remove himself from the hug pile. "He mentioned letting Echo visit."

Really? I pull away, bouncing on my toes.

"I was thinking you and she could work on the females while Chev and I focus on Mammon," Aziel continues.

That sounds amazing. I haven't seen Echo since the awkward apology inside the shifter meeting cave, and I desperately need some girl talk.

I'm sure Kato isn't happy about his daughter coming here, but he's taken a back seat since being urged into retirement. Chev's been owning all conversations with Aziel.

"Silas, can you send me the final amount you got the Lust council to agree to?" I ask.

Silas releases Aziel with a nod. "Of course."

Gray continues to hold Aziel, and the Wrath awkwardly shifts before wiggling free and making his way into our closet. I follow and sit on the edge of the bed, taking a moment for my racing heart to slow when another bout of nausea hits me.

This whole baby thing isn't as fun as I thought it would be.

I haven't spent much time thinking about the fact that I'm going to be a mother. The idea of children was never something I let myself wish for, the fear of having a female too great a risk. A small part of me is still scared, fearful of the world our child will be born into, which only further urges me to push for action to be taken toward securing the females and instilling new regulations.

I want my daughters, if I have any, to be born into a world where they don't fear the actions of men.

"If you want to rest, I can ask Echo to come over later," Aziel offers, stepping out of the closet.

He's dressed in a pair of blue slacks and a white button-up shirt, and Gray gives an appreciative hum as he walks past and steps into the closet with Silas. I enjoy it when Aziel dresses up, too, and I can't help but smile as Aziel's cheeks turn a light shade of pink.

He's shy.

"I'm okay, I promise," I say, pushing off the bed. "I want to see Echo."

Aziel doesn't look convinced, but thankfully, he doesn't argue as I make my way to the closet and pick out something to wear. Silas and Gray bicker quietly amongst themselves, and I slip around them before tugging on a loose dress and pulling the pair in for a goodbye kiss.

"I'll see you tonight," Silas says. "I love you."

My heart thumps every time he says that, and I flush as Gray points it out. Gray's always trying to embarrass me, and I step out of the closet before he takes it upon himself to say anything else.

I head downstairs, pointedly avoiding the dining room and kitchen as I make my way to my office. Rock and I have been working on some plans for the facilities these past few days, and my office is a bit messy.

A quiet knock on my door draws my attention, and I spin just as Silas steps inside.

"Hey," I say, shocked he's here. "I thought you were going to Lust with Gray."

Silas nods. "I am, but I wanted to speak with you first."

Well, isn't that ominous. I clear my throat and sit on the edge of my desk, waiting to hear what he says. I was under the impression things were getting better, the two of us no longer on edge around one another, but maybe I misread the situation.

Silas makes his way to me and grabs my waist. His grip is light, and he sighs before shutting his eyes and dropping his forehead onto mine.

"I'm so sorry, Charlie," he whispers, his voice rough. "You've been so patient with me, even when I don't deserve it. I abandoned you when you were forced into Lust, and I can't express enough how ashamed I am."

Silas clears his throat, our bond pulsating with pain and regret, and my heart swells as I cup his cheeks and look him in the eye.

"We both fucked up, Silas, and you have no idea how sorry I

am, too," I promise him. "I love you, and I'm not angry with you. I understand why you did what you did, and I'm happy to be here with you today. You make me happy."

His guilt pours into me, and I readjust my grip on his cheeks with a quiet sigh.

"Our relationship wasn't equal," I say, "and there was a lot we needed to work through, but that doesn't excuse cheating. I deserved your cold shoulder and every bit of doubt and caution you threw my way."

Silas doesn't look pleased as he pulls away, his wide, black eyes staring into mine. He won't get the response he wants out of me, and I won't be mad at him to make him feel better about his unnecessary regret.

Instead, I trail my fingers over the mark I left on his neck, hoping he can feel my love for him. It's all-consuming, and I'm so grateful to have him in my life.

"Aziel." Chev's loud voice echoes down the hallway just outside my office. "I have arrived!"

Silas rolls his eyes as he pulls away from me. "I should get going," he says. "Don't push yourself today. If you're not feeling well, take time to rest."

"Of course," I say.

We both know I won't do that, and Silas shakes his head before vanishing.

I hop off my desk just as Chev and Echo peek into my office. The female shifter beams as she pushes past her brother and steps inside, and I can't help but laugh as Chev glares at the back of her head. Those two are always fighting.

"Aziel's in his office," I say.

Chev smacks his tongue against the roof of his mouth, the man clearly upset about his lack of formal welcome at the portal. He was probably expecting Aziel to stand outside it like a coat rack.

"Thanks, Charlie," he says, spinning on his heel.

I shift my attention to Echo, my lips curling before I lunge forward and yank her into a tight hug. She squeezes me back, her hold so tight, I groan.

"I missed you," she says, lifting me a few inches before swinging me back and forth. "And I'm eager to get to work."

Echo takes the words straight out of my mouth, and we make our way to my desk as she fills me in on everything the shifters have been working on while my males and I have been distracted with Lust and the war with Mammon.

"The Seekers organization already has one or two secure housing facilities built on each realm. They use them to hold females before they're sold…" She trails off awkwardly, seemingly not remembering until just now that I spent time in one before being purchased by Aziel. "The buildings are good, and the security measures are top tier. We plan to repurpose them into rehabilitation facilities."

That makes sense.

"What do you plan to do with the Seekers employees?" I ask.

Echo shrugs. "Chev wants to, and I quote, 'crush them,' but the official plan is to replace them with shifters. We'll need bodies both inside the facilities and in the corporate offices, and, over time, we'd like to begin employing women."

I bounce in my seat, beyond excited. "This all sounds so amazing." I clasp my hands together. "I'm sure you've already heard that Silas secured funds from the Lust council, so that'll be a huge help."

Silas said he would send me the details, and I gesture for Echo to pull up a chair as I grab my computer and check my messages.

As promised, there's one on top from Silas.

Echo and I get to work reading through it, and we print out and mark up several documents for her to bring back to the shifters. I'm eager to join meetings with them, but Aziel has been anxious about me leaving home until everything is settled with Mammon.

I don't love it, but it's not an argument worth having.

I understand why he's nervous, and I don't mind waiting a few days until he feels he's got things under control.

Echo and I work for several hours, but it gets hard to focus when Chev and Aziel grow loud. I don't understand what they say, but their voices travel down the hallway and into my office.

It's excessive, and after twenty minutes, Echo and I make eye contact.

"I have no idea." I sigh, answering the unspoken question.

When a bang vibrates my desk, I stand and storm out of the room, determined to figure out what they're up to. Aziel and Chev are in the hallway outside the portal, and both men freeze as they spot me.

The large chest they're carrying drops to the floor.

"What's going on?" I ask.

Aziel straightens up, pretending he wasn't just hunched over trying to sneak the chest into the shifter lands.

"Aren't you supposed to be discussing Mammon?" I pry, cocking my head to the side.

Chev clears his throat, looking awkward as he gestures for Echo to come over. She brushes past me, and Chev orders her to help him lift the chest.

I watch, intrigued, as they carry it through the portal.

"What's in that?" I ask the second they disappear.

Aziel shoves his hands in his pockets and rocks back on his heels, his eyes darting around before he sighs and turns into his office. I'm quick to follow.

"There are jewels in there," he says. "The shifters don't believe in banking systems and prefer to have their money in physical forms."

Of course they do. That doesn't explain why Aziel was giving Chev money, though, which we both know is my next question. I open my mouth to ask, but the words die in my throat as I scan the papers cluttering the top of Aziel's desk. At least a dozen maps are scattered on it, each marked with ink.

It's messy, but Aziel seems to understand where everything is as he pulls out one of the larger maps and sets it on top. It's of the Wrath lands.

"Mammon's soldiers are stationed at these red points here," he explains, gesturing to the markings along the border. Many of them have been erased and moved inward.

"She's been getting more aggressive?" I ask. "I thought you said she was pulling back."

Aziel runs a hand through his hair, and the tugging of our bond tells me I'm not about to like what comes out of his mouth next.

"Most of her warriors are mid-level demons, so they can teleport, but not far," Aziel says, his knuckles turning white as he grips the desk's edge. "Our home is far enough away from the border that there hasn't been a huge concern with them trying to enter our home, but with them moving in, I have a feeling that's what she's planning. Mammon knows she won't win in a war against us, and I can only think of one reason she wouldn't be retreating."

Our bond almost hurts with how hard he's pulling on it, and I step to the side and press my body against his in the hopes of calming him down. I'm here, and I'm okay.

"I killed her eldest son years ago, and she wants to hurt me just the same." Aziel releases his desk and pushes my hair behind my ear.

I never thought I'd see the day Aziel would touch me with such love. He's still grumpy, always annoyed by our males and me, but there's tenderness behind it.

Even when he's trying to hide it, the bond gives him away.

Aziel seems to sense the direction of my thoughts as a tight smile spreads over his lips, his eyes crinkling at the corners before he turns back to the map. He pulls out another one, a zoomed-in version of the southern border, where most of Mammon's troops are.

I look over it, my interest piqued by the large, black circle Aziel's crudely drawn over a relatively large cluster of red spots.

"We're launching an attack here," Aziel explains. "This should take out about thirty percent of Mammon's troops, and it'll have the ogres pulling out for good. Gray and Silas will be coming with me, and I'd like you and Rock to stay with Chev and Echo until the attack is over."

My heart lurches.

"Why do Gray and Silas need to come?" I ask.

Aziel runs his thumbs across my cheekbones. "Silas's brain is an asset, and I'll need his support. Gray will be there on behalf of Lust. My people need to see him as a ruler, and if he's not there, it'll reflect poorly on him in the eyes of the Wraths."

I struggle to swallow past the lump in my throat. "Have you talked to Silas and Gray about this already?"

Aziel shakes his head. "I wanted to talk to you first."

My heart flutters, happy he's considering my feelings rather than deciding for me. I appreciate the gesture, and I scan the map with a heavy heart. I can't ask them to stay here, and I'm sure nobody would ever expect them to let me leave the estate without them. I'll be safe with the shifters.

Even if Mammon knew I was there, it would be hard for a Greed to find me without being caught by one of the shifters.

"For how long?" I ask.

I hate being away from my males, and I've grown accustomed

to having them around.

Aziel's cheeks cave into his mouth as he debates an answer. "Not long. I'm hoping only a few days. We'll leave tonight."

"Promise me you'll be safe," I order. "I expect all three of you to return in perfect condition."

Aziel smirks. "I promise."

We go over the details of the attack, and I ask no less than a thousand questions before Aziel and I make our way upstairs to pack some clothes for my stay with the shifters.

He lingers in the doorway as I grab a bag and begin packing. I don't know where my leathers went, Gray or Silas probably having moved them at some point, so I stick to the athletic clothing I usually wear.

They're comfortable, and they give me a good range of movement.

Aziel pulls out his phone to send some messages, and a few minutes later, Gray and Silas appear in the bedroom. They look angry, and they pull Aziel out of the room without so much as a glance in my direction.

I continue packing as Gray's loud voice travels down the hallway.

He isn't happy with Aziel's plan to send me to the shifter lands. I don't love it, either, but I dislike the idea of being murdered more. Besides, I miss my cabin, and I haven't checked my traps in a few days. Although maybe it's time to give them up.

I'm pretty sure I left them in a giant patch of poison ivy, and I'm not in the shifter lands enough to justify keeping them.

I absentmindedly rub my stomach. There's still no bump to my belly, the skin just as it was before I found out I was pregnant, but I hope there'll be something to feel soon.

My lips curl as I imagine what it'll feel like to have my belly stretch around a baby. Gray's probably going to be all over it. He already is now, and there's nothing even to see.

A quiet creak of the bedroom door draws my attention, and I roll my eyes as I turn to see what agreement my males have come to. Instead, an unfamiliar demon stands in the doorway. He's relatively tall, probably standing around six or so feet, with strong features and short, black hair.

I shake my head, my mind going blank before I open my mouth and scream.

The noise hurts my throat as it erupts, and I slam my back against the dresser as my males come busting through the door. Aziel's on top of the stranger before my eyes track the movement, tackling him to the floor before he freezes and laughs.

I place a hand over my chest, struggling to breathe as Gray rushes over and pulls me into his arms.

"That was such a good scream," he says, completely ignoring the strange man who's welcomed himself into our bedroom. "You should have used it when Shay took it upon herself to sneak in and meet with you."

Aziel climbs off the demon and helps him up. The man pops to his feet with a snort, adjusting his clothing before turning toward me.

"It's me," he says, stepping forward.

I move back, pulling Gray with me. I don't know what this man has said to convince my males that I know him, but I definitely do not.

"Charlie," Gray whispers, running his hand down my arm. "It's Rock."

The words take a long moment to sink in, my panic making me slow. Rock? Rock is a shadow, and the demon standing before me is very much solid.

"I solidified during the ceremony," the demon explains, lifting his hands in a gesture of peace. "But you were asleep when it happened."

I do faintly remember Rock telling me all about the different ways he could become solid, but I still don't believe this man is my shadowy tutor. I'm not sure where Rock disappeared after the ceremony, but he's always venturing off on little side missions for my males.

"Oh, come on, Charlie. I know you recognize my voice." The man laughs, clearly finding humor in this. "If it helps, I can tell everybody about the time you were so sore after training with Echo, you needed my help sitting on the toilet?"

Aziel raises a brow, his lips twitching as he clears his throat and begins reviewing all the clothing I've packed. Even Silas makes a noise, his angry expression cracking as he joins Aziel by my suitcase.

It's not that funny.

Gray's the only one who doesn't laugh, his comforting hold remaining.

This stranger does sound like Rock, and only Rock would know that story. I suppose my males would be able to tell if it were an imposter, too. They've got better senses than I do, and they can probably smell that it's him.

Rock holds his hands out to the side and does a spin, showing off his new body. The action feels very him.

"What are you now?" I ask.

Rock's smile widens.

"I'm technically a Wrath, but Gray has agreed to let me become a Lust demon," he says, bouncing on the heels of his shoes.

He looks so excited, and I can't help but mirror the emotion. Rock deserves it, and he'll make a good Lust demon. He got around quite a bit in his shadow form, and I can only imagine how many more people he'll attract as a full-bodied demon.

Especially one who looks like him.

It doesn't look like he's shaved in a good week, and the facial hair makes his sharp jawline stand out.

I purse my lips, letting my eyes trail down his frame.

Rock wears his signature black robes, so it's hard to know what his body looks like, but from the few hugs he's given me and the many times I've run into him, I know he's sturdy.

I jolt when Gray pinches my elbow, my face turning red.

"What?" I hiss, playing dumb.

Aziel walks to the dresser to grab clothes while Silas sits on the edge of the bed.

"Charlie's got the hots for me." Rock laughs, meeting Gray's eye.

I scoff before moving to stop Aziel from changing up the entire wardrobe I packed. There's a difference between being curious about what my best friend looks like versus having the hots for him.

Rock's good-looking, and I love him, but I have no interest in anything romantic or sexual with him. Especially after all the detailed stories I've heard about him and his females.

Aziel pulls out all the tops I packed so he can shove different ones inside. Some belong to Silas and Gray, but most are his.

Silas chimes in, pulling me onto his lap as he continues his earlier argument with Aziel. "I'm still not happy about this."

The Wrath doesn't seem to care, and he shrugs before zipping up my bag and tossing it to Rock.

"We've taken a vote, Silas, which was your idea if I remember correctly," Gray says, his voice soft as he approaches and drops to his knees before us. "We'll come to get you as soon as possible," he promises me.

He pushes up my shirt and places his hands on my belly, feeling the skin before leaning in to kiss it. My face flushes, and I run my fingers through his hair with a smile.

"Promise to be safe," I demand, releasing him as Aziel joins in.

Both men hover over my stomach, completely ignoring me. Even Silas reaches around to touch it, but I don't mind. I can feel their love for me through the bonds, and I share their excitement over our future.

"I promise, my love," Silas whispers, his voice soothing.

His lips make contact with my temple a second later, and I instinctively clench my thighs as my body reacts to the feeling of all three of them surrounding me like this. I don't mean to, and I hurry off Silas's lap before they feel obligated to be intimate with me.

I know they would gladly do it, but I want them to recover first. The ceremony took a lot out of them, way more than it did me, and the last thing I want is to rush my males.

"Come on, Charles," Rock says, using the nickname I hate. "Chev told me Emily was going to leave dinner in the cabin for us, and I want to eat it while it's fresh."

I give my males one last squeeze before following Rock downstairs to our portal. Aziel, Silas, and Gray follow me to it, and I try my best not to be dramatic and cry as I say my final goodbyes.

My males will come and get me soon.

Everything will be okay.

Chapter Sixteen

CHARLOTTE

MY IRRITATION REACHES an all-time high as I lift my sheet of paper in the air and try to make sense of the sloppy handwriting. It's impossible to make out any of the letters, let alone translate them.

Silas ran all the documentation the Wraths had saved from their rehabilitation facilities through a computerized translator, which has been an enormous help. Still, there are some things even it couldn't pick up on.

The Wraths have horrible handwriting.

"Let me help," Rock says.

I frown. "Good luck."

I slide the paper in his direction and point to the section I'm struggling to read. Echo leans over to see, her nose wrinkling as her eyes dart along the page.

I sit back in my chair and peer around the meeting cave. It's a bit chilly here today, and I'm glad I brought my sweatshirt. It's technically Aziel's, and it's a good ten sizes too big, but it keeps me warm. The shifter leaders sit around the table, the cold not seeming to bother them as they pore over paperwork and debate their plans for the rehabilitation facilities.

"I think it would be best for me to check in with Aziel," Kato says, tapping his fingers against the table.

He's been complaining all morning about not being invited to assist in Wrath.

I didn't realize Chev was purposefully keeping information from him, and when Kato asked why I was staying here for a few days, I didn't think twice about sharing the truth.

It wasn't until Chev was grimacing and shaking his head that I realized my mistake, but by then, it was too late. Kato was gobsmacked, and after accusing Chev of keeping secrets, he seems to have settled into a minor depression.

"You're retired, Dad," Chev says, reaching for a piece of fruit sitting in the bowl at the center of the table. The shifters are always eating. "That means you relax and enjoy old man pleasures."

Kato grumbles.

"I have no idea what this says," Rock admits, sliding the paper back in my direction.

Damn.

Kato grabs it next, eager to try, and Rock sets a glass of water on the table in front of me a second later.

"Drink," he says.

It seems Rock's taking his orders from Gray quite seriously, and while it's very sweet, it's more than a little unnecessary. Water is good for me, but I don't need to drink a full glass every hour on the hour. It's neurotic, and I'm pretty sure Gray read one 'best practices for pregnancy' article and took everything to heart.

"When is Aziel leaving?" Kato asks Chev.

Kato clears his throat and stands a moment later, and I raise a brow as Chev stands to match his father. They've been bickering all morning, and I'm interested to see who will back down first.

"They've already left," Chev says, walking around the table.

He grabs his father's shoulders and forcibly pushes him back into his chair. "Now, please relax. I understand you want to help, but it's time for you to accept your position."

Kato scoffs. "I'm old, not weak."

My lips twitch, and I lower my head so he can't see my smile. I don't think of Kato as old, the man looking no older than thirty-five, but I don't question it. The shifters have a unique culture around retirement.

Just one month ago, Kato was considered the strongest shifter among them all, but the second he handed his title to Chev, everybody began to treat him like a frail, old man.

Echo's explained it's the shifter's way of keeping their elders safe.

You push them out when they're still strong, letting them go through denial while they can still defend themselves, so that by the time they're truly weak, they've accepted their positions and don't try to thrust themselves into the middle of battle.

The shifters have a long history of men who are too old to fight trying to help protect the pack in times of trouble, their interference unnecessary and distracting.

The way they handle it is genius, even if Kato seems to be struggling.

He clearly doesn't like the new perception of himself, but Chev's more than a capable leader. The pack is in good hands.

Echo reaches across the table to grab the document Kato has abandoned. I hope she can make sense of the messy scrawl, but after only thirty seconds, she flicks it back toward me with a frown.

"I give up," she huffs.

Well, fuck.

This page is part of an extensive document on the safety protocols used within Wrath's facilities, and it's important. I suppose I could always ask Aziel about it when he's back, but he's going to be busy for who-knows-how-long, and we don't have time to wait.

The shifters are eager to get the ball rolling, and we've just about finished our planning.

We know exactly what we want to do and how we want to go about it, but we need Aziel's focus to begin. The shifters don't have the population numbers to take over the Seekers facilities, and their strongest warriors are still assisting Aziel in Wrath.

Thankfully, the shifters don't seem to blame Aziel, recognizing things with Mammon are out of his control. If they do blame him, though, they're doing a good job of keeping it from me.

"Let me take a look," a shifter across the table offers.

I'm pretty sure his name is Otto. He's a friendly, brown-haired, hazel-eyed deer shifter, and he's clearly been putting in hours of work here.

We estimate that six new facilities will need to be built to support the sudden influx of females, and he and two other shifters have been working on deciding the best places to put them. Most realms have one or two, but that won't be enough to support the entire population of purchased females.

There were discussions of staggering the rehabilitation of females, but that was quickly shot down. We can't, in good conscience, pick and choose which women get saved first, and we want to move them all in one big swoop.

We don't want to give men the opportunity to hide or kill their females.

Otto pushes his paperwork aside as I slide over the one sheet we've been struggling to translate.

A large map of the dragon realm sits before him, with several high-density areas marked. The dragons are a dangerous species, even more elusive than the shifters, and nobody's particularly excited to work with them.

Given the feminine handwriting mixed within Otto's scribbles, I have a feeling he's been getting help from his mate.

I haven't had the pleasure of meeting the mates of the other shifter leaders, most of them still wary around me. I've only spent time in Chev's pack, so the others don't know me well.

Otto frowns as he types away at his translator, his eyes narrowing as he tries to make sense of the text. Every handwritten Wrath document we've come across is nearly impossible to read, their handwriting entirely illegible.

"Don't forget about your water," Rock says, nudging the still-full glass in my direction.

I can't help but laugh as I grab it and chug the contents. The shifters have fantastic water, their lands unpolluted and the rivers clean. The human climate was ruined long before the decline, and our water sources are permanently damaged.

They have to import it now, and it's stale and smells eerily similar to feet by the time it arrives.

"Are you having a boy or a girl?" Kato asks, shifting his attention to me.

I instinctively place a hand on my belly. I have a feeling my males know, their damn noses able to pick up on everything inside my body.

"I'm not sure. I want it to be a surprise," I admit.

Kato chuckles, his eyes crinkling. "My Emily once said the same thing, but she changed her mind two months later and threatened to cut off my fingers and burn my axe if I didn't tell her."

The room erupts into loud laughter, and Otto slides my document back in my direction with a defeated shrug of his shoulders.

"You were a good baby, but very loud," Kato continues, turning to Chev. "You had lungs of steel and sure loved to use them. When you were only a few months old, you got stung in the butt by a tree bug and cried for *hours*!"

What's a tree bug?

Chev looks embarrassed, his cheeks tinting pink as he waves away his father and returns to work.

Kato loves to talk about his family, but it seems he's not the only one as the wolf shifter across from me launches into a story about his baby niece.

I like the wolf shifter, Levi, but he and Kato don't exactly get along. Levi's convinced Echo is his mate, and Kato's been working hard to keep his daughter hidden from Levi ever since. Echo seems all on board with that, too, the woman quite vocal in her desire to remain a 'free bear' for a few more years.

"My niece likes to fold in half and put her toes in her mouth," Levi says, pressing his hands together to show the fold. "And I'm very much looking forward to telling her mate about that when she's older."

I place a hand over my stomach and lean back in my chair.

We've been holed away in this cave all day, and I could use the break.

Otto begins telling his own story about his children, and I do my best not to look horrified when he casually lets it slip that he has eight of them. He sounds a lot like Gray, and I admire the patience he must have to raise so many children, but that's not going to be me.

I'm thinking three, max.

My smile falls as I turn and spot Chev, the man catching my attention as he tries to slip out of the room. He looks upset as he disappears, and I carefully stand before following him out.

I suck my cheeks into my mouth as I navigate the dark cave,

my bonds helping my eyesight but not so much that I can easily walk through here. Chev is loud as he heads toward the exit, and I follow the sound for direction. I'm sure he can hear me doing exactly that, and he seems to stomp even louder.

"Chev?" I ask, rounding the final corner that leads to the cave opening.

The giant shifter leans against a wall, refusing to meet my eye. He doesn't need to, though, for me to see the wetness on his cheeks.

"You should go back inside," he says, wiping roughly at them.

I shake my head, refusing. Chev's a fool if he thinks I'll leave him when he's so upset. Chev has always been vocal about his excitement to find his mate, and I'm sure it's hard to sit around and listen to all his peers talk about the one thing he wants so badly.

Chev turns to peer into the woods, the sunlight bouncing off his tears.

"You'll find her soon," I promise, touching his back. "And you'll have your own little hoard of shifter babies you can fawn over."

He shrugs. "Some shifters never find their mates," he says, clearing his throat when it cracks. "They search high and low, but it never happens. Our mates are everything to us, so we never stop looking."

Wind rustles the trees, and I wrap Aziel's sweatshirt tighter around myself.

"Some unlucky shifters find their mates too late and miss the opportunity to have children. I don't want that to be me."

I'm confident it won't be, but that's not what Chev wants to hear. He's still young, maybe only a few years older than I am, and he has so much time to find his mate. The shifters can detect them through sight alone, and I'm secretly hoping he'll find her through our work with the females.

She exists somewhere. It's just a matter of figuring out where.

If worse comes to worst, we can take pictures of the females in our facilities and have him scan them until he recognizes her. It's probably unethical, but I'd be willing to bend the rules for Chev.

I'd do anything for him.

The bear shifters risked their lives to hide me from Mammon, no questions asked. Not once did they treat me as anything other than a welcome guest, and they even went as far as to fight for me when I was kidnapped and taken to Lust.

Chev and I stand beside one another in silence, and I hope my presence is comforting rather than intrusive. I'm just about to ask if he'd like me to leave when he reaches out and places a hand on my stomach.

His fingers press into my sweatshirt, and he's careful not to touch my bare skin. I let him, clasping my hands behind my back. I've caught Chev staring at my belly a few times, and I know he's interested in it.

Shifters are insanely protective over their pregnant mates, and they'd probably try to fight Chev if they ever caught wind of him looking at a female's belly. I doubt my males would be too offended about Chev touching it over my clothing, and I can tell he's curious.

"Aziel's always talking about how excited he is," Chev says. "The fool can't get through an hour of work without talking about you and the baby."

I breathe out a laugh, my cheeks warming at the information. Aziel doesn't show as much outward affection as Gray and Silas do, and even though I know he loves me and is excited about our child, it's still comforting to hear he's been gushing.

I'd pay good money to see it, and I wonder if his lack of visible excitement is because he's the biological father.

Gray can't keep his hands off me, the incubus always trying to sniff and be close to my belly, and even Silas goes out of his way to touch me. Aziel probably already feels connected with our child and doesn't need extra reassurance the baby is his.

Fear of Gray and Silas rejecting our baby grows the more I think about it, the possibility low but still there. They'd never do anything intentionally, but a small part of me is terrified they won't genuinely love and view our child as theirs.

"My baby!"

Chev snatches his hand from my belly, and I step aside to make room for Kato. The large shifter barrels between us, and a loud gasp slips from his lips as he spots the dried tears on Chev's cheeks.

"It's okay, my perfect boy," Kato coos, immediately pinpointing the cause of the tears as he grabs and yanks his son into his arms. "I promise you'll find her."

Chev groans but simultaneously, he wraps his arms around Kato's waist and returns the hug. The two are close, and I'm sure Chev's previously expressed his fears to his dad.

I wouldn't be surprised to hear Chev had similar fears before meeting Emily. Shifters aren't exactly known for their patience.

"It's only a matter of time," Kato says, squeezing Chev tightly, "and she will be perfect and worth every day of waiting. Just like your mother is to me."

I chuckle, loving the love between them, before excusing myself and making my way back inside.

Rock's taking another crack at translating my document when I return, the demon our best hope at deciphering it. I pause in the doorway, beyond happy to see a room full of men working hard to save the females.

The shifters are dedicating so much of their time and resources to this, and seeing their passion for this task fills me with insurmountable joy.

"I need to wrap up soon," Otto says, breaking the silence. "My mate will kill me if I'm home late again."

His words are met with quiet agreement, all the shifters admitting they must leave, too.

Still, nobody moves. Most of the men were already here when I arrived this morning, and given the sheer amount of work they've gotten done since our alliance was finalized, they've been putting in a lot of hours.

"I think I've got a few words," Rock says, reaching for a pen.

His handwriting is shit, too, and I suck my cheeks into my mouth as he scribbles a rough translation on a blank piece of paper. The Wraths are so fucking brilliant, but they need to invest in teaching children how to write legibly.

Chev and Kato return shortly, their presence capturing the attention of the other shifter leaders. It's evident by the hesitant glances that they've realized why Chev left, but thankfully, none address it.

It only takes a few minutes for things to return to normal, and we work in relative silence for a good two hours before Otto stands and stretches his back. "I really need to leave now."

The others grudgingly agree.

"Will you be here tomorrow, Charlie?" the wolf shifter asks.

I nod. "Bright and early."

Rock groans, and I smack at his arm, much to the room's pleasure. The shifters enjoy watching me 'demolish' Rock, and I have a feeling it's because he's a demon. Rock's a good sport about it, though, even if he's not a morning person, and he voices no complaints as he stands and helps me pack up.

He knows better than to complain if he wants Emily to bring him Ucka meat for dinner.

Chapter Seventeen

GRAY

AZIEL LAUGHS AS I wipe a speck of blood off his cheek, the man not caring if my actions have the seven generals sitting around the large stone table looking at him funny. He usually does a better job of cleaning himself before these meetings, but it seems he forgot today.

Luckily for him, I'm here to help.

"I'm excited to have you back," I say.

Aziel and Silas left two days ago, the pair leading separate missions along the Wrath border. Aziel's was successful, and he arrived a few hours ago with blood-splattered skin and a victorious smile.

Aziel's ugliest, tattooed general scoffs. "We're in the middle of a meeting."

The Wrath generals have been more argumentative than usual, and they've been pushing Aziel's boundaries after hearing the details of the Lust ceremony. I suspect that's the reason Aziel chose to lead a unit into battle instead of remaining at home base and sending one of his generals, but I won't insult him by asking.

He wants the respect of his people, and I won't mock him for it.

I should've known the council members would never keep quiet about the ceremony, and I'm willing to bet they've been excitedly telling everybody who will listen how Aziel bent for me. I'm pretty proud of it, but unfortunately, it negatively affects how Aziel's generals view him.

I turn toward the door as Silas comes storming in. He's also covered in blood, maybe even more than Aziel, and I can barely contain my excitement as he makes his way into the room.

Aziel hasn't sent me out to fight as he's done with Silas, and I've been stuck at our main camp near the southern border of Wrath. I prefer to spend my time at home base, and I know I'm only here as a figurehead, but I still take offense.

Fighting's never been my thing, but I'm more than a morale booster.

"Mammon's cleared out her two strongholds near Black River," Silas says, gesturing for the general sitting on Aziel's right to move.

The Wrath scrambles to his feet. I thought it was a bit cocky of him to claim the spot to Aziel's right in the first place, and I'm happy Silas isn't letting it fly. He locks eyes with the general as he sits, the silent message loud.

Aziel doesn't even notice the interaction, the man too busy poring over the maps on the table.

"What about the ogres?" Aziel asks, grabbing his marker to strikethrough the two strongholds Silas was sent to take care of. "We heard reports that they were camping out on the peak."

I go to the water jug along the far wall and fill a glass for Silas. The fate doesn't look injured, which is good, but I'm sure he hasn't been eating or hydrating as well as he should be. We don't need as much food to survive as the weaker species do, but it's still good for us.

Silas was gone for two days, and he needs to replenish.

I promised Charlie I'd take care of our males, and I'll be damned if I slack on my duties. I have a reputation to uphold as her favorite mate, and letting Aziel and Silas be dirty brutes will surely hurt that.

"We didn't come across them, but we saw smoke rising beyond the lower mountains," Silas says, downing the water I hand him. "We had too many injured to continue the journey, but I'll take a new unit of men there tomorrow to check it out."

A small part of me knows I should be embarrassed by how aggressively I'm serving him and Aziel, but it's hard to control the urge. It's not usually this pronounced, even among the strongest Lust demons, but my stress seems to be making it worse.

Silas dips a cloth into his cup and wipes his face clean, and I watch to ensure he's doing it correctly before turning and sitting in the chair on Aziel's left. I only lower halfway before one of the generals grabs my wrist.

"Water," he orders, jerking his head toward the jug.

I stiffen.

"I'd suggest you remove your hand from my mate," Aziel mindlessly says, searching underneath one of his maps. "Where the fuck is my red marker?"

The general doesn't release me.

I have half a mind to shake him off, but I remain still and let this play out. My inner incubus likes to be pampered, and seeing Aziel's wrath come out to protect me always gets me going. It's been almost a week since the feeding ceremony, and I'm growing hungry.

Aziel's eyes dart toward my wrist, checking to see if his order's been followed through, as he adds a red marking to the spot Silas points to on the lower mountains. The hand on me tightens, and I smile as the general's nail cuts into my wrist.

I smell the blood immediately, and I can tell Aziel does, too, as his marker drops onto the map.

He moves quickly, and Silas leans back in his chair to watch Aziel grab the general's hand and physically pry it off me. The general screams as his fingers are bent backward, and he looks to the other Wraths for help.

They don't so much as flinch as Aziel breaks every finger on his hand.

Aziel's pupils dilate, and I lick my lips as he grabs the back of the general's neck and shoves the man's face against the stone table. I like the way Aziel's back flexes beneath the fabric of his shirt, the muscles stretching against the material.

He looks good.

Arousal pools in my lower abdomen as the demon clutches Aziel's wrist, fighting with his broken fingers to try to pry the hand off his neck. His face turns red, and I watch for a moment longer before approaching the two.

Now's not the time for Aziel to kill his men, even if I'm glad he's finally losing his cool.

He's been noticeably calmer since bonding with the three of us, and it's good for his people to see his wrath and know their leader is still the powerful man he's always been. He may have a better temper now, but he won't stand for disrespect.

I press myself against Aziel's back and breathe him in, enjoying his scent as I grab his hand and gently pull it off his general. Aziel fights me at first, unable to control it, and I press a soft kiss to the back of his neck before trying again.

This time, he lets me move him, and I curl my fingers around his so he doesn't lash out again.

"Please," the general begs, tripping over a chair as he scampers away. His eyes dart between Aziel and me. "I'm sorry."

He doesn't know whom to speak to, and I shoot him a cocky

smirk.

"It seems like it would benefit you to be nice to me," I say, trailing my hand down the front of Aziel's body.

My Wrath King vibrates as he struggles to calm himself, and the general finally seems to grow half a brain as he climbs to his feet and hurries out of the room. I'm faintly aware of the other generals following, their stench of fear filling the small space.

I know Aziel enjoys it, but I'm not a fan.

I wrinkle my nose and bury my face in his hair to try to avoid it. I don't like the negative emotions, and I continue running my hand over Aziel's chest and stomach until something much sweeter fills my lungs. It's his lust, and I inhale it like the good incubus I am.

I lick the marks on his neck as my fingers reach his zipper. Aziel's already hard, and I let out a low moan as I slide my hand down his length.

"I'm hungry," I whisper. "It's been almost a week since the ceremony."

Aziel shivers, his arousal growing.

I've been avoiding feeding for as long as possible, but I'm beginning to grow shaky. I need it.

My lips curl into a sneaky grin as I shove my hand down the front of Aziel's pants and take hold of him. He grunts, his hips twitching before he spins us and pushes me face-first onto the table.

I bend at the waist, eager to see what he will do.

My pants are ripped down a second later, and I peer out the door the generals left through as Aziel grabs my shaft to squeeze out my arousal. It flows from me so easily now, covering his hand with only a few strokes.

"You make so much for me," he says.

Clothing rustles to my right, and I turn just in time to see Silas undo his pants and pull out his cock. He meets my eye, and our bond vibrates as he watches Aziel bend me over. I wonder if he knows I intend to feed on him next.

I expect Silas to stroke himself, but instead, he lightly rubs Aziel's mark on the side of his shaft. The mere touch turns him into a panting mess, and I watch him through heavy eyes as Aziel strips and lines himself up with my ass.

"Look, baby," Aziel says, drawing my attention.

He presses his chest against my back before curling his fingers around the front of my neck and lifting my head.

I blink, angry Aziel's not already inside me as I lock eyes with one of his generals. The man stands in the doorway, his eyes flickering quickly between the three of us. He excused himself before Aziel got angry, and he looks beyond shocked that this is what he's returning to.

Aziel chuckles as I moan, unable to look away from the general as Aziel begins to fill me. He moves slowly, allowing me time to stretch around him. My body adjusts quickly, and within seconds, his hips meet mine.

"This is what you like, isn't it?" Aziel asks, his warm breath hitting my ear. "Silas told me what Asmod's power is doing to you." He pulls out to the tip before rocking back in. "You want an audience."

A small part of me is mad at Silas for opening his big mouth, but it's hard to stay angry when Aziel's filling me so perfectly.

"You want my men to watch me fuck you." Aziel moans as he slams into me, his hips smacking my ass. "You want them all to know I'm yours, and you want me to publicly claim you."

I have no words, and I continue staring at Aziel's general as my chest rubs against the table. I can faintly make out the scent of the general's arousal, but he's too far away for me to truly feed off it.

"You want everything to be about you, don't you?" Aziel continues, sliding his hand down my spine. "My greedy fucking mate."

The general steps into the room, his eyes still on me. I grin as his action draws the attention of both my males. They turn in his direction, and something in Aziel's and Silas's expressions must frighten him as he spins and runs out of the room like a fire's been lit under him.

I love it when they get possessive over me, and I drop my head onto the table as I feed.

Each of Aziel's thrusts rubs my cock between my stomach and the table, and it feels amazing. I can't help but rock back against him, eager to be filled every time he pulls his hips back.

Aziel laughs at my desperation, but I don't care. I needed this.

"More," I beg, not caring who can hear me. "Please, Aziel. More."

Aziel grunts, tightening his grip on my wrists.

His movements grow unsteady as he fucks, and I clench around his length as I feed off his and Silas's thick lust.

"Fuck, Gray." Aziel moans, planting his hands on the table on either side of my head. The drag of his cock is everything to me, and my legs shake as his orgasm builds. I can taste it on my tongue, and my eyes roll back as Aziel fucks himself deep into me and stills.

He grunts, and I happily feed as he fills me with his cum.

"Thank you." I gasp as he pulls out.

"You don't have to thank me for feeding you, Gray."

I hum, too content to argue with him. That's exactly what I needed, and I already feel so much better.

"Gray..." Silas says, drawing my attention.

His chest and neck are flushed, and he continues rubbing at the mark on the side of his cock as I straighten up. He's such a good boy, waiting patiently for Aziel to have his turn before begging for me. Lust pours from me as I approach my fate, and I place a hand on his chest before straddling his thighs.

He releases his cock and curls his hands around the armrests of his chair, gripping the wood so tightly, I'm surprised it doesn't crack.

"How long do you think you can fuck with that mark?" I ask.

Aziel watches with poorly concealed interest as Silas fumbles for an answer.

"I don't know," Silas admits, shame thick in our bond.

He's embarrassed, and I love it. He does, too.

"Maybe five minutes," he eventually decides.

I doubt he'll even be able to last that long. It's a shame, too. I used to lie awake at night whenever Silas had one of his females over, and he could last for hours. His partners loved it, loved how long they could use him.

"You're useless, Silas." I chuckle.

He gasps, his red flush deepening in color. I lean in, bringing my lips to his ear. "How can you expect Charlie to love you when you can't even pleasure her? How do you expect me to love you? I'm an incubus, Silas. I need to fuck."

Aziel rounds Silas's chair, and we make brief eye contact before he crouches and brings his mouth to Silas's other ear. "Don't listen to him, baby. Your cock is so fucking big, and Gray's a whore for it. He's obsessed with you. He can't get enough of you."

Silas's eyebrows pull together as he throws his head back, a low moan slipping from his throat as his hips jerk beneath me. He loves praise just as much as he loves being talked down to, and the scent of his arousal is achingly strong as I grab his cock and sink down on it.

Aziel continues to talk to Silas. "See, he can't stop himself from sitting on you."

I moan as Silas stretches me, and I plant my hands on his shoulders before rolling my hips. The fate white-knuckles the armrests of his chair, and within thirty seconds, he grabs my hips to try to stop me.

"Gray, please," he cries, pressing his forehead against my chest.

Aziel leans forward, happy to watch our fate embarrass himself. The poor guy isn't even going to last a minute.

Silas tightens his grip on my waist, trying again to stop me, before his hips jerk upward and he cums. I continue to fuck myself on him, my body begging for release.

It's so good.

"Do you think you can go again, baby?" Aziel asks. "Gray's going to need more than that."

"Fuck," Silas curses. "Yes."

His fingernails cut me more than Aziel's general ever did, but I love it.

"Please, Gray," Silas begs, his voice low as his desperation grows.

I force out my lust so his cock stays hard. He cries, but I can feel his love for it through the bond. He likes being embarrassed, and he enjoys the humiliation of being unable to fuck for long.

Silas cums two more times before our bond tells me it's time to stop, and I pull back my lust to let him grow soft. He slips out of me, plenty of cum coming along with it, but I remain on his lap as I push his hair out of his face and pepper his cheeks with kisses.

"That felt so good, Silas," I say. "Thank you."

He wraps his arms around my waist and pulls me against his chest, and I continue to play with his hair while he pants onto my shoulder. Aziel plants a quick kiss on the top of his head before returning to the table. I have a feeling he's looking at his maps, but I don't turn around to confirm my assumption.

"Was that okay?" I ask.

Silas nods, and after another few minutes, he releases me.

His face is still red, but the tumulus emotions that zipped through our bond have settled. I give my still-hard length a quick squeeze before climbing off Silas's lap and reaching for my pants.

"You don't want to finish?" Silas asks, reaching around my waist.

I huff, smacking his hand away from my goods.

"No. I'm going to wait for Charlie," I say, grinning as my two males frown and exchange glances.

Charlie doesn't expect us to refrain from intimacy with one another while we're gone, but I have a feeling she'll be pleased to learn I waited for her like a good mate. Aziel and Silas seem pissed as they realize what I've done, but I shrug their anger away and finish dressing.

I get to feed, and I get to be Charlie's favorite male upon our return. This is perfect for me.

"You're a bastard, Gray." Silas snorts, making no effort to pull up his pants.

Sweat drips down his temple, and I bend to kiss his cheek. He turns last minute, so I connect with his lips instead, the man stealing a kiss just as I stole his abstinence.

"I love you," I whisper, tucking his dick away and pulling up his pants.

"We should send a unit out to the lower mountains tonight," Aziel says, effectively ruining the moment.

The Wrath generals return shortly, their timing and arousal telling me they listened to and enjoyed the show. They liked hearing Aziel prove his virility, and they may have even learned a thing or two they can take home to their spouses.

They should be thanking me.

Aziel does an excellent job pretending our little break didn't happen as he jumps back into work mode, and the generals nod in my direction as I leave the room to ensure the men harmed on Silas's mission are healing properly.

Good. It's about time they show me a little respect.

Chapter Eighteen

CHARLOTTE

THE COT ROCK sleeps on creaks as he sits up, and I pretend not to hear it as I glare at the ceiling.

"Are you sure you're okay?" Rock asks.

The cot gives another groan. The thing is barely able to support his weight, and it whines whenever he so much as *thinks* about moving. I've offered to switch places at least a hundred times, but he pretends he can't hear me when I ask.

It'd be a good excuse if he weren't a demon with impeccable hearing.

Sighing, I turn in his direction. He looks pitiful as he waits for my response, and I force a smile before nodding.

"Silas warned me that I might feel some mild cramping," I say, squeezing the soft flesh below my belly button. "He said it's common for human females."

Rock's eyes narrow as his nostrils flare. He's trying to smell me, and I wave him away when he moves to get closer. There's wetness in my underwear, and I don't want him getting close enough to smell it.

Bleeding is normal, too.

Silas didn't tell me that, but I know it.

Everything is okay.

"I'm fine. Honestly," I promise, resisting the urge to wince as another cramp spreads through my lower abdomen and back. "Do you know how to block a bond? I don't want them to feel it and worry."

My males could be in the middle of a fight, and the last thing I want is for them to realize I've got some tiny little cramps and get distracted. I don't know what I'd do if they got hurt because of me. They already muted their ends of the bonds, and I hope that means they won't feel any changes I make to mine.

Rock looks disappointed by my question, but I don't care. I asked him how to block my bonds. Not for a lecture.

"Charlie?" Rock asks.

He sighs as he takes note of my pointed stare, and his cot creaks as he sits up further.

"There are a few ways to do it," he finally gives in and says. "Some people imagine building a wall between themselves and their mate, and some think of it as tying a knot. It's instinctual, like breathing. You have to focus on the bonds and tell them what to do. They'll listen."

That makes absolutely no sense.

I give a jerky nod and lie back down. The ceiling is a beautiful dark wood, and I stare at the beams for a long minute before shutting my eyes and searching for my bonds. I've gotten pretty good at finding them, but I've never tried to stop my emotions from getting through before.

I resist the urge to tug on the bonds, scared my males will sense it, and instead, I focus on shutting them out. It feels wrong at first, but I imagine tying my bonds into knots until I feel Aziel's and Gray's close. It takes longer to cut off the connection with Silas because the bond is new, but I get it after a few minutes.

My chest deflates once it's done, and I wipe away the tiny bead of sweat that accumulated on my upper lip from the effort.

Another cramp hits me, and I gently massage my lower abdomen until it disappears. I refuse to let Rock's concern get to me as I think through all the work we need to do tomorrow. We've made significant progress these past few days, and at this point, we have a pretty comprehensive action plan.

Implementing everything will be a different story, but that's not my focus. I'll leave the fighting to Chev and my males.

"Charlie?" Rock says, drawing my attention.

I grunt.

"Stay here."

He's up and out of the room a second later. I sit up, alarmed, and stumble to my bedroom door just as he rushes out the front door of our cabin. He slams it shut behind him, the loud bang of the wood startling. *What the fuck?*

My pulse races, and I keep my footsteps light as I tiptoe to the front window and peek outside. There's nothing but black out there, and Rock is nowhere to be seen.

I lean closer to see if I can spot him between the trees, but a low growl has me jumping back. It emerges from deep within the woods, and it sounds fucking terrifying.

What's going on?

I want to flick on the porch light to get a better view of what's out there, but I don't want to draw any attention to my cabin. It's dark in here, and I hope that keeps my space inconspicuous.

There's another loud noise from outside, and I rock back on my heels as I wait for Rock to return and explain what's going on. It would be stupid of me to go outside when surrounded by shifters who could kill me with a flick of their wrists, and I hug my arms to my chest before stepping farther into the living room.

Another growl vibrates through the air, and I stiffen when I realize it's come from behind me. Somebody's in the cabin, and I highly doubt they're friendly.

I have half a second to think over my next move before I rip open the front door and run outside. I'd rather be outside with Rock than inside with some mysterious, angry shifter.

I make only one step onto the front porch before something barrels into me from behind. My feet fly up from underneath me, and a sharp ache travels up my back. My mouth opens, but pain prevents any sound from emerging as I flip over the porch railing on my left and land on the hard ground.

The drop isn't far, but a splitting burn spreads along my hip and elbow from my less-than-graceful landing.

There's a series of loud howls from deep within the woods, but I barely notice it as the bear shifter who just shoved me jumps off the porch. Its sharp teeth are only inches from my face, and its bright, blue eyes bore into mine as bloody drool drips from its mouth onto my neck.

The bear snarls, and I scream.

The shifter's eyes widen milliseconds before its head is yanked backward, and I kick at its chest in a panic.

Rock stands behind the giant bear, and he rips the animal off me before snapping its neck.

"Go back inside," Rock orders.

I don't hesitate, and my legs carry me toward the safety of the cabin a moment later. The porch steps are on the opposite side of where I fell, and I scan the distance before jumping and climbing up the side where the shifter threw me over and broke the railing.

This will be quicker.

Another bear comes storming onto the porch just as I climb back on it, its eyes locked on me. I can never tell who is who in their animal forms, and I curl my fingers around the wood as the bear blocks the front door of my cabin. My body is frozen in fear, and I instinctively shut my eyes.

Fuzzy legs brush my sides before covering me, the shifter placing its body entirely over mine. A low growl seeps from its throat, and I take the fact that I'm still alive as a good sign and make myself as small as possible underneath the creature.

It's hard to breathe through my panic, and I wrap an arm around my stomach as another cramp hits. This one's a bit more painful than the rest, and the shifter above me seems to sense my pain as it whines and lowers until I'm squished between the wooden porch and its belly.

"Shit," I say, unable to see clearly through its fur.

What I do spot, though, has me stilling. Two giant shifters, both larger than the one who attacked me and the one currently lying on me, come tumbling out of my cabin. Their fur is matted with blood, and the shifter guarding me backs us up against the side of the porch, keeping us hidden as the two larger ones snap at one another's necks.

I wince when one gets a good bite and sinks its teeth into the other's throat.

There's a sickening crunch followed by a loud whine, both shifters crying as the teeth sink in deeper. My hands shake as I grab the legs of the bear in front of me, holding his ankles.

What's happening? There are no demons or ogres around, only shifters attacking other shifters. I spot a goat and a bison among them, but they get taken down quickly. They're no match for the larger, stronger bears.

A big cat shifter jumps onto the porch and lunges for the man on top of me, but the bear only needs to make one powerful swipe of his paw to have the cat falling limp.

Are the shifters in the middle of a war or argument I didn't know about? There's no way it's a coincidence they've started attacking right outside my cabin, and I'd be a fool not to realize

I'm a target.

Mammon probably got to them.

Another cramp has me digging my nails into my protector's ankles, probably drawing blood, but he doesn't react.

"Charlie?" It's Chev's voice.

I stick my head out from underneath the shifter I'm hiding under, but I'm too close to the fighting to risk leaving his safety. Chev spots me quickly, though, his eyes locking with mine before he rushes forward and yanks me out from underneath the bear.

Whoever was protecting me is gone in a heartbeat, a terrifying noise slipping from his chest as he storms off to fight. Chev throws me over his shoulder and sprints away from the action. He's naked, his leathers probably having ripped during a shift, and I grab his hips to keep my face from smashing into his butt.

"What's going on?" I ask, struggling to make out anything in the dark.

The moon provides some light, but not enough.

"Fucking Vont," Chev says, handing me to a bloody, panicked Rock. "Take her to my home."

He's gone before either of us can question it, but Rock immediately follows the order and brings me toward Chev's cabin. He can move much quicker than I'd ever be able to, even when carrying me. Shifters move to the side to let Rock through, the men forming a line around the central pack lands as they protect their females and children.

Rock shoves Chev's door open and sets me on my feet before rushing toward a bloody, half-naked Echo. Three men surround her, and Emily holds her daughter's head in her lap as the men work on Echo's mangled leg. It looks like the muscle has been stripped clean from the bone, and my stomach roils as I stumble forward and drop to my knees next to her.

Who would do this? The shifters revere their females, and

Echo is, by far, a favorite among them.

Echo screams as the shifters work to fix up her leg, and I fight the urge to puke as they press the torn-up skin together and staple it in place.

"Is she okay?" I ask, glancing frantically between Emily and the three shifter men working on her.

Emily looks frazzled, her leathers on backward, and she pushes Echo's sweaty hair off her forehead before responding.

"She will be. We've had men watching Vont because of his ties to Mammon, and he and a few other shifters attacked them tonight. Echo saw and ran to your cabin to warn you, but she's not a fast runner, and they caught up quickly."

Vont and his men did this to her? To his niece?

Rock must have heard her screaming, and that was why he ran outside.

"I took four of those fuckers down," Echo chokes out between sobs. "I didn't even need my sword."

Emily runs a shaky hand through her daughter's hair.

"Fuck yeah, you did," she says, her voice weak.

Vont was never happy with me being here, annoyed his brother was going against his mate by offering me protection, but I never in a million years imagined it would come to this. Kato always made it sound like Vont knew Mammon wasn't making the right decisions and didn't support her, but I suppose it's well-known how desperate the shifters are to please their mates.

There's an actual war between the Wraths and Greeds, and at the end of the day, Mammon is still his mate.

Echo screams as her leg muscles begin to reform, and I have to look away before I get sick. She's healing quickly, and Rock comes up alongside me to examine my hip and elbow.

His touch on the wounds hurt, but it's easy to ignore it with everything else going on.

He wipes away the blood that drips down my forearm, and his eyes meet mine before carefully pressing a wet cloth over the cut. I hiss, but I don't pull away as he bandages it up.

I didn't even realize I was bleeding.

"I'm so sorry, Charlie," he says. "I heard Echo scream, but I didn't realize it was because of an attack. I came back to you as soon as I realized."

His voice cracks, and I give his arm a tight squeeze.

"You didn't know," I assure him. "It's okay."

Rock works his jaw side to side before shaking his head. This was a shock to both of us, and he had no idea Vont was coming for me. The shifters have been watching him, and he hasn't made any moves before. I was here for weeks when I ran away from Mammon, and he never tried to hurt me or give Mammon information on my whereabouts.

I glance at the front door, waiting for Chev and Kato to return. It's quiet out there, Chev's cabin too far away for the sounds of fighting to reach it.

I have a feeling the two large bear shifters fighting just outside my cabin were Vont and Kato, and one had his teeth sunk deep into the other's neck the last I saw. My only comfort is that Emily is okay, and she would surely sense if Kato were hurt.

Rock keeps me distracted as he bandages my arm, apologies continuing to slip from his lips every time I wince or cringe. My pain is nothing compared to what's happening with Echo, and I remind myself of that every time he digs out a pebble lodged in my skin.

Echo's cries quiet as the deepest parts of her leg heal, her pained screams shifting to slow, deep breaths and low grunts. The male shifters filter out as they're no longer needed, each rushing to return to the fight.

I'm assuming they were the ones who brought her here. With

so much of her leg gone, walking here herself would've been impossible.

"Let me look at your hip," Rock says to me, pulling up the hem of the shirt I'm wearing.

I shift my position and pull down the side of my sleep shorts. The skin there is relatively unharmed, more of a scrape than anything else. Rock seems relieved, and his shoulders roll inward as he leans forward in search of any debris he needs to pick out.

He gets a few inches away from my stomach before stiffening.

"Is everything okay?" I ask.

Rock takes too long to respond.

"When was the last time your stomach was smelled?" he asks.

What? I blink, trying to remember. My males were all over it before I came here, but that was a few days ago.

Rock leans closer and cups my lower stomach. I'd usually feel weird about him putting his bare hand on such an intimate part of my body, but it's low on the list of things I'm worried about right now.

I shake my head, my heart pounding. What's going on? I move to get up, not liking this, but Rock drops a hand on my shoulder to keep me seated.

"This isn't funny," I say, already on the verge of tears.

Rock licks his lips and brings his face to my stomach again. I push him away, wanting him to stop, but he ignores my attempt before gently pulling me to my feet.

My throat runs dry when he guides me into a bedroom away from Emily and Echo. It's small but cozy, and I eye the rumpled sheets and shelves full of knickknacks before turning toward Rock.

He gestures to the bed, and I'm faintly aware I'm getting blood on Chev's sheets as I lower myself onto the mattress. Rock crouches by my feet and grabs my hands, which I absolutely hate, and I work my jaw from side to side as another cramp steals my breath.

No.

It's painful, but cramps can happen during pregnancy.

"Charlie," Rock says, pausing to clear his throat. "You smell wrong."

I shake my head, refusing to listen.

"I smell like Aziel," I argue. "That's what everybody tells me. My natural scent changed after the bondings and pregnancy. I won't smell the same way I used to."

Rock looks pained, and he sucks his cheeks into his mouth before readjusting his grip on my hands. His palms are sweaty.

"Charlie—" he begins.

I push him away, not wanting to hear it. We have more important things to worry about than him being forgetful and not remembering how scent is supposed to change.

Chev and Kato are just returning as I storm out of the bedroom. Kato looks pretty banged up, a large chunk of his shoulder missing. Chev is in better shape, with only a few minor cuts and scrapes covering his skin.

They rush over to Echo, fretting over her now-healed leg. Emily's voice is low as she whispers to them, probably informing them about Echo's injuries, and they appear solemn as they nod and help the female shifter to her feet. Both men look haunted as they turn toward me, and Echo wraps an arm around their shoulders for support as they carry her to the couch. She drops onto the cushion with a huff, her eyes already half-shut as she slumps to the side.

I'm sure healing a wound that big took a lot out of her.

Chev and Kato continue to stare at me, and I clasp my hands behind my back with a frown. Why are they looking at me like I've just sprouted four heads? Rock wraps an arm around my waist before leading me to the bathroom, his grip on my hip tightening as another cramp has me fighting the urge to double over.

"I'm calling Gray," he decides.

I sit on the toilet seat and bring my head between my knees, and Rock rubs my back as he wrestles his phone out of his pocket and calls Gray.

This isn't happening.

"Gray?" Rock says into the phone. "We're going to need you here. Charlie's—" He pauses as if he's been cut off, but his phone volume is too low for me to hear. "No, she's—" Rock pulls his phone away from his ear and checks the screen before shaking his head and shoving it back into his pocket.

"Is he coming?" I ask.

"I think so. He hung up on me."

I grab my thighs and straighten my spine, not wanting to look pitiful.

This bathroom is surprisingly cluttered, with feminine beauty products lining the shelves. Everything's unopened, and I battle tears at the sad sight of Chev's hoarding. He wants a mate so badly.

Another cramp steals my thoughts, and I squeeze my thighs as I fight through it. My underwear is wet, but I refuse to take off my pants and look. I'm not ready to see what I already know is there. Instead, I hang my head between my knees, letting Rock massage the back of my neck. It feels good, and it offers a distraction from the pain.

My muscles tense as another pair of hands join Rock's, and I squeeze my eyes shut as somebody lowers themselves to the floor in front of me. Gentle hands urge me to sit up, and I choke back a sob as Gray lifts the hem of my shirt and buries his face in my belly.

His hair's damp, and cool water drips down my fingers as he

kisses my stomach and pulls me onto his lap. No words are spoken—none need to be—as he teleports us into our bathroom back home. It doesn't bring any comfort, and I step away when Gray tries to remove my clothes.

I don't want him to see me, especially the mess that's become my underwear and inner thighs.

"It's okay, my love," Gray urges. He pulls open the shower door and turns on the water. "We need to clean you up."

He reaches for me again, but I sidestep him. Gray sinks his teeth into his bottom lip before grabbing my arms and pulling me underneath the shower stream. I gasp, shocked as my clothes grow soaked.

"Gray!" I say, shoving at his chest. "I can do this by myself."

He kisses my temple before ripping my shirt from the back and tossing it into the corner of the shower. It lands with a wet splat, but when I turn to look at it, Gray grabs my chin and refuses to let me.

"Look at me," he orders, sliding his hands to my waist.

My bottom lip trembles, and I fight back tears as Gray removes the rest of my clothing and nudges my legs apart. He runs his hands up and down my thighs, cleaning the blood.

"Is Ephraim okay?" I ask.

Gray doesn't answer.

He continues cleaning my thighs before reaching for my soap. He doesn't hog the water for once, keeping me under the spray as he stands beside it in soaking-wet clothing. That realization has my knees buckling, but Gray quickly catches me before pulling me tightly against his chest. He squeezes me, letting me cry as I finally accept what I already know to be true.

I'm losing the baby.

"Don't tell Aziel and Silas until everything with Mammon is over," I beg, the words practically incoherent as I try to speak through cries.

I can tell Gray's unhappy with my request, but it's a hill I'm willing to die on. We need to wrap things up with Mammon, and there have already been enough setbacks. They'll abandon the mission to be here with me if they hear about the baby.

We can't have that.

I'm one person, and my well-being is nothing compared to the millions of females counting on us to improve things. I won't let my males abandon them.

"Charlie, I don't—"

"Promise me," I say, interrupting. "You know this will distract them, and we need to focus on the big picture."

Gray works his jaw side to side before nodding.

I hesitate before looking down. My blood's been cleaned, only a few red drops on the floor where the water doesn't hit. Other than that, everything looks the same. I wasn't showing, but I still run a hand over my stomach in search of something.

Gray copies me, placing his fingers over mine before dropping to his knees.

I watch, wiping roughly at my cheeks as he kisses my belly.

"I'm sorry," I choke out.

"No." Gray's fingers tighten where they hold my waist. "This isn't your fault, Charlie. Nothing you did caused this, and there's nothing we could've done to prevent it," he promises, bouncing back to his feet and cupping my cheeks.

His eyes grow wet, and a tear slips out of the corner of his eye before getting washed away by the shower spray.

"Ephraim just wasn't meant to be," he continues, pressing his forehead to mine.

We all knew this was a possibility, but a small part of me thought I'd be lucky. I thought their bonds would make me stronger.

Gray turns off the water and ushers me out of the shower. He wraps a fuzzy towel around my shoulders and pats me dry before stepping out of his wet clothes and haphazardly throwing a towel around his waist.

I mindlessly follow him into our bedroom, and I linger awkwardly as he grabs me a pair of his briefs and a pad. He doesn't say anything as he helps me step into them, and I try my best to ignore why I need them in the first place.

"Silas and Aziel are going to wonder where you are," I say.

Gray shrugs before pulling back the covers and urging me to climb into bed.

Everything feels surreal, and I curl against him as he turns on the TV for background noise. We lie like this for a while, neither of us knowing what to say.

There's nothing *to* say.

Gray glances at me every few seconds, clearly worried. I pretend I don't notice, instead listening to his heartbeat and counting the seconds.

"I need to go do something," Gray abruptly says, brushing my hair out of my face.

I turn, taking in the sight of his red eyes and splotchy cheeks before nodding. He was so excited for our baby, always talking about all the things he wanted to do with them and how they'd love him more than our other males.

Seeing Gray's teary eyes is crushing. He never cries.

Well, not usually.

He gives me another kiss, this one firmer than the last, before disappearing. I wrap my arms around my waist, hugging myself as I pull my knees to my chest and bury my face in them.

What good am I if I can't give my males children?

I know they won't blame me, but that doesn't mean they won't be disappointed. Silas has been hoarding parenting books in his office, marking them up and forcing Aziel and Gray to read the parts he deems essential.

My face scrunches as another cramp spreads across my lower abdomen, and I squeeze myself in a sad attempt to stop it. Minutes pass, and I eventually untuck myself while waiting for Gray to return. Where did he go?

Maybe he wants space.

I bet that's it, and I roll onto my side and curl into a small ball under the covers. I miss my males, and I hate that Gray left me alone. I'd rather be in the shifter lands with Rock than in this bed alone.

My tears don't stop despite how hard I try to get them under control, and I burrow even further under the comforter to try to escape it all.

"Baby?"

I ignore Gray. He's been gone for a good hour, and now *I* want to be alone.

I don't need him, or anybody.

"Can you sit up for me? I stole something for you," he continues. He stole something for me? I'm not interested in it, and I roll away as another cramp works through me.

I groan, desperate for some relief. I thought period cramps were bad, but they're nothing compared to this.

"Oh, my sweet girl," a feminine voice says.

I freeze, too scared to move.

The top of my head grows cold as the covers are pulled back, exposing my curled form to the room. Thin hands I'd recognize anywhere slide down my cheek. I gulp in complete disbelief as the bed dips and my head is pulled against a soft chest.

"Charlie," my mom breathes.

I turn and wrap my arms around her waist. She smells like home, and I cry into her lap as she tucks my hair behind my ear and fixes my eyebrow like she's done since I was a child. I've been blocking out the memory of the last day I saw her and my dad, living in blissful ignorance, and I feel the weight of it press into me as she holds me.

My dad's dead, and I never really thought I'd see my mom again.

My sobs become incoherent, and I feel like a baby as I curl against her.

"Gray filled me in on what happened," she whispers, clearly not caring that I'm getting snot all over her shirt. "You're going to be okay, I promise. I'm here, my sweet girl, and I'm not going anywhere."

Silas said removing her from the facility would draw unwanted attention, but I'm selfishly glad Gray went against Silas's wishes and brought her here. She makes everything better, and I let myself sink into her comforting hold as another set of sobs shakes my body.

"I'll get you two something to drink," Gray says. His shirt is slightly torn, and his hair is all messed up, like he had to do a bit of fighting to get to my mom, but otherwise, he looks unharmed.

He prods me through the bond, and I squeeze my eyes shut as I try to figure out how to open the barrier I put between us. It takes some effort, and my mom seems to think it's another cramp as she coos and speaks soothing words until I relax.

I'm bombarded with emotions the moment I open my bond with Gray, and I grab as much of him as I can and pull.

He pulls back before leaving the room, and I turn to my mom.

"I missed you," I whisper, forcing myself into a sitting position.

Mom looks the same. Her grays are a bit more prominent, but she seems perfectly healthy. A small part of me feared Silas was exaggerating when he said the facility treated her well.

"I've thought about you every day," she admits, her eyes filling with tears before she chokes out a laugh and blinks them away. "Some demon, not Gray, visited me a few months ago. He told me he'd bring me to you soon, but I didn't believe him."

She snorts, wiping at her cheeks. "He was pretty intense, and I thought he was lying. I put him on a block list so he couldn't visit me again. Gray says that one was Silas, and that you've got a few men in your back pocket."

Despite my sour mood, my lips curl into a small smile as I nod tentatively. Silas can be intense, and I don't blame my mom for getting a bit freaked out.

"There're three of them," I say. "Gray, Silas, and Aziel. They're a bit intimidating, but they treat me well."

Mom pushes my hair behind my neck to better look at the marks littering my skin. "And what's this?"

I flush, moving my hair back over them. "That's private."

She raises a brow but doesn't push. At least, not for now. Mom can be persistent when she wants to be, and I'm sure this isn't the last I'll hear about my marks.

I grab her hand and squeeze as another cramp comes. When it's over, we fall into silence. I don't know what to say. I've imagined what our reunion would look like since the day I was taken, but never did I think it would be like this.

"Did you know I had two miscarriages before you?" Mom asks, pausing when Gray steps inside with tea. "They're scary, but it doesn't mean anything is wrong. You came after, and you were a healthy, chubby baby."

She offers Gray a soft smile, a sharp contradiction to the hard eyes that scan him. Gray might have brought her to me, but it's clear she's wary. I don't blame her, and Gray doesn't seem to, either, as he sets our drinks on the bedside table, kisses my temple, and turns to leave.

I reach out and snatch his hand, refusing to let him. "Stay."

Our bond hums, and I bring the back of his hand to my lips. Gray beams, curling his fingers around mine before climbing on the bed and sitting cross-legged on my right.

My mother watches, the woman ever-so-vigilant. "So, how did this come to be?"

Chapter Nineteen

AZIEL

SILAS NUDGES MY shoulder as my Wraths massacre the remaining Greeds. I'm far enough away that the scent of death and fear isn't provoking me, and I lean against Silas's side as we watch.

A few of Mammon's soldiers decided to try to fight, the fools not realizing the rest of her army had already left.

The Greeds scream and run like scared children, the sight enticing, and I step forward to join before Silas grabs my wrist to stop me. I frown, clenching and unclenching my fists as he pulls me in the opposite direction.

"Not now," he says, leading me away from the battle. "I want to get home to Charlie, and you getting violent will only prolong that."

I huff, knowing he's right but not happy about it. I can't wait to see Charlie again, but pulling myself away from such an exciting fight is still hard. I won't be able to stop once I start, and I'm more than ready to go home. I've been tempted to go to the shifter realm a few times to see Charlie, but the travel would have weakened me, and I needed to retain as much of my strength as possible.

It's hard being away from her, and I've been missing Gray, too.

He left two days ago to fix some urgent issue in Lust, and we haven't heard from him since. Still, I can't wait to go home and see him.

Even during all those years with Silas and then Gray as my friends, I've never had somebody to come home to like this, and I can't help but smile as I wrap my arm around Silas's shoulder and teleport us back to the main base. The entire place is a party, but I ignore it and make my way to the meeting hall.

My generals are already waiting for me, and they rise from their chairs before bowing their heads as I step inside.

Good.

It's about time they begin treating me with respect again, and I give Silas's shoulder a happy squeeze as we head to our seats. He's been a massive help with this, but that's nothing new. Silas has always been my voice of reason, and he more than makes up for any shortcomings I may have as a leader.

He's better than I am, but it would inflate his ego too much to hear that admission from my lips. Besides, I'm pretty sure he already knows.

"What's the update?" Silas asks, taking charge of the meeting.

I let him, and I busy myself with the plates of food left out for us. Silas doesn't like the vegetables we were served, and I frown before scooping them from his plate and replacing it with the meat from mine. Gray's usually the one who coordinates our meals, making sure the cooks are serving something everybody likes, and I always forget how much I appreciate the forethought until we're given a meal we have to shift around like this.

"The ogres have cleared out, and Mammon's men are actively retreating. The shifters sent word that her mate was executed, and our informants have confirmed she's in mourning."

Her mate? I tap my fingers against the table before reaching for my phone to see if there's any word from Kato or Chev. Shifters aren't easy to kill, and something big must have happened in the shifter lands if Vont is dead. Chev never answers his phone, the man firmly against technology, but I still give him a call.

He answers on the second ring.

"What happened with Vont?" I ask. "Is Charlie okay?"

Chev sighs. "Charlie is with Gray."

Silence fills the line as I wait for him to update me on Vont. The shifters don't like to discuss their private business, but when it involves my mate, I'm sure as fuck going to figure it out.

"Vont made an attempt for Charlie," Chev eventually admits. "She wasn't hurt, and the situation has been handled."

Silas places a hand on my forearm, the man probably sensing my rapidly growing rage.

"Why the fuck didn't you call me earlier?" I ask.

I can practically feel Chev rolling his eyes through the phone, which only further works me up.

"Gray asked us not to," he says. "I'm hanging up now. Goodbye."

The line goes dead, and I slowly lower my phone to my side before clenching my fists. The metal warps, and I drop it onto the ground before turning back to my generals. I thought Gray had an urgent matter in Lust to see to, not one affecting our mate. He will be answering for this later.

"Continue," I hiss through clenched teeth.

My generals exchange glances, and I catch a slight whiff of fear before I spin and pace the length of the room.

What was Gray thinking? Does Silas know?

I turn toward the fate, my eyes narrowing as I stare him down.

He blinks, glancing in my direction before raising a brow and facing me dead on. I don't like his silent challenge, and I suck my cheeks into my mouth as he crosses his arms over his chest and raises a brow.

Fucking bastard.

"Yes?" he asks.

He definitely knows something.

Working my jaw side to side, I turn toward the general I ordered to figure out what was happening in Lust. I didn't like the idea of Gray feeling like he needed to handle these situations by himself, and I wanted to ensure nothing so serious was happening that Silas or I needed to intervene.

"What have you got on the issue in Lust?" I ask the general.

Silas was annoyed when I did this, but now I'm pleased I did. I turn to the man I gave the assignment to, annoyed by the way his face turns red.

"I couldn't find anything," he admits.

Of course he couldn't. Because there probably isn't anything to find.

I nod, making brief eye contact with Silas before running my hands through my hair and sitting at the table. Charlie is okay, and I can contain myself for twenty minutes to finish up here.

"Mammon has given her men orders to return home," my top general, Raum, says, "and we're confident she has no plans to regroup and attack in the near future. With funds from Lust being cut off and the ogres stepping back, she can no longer afford the cost of the fight. She doesn't have the resources or men."

"Let's send the shifters home, but I want to keep Wraths on the borders," I decide.

I don't trust Mammon not to try to pull something in a desperate, last-ditch attempt, especially now that her mate has been killed. I had nothing to do with it, but I'm sure she still blames me. It's easier to do that than accept the fact that her decisions were the direct cause of Vont's death.

"And let's remove the evacuation notice on the border towns," I continue.

My warriors nod, and they share some additional information on Mammon before taking their leave. A few will remain, but most are going home to see their families. They'll rotate shifts these next few weeks, at least until we're confident Mammon isn't planning another attack.

Then we can lower our border units back to where they were before this mess.

My hands clench and unclench by my sides, and I wait until the last of my men are gone before turning to Silas.

"Tell me what you know," I order.

Silas presses his lips together, looking mildly annoyed.

"I don't like what you're suggesting," he says. "I know just as much as you."

I snort and lean back in my chair. "You're a fate. You know much more than I do."

Silas's lip twitches, but it's the only reaction I get. He's got a big ego, and I'm unintentionally feeding right into it. I don't care, though. He knows something, and I don't like that he's keeping secrets from me.

I shut my eyes and seep into his brain, searching for the answer myself. I'm faintly aware of him pushing at me, trying to force me out, but he should know by now that's not going to work.

His mind's a fucking maze, and I move around until I find the memory I'm looking for.

He's standing next to me when Gray gets a phone call, and he watches Gray's smile fall as he listens to whatever the person on the other line is saying. I'm busy speaking to Raum, and I don't notice the exchange.

Silas briefly debates capturing my attention and pointing it out, but he decides against it at the last moment. Gray's his own man, and Silas has been trying to be better about his prying.

He can't hear the conversation from the distance, but he can tell by Gray's face that it's nothing good.

I dig in deeper, watching through Silas's eyes as Gray hurries over to us and says he needs to leave. Silas turns to me as I demand he tells us why. He gets the feeling Gray is lying as he gives an excuse about Lust, but he decides not to push it as Gray leans in and smashes their lips together.

Silas is proud, and he's happy Gray's taking the initiative to solve problems himself.

He also thinks my pouting is cute when I get frustrated by the lack of detail I'm receiving.

I clench my jaw as he compares me to a lost dog.

Gray's gone a second later, and Silas is annoyed when I immediately turn to the nearest general and order him to figure out what's going on in Lust. He's disappointed in me, and I feel mildly guilty as I pull myself out of Silas's mind.

"You think I'm a bad mate," I say.

Silas cocks his head to the side, scanning my face, before sighing and shaking his head.

"That's not true," he argues. "I just think you should give Gray more credit. He's come a long way, and you're too busy worrying over him to see that. Even if he was lying about Lust, you should trust he's doing it for a good reason. You wouldn't question it if it were me."

I frown, hating that he's right.

"Are you going to apologize for forcing your way into my head?" he continues.

Silas grins at the glare I shoot in his direction, and his smile widens even further when I suck in a sharp breath and mumble an apology. It's all he'll get from me, and he should be grateful.

The bond between us is still new, and I sink my teeth into my bottom lip as it warms. Silas seems to feel it, too, if his reddening cheeks are anything to go by. His fingers twitch before he places a hand on my shoulder and leans in.

Being intimate after so long of being nothing more than friends feels weird, but I can't say I don't enjoy it.

I curl my hand around Silas's neck and pull his mouth down on mine, easily taking control as I slip my tongue between his lips. He lets me, a low moan emerging from his throat as I taste him.

It's nice, and he relaxes against me as I pull back and move my mouth to his neck. The bond between us is on fire, and I moan into his skin as I lick up the column of his throat.

"Gray will have our heads if we get carried away," I say, stepping back.

Our incubus is greedy—and petty.

He's usually able to contain it, but he's been struggling and I'm not trying to make that any more challenging for him. Even when he lies about the whereabouts of our female. I bet he's been at home with her this entire time. I'd bet my fucking life on it.

Silas rises from his chair and steps away. I smell his arousal, and I watch with interest as he reaches into his pants to adjust himself. The mere touch has him stiffening, the poor man probably accidentally touching his mark.

"Do you like my mark?" I ask.

He glances at me out of the corner of his eye. I know he does, but I still like to hear it.

"Yes," he says.

Good. We fall into a comfortable silence as we begin tidying up the room. Files from the last few days are scattered about, the place growing messy after Gray left. He was always good about keeping things neat for Silas and me.

I light the private, handwritten notes and plans we no longer need on fire before roughly folding up the ones we want to save. I'll reorganize everything when we get back, hopefully with Gray's help.

I'm in too much of a hurry to return to Charlie to worry about making everything perfect.

"I couldn't do any of this without you," I admit as we pack the last items.

Silas pauses, his head snapping in my direction before he shrugs and pretends like my compliment doesn't have the bond between us twisting. I've always known he likes praise, but I didn't realize how much until our marking.

I wish I had done it more over the years. It clearly means a lot to him.

"This should be good enough for now," I say, eager to get home. "We can finish up the rest tomorrow."

I'm hoping my mates are home, and I'll kill Gray if he sends me on a wild goose chase looking for them. He's constantly bouncing around and going missing, but I don't want that for Charlie.

Especially while she's pregnant. Teleporting isn't easy for her body, and I don't like the risk it imposes on our baby.

Plus, not that I'd ever tell Gray this, but he's not very good at it. He's getting better, but it's still choppy.

Silas bundles up the files he's decided to keep before snatching up his laptop and a few maps. I do the same, and I knock him on top of the head with a rolled-up map before disappearing.

I'm going to beat him home.

We end up in my office simultaneously, and I narrow my eyes before dropping my things on the floor and sprinting out of the room. We haven't done this in a good four hundred years, and I'm glad he's on board as he runs after me. He used to win this game when we were young, but my legs are much stronger now than they were back then.

I don't hear anybody in the offices or the library, so I avoid that direction and make my way to the stairs instead.

Silas wraps his hand around my bicep and shoves me against a wall, and I bellow out a laugh before lunging for his back. He easily avoids me, his feet sliding against the floor as he makes a sharp turn and sprints through the dining room.

"You bastard," I shout, running behind Silas.

Since when did he start playing dirty?

I keep my ears peeled for Charlie's heartbeat as Silas and I race through the house, our quick movements scaring the shadows. I'm faintly aware of one dropping a plate as I twist around her, barely avoiding barreling into her shoulder as Silas begins climbing the stairs.

My lips curl as I grab his ankle and yank, watching his arms flail just seconds before his face smacks into the wood. There's a loud crack, but he'll heal quickly, and I jump over his sprawled form without a second thought.

We could teleport to Charlie and Gray, but it's more fun to race.

Silas is up again a second later, his feet pounding into the ground. I laugh, glancing at him over my shoulder before making a sharp right as I pick up Charlie's heartbeat.

She's in the guest room.

There are two others with her, probably Gray and Rock, and I push my legs to speed up as I ram into the door and break it off its hinges. There's a loud shriek, but it goes in one ear and out the other as Silas follows right behind me, his body slamming into mine and causing us to tumble to the floor.

I'm out of breath, and I shove Silas off me before rolling over and pinning him. He's red in the face, and he knees me in the thigh as his teeth snap at my shoulder.

I have one of his wrists in my hand and fight him for control of the other when I freeze.

Silas doesn't seem to realize, and he rips his arm free of my suddenly loose grip before he shoves the palm of his hand upward against my nose.

Immediately, there's blood, but I pay it no mind as I turn toward the stranger in my home.

It's Charlie's mother, and I bounce to my feet as I glance between her, Charlie, and Gray. What the fuck is going on? Silas is next to me a second later, a question falling from his lips before he quiets and sits back down.

I turn to him, confused, before shifting my attention back to Charlie.

Her face is red and her eyes teary, and I scan her body before settling on the hand resting on her belly. That's not right. I step closer and breathe her in.

She doesn't smell right.

"Aziel," she whispers, falling silent when I step back.

No.

She's supposed to smell like me. She smelled like me when we left.

I swallow past the lump in my throat, my eyes darting between her, Gray, and Silas for confirmation. Gray pulls her into his arms, and Silas teleports to her side and cups her cheeks.

He's whispering something to her, but I don't listen.

All eyes turn to me as I take another step back. I wipe my face, cleaning up the blood from the broken nose Silas gave me just seconds ago.

With it healed, I can smell Charlie better, and I wince as the putrid scent of death fills my lungs. I don't like it, and I shake my head before glancing at Gray again for confirmation.

He nods, his only response, and I blink before turning and

leaving the room.

I'm teleporting the second I cross the doorway, taking myself to the one place I know will make me feel better.

It's dark and cold, and I breathe in the familiar scent before searching for my first victim.

I missed the pits.

Chapter Twenty

CHARLOTTE

I TRIP OVER a tree root, too busy looking around to focus on where I'm stepping.

Mom squeezes my hand, stabilizing me before letting go and stomping after Silas.

We've been wandering around these woods for hours now, with no sign of Mom's mysterious elven friend to be found. She says he's a powerful elf and can help us secure an alliance for their technology, and I'm excited. The elves are one of the final puzzle pieces we must secure before officially launching our takeover of the Seekers organization.

The elves have the technology we need to effectively find and remove purchased females from the homes of the men who purchased them. We want to move quickly once we've begun. We need to.

Word will spread quickly, and we don't want to give males time to hide or injure their females. Chev is scared the rougher species, like the ogres, will choose to murder their purchased women instead of giving them up, and that's not a risk I'm willing to take.

We need that technology.

"Are you sure he's here?" I ask.

I still can't believe Mom managed to meet somebody while trapped in the facility, but I'm not ready to pry. I'm unprepared to accept and face my dad's death, so I'm not asking for details about Mom and Niven's relationship.

I can't.

Maybe when this is all over, I'll let myself feel, but I'm just not ready yet.

"What if he's not happy we're here?" I say, glancing between Silas and Gray.

They both walk a few feet ahead of me, and my mom shoves her way between them before storming ahead. Gray takes that as his opportunity to return to my side, and he slips his hand into mine with a wide smile. Our bond tugs, the incubus making a pointed effort to reach me through it.

Things have been tense since the loss of the baby, especially since Aziel left, but I'm refusing to dwell on it.

We have work to do.

"I know where I'm going," Mom says, shooting me a sharp look over her shoulder. "Niven is a dear friend. He wouldn't have given me his address if he didn't want me to visit."

Silas lifts a hand to stop us, and Gray wraps an arm around my waist. His hold is possessive, and he squeezes me tightly to his chest as we wait for further direction from Silas. Sneaking into the elven lands is a little risky, and I know Gray and Silas are pissed that I demanded to be brought along.

It was a better option than leaving me at home by myself, though.

Aziel is nowhere to be found, and Silas refuses to let me step onto the shifter lands after the incident with Vont. The other day, he caught me looking at the portal and got all red in the face.

The color refused to go away even as I assured him I wasn't planning on sneaking out.

I honestly wasn't, and I was only looking because I'm worried about Rock. He wasn't wearing the ring that helps him teleport when everything happened with Vont, and while I know the shifters wouldn't hurt him, I don't trust them not to lock him up in the cabin again. They're probably ramping up security after the attack.

"How did you even meet Niven?" I ask.

Mom shrugs, her face turning red. "He said the human realm called to him, and he wanted to tour the facilities there to learn about the Seekers technology."

I press my lips together. Silas told me he saw her being *intimate* with an elf, and given how weird the blessed breeds are about sex and mate bonds, I have a feeling this Niven feels something beyond friendship for my mother. Does she know that?

Anger boils inside me, and Gray and Silas soothe me through the bonds. My rage isn't rational, but I can't help it. My dad was a good man, and a small part of me wants my mom to be alone forever to honor his memory.

Even if I know it's not fair.

I glance at my feet and shift my stance until Silas gestures for us to continue walking. The elven lands are dangerous, and my males are being cautious. They didn't expect my mom to have such a rough idea of where Niven's home was, and they thought she was giving them instructions directly to the correct location.

It appears she thought she was doing that, too, and I can tell she's pissed to have been brought into the middle of the woods.

Gray glues himself to my side as we walk, the man practically carrying me through the woods. We haven't spoken about the baby, or lack thereof, since Aziel left, but I can tell it weighs on his mind.

It's the elephant in the room, but I appreciate him not pushing the topic.

I accept our baby's gone, but I don't want to discuss it. We'll have time to mourn when everything with the females is settled. It's not healthy, I know that, but I've never been known for my mental stability.

"Maybe he gave you the wrong address?" I say.

Mom spins and glances at me before sliding her eyes to the large incubus that holds me. She's not the biggest fan of Gray, but she's been keeping her opinions to herself.

"I know where I'm going, Charlotte," she says.

I purse my lips, dropping the subject.

I can tell she's embarrassed that her instructions didn't take us directly to Niven's home like she thought they would, but we've been walking around for hours, and, eventually, we'll have to call it. Silas warned that the elven lands are especially dangerous at night, and we need to be out of here before the sun goes down.

We walk for another ten minutes before Silas holds up his hand to stop us again. We all freeze, and he cocks his head to the side before disappearing.

I don't like when he's out of sight, and my heart pounds in his absence.

Gray pulls me tighter against his side as we wait for Silas to return, his thumb rubbing relaxing circles into my waist. He always seems to know what I need, and I accept his comfort with a quiet sigh. I know I'm being clingy, Aziel's disappearance making me paranoid about my other males leaving, but Gray and Silas have been exceptionally understanding.

"These are Niven's lands, and he's not going to hurt us," Mom says, ignoring Silas's order and storming ahead.

I shrug, mostly agreeing with her even if Silas and Gray don't.

Gray hisses and reaches for my mom, his arm tightening

around me before he lifts my feet off the ground and hurries after her.

"Patty," he says. "Get your ass back here."

She ignores him, which is unsurprising, and I hold back a laugh as he huffs and continues chasing her. Gray usually gets along with everybody he meets, but for some reason, it's not working for him and my mom. They don't actively dislike one another, but there's not a budding friendship on the horizon.

I have a feeling it has to do with him being an incubus. Mom made assumptions when I told her how I came to meet Gray, Silas, and Aziel, and no amount of my assurances seem to be getting through to her. She's convinced they took advantage of me, and while I'm willing to admit there were a lot of issues regarding our power imbalances and my lack of options, I'm confident they're whom I want.

"Patricia Myers!" Gray hisses.

I suck my cheeks into my mouth. She doesn't like being called by her full name.

Mom spins around. "Listen here, you—"

Silas returns just as I open my mouth to stop them, his presence thankfully ending the impending fight.

He glances between us, visibly annoyed we didn't stay still. "There's a house ahead with a man sitting on a porch. He already knows we're here, and considering we haven't been attacked, I'd say we're good to go ahead."

My mom shoots Silas a cocky look and marches ahead.

Silas and Gray remain behind, and I turn and rub Gray's chest.

"She'll warm up to you," I whisper, kissing his cheek. "I'll talk to her when we get home."

Our bond tightens, and Gray lets out a quiet groan before shaking his head and cupping my chin. He smooshes my lips together before ducking and kissing me, the goofy action making me smile.

"Don't. She has every right to be mad at me. I purchased you to be used, and I don't blame her for being upset," he says, squeezing my cheeks before releasing me and following her into the woods. "I'll win her over. Won't I, Patty?"

He shouts the words loudly, so there's no way she doesn't hear.

Her pace quickens as she attempts to escape Gray, and I roll my eyes before turning to Silas. He looks tired, and I don't hesitate to wrap my arms around his waist.

"Is he the man you saw?" I can't help but ask.

Silas returns my hug with a tight one of his own. It feels good to be in his arms, and I let myself sink into it. There was a time I never thought I'd get to experience it again, and I'm overcome with nothing short of relief every time he doesn't push me away.

I can't help but wonder what he even sees in me. He's as old as dirt, and he's undoubtedly come across hundreds, if not thousands, of women who could do much more for him than I can.

"It was," he admits. "Fate can be ruined, made worse, if you speak on things that shouldn't be known."

I rest my chin on his chest.

"Is that your nice way of telling me to keep my mouth shut?" I tease.

Silas shrugs, and I let out a quiet laugh before lifting on my toes and kissing him.

"I wish I could put into words just how much I love you," I say. "You mean everything to me."

I'm disgusted with myself whenever I think back to the things I did with Kato and Emily, and I'm desperate for Silas to know and understand how much I regret it. I know what I did was wrong, and I worry I'll never truly be able to express just how sorry I am.

Silas brushes my hair behind my ear before bringing his hand to my chest.

"I can feel you, baby," he says. "I know."

His lips curl at the corners before he lifts me off my feet and carries me to Gray and my mom. Their loud bickering makes them easy to find, and I deflate as I listen. All they do is huff and puff around one another, and it's frustrating.

We walk for another few minutes before I spot a house through the trees. It's quaint, a single-story farmhouse with brick siding and a large, wrap-around porch. My mom always joked about how she wanted to live in a home like this in the country, but we could never afford it.

Silas sets me on my feet, and I awkwardly pull at my underwear and fix my bloody pad before hurrying toward Gray. My mom tries to speed past him, but he grabs her hand and refuses to let her run ahead. I agree it's probably the right thing to do, but she's not pleased.

She turns to him with a snarl and tries to rip his hand off her, but Gray doesn't budge.

"Stay with us," he quietly says.

Gray's annoyance hits me through the bond, but I appreciate him going out of his way to keep her safe.

My mom fights harder the closer we get to the house, and I fiddle with the hem of my shirt as I eye the man sitting on the porch. He's wearing long, deep purple robes, the color accentuating his violet eyes and dark skin. I don't remember any of the elves I've ever met before having violet eyes, and I do my best not to gawk as Niven rises halfway out of his chair and gives my males and me a slight bow. A strand of his long, dark hair falls into his face, and he smoothly pushes it away as he straightens back up.

He rises to his full height as he shifts his attention to my mom, and a wide smile spreads over his face as he lowers into a deep bend.

Why does she get the better bow?

Mom continues to try to wrestle her arm out of Gray's hold, and Niven's attention flashes to their connection before his eyes shift into a dark brown. That's the color I remember seeing on the elves I briefly met when I was with Mammon, and I press my lips into a firm line as Gray releases my mom.

She hurries up to Niven and pulls him into a tight hug, and Silas places a hand on the small of my back as he guides me forward. My palms are sweaty, and I nervously wipe them on my shirt as Niven's eyes flicker back to violet. I trip, convinced I'm hallucinating.

"Our eyes are our souls," Niven says, his voice like a song as he answers my unspoken question. "We prefer to keep them hidden."

What does that mean?

"But we're unable to do so in front of fates," he continues.

Silas goes rigid, his grip on me shifting from soft to mechanical as Niven releases my mom and gestures for us to join him on the porch.

"And this must be your lovely daughter?" Niven asks my mom.

Mom licks her lips. "This is Charlotte, and her…" She trails off as she glances at Silas and Gray.

"We're two of Charlie's mates," Silas smoothly interjects.

Niven's eyes continue to flicker between violet and brown. He looks mildly annoyed by it, and he dips his chin in acknowledgment before sitting back down in his seat. My mom takes the spot right next to him, the two so close, their knees are touching.

I'm not a fan.

"We can't stay for too long," Mom says.

Gray turns and walks back toward Silas and me, refusing to approach the house until I'm sandwiched between the two men. They each place a hand on me, probably preparing to teleport me away the moment something goes wrong.

I trust my mom, though, and I plaster what I hope looks like a friendly smile on my face as I follow Niven onto the porch.

"It's nice to meet you," I say, holding out my hand.

The man glances at it before sliding his gaze to my mother. She chuckles, and Niven awkwardly shakes my hand. He releases me immediately, and I pretend I don't notice how he wipes his palm on his pants afterward.

"I'm sure you've heard about everything happening between Wrath and the shifters," Mom starts. She waits for Niven to nod before continuing. "Well, my daughter here is the cause of all that, and I was hoping we could chat with you about getting support from the elves."

Niven sucks his cheeks into his mouth, contemplating.

I'm taking it as a good sign he doesn't immediately shoot us down, and I lower myself onto the small porch swing between Silas and Gray. Their thighs squeeze me in, the three of us barely fitting and most definitely looking peculiar, considering there's ample seating for us all, but I don't complain.

"There has been much back and forth between Mammon and Aziel," Niven explains. "We feel it's been a waste of our time, and we do not wish to get in the middle of it."

I suppose that's understandable. Mammon made them many promises, and I'm sure they were frustrated when she decided to abandon the cause in lieu of starting a war with Aziel. We've been doing our best to work quickly, but this project is taking longer than we initially thought.

There have been quite a few setbacks along the way.

"We've been working with the shifters on final plans, and

we're ready to set things into motion," I say, my face warming as Gray and Aziel both set their hands on my thighs.

We're waiting for Aziel, but we have no idea how long he'll be gone. Silas and Gray are convinced he went to the pits, but neither wants to go there to confirm. Fates are hunted by the other demons, so it's much too dangerous for Silas to go, and Gray isn't a very good fighter.

I fear he'd be killed rather quickly.

"When the elven leaders met with Mammon, they agreed to share technology," I say. "We want to know if that offer could still be on the table."

Niven clasps his hands together and leans back in his seat, his purple robes swishing around his legs.

"I'm not in a position to make those decisions," he says. "I am not an elven leader."

Silas clears his throat. "Yes, you are."

He doesn't follow up his words with an explanation, and Niven presses his lips together as he glares at my fate. Given Niven's reaction, I have a feeling Niven's position, or something relating to it, is meant to be a secret. Even Mom looks mildly surprised.

Silas probably only knows because he's a fate, and he's probably seen Niven during one of his visits to the fated world.

I've gathered the fates can be selective over what Silas sees, explicitly choosing the items he will need in the future. Sometimes I think they show him things he doesn't enjoy, too, if his occasional jolting awake is anything to go by.

He refuses to talk about what he saw, which I've accepted.

"I will set up a meeting with our leaders to discuss," Niven says, continuing to stare at Silas. "We will have an answer for you shortly, and I'll reach out once they've come to a decision."

The tension between us is thick, and I nervously clear my

throat before forcing a wobbly smile onto my lips.

"We would appreciate that, and we're more than happy to meet with the council to go over our plans and answer any questions," I say.

We've sent the elven council many messages, but they respond with only a templated response stating they will reach out once they have something to share. The elves know Mammon and Aziel are fighting, and they aren't interested in humoring either one of us.

"I'll keep that in mind," Niven says, still staring at Silas.

They're making things awkward.

"Wonderful," Gray chirps, not helping.

My mom shoots Gray the sideways look she does every time he speaks, her eyes crinkled in the corners and her lips pursed. I want them to get along, and I hope they find common ground soon.

"Would you like to remain here with me, Patricia?" Niven asks, turning to my mom. "I have a spare room decorated to your liking."

Decorated to her liking? How does he even know what she likes, and why would he do that?

I suck my cheeks into my mouth and turn to investigate the wooded area surrounding Niven's house. The trees here are beautiful, some of the largest I've ever seen, and it might even put the shifter forest to shame.

"That's very kind of you to offer, but I'd like to stay with my daughter for now," Mom says.

My lips twitch as she rises from her chair and smooths her hands down the front of her dress. Niven watches her every movement with an intensity I don't appreciate, and my mom flushes as she notices it. She used to flush like that for my dad, too, and I debate saying so before biting my tongue.

Mom deserves to be happy.

Dad would want that for her.

I stand, Silas and Gray quickly copying me, and go to Niven. He didn't like my handshake earlier, so I give an awkward half-bow instead. I'm sure I look far from graceful, and Niven visibly holds back laughter as I turn toward my males and gesture for them to do the same.

Gray bows without a second thought, and Silas hesitates before lowering.

Niven gives a bow back, and Gray grabs my arm and teleports me home a moment later. I plant my hands on my knees as the world materializes around me, and Gray rubs my back as Silas returns with my mom.

I fucking hate teleporting.

Chapter Twenty-One

SILAS

I KEEP TABS on Charlie and Gray through my bonds as I materialize inside the pits. I don't want them to wake up and grow worried when they realize I'm no longer in bed, the two acting especially clingy lately. They're all over one another and, in turn, all over me.

I love my mates, I love them so fucking much, but they're driving me crazy.

They're trying hard to hide how much Aziel's disappearance has hurt them, but neither is particularly successful. Charlie's been silently crying in the shower each morning after waking up and discovering Aziel still hasn't returned, and I've caught Gray trying to sneak off to the pits twice.

Aziel leaving crushed them, Charlie especially, and I hate him for making her think he's angry with her for the miscarriage. The idiotic Wrath has never been good with emotions, especially pain, but he needs to find new coping mechanisms.

It's not good for our family.

I warned him this could happen, and I made it wildly fucking clear how sensitive human pregnancies can be in the early weeks.

I scoff and kick a rock before ducking underneath a whizzing arrow.

The pits are dangerous for any demon, but they're especially bad for me. I'm a hunted species, and while Aziel's claim of me provides some protection, the pits are a free-for-all. There's nothing anybody could do if I were harmed or killed, and all the demons in here know that.

It reeks of death here, and what was once a sprawling Wrath city is now nothing more than busted-up buildings and rubble. I can smell the blood and excrement from here, and I wrinkle my nose as I make my way into the center of the street. I'm between two large buildings, one that looks to have once been a bank and another that was potentially a restaurant.

Aziel's father made this place long ago to feed his cruel desires, and the Wraths fucking love it. Even if most of those who come here end up dying.

At some point, it became an initiation ritual among young Wraths. They need to spend an entire day here before their communities accept them as a true warrior, and Aziel's been trying to get that situation under control for years now.

He doesn't want his people to come here, but his constant presence isn't helping.

Stupid Wrath.

He should have known better than to abandon Charlie, and this is precisely why we didn't want to tell her she was pregnant in the first place. Had we kept quiet, she probably wouldn't have even known she was with child. This entire thing would have seemed like nothing more than a late period.

"Aziel, where the fuck are you?" I shout, drawing plenty of attention to myself.

He'll come to me.

I duck under another arrow, this one closer to my neck than

I'd like it to be.

"Aziel!" I scream into the blackness of the pits.

I've never come here before, usually letting him sort his shit out on his own time, but I don't have the patience. We have a female to care for, and his absence is actively hurting her.

My lips curl into a grin when an arm wraps around my neck and yanks me against a hard chest. I stumble, not having expected Aziel to be quite so sneaky, and I reach up to grab his wrist as he drags me away.

I'm pulled into a thin alleyway, the space barely wide enough to fit us.

"What the fuck are you doing in here?" Aziel asks, tightening his arm around my neck.

I huff, pissed he has the audacity to ask me that.

"It's time for you to come home," I say, shoving at Aziel until he releases me. "You're running away from your problems like a child, and I'm not going to sit back and let you make a fool of our bonds." I spin to face him the second his hold lightens.

"I'm making a fool of our bond?" He scoffs, pushing my chest.

I stumble back a few steps before moving forward until we're toe to toe. I'll give him a fight if that's what he wants.

"You know, I've had the feeling you've been hiding something from me," Aziel says, his voice unnervingly hoarse. "I thought it was about Gray, but that's not it, is it? I let our bond lull me into trusting you, but you can't be trusted."

Aziel grabs my chin, his fingers digging into my cheeks. "No, you can't be trusted because you're a fucking fate. A fate who knows everything but does nothing."

He squeezes my cheeks before releasing me, and I run a hand through my hair, not bothering to deny his accusation. Aziel's not dumb, and I won't insult him by pretending I don't know what he's talking about.

We've often argued about my lack of involvement in things, the worst being when I didn't stop Gray from forcibly bonding with him. The fates don't work like that, and going against them only worsens things.

My entire purpose is to facilitate within the physical world when they can't.

"You knew," Aziel spits. "You knew our baby was going to die."

My throat runs dry, and I numb the bonds in my chest so nobody feels the sharp sting of self-loathing that rushes through me. I didn't know for sure, but I could tell something was wrong the last few times I entered the fated world. They're usually open, encouraging me to search, but they've been hiding from me.

I've never seen Charlie's fate, or that of any of my males, but the risk of me stumbling upon it was still too high for them. The fates didn't want to risk it, and I knew something wasn't right. They don't hide unless they're keeping something from me, and they don't do that unless it will affect me directly.

It wasn't hard to make assumptions, and I've only been able to think of one reason why.

I clear my throat, hoping my voice comes out level.

"You two killed Asmod," I say, clenching my fists as my eyes grow wet. "He was a royal, and you knew his death would upset the balance. The fates had to respond. They couldn't let it go unpunished."

Aziel scoffs, his fist crumbling the cement wall behind my head. I don't flinch.

If he wants to hit me, so be it, but that won't change what happened. I don't control the fates, and I had no part in their decisions. There's nothing we could've done to stop it, and speaking up would've only made things worse.

The fates would see it as a betrayal, and they'd punish me for it.

They'd punish all of us for it.

Giving Charlie an early miscarriage was a weak punishment, and we all know it. The fates went easy on us, an action that goes against everything they stand for. Killing Asmod was huge, and a proper punishment would have been to let Charlie carry the baby full term before killing them both.

I'm sure the only reason they didn't was because they have larger plans for her.

Plans I'm not privy to due to our close relationship.

"You're a fucking coward, Silas," Aziel says, his voice full of poorly concealed hatred. "You sat back and let us go off to fight Mammon knowing full well that something was wrong."

The dried blood around Aziel's hands cracks as he clenches and unclenches his fists. I stare at them, waiting to see if he'll hit me. We've never fought before, at least not over something so serious, and I'm interested to see what he does.

Seconds pass, each one longer than the last.

"Are you going to hit me?" I ask.

Aziel shakes his head, his chest deflating. "Never."

He sure looks like he wants to, though.

"You don't know what it's like to be a fate," I whisper, my voice cracking. "Do you think I *wanted* to sit back and pretend everything was okay when I could guess our fucking baby was going to die?"

Aziel's throat bobs, and his eyes widen as I shove at his chest and press him back against the wall.

"I didn't ask to be a fate, and you don't get to act like you're the only one hurting," I continue. "Our mates are at home convinced you hate them. Charlie's crying herself to sleep every night because she's blaming herself for something she had no control over, and what are you doing?"

I curl my right hand around Aziel's neck, pinning him in place. "Running around the pits so you don't have to acknowledge you're upset?" I let out a dry laugh and release him, my emotions frazzled.

Aziel's chest expands as he sucks in a deep breath. I watch, mirroring his action.

Being a fate is agonizing at times, and I have absolutely no fucking control over it.

Meeting people and knowing exactly how and when they'll die, knowing all the pain they'll feel and the millions of mistakes they'll make, isn't fun. I can't make friends for fear of seeing things I shouldn't, things that will haunt me whenever I'm around them.

I can't sleep at night without going into the fated world, and I can't go into the fated world without learning something horrifying.

My brain is full of answers to questions I never asked and don't want to know, but there's absolutely fucking nothing I can do about it. The scarcity of fates means all the extra work is put on me. I need to know everything to make up for the shortcomings of those who have been killed. I don't want to do it, and I don't want to know.

I want to turn my brain off.

I don't realize I'm crying until Aziel pulls me against his chest, his arms wrapping tightly around my waist. It only worsens things, and an ugly sob bubbles up out of my throat despite my attempts to keep it down. This isn't about me. Charlie and Gray are the ones who need comfort.

I'm fine.

Aziel curls one hand around the back of my head while the other runs down my spine. The blood on his skin and clothing smears over me, but I hardly notice.

"I'm sorry," I choke out.

"No," Aziel says, tightening his grip. "I know it's not your fault. You had no control over their decisions, and I shouldn't have left. It's me who fucked up."

The bond between us pulls and twists with emotion, and I let Aziel hold me until it settles. He buries his face against my neck and breathes, his body shaking as he struggles to calm himself before he licks over Gray's and Charlie's marks.

The action forces a dry laugh from my throat. He's like a dog, constantly eager to sniff and mark his territory.

"Come home," I say, pulling out of his embrace.

My face is wet from blood and tears, and I turn away in a sad attempt to hide it. I don't like being vulnerable, especially in the pits, where I'm sure we've got hundreds of eyes on us at any given moment.

"I know you fell in love with our child, but you can't run away from everything that makes you upset," I quietly remind him. "That may have been what we used to do, but I don't want us to be like this with Charlie."

She deserves better than that.

Aziel cups my cheeks and stares into my eyes, his touch notably softer than it was when he first grabbed me. His black eyes are glossy, filled with unshed tears, and one falls down his cheek as he leans in and presses his lips against mine.

The world around us disappears, and a second later, we're in Aziel's old bedroom.

It still smells of him in here, and I step away and wipe at my cheeks as I turn and look around. Now that he's no longer using it, large shelves and bookcases have been installed along almost every wall. They're filled with hundreds, if not thousands, of trinkets.

"Where did all this come from?" I ask.

Aziel shrugs. "I cleaned out some closets around the manor," he admits. "So we can have a dedicated space for cleaning supplies."

My lips twitch, and I shake my head as I go to his closet to grab a fresh pair of underwear and a shirt to change into. I smell like the pits, and my skin is covered in dried blood where Aziel touched me. Aziel grabs a pair of fresh underwear for himself before following me into the bathroom.

He strips and tosses his clothes in the trash, and I turn on the shower.

Blood is crusted over his entire body, and I grimace as I gesture for him to get in the shower first. He does, and blood immediately flows down his body and swirls into the drainpipe between his feet. I wait until he's mostly clean before joining.

"What should I say to her?" Aziel asks after a moment.

That's a good question, and I wish I had an answer.

"Tell her the truth," I suggest, cleaning myself.

Charlie's not unreasonable, and she'll understand Aziel's fear. It's been only the three of us for a long time, and sometimes we make mistakes. He knows running away wasn't the right thing to do, and an apology goes a long way in the eyes of our female.

"Are you going to tell her about me?" I work up the courage to ask. "About the fates?"

Aziel turns to me, and his eyes soften before he drops his gaze to the floor and shakes his head. I gulp, my pulse racing with fear. I don't want Charlie to be afraid of me, frightened of the things I see and how much I know.

More than anything, though, I don't want her to blame me for the miscarriage. I suspected, and Aziel's right in saying I'm nothing more than a coward who knows everything but does nothing. She'll be disappointed in me, ashamed even, and I don't think I can live with her resentment.

"Silas, what I said earlier…" Aziel reaches for me, his hands raising into the air before he hesitates and awkwardly drops them back to his sides. "I didn't mean any of it."

I shrug, refusing to look him in the eye as I suck my cheeks into my mouth. He did, and that's okay. I can't be angry with him for acknowledging what we both know to be true.

"Look at me," Aziel says, taking hold of my shoulders.

He pushes my wet hair out of my face and stares, his eyes scanning every inch of me. It makes me uncomfortable, and I shift awkwardly while I wait for him to speak.

"I'm so sorry, Silas. I know how hard being a fate is, and I was beyond cruel to say those things. You're a good male, worlds better than Gray and I combined, and we are so lucky to have you." He pulls at our bond until I open it and let him feel me. "I love you, Silas, and I didn't mean what I said. We won't speak about it again. Nobody has to know."

I shift my weight from foot to foot.

"Nobody will know, okay?" Aziel continues. "You did nothing wrong, and if it weren't for you being such a loyal fate, I know our punishment would've been worse. Charlie killed Asmod, and that's not your fault."

I reach around him to shut off the water, not wanting to hear any more of this.

"Say it," Aziel orders, grabbing my wrist when I try to leave. "Say it, Silas."

I lick my lips and glance at the ceiling before looking at Aziel. He seems earnest, and he opens his bond entirely so I can feel the truth behind what he says. It shocks me, and I clench my jaw when my bottom lip quivers. He honestly doesn't blame me?

Aziel pushes my hair behind my ears, touching me like I'm a wounded animal. "Say it, baby. Say that you know it's not your fault, and you didn't do anything wrong."

My voice shakes when I finally work up the courage to speak. "It's not my fault, and I didn't do anything wrong."

Aziel hums, quietly approving before letting me go. I spin around, eager to dry myself off, get dressed, and return to bed. Charlie and Gray are still asleep, their bonds peaceful, and I do my best not to let them feel my struggle as I tug Aziel's shirt over my head and pull his underwear up my legs.

The Wrath stares at me, clearly concerned over my mental state, but I ignore it.

I've been dealing with this for hundreds and hundreds of years, and I've long since accepted there's nothing I can do about it. Having my mates helps, and the good days are finally beginning to outweigh the bad ones. I see a good man's death one night, but the next morning, my female is chattering excitedly about her plans for the day while my incubus shoves food down my throat.

I'm happy.

Aziel follows me out of his private wing and into the one we share. Charlie's sound asleep, her back pressed against Gray's outstretched arm, and I smile down at them before climbing in on the end, leaving Aziel room to squeeze in next to her.

Chapter Twenty-Two

CHARLOTTE

A WARM BODY crawls over me, and I groan as I shove at it.

I'm too tired to deal with whatever Gray and Silas are doing. Gray's constantly waking me up with a foot in the back, and Silas always tries to suffocate me with his cuddles. Neither of which I'm particularly excited about right now. I need room, and I roll into Gray's space to try to avoid Silas. It won't take long for Gray to get too hot and push me back against Silas, but I'll deal with that then.

I miss the days when Gray was desperate for my affection and too scared to be mean to me at night. He'd hold and squish up against me even though he hated it, silently suffering like a good male.

He cherished whatever he could get, but now I get a rough palm shoved against my shoulder for forced distance.

He's sure grown comfortable.

A heavy body lowers on my back before a warm hand wiggles between the mattress and my stomach. I bury my face in the sheets, my jaw clenching as the hand settles against the skin directly below my belly button.

I don't like being touched there, and I throw my elbow against who I'm pretty sure is Silas before rolling even further onto my stomach. There's nothing in there for them to feel, and failure washes over me every time they do.

"Charlie?"

My body goes painfully rigid, every muscle tensing.

Anger flares in my chest, and I debate getting up and leaving the room before spinning around to face Aziel. He lifts, removing his weight from my back so I have room to flip around. I stare at his chin as he sits farther down on the bed, giving me space.

I try to make eye contact, but the second I take in the pain reflected in his irises, I lower my gaze to his chest.

This is easier.

He's wearing only black underwear, and I quickly scan his exposed skin for any injuries. There aren't any, thankfully, and I pull the sheets to my chest when I feel his eyes on my bare skin. I don't like to sleep with clothes on, and I feel vulnerable being naked in front of Aziel right now.

"Aziel," I breathe, unsure what else to say.

What is there to say? He left, ran away the second he learned I lost our baby. We were all hurting, but instead of sticking around, he ran away. I understand needing some space, but he's been gone for almost four days.

Four fucking days.

We haven't heard a word from him, and if it weren't for the bond between us that twists with anger and betrayal, I'd have no idea whether or not he was dead.

I also have no confidence that he plans to stay.

Will he run off to the pits every time he gets upset? Will I have to spend the rest of our lives constantly afraid of setting him off? Having to cherry-pick the information I give him and ensure he receives it at just the right time?

That sounds exhausting.

Knowing Gray is also beyond hurt, I give his shoulder a gentle shake. He huffs, shoving at my hand before his nostrils flare and his eyes spring open. He's sitting up a second later, his arm wrapping around my waist as he pulls me back against his chest.

He wraps his arms around me, squeezing me tightly before deciding that's not enough and lifting me over his thigh so I sit between his spread legs, my back to his chest.

I let him, happy with the protection against Aziel.

I may be angry with the Wrath, but it's nothing to the incubus's current fury.

"What do you want?" Gray snaps.

I let my head rest against his chest.

Aziel can't run away for days only to return in the middle of the night and crawl into bed like he hasn't done anything wrong. He especially doesn't get to wake me up with his grabby hands.

"I'm sorry," Aziel says, reaching for me before deciding better and placing his hand on Gray's knee.

Gray shifts but doesn't push him off.

"I'm so sorry. I shouldn't have left," Aziel continues, rubbing his thumb along the inside of Gray's knee before inching slightly closer to me. "I was scared, and I made a stupid decision."

I gulp, turning toward Silas.

He lies on his side facing us, his black eyes closely watching our every interaction. There's something off about him, our bond weaker than usual, and I grab his hand to pull him closer. Aziel left all three of us, and I don't want Silas to feel like Aziel's apology is only directed at Gray and me.

Silas deserves one, too.

The fate slides underneath the covers toward us, quickly taking me up on my silent offer. I can tell he's trying to clock my emotions. He's prodding a bit through our bond, too, but it's nothing compared to Aziel trying to barrel his way through the barrier I've put up between us.

The one I put between Silas and Gray has been down since they returned, but I'm not ready to do the same with Aziel. I'll forgive him the moment I feel his pain, but I deserve to be angry, too.

I'm not stupid. I know he's hurting. Aziel's never been very good with his emotions, and he's gone to the pits several times since we met, but I thought things were different now.

We're bonded, and he can't just up and leave whenever the mood strikes.

"You left us," I say, my voice cracking.

Aziel's lips purse, and I fight the urge to cave in when he drops his chin to his chest like a scolded child. It's hard to stay angry with him when he looks so heartbroken and lost, but it doesn't make up for his actions. I would've been more understanding if he'd been gone for a few hours, or even a night, but it was four fucking days.

We've managed to secure our alliance with the elves in that time, and we've been giving every excuse possible to the shifters so they don't think we've pulled out.

Aziel clears his throat and inches closer.

"I never want to hurt you guys," he whispers, glancing at Gray before carefully moving his hand to me. "You three are my entire life, and hurting you is the last thing I want."

He places his hand on my thigh, and I sink my teeth into my bottom lip to prevent it from trembling.

"Then why did you?" I ask.

Gray smooths a hand down the back of my head, and Silas leans over and kisses my shoulder. His lips linger, his wet hair tickling my cheek. Why is his hair wet?

"I don't know," Aziel says. "I just... I was so excited for our baby, and when I realized it was gone, I just didn't want to feel."

His fingers slide to my stomach. I stopped bleeding yesterday, minus a bit of occasional spotting, and I watch through narrowed eyes as Aziel reaches for the sheet and slowly pulls it down to expose my bare chest and belly. He places his palm flat on my lower abdomen, and I stiffen in Gray's arms as he feels what no longer exists.

I don't like being touched here, but I'll let Aziel have his goodbye.

Silas rests his head on my shoulder before copying Aziel and placing a hand on my stomach. Both men feel it, running their fingers over the skin. It doesn't last long, and I let out a breathy laugh as Gray reaches around me and shoves their hands aside.

He spreads his fingers, taking up all the room with an angry huff.

I place a hand on Gray's thigh, rubbing it as I use my other hand to gently pull him away to make room for Aziel and Silas. The incubus was possessive over the baby, but it was theirs, too.

He can't hoard it, even if he wants to.

Aziel doesn't hesitate to return his hand to my stomach, his calloused touch light before he leans in and kisses my skin. I know what he's doing, and I look away as he smells me. Gray and Silas have done this hundreds of times, smelling my belly in the hopes they detect a hint of Aziel.

They never do, and Aziel won't, either.

I swallow the cry threatening to tear out of my throat as Aziel's eyelashes grow wet and a tear slides down his cheek. It's hard to see in the dark room, but I feel it when it falls from his chin and lands on my stomach. He prods me again through our bond, silently begging to be let in, and I run my thumb over his cheek to wipe away a second falling tear.

"Does it hurt?" he asks.

His voice cracks, the sound breaking my heart.

"She's fine, no thanks to you," Gray hisses from behind me. "Her true males were here for her, and we made sure she was as comfortable as possible."

Aziel looks devastated, his lips opening in a quiet gasp before he clears his throat and glances away.

Gray's made his anger toward Aziel no secret these past few days, cursing the Wrath whenever he gets the opportunity, but I don't feel the same way. Silas and I have agreed not to get involved, letting them sort out their issues themselves, but Gray claiming Aziel isn't one of my true males is too far.

I pull Gray's arms off my waist and move toward Aziel.

Despite my better thoughts, I let the barrier between our bond down. Immediately, I'm bombarded with emotion, the intensity of it overwhelming. I'm faintly aware all three men surround me as I wrap my arms around Aziel's shoulders and climb on his lap.

He smells fresh, and I notice for the first time that his hair's wet, too. It tickles my cheek, and I curl my hands around the strands to keep him from pulling away. Aziel returns my hug with a tight one of his own, burying his face in my neck with fevered apologies.

"I'm so fucking sorry, baby," he whispers. "Please. I'm so sorry."

He prods our bond a moment later, the man desperate to feel and understand my emotions.

I sigh, relaxing against him. "You can come in."

Aziel pulls back, his eyebrows furrowed in question. I lick my lips, the corners quirking upward before I roll my eyes and tap my temple.

"You still want access to my head? I'm giving you permission," I explain.

Aziel's pained expression shifts, and he beams as he shuts his eyes and pulls me back into his arms.

It only takes a few moments before I feel *something* in my head. It's unnatural, like a headache that I'm not actually feeling. There's a slight pressure in my skull, the feeling uncomfortable but not necessarily painful. I always imagined it would hurt, and I rest my forehead against Aziel's shoulder as I let him pry.

The pressure grows, and after a few seconds, I tap him on the side of the head. He doesn't stop, and Silas takes that as his cue to step in and knock him harder. I flinch as Aziel's head is whipped to the side, and I offer a timid smile as he blinks and glares at the fate.

Silas shrugs, clearly unconcerned, as he grabs me by the hips and gently guides me into his lap. I can't help but laugh at their antics, secretly liking the way they all fight over me. It feels nice to be wanted, and I curl against Silas with a contented sigh.

"Don't fucking touch me."

I should've known the peace wouldn't last long.

Silas, always so nosy, shifts to watch Gray kick at the approaching Aziel. The Wrath takes it in stride, and he pins Gray's legs to the bed before climbing on top of him. It's borderline amusing to watch Gray try to fight Aziel, the incubus's strength paling in comparison to the Wrath's.

"Gray, please, baby," Aziel murmurs, knowing precisely what to say to calm Gray down.

Gray loves his pet names, and I can practically see his anger depleting as Aziel throws himself on top of Gray and whispers every sweet thing that comes to mind.

"My love, I'm so sorry," Aziel pleads. "You're so much better at these things than I am. I know that, but I want to be better. Please, baby, let me in so you can feel how sorry I am."

I raise a brow. Who knew Aziel would be so good at begging?

Gray grunts, continuing to try to fight Aziel. I burrow my face into Silas's chest as Aziel seems to have enough and pins Gray below him. Their relationship is weird and—frankly—pretty unhealthy, but it seems to work for them.

"Get off me, you fucking oaf," Gray hisses, his limbs flailing.

The sheets twist around them, and Aziel roughly rips them off to expose Gray's naked body. The two men continue to fight, and Silas smoothly moves us away from the pair when Aziel manages to wrap every one of his limbs around Gray, trapping him like a spider.

Gray's face is red as he fights, and after a moment's hesitation, he throws his elbow into Aziel's chin.

They become a blur, and I curl my fingers around Silas's wrists as Aziel throws Gray over his lap and brings his hand down hard on the incubus's ass. A loud echo rings out from the strike, and I'm even more surprised when Gray slumps, letting it happen.

He whines, and Aziel spanks him four more times in rapid succession.

Silas trails his hand down my spine, circling each vertebra as we watch Aziel spank Gray. I've always known Aziel's got a dominant streak in him, but I never thought I'd see the day where he very literally spanks Gray. Why is he doing that?

When Gray tries to look at us, Aziel grabs his head and forces him to stare at the mattress. Gray lets out another whine, and Aziel hums as he runs his hand over Gray's reddening ass.

I jolt when he abruptly spanks him again.

I don't doubt that I'd crumble under the force of the strikes, but Gray takes them in stride.

"I'm sorry." Gray eventually gasps, his back arching as Aziel comes down with a particularly hard one. "Please, I'm sorry."

He wiggles on Aziel's lap, and Silas kisses the side of my head as Aziel smooths his hands over Gray's raw skin.

I turn toward Silas, watching his reaction. Is this what he

likes? I know my males have been taking things slow with me, especially Silas. He's terrified of scaring me away, convinced I'll be uncomfortable with his wants.

Gray doesn't seem to have any sexual preferences, the incubus enjoying whatever's thrown his way.

He's submissive to Aziel, but he tends to take charge of Silas and me.

Silas and I feel we're on a level playing field most of the time, but I'd like to learn how to dominate him. I know that's what he enjoys the most. Should I try to spank him? He likes it when I pull his hair, but I don't possess even a tenth of the demons' strength.

I could never hit Silas as hard as Aziel did Gray, even if I wanted to. It would never be satisfying for him.

Aziel interrupts my thoughts. "That's enough, Charlie."

The pressure is back in my head, and I spin toward the Wrath with a frown. I'm most definitely going to regret giving him access to my thoughts and memories.

Gray's putty in Aziel's arms, and he sighs contentedly as Aziel lies on his back and pulls Gray overtop him. For the first time in days, my bond with Gray is genuinely relaxed, the man finally letting go of his anger.

I stare at his half-shut eyes, and a slight smile spreads over my lips as Aziel pulls back the covers for Silas and me.

We slide in next to him, and Silas refuses to let me go. I won't be able to fall asleep like this, but it's only a matter of time before he rolls over to Aziel, anyway.

Those two are the cuddlers.

"We got the elves while you were gone," I blurt out.

Aziel peers at me over Gray's shoulder. He appears shocked, and I love it. We were productive while he was off doing whatever he does at the pits, and I want him to know it. Aziel tried several times to contact the elven leaders, but he was immediately rejected each time.

It feels good to have been able to do something he couldn't, and it feels even better that my mother facilitated the entire thing.

Aziel clears his throat. "How?"

"My mother knows somebody who knows somebody," I say.

Aziel cocks his head to the side, and I preen as his pride seeps through our bond. Humans may not have the physical strength and abilities of demons, but we know how to get things done.

"No more leaving like that," I continue, forcing my voice to sound firm.

Aziel doesn't hesitate to nod, the motion jerky and quick.

"It won't happen again."

It better not. Next time, I'm making him sleep in his old room. Two nights in there for each day he's gone. I'll have loud sex with Gray and Silas, too, just to piss him off.

Chapter Twenty-Three

AZIEL

GRAY GLARES AT me as I type into my computer, his attention distracting as I struggle to find the proper wording for my message.

I'm impressed by the work my mates completed in my absence, and I've got a lot of catching up to do. The shifters are ready to move forward, and the elves are willing to provide their technology and install their systems into the Seekers database the moment we've taken over their offices. I've become the bottleneck.

Silas walked me through the treaty with the elves this morning, and my lips curl as I recall how eager he was to show me everything they did.

The Wraths have never had so many alliances, and it feels nice.

It's a positive change from the hatred my kingdom has always been met with, even if the treaty is technically between the elves and Lust. The small men refuse to let the word "Wrath" touch any of the contracts, but I'll take what I can get.

Everybody knows I come with Gray, and vice versa.

The elves only ask for intimacy training from the Lust demons, which is probably the most straightforward deal we've ever made. Succubi and incubi love to do these things, and even before this, they've practically fought over the rare opportunity to enter the shifter lands and teach the young adults about sex.

Gray went once, and he felt on top of the world for weeks afterward.

I'm willing to bet he'll also feel great about the elves, and he'll undoubtedly spend the next hundred years talking about how he is the sole reason the elves began producing females again.

At least, I assume that's why they want the intimacy training. It's rumored that the elves don't frequently have sex, and when they do, it's painfully bland and clinical.

The Lust demons will change that for them, and Gray will be over the moon.

The incubus continues to glare at me from across the room, and I sigh as I move my computer mouse to light up the screen.

I'm in charge of alerting the Seekers that they're to evacuate their building. A conglomerate of wealthy businessmen runs the organization, but none individually are particularly powerful. If they try to fight back, I'll kill them off one by one.

I don't care if it makes Silas and the fates upset.

Effective today, the Seekers will no longer be tasked with finding and collecting females. The shifters will take over the day-to-day handling of the facilities the minute we get the Seekers out of their headquarters, and they'll begin work immediately.

The Seekers employ men of all species, and it's a guarantee that the moment we take over, every realm will be alerted by the end of the day. Nobody will be happy with our actions, but with Wrath, Lust, shifters, and elves all backing the decision, I don't think anybody will try to push back.

I bet Levia wishes he hadn't gone behind my back to try to

secure a deal with the ogres. The King of Envy has been quiet lately, hiding away until his betrayal blows over. If he tries to intervene in our plans, I'll kill him.

Gray continues to glare, and I continue to ignore him.

If he doesn't let up soon, I'll spank him again. I like the way he submitted to me, and I look forward to the opportunity to do it again.

Clearing my throat, I shake my head and force my focus back to my computer. Now's not the time to get myself worked up. I've got too much work to do.

Besides, I know Gray won't give in to me anytime soon.

He's angry, and when he's angry, he's petty. Charlie needs time to heal, and Gray's made it clear he intends to feed on Silas exclusively from this point forward. I'm not pleased with his decision, but I have no right to complain. Not after I left them.

What happened to the days when he was begging for me?

Charlie and her big, bug eyes ruined everything.

"Stay out of Charlie's head," Gray finally snaps.

He's always finding something to be pissed about, but this doesn't involve him. Charlie's my mate, too, and he doesn't get to sit around acting like every aspect of our relationship has to go through him.

Charlie gave me permission knowing full well the repercussions, and if I want to spend every night replaying her entire life for myself, I very much will.

Ignoring Gray, I send an email for Silas to review. It's the message I plan to send to the Seekers, informing them of our decision. I figure it'll be best to give them notice over the computer before showing up in person.

It gives them time to be angry in private.

Gray's best with words, and he's usually the one to wordsmith our notices, but I fear he'll demand an arm and a leg in payment for his services.

Gray shifts his weight from foot to foot, clearly unamused with my lack of response, before stepping farther into my office.

"Did you hear me?" he asks.

I pinch the bridge of my nose and suck in a deep breath. I hate Silas's stupid fucking breathing exercises, but I force myself to do them anyway. They help more than I'd care to admit.

"Yes, Gray, and I heard you the last ten times you demanded I stay away from Charlie," I say.

Gray crosses his arms over his chest, and I tilt my head to the side as I listen for the female in question.

She and her mom work hard in her office, poring over paperwork with Rock. The poor demon got stuck in the shifter lands, and he practically sprinted through the portal the second I opened it this morning to speak with Chev.

Rock hardly seemed upset about the closed portal, though, and when I saw the mess he made of Charlie's cabin, I can see why. He's turned it into his own space, and he even convinced Chev to bring him new furniture so he could redecorate.

I have a feeling I'm going to be receiving a bill for that in a few days, but I'll pay it if it keeps Charlie's friend entertained. Rock's good for her, and I'm glad Silas chose him as her tutor.

"When was the last time Charlie did her lessons?" I ask, turning to Gray.

He looks taken aback by my question, and he blinks a few times before shrugging.

"It's been a while," he admits.

I don't like that, and I make a mental note to get her back on a regular schedule.

Charlie's life has many moving pieces, and I read that most humans thrive off routine. It's not a need demons have, but I can tell Charlie likes it in the way she demands we go to bed at the same time and eat three set meals a day.

"I have problems," Silas shouts, barreling through my office door.

He pauses for a minute as he takes in Gray's attempt to intimidate me, the incubus now hovering over my desk with a stern glare. It's cute, and it makes me want to bend him over.

"Shouldn't you be in Lust?" Silas asks, walking around Gray so he can set his computer on my desk.

Gray continues to glower, his stern expression cracking as Charlie and her mom get worked up about something and grow loud. All three of us fall silent to listen, and I enjoy the way the two women speak so freely with one another.

I'm not in love with the fact that Charlie's mom is living with us, as the woman is headstrong and bossy. I also don't like how rude she is to Gray, constantly belittling him. I can tell the woman wants to do it to me, too, but she's smart enough to keep her mouth shut.

Silas is the only one she seems to like, odd considering how much she disliked him when they first met, which I think is bullshit.

I'm twice as nice as Silas.

Still, I can't wait for her to leave. She's welcome to visit whenever she wants, but this is my home and I'm tired of it being infiltrated.

First, it was Charlie, the female bouncing around, claiming my space as hers. Then Rock, the shadow-turned-demon an absolute menace to my life. Then it was Chev, the shifter constantly helping himself to my home. Now it's Charlie's mother.

I might have to buy myself a second home to hide from them all.

"I thought you were meeting with the Lust council to discuss the elven treaty today?" Silas asks Gray.

Gray shrugs, unapologetic.

"I'm making sure Aziel doesn't leave again."

I run a hand through my hair, guilt warming my bones. I've learned my lesson, and I have no intention of leaving.

Silas shakes his head before running a hand down Gray's back. He knows how best to comfort Gray, and I fight the urge to eavesdrop as Silas leans in and whispers a few comforting words in his ear.

Gray's jaw clenches as he turns and looks away, but after a few seconds, he nods and vanishes.

"How long do you think it'll take him to get over me leaving?" I ask.

The bond pulls as Gray teleports away, and I rub at my chest until it settles once more.

Silas purses his lips. "A while. You really hurt his feelings. Charlie's, too."

Silas doesn't hold anything back, never has, but I wish he'd lie to me at times like this. I know how much I fucked up, but I want things to return to normal.

Maybe I should try to take Gray on a date.

Charlie, too.

I've never gone on one, but starting a tradition with all three of my mates might be nice. Charlie and Gray would like it, and I think Silas would, too.

"You said you had a problem?" I ask, changing the subject.

Silas groans as he walks around my desk and opens his computer. On the screen is the carefully crafted message I just sent him, and I lean back in my chair as he launches into an entire fucking lecture about it. It's hours before we've got it in a place we're both satisfied with, and I slide out of my chair and lie flat on my back the second after I hit *send*.

"Well, there's no turning back now," I mutter.

Silas lies on the floor next to me, his shoulder brushing mine.

I fish my phone out of my pocket and send a message to my elven contact, letting him know we've notified the Seekers. The elves will now lock out the Seeker databases, preventing them from erasing any important files or sending out any mass communications.

They'll also be remotely locking the portals within all the Seeker-owned female collection facilities.

There are a few realms that force the Seekers to house women until they are 'of age' to be sold, and we want to prevent anybody from trying to sneak them out during the transition. I'm hoping the Seekers kept files on lineage and we'll be able to unite mothers with young daughters, but the elves are convinced that information hasn't been recorded.

Still, we will try our best to reunite families.

Many fathers of daughters have been killed, typically because they tried to hide their children as Charlie's father did, but most mothers were spared.

I slide my hand across the ground until I reach Silas's arm, and blood rushes to my cheeks as I slide my fingers against his. He takes the hint and clasps my hand, and we stare at the ceiling until we hear the *ding* of a response come through my computer.

I sit up to check it.

The Seekers have responded already, and they spit threats I know they won't follow through on. I scan the words before reaching for Silas and grabbing his hand. I tried it his way, being civil over email to give them time to react and respond, but now it's time to do things the way I want.

"You're killing me, Aziel," Silas says, snatching up his computer and phone.

I grin and squeeze his hand before teleporting us to the

Seekers headquarters. It's a three-story building in what used to be the nymph realm, but the Seekers took over after the nymphs went practically extinct. Giant floor-to-ceiling windows span every wall, showcasing the thick woods beyond. I've heard this realm is relatively uninhabited now, which makes it the perfect place for the Seekers to operate.

Most rulers don't even know where the headquarters are, but I was called in for a private meeting about eighty years ago, and the men in charge were dumb enough to ask me to meet them here.

All eyes are on Silas and me as we walk through the building.

It's easy to ignore, and I enjoy the view from the windows as I head toward the top floor of the building. Silas trails behind, the man so close, I can feel his body heat through my shirt. He enjoys fighting more than he lets on, and he happily follows as I climb the stairs and push open the door to the executive board room.

It's chaos inside, red-faced men in stuffy suits sitting around a wooden table. Power fills the room, each man seeping what he has. It's nothing compared to mine, and I linger by the door, watching.

All arguing comes to a screeching halt as my presence is noticed.

I smile, loving the fear that seeps from their pores.

"Aziel," Toruuk, the current man in charge, says.

The ogre is known for his bad temper, and I raise a brow as he pushes out his rounded stomach to appear larger. Ogres are relatively short, but they're quite sturdy.

My smile widens, and I nod in greeting before stepping up to the large, round table.

"It seems you've got some issues with my announcement?" I tease, pressing my palms onto the top of the table.

Toruuk pushes back his chair with a shout. He looks rumpled, his gray skin covered in a thin layer of oil and pointed ears pressed flat against his bald, oval head.

"I've been running this organization for seventy-eight years, and if you think you can march in here throwing around your name and take it, you've got another think coming. Over my dead body will I let you—"

His words are cut short as I teleport behind him. I wrap my hands around his neck and jaw before twisting. The man has a thick neck, but disconnecting it from the rest of his body doesn't take too much force.

Silas rolls his eyes, an action I think I will begin punishing him for, as he sets his computer on the table and opens it up. Fear saturates the room as Toruuk's body falls to the floor, and I shut my eyes and suck in a calming breath.

There's no need to get all worked up right now.

Half the executives in the room are gone when I open my eyes, and I level my stare with the few brave ones who remain.

"Does anybody else have any issues?" I ask.

My question is met with silence and vigorous shakes of heads.

"I'm happy to hear that. Honestly. Very pleased," I say, making eye contact with each man. "I want this building emptied within the next hour."

People fumble over themselves to leave, and I wait until the room is empty before turning toward Silas. He frowns at me, his eyes darting toward the body on the floor.

I promised I wouldn't kill anybody, but talking was too slow and ineffective. I'm not here to make friends, and Toruuk was a piece of shit, anyway. All the ogres are.

Silas remains quiet, thankfully, and returns to his computer. I stand behind him, watching as he connects to the portal located on the first floor of the building and adjusts the settings. The elves supplied us with the information we needed to take control of the Seekers' portal remotely, which will be a huge help.

We leave the option for departure open, but Silas restricts entry so only the portals in our manor and Charlie's cabin can connect here.

"All set," Silas says, closing out the application.

I nod, pleased.

"Can I use your phone?" I ask.

I forgot mine, not unusual for me, and I tap my foot against the ground as Silas fishes his out of his pocket and hands it over. It lights up to reveal a lock screen, and I press my lips together as I stare at the keypad.

He's never had a password on his phone before.

Silas takes the phone as he sees my confusion, his lips twitching as he types in the code and hands the device back over. I suck my cheeks into my mouth, shifting my weight from foot to foot before giving in and asking.

"Why do you have a password on your phone?"

Silas raises a brow. "What?"

He's laughing, but I don't think this is very funny.

"Gray and put a code on both his and my phones after Charlie used his to contact Shay. It's his birth year, and it's been there for months," he says, still laughing.

Straightening my shoulders, I do my best to pretend I'm not embarrassed about asking as I step out of the board room and head to the ground floor. Men scamper throughout the building, desperate to grab their things and escape. I'm sure it didn't take long for the news about Toruuk's unfortunate death to spread.

Movements quicken as I walk through the building, and it's cleared out after only a few minutes. Paperwork and random knickknacks litter the floor, and I even spot an abandoned blue sneaker underneath a table.

I take a moment to enjoy the silence before calling Chev.

He takes forever to pick up, and I tap my foot impatiently

against the ground while I wait.

"Silas?" he asks as the line connects.

"It's Aziel. The portal's ready for you," I say, hanging up the second the words are out of my mouth.

Chev likes to chat, and if I'm not abrupt, he'll try to initiate an entire conversation of nothing. Sometimes I like it, enjoying having my mind taken off work, but now's not the time. Minutes pass, and I kick off the wall as the first shifters step through the portal's blue haze.

The giant men bounce around, clearly excited as they explore the building.

Twenty shifters step through the portal before Chev and Echo appear, and I wait patiently as they take their sweet time looking around.

Silas joins me just as they finish.

"This was quicker than I thought it would be," Chev says.

"I can be persuasive," I say, shooting Silas a glare when he snorts. "Besides, we always knew this would be the easy part. It's what follows that's going to be hard."

———

Chev storms into my office, drawing my attention. Charlie really needs to remember to turn off our portal once she's done with it.

"Tonight, we celebrate," Chev says, dropping a hand on my desk.

I'm only half-listening, and I pretend to contemplate his idea before shaking my head and turning it down. I know how the shifters celebrate, and I have no interest in participating.

"I'm busy," I say.

Today was a long day. We spent all morning working with the elves to locate the females within the dragon realm, their technology so advanced, even I have trouble understanding it. The elves have been collecting and storing the genetic markup of every individual who uses the portals for years. Given that's how most beings travel, they've collected a significant amount of data from almost every realm.

It's terrifying, and if I weren't so desperate for the information, I'd be making plans to eliminate it.

I probably will in the future, but that's a project I'll set aside for now.

The portals have given the elves a general idea of how many females are within all the main metropolitan areas, and they're using housing records and infrared satellites to confirm the location of the women. Things get a bit spottier in the rural areas, but the satellites help fill the gaps of information the portals cannot provide.

Once the elves have a woman's exact location, they can create a temporary portal underneath her. The portals aren't strong enough for long-distance teleportations, but it allows for a significant number of women within a small radius to be moved to a secure location where the shifters can grab and escort them to a stronger, stable portal that can bring them to a secure facility.

Females in rural areas need to be manually pulled from their homes, but that's where the strong demons are coming in. Gray and I are *handsomely* paying demons who can teleport across realms, and when the elves home in on the general area of a female, a demon is given the coordinates and sent out.

We've spent the past two days testing it, stealing females from the human realm. Human senses are too weak for the men to feel the energy shift of a portal being created in their homes. They simply think their females ran away or got stolen.

Our tests have been successful, and today, we finally launched our first large-scale rescue.

There was much debate on whether we wanted to begin with the ogres or dragons, both species known for their violence, but we decided on dragons.

We cleared their six largest cities in one day, and over two thousand females are being moved into rehabilitation facilities. The female shifters are with them now, informing them of what's happening and calming them down.

Charlie is ecstatic, even if she's disappointed she can't be there.

These women are scared and occasionally hostile. They don't trust us, and many of them are attacking. Charlie is too weak, and those women will be able to sense it. They'd go for her, and I won't take the risk.

"We need to celebrate, Aziel." Chev huffs, placing a hand on my shoulder.

I brush him off, not in the mood.

One of my generals sent back word that the ogres have begun murdering their females in anticipation of our collection, and the females owned by dragons we've yet to get to are facing similar fates. We have people working around the clock, but we can only move so quickly.

"Women are dying," I say, showing Chev my screen.

He doesn't look at it.

"But more are being rescued, and we knew this would happen. You've been nonstop working for days, Aziel, and I can see you're about to explode." He grabs my head and then lifts his hands out to replicate my head exploding. "Your mates are worried about you."

I brush his hand off my head. He doesn't know anything about how my mates are feeling.

"Echo told me all about it. Charlie tells her everything."

Maybe he *does* know something about how my mates are

feeling. They've been telling me for days to take a break, at least for a few hours. I've hardly seen them since we took over the Seekers' headquarters, and I've already fallen asleep in the nymph lands twice this week.

"I will have one drink with you," I say, giving in.

One drink, and then I'll go home and get a few hours of rest. I don't want to, but I'm eager to get everybody off my back.

Chev beams and fixes his leathers before spinning and storming out of my office. I glare at his back, annoyed, before making my way to the bedroom. Charlie, Gray, and Silas are up there watching a movie, and I push open the door to see them cuddled on the bed together.

Gray beams as he notices me, and I flick on the bedroom light as he pats the spot on the bed next to him.

"We can start it from the beginning," he offers, inviting me to join.

I shake my head. "Chev has invited me out."

I expect to be met with disappointment, hopefully enough that I can go back to Chev and say my mates are too upset and I'm unable to go, but instead, I'm met with raised brows and twitching lips.

Charlie is the first to speak. "I hope you two have fun."

This is not the reaction I want.

I shift my weight from foot to foot, waiting for somebody to speak up and tell me not to go, before scratching the back of my head and leaving. This is bullshit, and I give them all mildly passive-aggressive, light yanks through my bonds before heading back downstairs to meet Chev.

Chapter Twenty-Four

CHARLOTTE

MOM LOOKS UP as I pass by my office, her eyes darting between Chev and me before she directs her attention back to her books. Silas loaned her everything he has on elves, and she's been spending every free minute reading them.

My chest tugs as I glance between her and the stack of books, a small piece of me still upset about her budding relationship with Niven, but it's getting better.

He clearly makes her happy, and I have a feeling she's been using the portal to sneak into his home whenever my males and I are busy. There's a glint in her eye I haven't seen in years, and she seems excited about the future for the first time ever.

We're making plans weeks and months in advance, which we've never done before. There was never a guarantee we'd ever have tomorrow, and it feels so fucking good to know that we do.

I lift a hand to my lips, signaling her to keep quiet, before sneaking down the hallway with Chev. The portal is just up ahead, and we're on a mission.

Silas appears out of nowhere and forces himself between Chev and me.

"What're you doing?" he asks.

Chev steps aside as Silas shoulders him, his lips curling down at the corners.

I lace my fingers with Silas's, loving him, even though he can be jealous. I don't blame him, and I understand where his distaste toward Chev comes from. The shifter's the spitting image of his father, and I'm sure Silas thinks of it every time he sees him.

It probably also doesn't help that Chev and Aziel have become such good friends. I just about choked on my spit when Aziel announced that he and Chev were going out together the other night. Aziel ended up coming home blackout drunk at some ungodly hour, waking all of us up as he struggled to change and get into bed.

Chev's been here practically every day since. It's usually to steal our food, but sometimes to speak to Aziel.

"Chev and I are going to visit Gray," I say, poking the panel next to the portal.

Silas raises a brow, looking surprised. I've never gone to Lust to visit Gray before, but I need to get over my fear of that place eventually. Things have finally settled there, and now that Valentine no longer has a claim to the throne, it's safe for me to visit.

Gray's been asking me to come for days, but I've been avoiding it.

Silas steps in front of me and begins messing with the portal settings. I peer around his arm, watching him add a Lust portal to the approved list.

"This will take you to the portal right outside Gray's office," Silas explains, stepping away. "It's heavily guarded, so don't think you'll be sneaking around without us knowing."

He's so dramatic.

Smiling, I lift on my toes and kiss his cheek. He's in an

exceptionally good mood today, and I have a feeling it has something to do with the twisting arousal that woke me up in the middle of the night last night. It was jarring, and I was surprised to find Gray and Silas missing from bed.

They returned twenty minutes later with swollen lips and messy hair, the pair pretending nothing had happened.

They've been doing that a lot lately, which I appreciated at first. Sex was the last thing on my mind after the miscarriage, but I understand Gray still needs to feed. He's been pulling Silas and Aziel aside daily for some private time, but I'm feeling ready now.

"Is Chev coming with you?" Silas asks as I turn the portal on.

I nod, glancing back at the nervous-looking shifter. "He says he wants to see Lust."

Silas laughs, which seems to offend Chev, whose cheeks turn pink.

"My mom was born there," he says, "and I'm part incubus. I don't think it's surprising for me to want to know what it's like there."

Silas hums, clearly not believing it, before leaning against the wall and crossing his arms over his chest.

"You're in charge of keeping Charlie safe until she finds Gray," he says.

Rock's usually my escort whenever I'm leaving the manor, but he's nowhere to be found this morning. I looked everywhere, too, and I'm glad I ran into Chev when I did. He was sneaking through our library, his lips pursed as he peered at all of Silas's books.

I'm sure Silas will smell the remnants of the shifter in the air the next time he goes in there, but I made sure to usher Chev out as quickly as possible. Silas is weird about his books, and I don't think he'd appreciate Chev stealing them.

Which I can tell is exactly what the shifter was planning to do.

"I will protect her with my life," Chev says, placing a hand over his chest.

I roll my eyes. "Let's go," I urge, stepping through the portal.

My anxiety grows the longer I put this off, and I want to get it over with. I tap my fingers against my thighs as I emerge in Lust, my gaze flickering over the long, red velvet rug covering the ground and the gold detailing on just about every dark wooden piece of furniture I can see.

The portal opens to a large, empty sitting room, and I tap my fingers against my legs as I spot the two guards standing nearby. They're tall, with long, dark hair and matching black uniforms. They also both look gravely serious, making me think they're Wraths. Aziel mentioned several Wraths were stationed here in case Mammon decides to try something.

"Charlie," the nearest guard says.

I jolt, spinning in his direction as Chev steps through the portal behind me.

I'm surprised he knows who I am, but I suppose there probably aren't a lot of human women using this portal.

"I'll take you to Gray," the guard continues.

Chev grunts, his hand hovering over my back as I follow the guard. He exits through a set of wide double doors on our left and turns right down a long hallway. Chev and I follow, both of us probably looking comically awkward as we peer into all the open rooms we pass.

They're full of sex, the Lust demons living up to their name, and poor Chev looks green as he takes it all in.

"Is it what you expected?" I ask, clearing my throat when it comes out croaky.

Chev frowns, his throat bobbing before he grunts and yanks me against his chest just as a naked man and woman come barreling out of one of the rooms. I can't breathe, and my face turns red as Chev screeches and dodges them.

The succubus doesn't notice or care about Chev's discomfort as she latches on to him, and he shoves her away before releasing me and running two shaky hands through his hair.

A loud laugh bubbles out of my throat before I can stop it.

"No. Absolutely not," Chev says, spinning on his heel and rushing back to the sitting room we just came from. "I'm leaving."

He disappears a second later, his large frame surprisingly lithe as he dodges guards and demons. I watch, waiting until he safely disappears into the sitting room, before turning back to the guard. Silas will give Chev a mouthful when he realizes he's returned without me, but I'm sure I'm safe with the guard.

The guard looks amused as he stares down the hallway through which Chev just disappeared, and he shakes his head before continuing to lead me to Gray.

The Lust demons give me a wide berth as they pass me, but whether that's out of fear of Gray or Aziel, I can't tell. Either way, I'm grateful, and I hurry behind the guard until I'm led into another large, red-carpeted and gold-detailed room.

There's a giant, platform bed in the middle of the space, and four—no—five demons are on it. They release loud moans as they fuck one another, and standing ten feet from the end of the bed, facing away from me, is Gray. His hands are clasped behind his back, and I linger in the doorway as I glance between him and the bed.

He's clearly intrigued by what he's watching, the man so lost in his private show, he hasn't noticed my arrival. I give our bond a slight tug, seeing if that captures his attention, and watch as his shoulders relax and he reaches up to rub his sternum.

Silas whispered that Asmod's power is bringing out his traditional incubus urges. The old Gray wouldn't have been interested in watching a show like this. He only cared to see us.

I'm not upset, especially since I know it's not his fault and he would never act on it, but seeing his interest in real life is a bit uncomfortable.

"Gray?" I ask, capturing his attention.

Gray jolts and shoots me a wide grin over his shoulder.

"Charlie!" He waves me over. "Come watch."

That's not what I expected him to say, and I glance between him and the bed before tentatively crossing the room.

"Sex shows are one of Lust's top attractions," he explains. "These actors will be performing in our high theater for the next few months, and I need to approve the act."

I run my tongue over my teeth and hug Gray from behind. He smells good, and I rest my cheek between his shoulder blades before sliding my fingers to his hips. He's hard, his length straining against the material of his pants.

Gray stills, probably frightened any movement will scare me away. I haven't touched him since before I lost the baby.

"It feels like you approve," I tease.

I shift and peer around his arm. The succubus on the bed spares us a glance, the dark haired, impossibly toned woman breaking character so she can peek at Gray and me. She scans Gray from head to toe, and I can confidently say I don't like the hunger in her eye as she looks at my male.

Gray once told me he's slept with many of the Lust women, and I wonder if she's one of them.

Our bond pulls as her gaze lingers on Gray's erection, and I take a firmer hold of his cock in a needy display of jealousy. It's mine.

Gray stiffens, his hand curling around mine.

"You're still healing, Charlie," he says, stroking the back of my hand with his thumb. "Don't rush yourself."

I don't like the rejection, even if it's coming from a good place in his heart, and I give him a harder squeeze.

Mine.

My need to claim him has me feeling eerily like Aziel.

I continue squeezing his cock as I slide my other hand under his shirt and up his torso.

"It's been almost three weeks," I say.

It's been a rough three weeks, but I'm feeling better. I'm ready to have sex again, and I want to feel close to my mates. I'm ready.

The succubus on the bed continues to stare, and I stare right back. Gray turns around, probably sensing my jealousy through our bond.

"Baby," he says, cupping my cheeks and tilting my face toward his. "I'm yours, and that's not going to change."

I glance again at the succubus on the bed. Now that Gray's not looking, she's more daring in her staring, and she goes as far as to smirk at me as she drops to her hands and knees and takes the man behind her.

The sight makes me angry, and before I can think better of it, I'm looping my hand around Gray's neck and yanking him down. His lips meet mine in a hard kiss, and I maintain eye contact with the woman as he grabs my thighs and lifts me.

She frowns, her cocky smile falling as I wrap my legs around Gray.

Gray dominates my mouth, slipping his tongue between my lips with a low moan. It feels good, and I rock my hips against his hard torso as I wrap my arms around his broad shoulders. Gray easily supports my weight and places his hands on my ass.

"You're naughty," he whispers.

I bring my mouth to his neck and sink my teeth into one of his marks, loving how he moans when I do so. Gray doesn't disappoint, and I take great pleasure in seeing the jealousy written plainly across the succubus's face as Gray begins carrying me out of the room.

Demons stare as he brings me to his office, the Lusts not known for their discretion. Some go as far as to stop what they're doing to watch.

All the Lust demons want Gray now that he's their king. They heard about his performance during the ceremony, and they want a taste. Aziel avoids coming to Lust because he gets so angry at all the needy stares Gray receives, the Wrath possessive over our incubus.

I continue kissing over the marks littering Gray's neck, enjoying how breathy he's getting.

His arousal is thick in the air between us, and I breathe it in with a low moan as he kicks open his office door and tosses me on the bed in the corner.

It's new, but I barely have time to take in the light-blue sheets or dark oak headboard before Gray flips me onto my back. He left the door to his office open, and a few daring Lusts step inside to watch as Gray rips off his shirt and reaches for mine.

I slide my gaze from them to Gray, my attention quickly captured by his smooth skin and muscular arms.

Gray likes the audience, a secret Silas told me is a side effect of taking Asmod's power, and I arch my back as he crawls on the bed. I don't mind the onlookers, and it's easy to ignore them when I've got such a perfect male on top of me.

"You're mine," I say, reaching for his pants.

Gray moans, the low noise thick with emotion. The succubus from the performance steps inside, her lips still curled into an antagonizing smirk. I've decided I don't like her, and I clench my jaw as I undo Gray's pants and shove my hand down the front of them.

"Fuck, Charlie." Gray gasps as I take hold of him. "I'm yours. You know that, baby. I'm all yours."

His pupils expand as he breathes me in, and a moment later, he removes my clothing. I lift my hips, eager to help, when Gray visibly hesitates. I know he's nervous about having sex with me, which I understand, but I'm okay.

I'm not the young, inexperienced girl I was when we met. I know what I want.

"Please," I beg.

Gray lowers, bringing his lips to mine, before removing the rest of my clothes. He does the same to himself, and I spread my thighs as he slots his naked body between them. He's hard, and his hips twitch as I curl my fingers around his length.

I love having a naked Gray in front of me, and I use his cock to pull him closer. Gray happily obliges, shuffling forward before grabbing a pillow and shoving it underneath my hips.

I missed this, missed him, and I roll my hips as he runs his tip up and down my slit, collecting the moisture before pushing in. Gray pauses and gives me a moment to adjust before continuing, a low groan slipping from his lips as he bottoms out.

"You feel perfect, my love," he whispers, his breath warming my ear as he begins thrusting into me.

I drop my head against the mattress, loving the stretch of Gray as I glance at the succubus from earlier. Her cocky smile has fallen, replaced with anger as she watches Gray fuck me. Good. It's about time she gets it through her head that he's mine.

I grab Gray's shoulders, my body rocking with the force of his thrusts.

"She's never felt me." Gray moans, glancing at the succubus. "And she never will. She'll never feel my cock, and she'll never hear me moan for her. She's nothing to me." He reaches between us to rub my clit.

I wrap my arms around Gray's neck, my fingers digging into his soft skin. He feels perfect, so thick and warm inside me, and I hold eye contact with the woman as he takes pleasure in my body.

Gray's fingers are rough against my clit, applying the perfect pressure until I'm squeezing my eyes shut with a low moan. I'm going to cum, but Gray already knows that. It only takes a few more seconds for me to cry out and release, and Gray loudly feeds as I orgasm.

I love it, and I lock my ankles behind his back as his thrusts begin to grow jerky.

"Fuck, Charlie, I'm—" Gray moans, grabbing my thighs.

I wrap my legs tighter around him. He's mine, and I want him to cum in me as he does with my males. He's always pulling out so his orgasm doesn't affect me, but I don't want that anymore.

"Cum in me," I beg, squeezing his hips with my thighs.

Gray plants his hands on the mattress on either side of my head before he drops to his elbows and stills.

I screech, digging my heels into his butt. It feels like every nerve ending in my body is electrified, and I'm pretty sure I'm accidentally cutting him with my nails as I bury my fingers into the muscle of his shoulders.

The noises that slip from my throat are barely human, and Gray drops atop me as my orgasm subsides.

It feels good until I need to breathe, and I tap his shoulder in a silent request for him to move. He's practically beaming as he sits up and stares down at me.

Well, he stares down at where he's inside me.

"Everybody, out," he orders.

The Lust demons pout as they filter out of the room. I sigh, content, as I relax into the sheets. This was just what I needed, and I can't help but smile as the chatter in the room vanishes. Gray flops onto his side and curls up against me, his head resting on my chest.

"I hope I put a baby in you," he eventually says.

My heart stutters, and I draw in a shaky breath before giving a jerky nod. My males asked if I wanted to be put on birth control after my miscarriage, but I've decided against it. My pregnancy with Aziel was a surprise, but I was still so excited.

My males will be excellent fathers, and I'm eager to start our family.

"What if I can't carry a baby?" I ask, voicing my fears.

I went to a female specialist doctor after the miscarriage to ensure everything was okay. The man ran no fewer than a thousand tests before deciding that the loss hadn't been triggered by anything specific.

There's nothing wrong with my reproductive system, and all my bits look good, but I still worry.

"You can, and will, carry a bunch of our babies," Gray says. "I want at least six, Aziel doesn't care how many, and Silas has mentioned two."

I laugh, patting his head. There's no way. The only one of my males I'd consider being an endless incubator for is Silas, and that's only because fates are so rare.

"Out of pure curiosity, how do baby Lusts feed?" I ask.

Gray snorts, probably sensing my worry.

"The need for that type of nutrition doesn't start until puberty," he assures me. "We'll be connected through bloodline, so they'll feed from a mixture of food and me. I'm really strong now, too, so all eight of my babies will have more than enough to sustain themselves."

The fact that the number has gone up doesn't go unnoticed by me, and I roll my eyes as he curls his hands around my waist, cuddling me. It's nice, but I just about jump out of my skin when another body joins us on the bed.

I gasp, my arms flinging to the sides until I realize it's just Silas. He licks his lips as he glances between Gray and me, and when intense arousal pulsates through our bond, my cheeks turn a thousand shades of red.

"How long have you been here?" I ask.

Silas shrugs, a smile toying at the corners of his lips.

"I teleported here about five minutes ago to bring Gray some paperwork, but you two were a bit… busy," he says, his smile growing. "I quite enjoyed the show."

Silas pulls me out of Gray's arms and into his. The incubus lets out a slight grumble before climbing off the bed to re-dress, and I pout as his naked body disappears behind layers of fabric. My males have been so busy these past few days, especially with everything happening in the ogre realm.

Almost everybody has been tight-lipped about it around me, probably out of fear of stressing me out, but Echo keeps me informed.

Uprisings in the ogre realm began the moment they learned Aziel and the shifters took over the Seekers organization. Once we began teleporting females out of the dragon realm, they began executing their females. They have an 'if we can't have them, nobody can' mentality, and we're running into issues getting demons onto their land.

The constant teleportation is hard on the Wraths, and the few Lusts we've tried sending in have gotten killed.

Aziel's implemented a speedy self-defense course for the Lusts to take before being sent out, but it's not going well. The Lusts are poor fighters, and Aziel has to stretch the Wraths thin to make up the slack.

The shifters help where they can, but considering they can't teleport, there isn't much they can do beyond protecting and collecting the females the elves bring to the large, sturdy portals. They're also busy trying to acclimate and fill the safest facilities first, the one in the human realm included. Four have already been brought to max capacity, and we anticipate having a fifth filled by the end of the week.

The dragons had more females than we anticipated, the creatures hoarding them, and now the shifters are working on building new housing facilities on their land for women to stay in.

Gray sits behind his desk and rifles through his paperwork, pulling me from my thoughts, and I lean my head against Silas's chest before pushing off him and sitting up.

"I should head back home." I sigh. "I've got an early morning with Rock."

My pesky tutor has been insisting we get back into a regular tutoring schedule, and we've agreed to meet three times a week for early-morning, two-hour sessions. I dread them.

"Stay here," Gray says, his eyes darting between Silas and me. "Both of you."

Silas trails his fingers up and down my arm, his gentle touch tickling. I'm painfully aware I'm lying naked in Gray's office, and Silas is still completely clothed.

"I need to get back to work," Silas says, ignoring Gray's demand.

Gray raises a brow, and his lips purse before he picks up his phone and calls in some woman named Sax. An unnervingly beautiful succubus steps into Gray's office a minute later, her black eyes darting between Silas and me before she turns and smiles at Gray.

Her hair is braided down her back, the long strands ending just above her butt, and she wears a skintight red latex dress. It's not unusual attire for Lust, but I curl my fingers around Silas's wrist as I take in her full lips and large eyes.

This is Gray's assistant?

"Yes?" she asks.

Gray gestures to Silas and me. "My mates need something to

snack on while they rest," he says, our bond twisting with arousal.

He clearly likes having us in his office bed, and Silas chuckles as I relax against his chest. I can't help it. The intense emotions Gray's feeding me makes it hard to resist the urge to lie here and relax with Silas. I miss my fate, and I spin into his arms as Sax disappears.

"Take off your clothes, Silas," Gray orders.

Silas hums, debating it, before giving in and releasing me so he can strip. We haven't spent much time together these past few weeks, and I need it. Gray seems to, too, if his commands for us to stay here are anything to go by.

Sax returns shortly with a tray of fruit, and she sets it on the edge of the bed before turning back to Gray. Our incubus isn't paying attention, the demon too distracted by something on his computer.

Silas clears his throat, drawing Sax's attention before gesturing to the door.

"That'll be all," he says.

Her lips twitch, like she's fighting back a frown. I cuddle against Silas and throw my leg over his straining erection, making a silent claim as Sax dips her chin and leaves, shutting the door behind her. As much as the Lust demons love Gray, they're obsessed with Silas.

They want him, but he's mine.

"Feed Charlie," Gray says, shooting Silas a sharp look.

Silas licks his lips, and his cock twitches against my thigh before he leans over and drags the fruit tray in my direction. I'm surprised he's not fighting harder to return to work, but I'm not complaining. I'll take a cuddly, obedient Silas any day of the week.

"Do you like when Gray tells you what to do?" I ask, sliding my fingers across his neck.

Silas's throat bobs. "I like having easy, tedious tasks that keep my mind busy. The fates are stressful, and it helps keep my thoughts away from them. You can tell me to do things for you, too. I enjoy it."

My pulse races, and I hope I appear nonchalant as I continue my prying. "Is it a sexual thing for you?"

Silas's lips twitch, the action telling me I'm not nearly as sneaky as I try to be. Still, he answers. "It can be."

Vague. He's always so vague.

Whenever Aziel or Gray ask something of him, he's more than happy to respond, but when it comes to me, all I get are half-answers that lead to more questions. It's incredibly frustrating, especially knowing I'd never judge him for what he likes.

I just let Gray fuck me in front of a room of Lust demons, for fuck's sake.

"Why are you so secretive around me?" I clear my throat when my voice cracks.

Silas grabs a berry off the tray and brings it to my lips, and I sneak a glance at Gray before opening my mouth and accepting it. The incubus is watching us from his desk, his gaze heavy.

"I've never cared how women perceived me," Silas says after a moment's hesitation. "It was never more than sex, but it's different with you."

Those words aren't as soothing as he no doubt intends them to be, and our bond pulls at the mention of him with other women. I by no means expect him to have been a virgin like Aziel, but it angers me that he was more open with those women than he is with me.

We're bonded, and I'm not going anywhere.

"Did you enjoy sex more with them?" I pry.

Silas frowns. "Of course not."

I'm not sure I believe that. They gave him what he truly

wanted, and he's just settling with me. Of course he would've enjoyed it more with them.

"What did you do with them?" I ask.

My anger only grows when Silas shakes his head, refusing to answer. He brings another piece of fruit to my lips, and I glare at it before opening my mouth and letting him pop it on my tongue. I'm unsure what compels me to do this, but I snap my jaw shut before he pulls his fingers out, biting their tips.

Silas hisses, his black eyes widening at my aggressive actions.

"Did they spank you?" I ask.

I haven't gotten the image of Aziel spanking Gray out of my head. It's something I'll never be able to give Silas, even if I wanted to. Humans aren't strong enough.

Silas shakes his head, silently refusing to answer my question. The action is answer enough, though, and I frown as he brings another piece of fruit to my lips. Silas is quicker with his retreat this time, his fingers just barely grazing my chomping teeth.

I shouldn't bite him, and I shut my eyes with a quiet sigh. I knew it. I'll never be able to give Silas what he wants, and in five years, he will regret having bonded with me.

Aziel yanks our bond, the sudden pain bringing to attention the slight pressure in my head. I didn't notice it until now, and I frown as I realize he's lingering around in my thoughts. He's always there, and he's gotten good at sneaking in without me knowing.

He probably did it while I was having sex with Gray.

I'm going to kill him.

My bond with Aziel yanks again, and Silas seems to misread my flinch as he frowns and brings his lips to my forehead.

"Spanking isn't the only way to cause me pain," Silas says. "My hair is sensitive. It hurts when you pull it, and I like that. I enjoy orgasm denial and overstimulation, both of which can be painful."

I sit up, surprised he's sharing this. I usually have to go to Gray to get this type of information, and I'm eager to hear more from the fate himself. Silas seems wary, scanning my face for any discomfort before continuing.

"If I do something that displeases you..." he continues. "Making me sit and watch you fuck Gray or Aziel would make me just as happy as you spanking me."

I clear my throat, my arousal growing at the thought. Silas seems to sense it, and the embarrassed flush of his cheeks disappears as a timid excitement takes over his features. Gray remains at his desk, but I'm sure his attention is on Silas and me.

It almost always is.

"And when I'm displeased..." I trail off and clear my throat, my face heating. "You'd want me to punish you?"

Silas shuts his eyes and sucks in a deep breath, and I reach forward to smooth my thumb over his eyebrow. Our bond hums, which I take as a good sign.

"Yes," he admits, shifting his position.

His hard cock is trapped between his stomach and my thigh, and I smile as I prop myself up on my elbow and apply more weight to my leg.

"What do you want me to do when you've been good?" I ask.

Silas takes a moment to answer, and I don't try to bite him when he pops another berry on my tongue. He grins as he realizes I'm no longer trying to attack him, and he rests his fingertips on my bottom lip before leaning in and kissing me.

"I want you to use me."

Silas's words ignite a fire within me, and I swallow past the lump in my throat before giving a firm nod. I can do that.

Chapter Twenty-Five

SILAS

MY HEART THUMPS as I feed Charlie another berry.

Her lips close around my fingers, her teeth grazing their tips, but she makes no effort to sink into my flesh as she did before. I don't mind the biting, though, the slight pain it brings exciting.

She's so nosy regarding my desires, always prying for my secrets, but I'm happy she doesn't seem off-put by what I've said. If anything, she looks excited. I've seen how she folds for Gray and Aziel, her quickness to submit leading me to believe she probably won't enjoy taking charge.

I love her either way, and I hate how she doesn't believe me when I tell her that. I like being dominated, but she acts as if it's the only sex I'm capable of enjoying. Anything with Charlie is a gift, and I don't need her to be something she's not just to please me.

My eyes fall shut as Charlie brings her hand to the back of my head. Her fingers catch on my hair, and I bite back a moan as she abruptly grabs a handful and forces my head back.

It's been a long time since she pulled my hair.

I can feel Charlie's arousal through the bond, her body

responding to mine.

I've been hard since I walked in on Gray fucking her earlier, and I bite back a moan as I recall how the incubus met my eye and wordlessly gestured for me to stand along the far wall and watch. The Lust demons peeking into the room gravitated toward me as I was cast aside, the men and women eager to feed off my arousal.

Charlie giggles, my female evil, as she releases my hair and trails her fingers down my chest. Her touch is teasing, and it tickles as she makes her way to where her thigh is pressed against my cock. Only the tip peeks out from behind her leg, and I moan as she traces her finger around it.

Fuck.

A bit of precum drips out, and Charlie spreads it around my cockhead before sliding her thigh away. I smash my jaw as she grazes Aziel's mark, a bolt of pleasure shooting up my spine.

"I purchased a few toys for your ass," I admit.

Charlie's heart flutters, and I curse as she crawls down my body and sucks the tip of my dick into her mouth. Her tongue is soft as she curls it around me, and I fight the urge to thrust into her mouth. She shifts onto her hands and knees, her ass up in the air, and I stare at the slope of her lower spine before reaching out to feel.

I could cry when she grabs my wrist and forces it onto the bed beside her.

Charlie pulls off me with a pop, her lips curling into a cruel smile.

"Toys?" she asks.

I nod. I've been collecting them since she promised me her ass.

"Show them to me," Charlie decides, sitting back on her heels.

It's hard to focus enough for a successful teleport when my dick is covered in my mate's spit, but I manage to make it to Wrath in one piece. I'm hurrying down the hallway of my wing before the world completely materializes around me, faintly aware of Aziel's presence in my head.

Usually, I'd fight for him to leave, but I'm much too busy for that right now.

If he wants to get lost in my head and killed by the fates, that's his business.

I rarely spend time in my wing anymore, but it's the perfect place to store everything that doesn't fit in our shared bedroom.

Specifically the books I want to keep away from Gray's grubby hands.

The velvet box I've been keeping the butt plugs in is sitting on the dresser just to the left of my door, and I pop open the lid to make sure Gray hasn't been messing with them before bundling it up in my arms and returning to Lust.

Charlie's still lying on the bed, her legs spread and her fingers rubbing slow circles over her clit. She and Gray stare at one another, and the incubus's lust is thick within the room as I sit on the edge of the bed and set my box on the sheets.

"Charlie," I say, drawing her attention.

She smiles and turns in my direction, and I press my lips together as she rolls over and crawls toward me. I like how this position makes her breasts hang, and I admire them before pulling open the box to show her what I've got.

I've bought a large variety of plugs, all in different sizes and colors. Aziel would be mad if he knew how much I spent on these, the cost equal to one of our shadow's yearly salaries, but it's my money to spend as I see fit.

Charlie turns bright red as she looks over them, and I glance between her and the plugs before reaching for the ruby that matches the current color of her cheeks. I listen to her heart hammering as I place it in her hands, and I close the lid so she doesn't get overwhelmed.

The ruby is small, a good starter toy.

"You want to put this in me?" Charlie asks.

I dip my chin in a jerky nod. "Yes."

I love the idea of her ass being mine and mine only. Gray and Aziel have already been notified, and despite how hard they laughed when I told them, they haven't tried to touch her there. At least not yet. Aziel will push for it at some point, the Wrath eager to claim every inch of our female.

I'll let him, but only after I've had my fill.

Charlie gulps and looks me over, her eyes lingering on my shoulders before trailing to my abs and eventually settling on my hips.

My cock twitches, and I stare Charlie in the eye as I curl a hand around myself. My palm presses against Aziel's mark, drawing a quiet moan from my throat as I thrust into my hand.

Charlie cocks her head to the side, her eyes wide, before glancing behind me. A warm body presses against my back a moment later, and I gasp as Gray slides his hands down my shoulders.

"Get on your hands and knees," Charlie orders.

I jerk, releasing my aching cock with a hiss before leaning forward and dropping my palms to the bed. Charlie's kneeling in front of me, and my abrupt closeness has her falling onto her back. I crawl over her, bringing my face level with her stomach.

Gray places a hand on my ass, teasing me with his fingers, and Charlie takes advantage of my distraction as she grabs my head and wordlessly guides my mouth to her sex.

I don't hesitate to lick her, eager for a taste. Gray's cum has pretty much all dripped out of her at this point, and it looks like she gave herself a quick wipe while I was off getting my plugs. I'm disappointed, and I whine into her flesh as I stiffen my tongue and press it inside her stretched-out sex.

I like when she tastes of my males.

Gray continues to tease me with his fingers, the incubus pressing against my hole but refusing to push inside. I rock back, wanting to feel him, but he pulls away with a quiet tut. The disappointment in his tone has my back breaking out in a cold sweat, and the sharp smack he gives my ass a second later has me fighting not to cum.

I love being spanked, always have. The burn feels good, and Gray isn't afraid to make it hurt.

"Stay still and keep your tongue out," Charlie orders me.

It won't take long for my jaw to grow sore in this position, but I don't care as I hold my mouth open and keep my tongue steady. Charlie holds my head and rides my mouth, her hips tilted so her clit repeatedly rubs against the soft, fleshy part at the center of my tongue.

My fingers twitch as I resist the urge to touch her, and in desperation, I fist the sheets to prevent doing anything out of instinct.

Gray waits until Charlie's on the verge of cumming to finally shove two of his fingers inside me, and I moan into her cunt. I want to cum, too, and my cock twitches in search of friction.

I jerk again, desperate for even a breeze to brush against my shaft, as Charlie finds her release. Her thighs squeeze the sides of my head, holding me in place as she rides her orgasm. I hold still, my jaw burning from keeping it open for so long.

Gray continues to play with my me, fingering me at a painfully slow pace. I'm excited to see what Charlie has planned for me, and I slowly lick her clit until she shivers and pulls away. She smells like me, just the way I like it.

"You can put the gem in me now," Charlie decides, giggling as she watches my face brighten.

I'd love that, and I can tell she senses it as I reach over and grab the toy.

"I want you to fuck me once you've got it in," she says, spreading her thighs. "But I don't want you to cum until I have."

My lips part with a low cry.

I don't know how long I can fuck her before cumming, especially when I've got Gray playing with my ass from behind. Moaning, I pop the end of Charlie's toy in my mouth.

Lube would be best, but I can tell she likes when I use my spit.

Charlie lets out a breathy gasp as I bring the ruby to her ass. I softly rub the pad of my thumb over her clit as I press the toy against her, urging her to relax enough that I can slip it inside.

I'm patient, pausing every time she clenches, but my cock hangs heavily between my thighs.

I'm growing desperate.

"Thank you, baby," I repeat, aching as I work the plug inside Charlie. My voice is embarrassingly hoarse. "How do you like it?"

Charlie pants, and I smile as I crawl over her. Gray quickly follows, kneeling on the bed behind me. I grab Charlie's hips before taking a moment to try to calm my raging body down. I quickly realize it's not going to work, and I line my cock up with her entrance instead.

She's soaked, and we both gasp as I sink inside.

I only push in a few inches before pausing, giving her time to adjust. I'm sure it's a lot having both me and the plug inside her.

"You feel perfect," I whisper, burying my face in her neck.

I'm not going to last long.

Charlie moans. "If you're good, I'll let Gray fuck you."

I wrap my hand around her head, holding her against me as I curl my back and drive into her. I want that, and I cry into the mattress as I try to hold back my orgasm. Her cunt strangles me, and the pressure against Aziel's mark is too much.

"Please, baby," I beg. "Please, please, please. I'm good." I continue to plead, wanting to feel Gray inside me while I fuck our female. "I promise I'm good."

Charlie gasps, her noises making my efforts to hold off my orgasm damn near impossible. I rub her clit faster in a desperate attempt to get her to cum, my thrusting growing jerky.

It feels too good.

Charlie grabs my back, her nails drawing blood as she drags them down my spine. She must be silently communicating with Gray over my shoulder, as a second later, the tip of his cock presses against me. I'm still relatively stretched out from his use of me last night, and it doesn't take much for him to bottom out.

I shove myself as deep in Charlie as I can, accidentally flattening her to the bed, as an orgasm races through me. It's impossible to hold back, and I cry into Charlie's neck before finding my mark and instinctively biting over it, reclaiming her.

Everything is silent as I lie on Charlie, too silent, and I fight back moans as Gray continues pumping into me, his hips smacking my ass with each thrust. It feels good, but it's impossible to focus on that when I've got a fuming female beneath me.

I was supposed to make Charlie cum first.

"I'm sorry," I whisper, ashamed. "I didn't mean to."

Charlie frowns, her eyes narrowing.

"He can keep fucking," Gray says, grabbing the front of my throat and pulling me back against his chest.

The action forces me away from Charlie, and I whine as my cock shifts inside her. Aziel's mark gets sore after I cum, and Gray knows that. His fucking pushes me into Charlie, and I cry out as Charlie plants her feet into the bed and begins to rock against me.

My thighs shake as I'm used from both ends, my breath sawing in and out of my lungs.

"You're *going* to make me cum," Charlie says, her eyes cold.

I look down, watching her fuck my cock in and out of her.

My cum drips down my shaft and into the sheets below, and I love it. I even catch sight of the plug underneath her, the red ruby catching the light every time she rolls her hips.

Gray's lust fills the air around us, and I desperately rub Charlie's clit before Gray cums in me. His orgasm will trigger mine, and I don't want to think about what Charlie will do if I cum in her twice before she gets a chance to finish. She'll be so disappointed in me.

All my mates will be.

"I love you, baby," I pant, struggling to breathe around Gray's tight grip on my throat.

Charlie jerks underneath me, her eyes rolling back as she wiggles on my cock. I could cry tears of relief when she finally clamps down around me, her walls pulsating as she finds her release. Gray feeds, his chest expanding against my back before he shoves himself deep inside me and cums.

I groan as it triggers my orgasm, and Charlie offers me a soft, sated smile as I drop to my elbows above her. Our noses touch, and she cranes her neck and presses her lips to mine as I jerk and spill inside her for the second time. It hurts, and every muscle in my body shakes as I struggle to hold my weight and prevent myself from crushing Charlie.

Gray seems to realize my struggle as he wraps an arm around my waist and gently guides me off our female. I collapse on my side next to her, needing a minute to collect myself.

Our bond hums, contentment thick within us as Gray spoons me from behind and Charlie curls up against my chest. I needed this, and Gray nuzzles into the back of my neck as he runs his fingers up and down my side.

"Thank you," I whisper.

Charlie giggles, the sound so fucking sweet, before she cups my cheeks and urges me to open my eyes.

"I love you, Silas," she says, entwining our legs together. "But it should be *me* thanking *you*."

Gray chuckles. "I agree."

We lie in silence for a long while, and at some point, I doze off. I'm not sure how long I sleep, but Gray and Charlie are still cuddling me when I wake up. My female sleeps quietly in my arms, and Gray rests his phone on the side of my head as he types out a message.

I lift my arm and knock his phone off me, annoyed he's using me as furniture.

"I need to get back to work," I say, running my fingers through Charlie's hair to wake her up.

We've been cleaned, probably thanks to Gray, and I clench my ass before groaning and sitting up. Demon genitals don't heal as quickly as the rest of our bodies, so I'm a bit sore, but I don't mind.

I like having the reminder.

Charlie rolls over, and I pepper her face with kisses as I reach for her plug. She winces as I gently pull the plug out of her, and a low sigh emerges from her throat when it's finally out.

"Did you like it?" I ask, setting it aside.

Charlie nods, her smile growing. "The pressure felt good when you were fucking me."

That's music to my ears, and I curl my fingers around her wrist before lifting her arm in the air so I can get a better view of her body. I want to make sure I didn't hurt her, and I'm relieved to see her skin is free of any red spots or tiny bruises.

"How much do you like this stuff outside the bedroom?" Charlie asks.

It's a good question, and I think it over as I slide off the bed and reach for my discarded clothing. Gray copies me, the incubus quickly tugging on his pants before returning to his desk. I appreciate him sticking around until I woke up from my nap.

"I like things that will lead to or somehow tie into the bedroom, but I want to be equal outside of it," I say before grimacing and backtracking. "Well, mostly equal. I occasionally like being told what to do."

Gray sits at his desk and curses under his breath, drawing my attention. His eyes dart over something on his computer, and he frowns as he clicks around with his mouse. We've all been swamped with problems this week, and Gray has a meeting with the council members later today to discuss Lust's participation in the shifters' female collection.

The council members aren't pleased with the number of Lust demons who have died this past week, and it sounds like they want to scale back their support. They're okay funneling money into Wrath, but they aim to draw the line at supplying physical bodies.

Lusts don't fight.

I've got a million files to look through myself, too.

The shifters have asked Aziel and me to step back, and they've even gone as far as to change all our access of shared documents to 'read-only' versions. They're afraid of us gaining too much power, and as annoying as it is, I understand.

We don't have the best track record when it comes to doing the right things for the females, and the shifters don't seem keen to allow for the possibility for history to repeat itself. We're kept informed, but we're banned from important meetings.

Aziel is pissed.

"Have you done all your studying for tomorrow?" I ask, turning to Charlie.

The shifters have urged her to take a step back, too, and Rock's been encouraging her to resume her studies. She's not pleased, but she isn't making a big fuss. The routine is good for her, and I think she secretly enjoys it.

Charlie groans and flops back on the bed, her eyes darting between Gray and me.

"I'm going to do it now," she promises.

I doubt it, but I don't say anything as I tug on my clothes and kiss her. Gray smacks his lips, signaling he also wants one, and I happily make my way over to him, too. His lips are soft against mine, but I teleport back home when I begin smelling his arousal.

He could go for hours if we let him, but I have work to do.

Chapter Twenty-Six

CHARLOTTE

I ROLL MY eyes as Aziel shoves Gray.

I spent hours begging all three of my males to agree to a game night, and I'm finally seeing why they were so against it. Gray and Aziel almost immediately began to fight, and Silas is winning after only three turns.

We sit on the ground around the coffee table in the living room, and I glance at the fireplace video we put on the TV for ambiance. Wrath is way too hot to light a real fire inside, but having it on the TV makes the room feel cozy.

My mom and I have also purchased about a million small throw pillows for the room, slowly transforming it into a dull room nobody wanted to be in into this fun hang-out spot. I'm sad she's decided to move into the elven lands and isn't here to enjoy it, but that's what makes her happy.

She's whispered to me that Niven is her mate, and I think I did a good job pretending to be surprised. I'd say I've done an even better job forcing myself to be happy for her. Seeing her move on from my dad is hard, but I'm slowly beginning to accept it. She deserves to be happy.

"It's not my fault you're shit at this game," Gray says, pulling me onto his lap so Aziel leaves him alone.

It works, Aziel lowering his arm, but I can tell the Wrath is fuming as he glares at Gray over my head.

I turn toward Silas, watching him grin happily as he lays down his card. He's in his own world right now, probably thinking about all the ways he's going to beat us. This is a human game, one I've played hundreds of times, and it should be me who's winning.

Aziel scans his hand before picking out his card. It's a point card, and I rush to set mine on top.

Gray hums, his eyes lighting up as he plays trump and steals the hand. It's not the move I would've made, and it will probably make the game harder for him in the end, but Aziel doesn't seem to realize that as he grunts and slams his hand on the table.

"I don't like this game," he says.

Silas and I ignore him, and I return to my spot next to Aziel when I notice Gray trying to peek at my hand. What a cheater.

"How's everything in Lust?" I ask.

Gray purses his lips, scanning his hand.

"Good," he says, placing his card down. "The council agreed to continue letting Lusts participate in the rescue missions. It's a buddy system now, where each Lust has a Wrath accompanying them. The Lusts bear the brunt of the teleportation, and the Wrath fights and grabs the female."

I nod, pleased to hear it.

Echo already told me all of this, but I don't want my males to know just how much the female shifter is telling me. Chev's been working hard to push Aziel and Silas out, and my males are foaming at the mouth for information. They'd never be able to keep what I tell them a secret, and Echo would stop sharing things with me if she knew I was telling my males.

"That succubus has been keeping her distance from me after

your little show," Gray continues.

Aziel frowns, looking confused, and I press my lips together. "Which one?" I ask.

Now it's Gray's turn to look confused, his head cocking to the side.

Silas places his card down before jumping in to explain. "Charlie doesn't like Sax, either."

As much as I didn't like the way that succubus performing the sex show was looking at Gray, there's also something about Gray's assistant that I don't love. All the Lust demons are trying to have a taste of my males, and I can't lie and say I'm not feeling a tiny bit insecure.

The succubi and incubi are drop-dead gorgeous, everything about them screaming sex. It's impossible not to notice.

Aziel slams his card on the table, a wide smile spreading over his lips before he shifts his attention back to us. He's getting really into this game, and I'm starting to think he doesn't quite understand what the "friendly" in friendly competition means.

Gray sets his hand face down on the table, drawing a quiet sigh from Aziel, before he crawls toward me and pulls me into his arms.

"Sax was Asmod's assistant for many years, and I need her help sorting through the thousands of files my father kept," he says, smoothing his hands down my back. "I know she misbehaves around me, and the moment she's no longer needed, I'll be hiring somebody new."

I lick my lips and glance to the side, embarrassed to so openly be talking about my insecurities.

"I know I'm not really in a place to be upset about your—"

Silas cuts me off. "You have every right to be upset," he says, seemingly sensing where my thoughts were traveling toward. "Your relationship with Kato doesn't mean you're not allowed to express concerns. You're allowed to be uncomfortable with us being around females who make passes at us."

I gnaw at my bottom lip, still feeling guilty. I feel like a hypocrite when I get jealous. It's not fair of me to doubt my males when I'm the one who messed up. I have no right to.

"Yes, you do," Aziel says.

What? Pressure in my head grows, and I frown as I realize he's listening to my thoughts. Is he ever not in my head? When did he even slip in?

My eyes dart between him and my cards, my jaw dropping.

I'm surrounded by cheaters, and I shake my head as I mindlessly toss a card on top of Aziel's. It's not a very good card, but I think he needs the win or he'll stop playing.

"I've made it clear to Sax that I'm not interested," Gray continues, not sensing the rising tension between Aziel and me. "You're the only female I want to be with, my love. You're my human."

He pulls me into a tight hug, his grip firm as he holds me against his chest. I love being held by him, and I grow soft with a quiet sigh.

"I trust you," I say, needing Gray to know my jealousy isn't because of him. "I'm just being petty."

I don't like how women look at him, but I know he'd never cheat on me. He'd never do that to any us.

Gray pulls away and shoots me a broad smirk, the man seemingly taking no offense.

"I love to be petty," he admits, laughing.

As if to prove his point, he picks up his cards and tosses one on top of mine. It's trump, and poor Aziel looks like he's about to scream as Gray takes the hand.

His end of the bond is twisting and turning with poorly concealed anger, but we all pretend not to notice. We also pretend not to notice when Aziel does one of his breathing exercises to calm himself down.

Silas's thigh rubs against mine, the man clearly happy with our game. We continue playing, and Aziel's face grows red as he loses another hand. I fight the urge to slam my head against the table when he and Gray begin fighting. Again.

"You're not playing this correctly," Aziel accuses Gray.

Gray shrugs, unconcerned. "I'm taking cards, aren't I?"

He's not taking any point cards, but Aziel doesn't seem to care about that. He wants us to take this seriously, and Gray is doing the exact opposite. I don't mind, and Silas is already playing three turns ahead of us, so I doubt he even notices.

But poor Aziel just can't let it go.

"Should we watch a movie instead?" I ask when Gray kicks Aziel underneath the table.

They're children.

Aziel hisses, his body jerking before he throws his cards down and stands. He's sprawled on the couch a second later, taking up more than half of it as he reaches for the remote. We rarely spend time in the living room, and I've made it a personal mission to have a family night here at least once a week.

My males work so hard, and if they insist I spend my time relaxing, I will drag them along.

Aziel makes room for me to cuddle against him, and Silas settles on my other side before throwing a blanket over us. Gray chooses to pout in the recliner, but I'm sure it's only a matter of time before he comes over.

There's not much room on the couch, but Gray knows how to weasel himself into a space he doesn't fit.

Nobody complains as Aziel chooses a movie for us to watch, but I make subtle eye contact with Gray and Silas when it starts. They blink, shrugging before turning back to the screen.

It seems I'm the only one shocked by Aziel's choice, but I suppose I shouldn't be too surprised by his apparent interest in crime dramas. He loves chaos.

My lips twitch as I recall the lounge room in his wing of the house. I bet he spent much time watching shows there, probably purposely avoiding Gray and Silas. He likes his alone time, and I can tell he's been growing antsy.

I give it one more week before he's hiding there, demanding to be left alone for an evening.

Gray doesn't move to join us as I thought he would, and a glance in his direction tells me why. The man's slumped, his mouth slightly open as he dozes off in the recliner.

I grin, holding back a giggle as he sleepily tugs off his shoes and pants.

More articles of his clothing are removed as the movie continues, the incubus yanking everything off in his tired state. Eventually, he's completely naked, and Aziel bends to grab a blanket and toss it on his lap.

"Thanks," Gray mumbles, haphazardly spreading the fabric over his legs before falling back asleep.

Being tucked between Aziel and Silas is comforting, and I shut my eyes and relax against them. It's been a long day, a long month.

We need this.

The bonds in my chest hum contentedly, and I softly rub at my sternum as Gray gets up and squeezes himself between me and the back of the couch.

We spoon with our heads on Aziel's lap and our feet on Silas's. Gray's taller, so his feet are dangling off Silas's thighs, but my toes barely reach them. Aziel mindlessly plays with Gray's and my hair, his thigh warm underneath our heads.

"This movie's awful," Silas says, peering at the screen

through his eyelashes.

He's been asleep for most of it, and I can't help but let out a quiet laugh when Aziel turns and shushes him.

Gray's chest vibrates against my back as he joins me in laughter, and Aziel grunts before flicking us on our foreheads. "Would you rather I put on a children's princess movie for you two?"

I shrug, but Gray takes him up on the offer.

"Put on one of the human ones," Gray says, reaching over Aziel's torso to snatch the remote. "I'd love to know what my Charlie was raised watching."

Silas mumbles something about getting a book before brushing Gray's and my feet off his lap and wandering out of the room. Aziel frowns, clearly annoyed, before crossing his arms over his chest and redirecting his attention to the screen. Gray selects a movie I immensely enjoyed as a child, and Silas returns a few minutes later with a book that looks even older than he is.

He smiles as I make that comment out loud, and he shoots me a quick wink before sitting in the recliner Gray once occupied and flicking on the tiny standing light next to it. I think he looks sexy when he's so relaxed, and I end up watching him more than the movie.

If he notices, which I'm sure he does, he says nothing.

Aziel massages my scalp, his eyes never leaving the movie he made such a huff over watching.

This evening is turning out to be everything I wanted, and I can't help but grin as Gray wraps an arm around my waist and gives me a tight squeeze. There's so much going on in our lives, but it's times like these when I feel the calmest. I love my males, and I'm so happy.

I hope I'm pregnant.

I can't help but imagine a baby cuddled up in Silas's arm as he reads his book, or crawling all over Aziel and Gray in an adorable demand for attention. I look forward to teaching a little me all about colors and animal noises, and I'm excited to learn everything about being a mother.

I think I'll be a good one.

"Can any of you smell if I'm pregnant?" I ask.

It's a scary thought, especially after the miscarriage, but I can't be fearful of that forever.

My question is met with silence, and I frown as I turn to peer at Aziel. He and Gray are visibly tense, and they refuse to meet my eye. I try not to take offense, and I turn to Silas, only to realize he's still reading his book.

I wait, but they still don't respond. Are they just going to pretend I didn't say anything? They hear my heart beating six rooms away, so I'm unsure what they think they're accomplishing here. I know they can hear me.

"I would like to be pregnant," I try again, my voice louder.

Gray pats my head. "Would you?"

What the fuck?

"What aren't you telling me?" I ask, sitting up.

Gray looks at Aziel and Silas, his eyes wide, before he licks his lips and turns back to me. My suspicion grows, these reactions not what they should be. My males haven't been smelling me or doing anything they did the last time I was pregnant, but that doesn't mean anything.

Silas didn't want them to tell me last time, and I'm sure after the miscarriage, he finally got them to listen.

My pulse races as I spin and glance at all three of my males.

"Whose is it?" I demand.

Chapter Twenty-Seven

AZIEL

MY TEMPLES POUND, and I rub at them as I read over Chev's frantic email. Shifters take everything too seriously, and I can never tell what's actually an issue versus what is Chev prematurely working himself into a tizzy.

I tap my fingers against my desk before opening the attachments he sent. It opens to shocking images, and I wince as my eyes flicker over the gore. A warning of what I was about to open would've been nice, and I scan the images before closing the attachments and deleting them from my computer.

Charlie loves to look through my things, and the last thing I need is her asking why I have images of beheaded females. We hoped only the ogres would resort to such drastic measures, but now the dragons are also participating.

We've almost entirely cleared their realm of females, but there are still a tricky few dragons we're struggling to track down. They're also the wealthiest ones with the largest female hoards, which is just our fucking luck.

Still, we're making great progress.

I'd love to assist more, but Chev and the elves are working

hard to keep me at arm's length. They don't trust my motives, which infuriates me. I've done nothing but bend over backward to correct our mistakes, and I'm eager for the evacuations to be completed.

We've shifted our attention to the ogres, funneling those women out as quickly as possible, and after that, we'll move on to the trolls. They're generally unfriendly little beings, but their attacks are more verbal than physical. They'll be easy to clear of females, and the shifters should be able to handle it themselves.

My Wraths need a break.

I've had to deploy a significant number of them, and they've been stretched thin. It hasn't looked good for me, especially after our attacks from Mammon prior to Vont's death, and my leadership is being called into question. There have been no formal complaints by the nobility or my generals yet, but I can tell it will happen soon if I don't get my kingdom back in line.

The Wraths are concerned that I'm favoring the shifters, putting their needs before my people because of my mate and her connection with them. They aren't entirely wrong.

Everybody knows by now that Charlie is my bonded, and even if we haven't yet introduced her as Wrath's queen, it's clear that's her intended position. My people aren't happy with it, most of them viewing her as too weak, but I just need to keep their anger at bay until we have a Wrath infant.

Charlie's made it clear she doesn't have much interest in leading my people if I die, and the moment we have a child who shares my blood, I'll name them my heir. Charlie's human genes are weak, and if the potency of our first child was any indicator, our future ones will be strong.

My people will love that.

Chev sends another email, this one with a plethora of capital letters and even more attachments. I lick my lips as I read over it, scanning for critical information.

We knew the more violent species wouldn't accept our new regulations without a fight, and I'm almost glad the ogres weakened themselves by fighting alongside Mammon. They're the only species with a large or strong enough army to put up a real fight, but now they don't have the means with which to attack.

The Queen of Greed has also been quite distant, but I'm choosing not to question it. My informants have told me she's been locked up in her bedroom since she received news of her dead mate. For all intents and purposes, it seems she's genuinely in mourning.

I would never have guessed her affection toward Vont was genuine.

I rub at my temples, my wrath pushing to be released as I take in Chev's panicked emails.

There are more uprisings than anticipated, and there aren't enough teleporting demons to keep up with the workload. I've gone out several times myself, but I can't just disappear for hours on end.

Too many people are reporting to me, and I need to be available.

Chev sends a third email, and I fight the urge to scream.

Charlie's new pregnancy makes me especially testy, and I'm having trouble controlling myself lately. I was worried about how my wrath would respond when I realized Charlie's babies aren't biologically mine, but the scent of my males in her hasn't bothered me.

The fact that there are two has me practically fucking feral, though.

I thought one child was scary, but now I'm ready to lock her away and hold her hostage until she delivers. I'd do it if I didn't fear the backlash I'd receive from my males.

Leaning back in my chair, I shut my eyes and suck in a few deep breaths, hoping to calm myself down.

It doesn't work.

My irritation continues to grow, and when I realize it isn't stopping, I seek out my bonds and stroke them. All three hum, and almost immediately, I feel my mates working together to settle me. It works, my pulse slowing and my blood pressure lowering.

My mates have gotten good at calming me, and I'm happy they don't bother me or make a big deal whenever I ask for it. It's just what I need.

Despite knowing I should reply to Chev, I shift my focus to Charlie. She's in Silas's office, begging him for information about her pregnancy he refuses to give. She's angry, but we learned our lesson the first time.

If we had our way, she wouldn't even know she was pregnant. We can smell the moment her eggs are fertilized, the hormones that spike within her a clear indicator. Still, so much can go wrong in those first few weeks, and we wanted to wait at least until she missed her period to tell her.

I blame Gray and Silas.

Both froze when she began asking about children, the two acting like complete fools and giving it away. Charlie's carrying two babies, and she smells of Gray and Silas like she once did of me.

We were made aware of her likelihood of having twins when we purchased her, the testing done at the human facility finding that her body often procures two eggs during ovulation. Still, it never occurred to us that it would lead to each of my males getting her pregnant simultaneously.

Gray's over the moon, while Silas is pretending to be calm. The fate isn't fooling anybody, though, and we can all feel his excitement through our bonds. It's almost as strong as his worry and fear, but the latter is an emotion all three of us share.

This time, we will be better with Charlie's pregnancy.

The doctor we took her to said many things could have caused the miscarriage, but stress is significant. We've taken as much as we can out of her life, much to her annoyance, and replaced her busy days with tutoring, food, and baths.

I've always believed it's best not to pamper Charlie incessantly, but I'm willing to do whatever it takes to keep our babies alive.

Even if it means I have to rub her calloused feet every night.

My lips curl as I listen to her try to manipulate Silas into discussing the babies, our female growing cunning in these recent weeks. She thought Gray was the weakest link for the longest time, but she's seemed to discover it's Silas.

Gray loves attention, good or bad, but Silas doesn't have the same desperate need for it. If she annoys him enough, he'll likely give in and tell her so she leaves him alone.

I'll kill him if he does, and I'm proud of how well he's tolerating her right now.

I give a yank of her bond, wanting her to come visit me. She always bothers Silas and Gray, but she usually leaves me alone when I work. I don't like it.

I want to smell her, and I curl my fingers into the armrests of my chair to stop myself from getting up and seeking her out. Charlie doesn't like when we're constantly sniffing her, and she has no issues telling us how annoying she finds it.

It's hard not to when she smells so much like us. I enjoy it, and I've been loving how Gray and Silas ooze from her pores. It's still faint, but soon everybody who comes near her will know.

They'll be able to sense immediately that she's ours.

A loud ping has me directing my attention back to my computer, and I release a sigh as Chev sends another impatient email. It's been less than five minutes since his last one, and I run my hand down my face in frustration.

God, he's annoying.

I type out a response as Charlie storms out of Silas's office and makes her way to mine. Her feet are loud as she stomps, and I pretend I haven't been listening to her for the past five minutes as she busts into my space and makes her way to my desk.

I expect her to stop in front of it, but instead, she walks around it and sits on my lap. I move back to make room for her, eager to feel her body on mine.

This is nice.

Charlie straddles me, the action bringing us eye level with one another, and I place my hands on her hips as she buries her face in my neck and sinks her teeth into her mark. *Oh?* I let her bite me, giving her leniency because of the babies in her, but I can't stop the hiss that slips out between my clenched teeth as hers tear open my flesh. She licks over the blood a second later, cleaning me as she pulls away and admires her work.

Already, I can feel it healing, and within seconds, I know my skin is back to normal.

"Do you feel better?" I tease, pushing her hair behind her ears.

Charlie nods, a guilty smile spreading over her lips.

"I don't know why I keep wanting to bite you guys," she admits, her cheeks turning pink.

I grin, enjoying her sudden need to claim us. It's a demon trait she's picked up on due to our bonding, but it's never been quite this prominent. I have a feeling it has something to do with the babies in her, her body struggling to adjust to the sudden surge in hormones.

I'm not worried, and I hope she keeps doing it.

I'd bite her back if I knew it wouldn't cause her pain. Her body isn't made to be marked, and I can't sink my teeth into her as I do with Gray and Silas. They like when I do it, and they heal within seconds, but Charlie would be torn up and bruised for hours.

My eyes trail to Charlie's belly, and I slip my fingers under her shirt to feel her bare skin.

"You're going to get so round," I say, excited at the idea.

I hope she does the waddle human females sometimes do when they grow large with babies. Charlie will be my giant penguin.

Charlie huffs, wiggling on my lap before climbing off and spinning so she can see what I'm working on. I've taken to communicating in the universal language so she doesn't feel we're hiding anything from her, and I sit back and watch as she fingers through my paperwork and reads over my communication with Chev.

A small part of me wants to be annoyed by her lack of trust, but I can't blame her for being cautious. I've let the females down before, and Charlie will ensure I don't do it again.

I grab her hand to stop her as she tries to click on an attachment Chev sent.

"No," I say.

Charlie tries to fight out of my grip, but I don't let go. This isn't for her to see, and I'm frustrated Chev sent them to me. I don't need to see the decapitated and mangled bodies to believe what he says in his emails. I take his word for it, and I don't want to risk Charlie or Gray stumbling upon these images.

They're sensitive, and it would be hard for them.

"They're images of dead females," I admit.

My lips graze the back of Charlie's neck as her muscles stiffen, and after a second, she clears her throat and moves on. I release her wrist, happy she's not pushing to see.

"Chev wants you to send more troops into the ogre lands?" she asks, reading over my email. "I thought you were already sending all the ones who can safely manage the long distance teleportations?"

Concern is thick in her voice, and my chest fills with pride as I flick through my emails and find the one I want her to read.

"He doesn't want teleporting demons," I explain. "He wants me to station Wraths on the ogre lands as a show of strength. He thinks it will intimidate the ogres enough to stop the executions."

Charlie's eyes dart rapidly over my message thread with Chev and Gray, and I press a kiss to the side of her head before continuing. "Gray's funneling Lust's money into our military reserve, and the Wraths who agree to defend are earning their salary and a half. It's now optional, but many are taking us up on the offer."

I've already spent a decent fortune on this, as has Silas, and I'd rather not drain my accounts if I don't need to. Gray got his council members to agree to a decent amount, but it's come at a cost Chev isn't too happy about.

We agreed to place a Lust-wide ban on the shifter lands, but the council wanted it dropped before agreeing to pay. It's still an 'at your own risk' endeavor, one many Lust demons don't return from. The shifter males will have to continue seeking out and killing the incubi and succubi they find wandering their lands, but I don't think the issue is as bad as Chev is making it out to be.

The shifters are strong, even those with weaker animal forms.

They're taught how to fight from a young age, and I'm pretty sure a young shifter girl could take down a full-grown Lust demon if she wanted to. They've been doing so for years already.

"Are you upset the baby isn't yours?" Charlie asks, her question jarring.

I reach around and cup her belly, letting myself fully feel the skin as I bury my face in her hair.

"The *babies* are mine," I say, curling my fingers into her skin.

"I don't care that our first ones will have the blood of Gray and Silas. They're still mine."

Charlie stiffens, but I'm too busy smelling the babies in her to try to understand why. They're pure, and already, I know I would do anything for them. She relaxes as I breathe in again, letting myself enjoy the scent while it lasts.

It's only a matter of time before she pushes me away and demands I give her space.

"Gray mentioned that only a Wrath will be your heir," Charlie says after a moment.

I snort. Leave it to Gray to say such ominous things without proper explanation. Silas's footfalls are quiet as he stands and approaches the wall separating our offices, moving closer so he can better eavesdrop.

"Fates can't hold a permanent position as a ruler," I explain, "and I'm assuming none of our Lust children would want to lead Wrath. I won't keep my title from any of our children, but I'm assuming only one with Wrath blood will be interested in it." As I finish, she seems to relax, and I enjoy how the bond between us settles.

I didn't realize Charlie was so upset about this.

"I'd like to be the next one to put a baby in you," I admit, kissing the mark Gray put on her neck. "But I'm not upset what's in there now isn't technically mine. I'm happy."

Charlie prods me through our bond, and I fight hard not to seep into her head. I've grown comfortable in there since she gave me permission, but I can tell she's getting annoyed. Well, she's always been annoyed, but it's beginning to grow genuine.

I'm taking it too far, and Silas has warned me that I need to refrain lest I find myself banished from our bed. He doesn't like when I enter Charlie's mind, and Gray has gotten good at kicking me out of his whenever he senses my presence.

She relaxes as she feels my love for the growing children in her. I'm genuine when I say I don't mind that they don't share my blood. They will be mine just the same, and I'm eager to be a dad. Gray and Silas think they'll be the best parents, but I know it'll be me.

Gray is too loud, and Silas gets annoyed too easily.

I am the perfect blend.

Charlie leans against my chest, and I drop my forehead onto hers when another email from Chev comes through. I have only moments to read it before I hear heavy stomping emerging from the portal in the hallway, and I enjoy the last few seconds of peace I have with Charlie before Chev comes barreling around the corner.

He storms inside my office with only the confidence a shifter can muster, his hands clenched into tight fists as he glares me down. "Why are you ignoring me?"

Holding eye contact with the irate male, I bring my lips to Charlie's ear. "I've always wondered what it'd be like to have a clingy boyfriend."

Chev's nostrils flare, and Charlie stifles a laugh before hopping off my lap. I pat her butt, thankful for her visit, before gesturing for Chev to sit.

"Morning, Chev," Charlie says, bringing her knuckles to his head.

He glares at me, and my lips twitch upward as he bends his knees so Charlie can better reach his forehead.

"Good morning, Charlie," he politely responds, knuckling her back.

I can tell it takes everything in him not to bark at her, and anger pours off him in thick waves as Charlie leaves the room. I watch her disappear and shut the door behind her, pleased she never asked me about our children's parentage.

It's about time she starts to respect the rules and limitations I put in place.

"I am not a clingy boyfriend," Chev says the moment we're alone.

Silas walks away from the wall, no longer interested in eavesdropping, and I lean back in my chair and cross my arms over my chest as Chev steps forward and lowers into the seat across from me. It creaks under his weight, and I momentarily wonder if buying smaller chairs would prevent him from coming here so often.

Chapter Twenty-Eight

GRAY

THESE PAST THREE weeks have been shit, and I glare at Aziel as he nudges me out of the way and steps into the shower, his shoulder rubbing mine.

He could have easily squeezed around me, and I hope he feels my anger as I move over and give him room.

"Can I help you?" I scoff, turning on a different showerhead for myself.

Aziel doesn't respond, the Wrath seemingly too grumpy for conversation.

It's been almost a month since we discovered Charlie's pregnancy, and the morning sickness is killing all of us. Contrary to its name, it seems it doesn't only affect her in the morning, and she was having a nasty bout all night.

It felt like she was rushing to the toilet every thirty minutes, our poor female's body betraying her.

It was my turn to stay awake and keep her company, but Aziel still got up and stole her from me every time.

He's getting annoying with his near-constant worrying, and I'm tired of him lurking over my shoulder whenever I'm caring for her. Charlie's my mate, too, and if I recall correctly, it was me she loved first.

He can't just come in and bully me out.

"Why are you mad at me?" Aziel asks, tipping his head under the shower spray.

I enjoy watching the water pour down his face and chest, and I lick my lips as my feet carry me forward. There was a time when he'd never let me see him in such a vulnerable position, and I scan his naked body with pride.

I always knew I'd win him over.

Aziel opens an eye to see what I'm doing, his lips twitching as I reach out and turn his warm water cold. His skin is covered in goosebumps almost immediately, but he makes no effort to change the temperature.

I forgot he likes cold showers.

"I'm not mad at you," I say, returning to my spray. "I'm just annoyed by your hovering."

Aziel hums, but he doesn't make any promises to stop.

Objectively, I know he can't. Aziel isn't exactly in control of his wrath at the moment. It's pushing at our bond, desperate to take over and do whatever it deems necessary to keep us safe.

His desperate need to protect us is cute, but it's still annoying.

The bathroom is silent as we shower, and neither Charlie nor Silas says anything when they join a few minutes later. Silas holds her waist so she doesn't slip, our female's limbs weak after spending so much of the night getting sick.

She doesn't look good, her skin pale and eyes full of exhaustion, and I clean her while Silas holds her steady.

She'll argue if we tell her to stay in bed, but we'll put her on Silas's office couch and cover her in blankets and pillows before giving her a computer to work. She'll be asleep in minutes. She always is.

For once, Aziel doesn't push me out of the way to try to care for her himself. I notice the way his hands clench and unclench as he watches, but he manages to contain himself and finally give us some fucking space.

I quickly work on Charlie, and Silas hurries to wash himself before leaving with her. I stay in the shower, needing another moment.

"Why don't you work from home today?" Aziel asks, turning off his showerhead.

I wish. There's so much to do in Lust, and I can't get anything done from home. I've tried before, and I almost always spend the entire day distracted by my mates. Aziel and Silas are good at tuning everything out and focusing when needed, but I don't have that same ability.

Sometimes I wish I were like Charlie.

Even with our bonds, her human ears are bad. She can't hear a damn thing most of the time.

"I'm too busy," I say.

Aziel doesn't push, and he runs a hand down my spine before leaving the bathroom.

Fuck.

I tug at my hair before slamming my palm against the wall and exiting the shower. I'm getting hungry, and it's only a matter of time before my mates notice the sinking of my cheeks and the darkening of my eyes. They're my first physical symptoms, but I hope to hold out for a bit longer.

I get little snacks as I walk through the hallways of Lust, but it's not nearly enough to sustain me.

I need so much more now that I've taken my father's power, and I need to feed almost daily to remain full. It makes me a nuisance to my mates, especially when they're busy and don't have time to carve out of their days for sex.

Rock's already in my office when I make it to Lust, but that's nothing new. He's taken up residence here, haughtily taking the master bedroom that once belonged to my father. Having access to that room shows his place as my righthand man, and I can tell he's taking advantage of that if the arousal coating his skin is anything to go by.

I can't even pinpoint just how many women he's covered with, and I roll my eyes as he pours me a big cup of coffee.

I take a sip, resisting the urge to moan.

"A riot broke out around the eastern portal last night," Rock says, getting straight into work.

Just my fucking luck. Valentine's been working hard to discredit my name, and while she hasn't been particularly successful, she's doing just enough to be a pain in my ass. Lust's brothel district is near the eastern portal, and it's one of the most trafficked ones.

"We were able to break it apart and bring in two of the leaders, but we still haven't been able to get our hands on Valentine," Rock continues, sliding some documents in my direction. "There were reports that she was there, but she fled before we arrived."

I flick through the reports, scanning for names and locations before setting them back down. Being King isn't as fun as I thought it would be.

"What do you want to do with the two leaders we brought in?" Rock asks. "We're holding them in the dungeon for now."

I have absolutely zero idea. Aziel would tell me to kill them, but Lusts don't respect shows of brute strength like Wraths do. My people will be angry, and it'll make me look scared. I tap my fingers on my desk, thinking through what I want to do.

If I let the leaders go, they'll be back causing trouble in no time.

"Put them on feeding probation," I decide. "For two weeks.

And put them on portal restriction for a month."

It won't be enough to kill them, but it'll be humiliating. Their skin will thin and turn gray in that time, and they'll grow desperate. The other Lusts will mock them, and they'll have trouble finding somebody to feed on once the probation is lifted.

They won't be strong enough to leave Lust and try to use their lure on a weaker species, either.

It's a suitable punishment.

Rock nods, and we move on to the next item. "You still need to sign off on this year's annual fair," he reminds me.

Shit. I completely forgot about that. It's been years since I've gone to the fair, and it's expected that I not only donate a significant amount toward it, but I also make an appearance with my mates. It'll be an all-day affair, and I need to give Aziel and Silas plenty of warning so they can take the day off.

"I also need to set up a meeting with Aziel and the council members to discuss the Wrath borders," I say.

The Wraths seem to think that our kingdoms are one because I'm mated to Aziel. They no longer want to pay for entry into my land and brothels, and we need to discuss how we want to move forward. The council members have made it clear they want the Wraths to continue paying, but Aziel's made good points in that they can't expect his people to protect us without offering anything in return.

We don't have to merge the borders, but we can grant Wraths a sort of citizenship that allows them access to our facilities without an additional fee.

"I'll set up that meeting for you." Rock pulls out his phone and makes a note of it. "I'll see if I can schedule something within the next week."

I shoot him a relieved smile. That would be a huge help.

"How's Charlie feeling?" Rock asks, changing the subject as

he calls for Sax to bring another coffee pot.

I shrug, not wanting to worry him. Rock may work for me, but his alliance remains with Charlie. The second he hears about her sickness, he'll be just as annoying as Aziel.

"That bad?" he pries, his eyes narrowing.

He's gone before I can answer, and I drop my head to my desk with a loud groan. There goes my righthand man.

I shouldn't be angry about it, and I'm usually glad Charlie has such a good friend in Rock, but I can't help but be pissed. I don't even know why I'm so angry, but everything happening today annoys me.

I should be happy Charlie has such a sound support system.

I *am* happy.

I love her wholeheartedly, and I'm glad so many others feel the same.

"Ephraim?"

Now's not the time for this, and I clench my hands into tight fists below my desk as Sax steps into my office. She's taken to using my old name recently, and I think it's an attempt to flirt. I don't like it.

Sax holds the pot of coffee Rock requested, and I force myself to shoot her a grateful smile before gesturing for her to set it on my desk.

"I go by 'Gray' now," I say, topping off my mug before taking a hearty sip.

Fuck, that stuff is good.

"How much did my father donate to the annual fairs when he was ruler?" I ask.

Sax grimaces. "I'm not sure off the top of my head. I can pull the records for you, though."

I nod. "That would be appreciated."

Sax lingers, but I pretend not to notice as I shift my attention to my computer. She's not the first female to stand around hoping I try for her, and I'm honestly surprised she hasn't given up already. Her use of my birth name only shows her desperation.

Does she expect me to be aroused by it?

I hate that name, and I love the new one I've chosen for myself. It's both an emotion and a color, and it's what my female associates with me.

"You're starving," Sax says.

I clench my jaw, my hand tightening around my mug. I'm fully aware of that, and I sure as fuck don't need it pointed out to me. Any Lust demon can sense it, my body drained, but my mates are tired and busy.

I won't bother them with my needs.

Being hungry isn't going to kill me, and I'm more than happy to wait. Well, I'm actually fucking miserable, but I will wait nonetheless. Coffee keeps my energy up, and it's usually manageable when I have more than an hour's worth of sleep.

Besides, it's not like I'm unaccustomed to starvation. I've spent the last hundred years in that state, all thanks to Aziel's refusal to let me in his dreams.

Greedy bastard.

Sax continues to stare, and I continue to ignore it. Why won't she go away? I've been trying hard not to be rude, but she's getting on my nerves. Charlie already doesn't like her, and I don't want to do anything to upset my female.

I've got a handful of emails waiting for me, including a fresh one from Silas, and I click on it as Sax walks around my desk. I shift to the side, avoiding her touch, and I sigh when she drops to her knees.

"Go away," I say, leaning closer to my computer.

Why's Silas sending me new budgets? What happened to the old ones? He said those were the final ones, but if that's true, what the fuck am I supposed to do with these? My lips purse as I scan the message accompanying his attachment, embarrassment flooding me when I realize these aren't new. They're the original, and he's reminding me to approve and share them with the council by the end of the day.

I think I was supposed to do this yesterday. How's he always so organized?

Sax places a hand on my thigh, and I snatch it up in the same breath. She cries as I twist her wrist back, and before I can stop myself, I shove her away.

"I *said*, go away," I repeat, turning back to my computer.

She cries, clutching her wrist as she scrambles to her feet. "It's my duty to ensure you're fed. You're our leader, and your female is failing you. She's weak, and—"

I cut her off. "Leave."

Sax laughs before lunging at me. I'm not expecting it, and I freeze as she sits on my thigh and tries to rock herself against me. Lust demons are typically quite bold, but this is absurd. It takes everything in me to stay calm as I stand and push her off my lap. Why won't she just fucking leave?

Aziel and Silas have told me I need to be nice to my people, but it's hard when they're constantly trying to hump me.

"You're going to fuck me, Ephraim," Sax says, straightening her spine.

I raise a brow, my anger growing as she continues.

"Did you know there's footage inside the brothels of Lust? I wonder how your female will feel to receive a video of you pumping yourself into other women. The things you said to them were filthy. Maybe Charlie can even learn a thing or—"

I cut her off, unable to control myself as I palm her forehead and slam her head against the wall. My bonds yank in alarm at the sudden hostility my mates feel from me, but I ignore them as I curl my fingers around Sax's throat. She blinks up at me, her eyes wide and panicked, as I yank out whatever part of her throat I manage to get my hand around.

She can't hurt Charlie if she's dead.

"Ah, fuck! Gray!"

Aziel's yanking me away a second later, his hands curling around my biceps before he teleports us to his office in Wrath. I kick at him, not wanting his distraction, but he's on me before I land any good strikes. He pins me to the ground, and I try to wiggle away when I feel him forcing his way into my head.

Nosy piece of shit. I push at him, beyond livid.

"You're starving," Aziel breathes, flipping me onto my stomach.

I hiss, my cheek pressing against the hardwood as he slides his hand around my front and shoves it into my pants. I'm hard, have been for days, and I groan as he grabs me.

"Smell me, Gray," Aziel orders, squeezing and tugging my length.

He licks my mark, and I inhale his arousal with a low moan. My body instinctively relaxes as it fills me, the scent intoxicating. I'd do anything for more, and I let him roll me onto my back with a contented sigh. He smells so good, and I bury my face into his neck as he pulls my cock out of my pants.

Our bond opens, the Wrath offering for me to take from him without the need for sex, but he should know by now that I'll never take his handouts.

Instead, I reach into his pants and take hold of him. He's already hard, and I slide my fingers over his length before spreading my thighs and urging him between them. Aziel quickly shuffles forward, and I pull his cock out and press it against mine to stroke us both at once.

"I'm sorry. I should've been paying better attention to you,"

Aziel admits, rocking into my hand. "Take what you need."

My arousal seeps out, acting as a perfect lubricant as I jerk us both in quick, hard strokes. Aziel kisses me the entire time, his tongue brushing against mine as I pleasure us. This is just what I needed, just what I've been craving, and I moan into his mouth as he finds his release.

His thick cum covers my fist, and I stroke myself with it before stiffening with a low cry. My back arches as I cum, and Aziel sinks his teeth into my neck as my orgasm forces another from him. I use my lust to draw more from his body, my hungered state making me greedy.

Aziel doesn't seem to mind, and he tousles my hair when I finally release us. His cheeks are flushed as he does up his pants, and I smile when he does the same for me. We've made a mess, and I hope he goes about the rest of his day reeking of me.

I want all his Wraths to smell it and know he's mine.

"I know it's in your nature to put us before yourself, but you need to speak up when you're hungry," Aziel says, wiping his hand on his shirt. "Silas and I are more than willing to feed you."

I suck my lips into my mouth before nodding. I won't do that, but I'll agree if it gets him off my back.

Aziel cocks his head to the side as he watches my response, his lips pursed before he grabs my chin and forces me to look him in the eye.

"I expect to see you in my dreams every night from here on out, Gray," he says, squeezing my cheeks until I timidly nod. "I don't care if you're full and it hurts. Until I can trust you to speak up, this is what we'll be doing."

He gives my jaw another tight squeeze before releasing it. I huff, rubbing my sore jaw as I rise to my feet. We've made a mess of his office, and I glance around before shrugging and teleporting back to Lust.

He wanted to force me into Wrath to feed me, he can clean it up.

Sax is gone when I return, and I breathe out a sigh of relief as I slam my office door shut and return to my computer. I hope she doesn't come back.

I didn't want to tell Aziel this in person, and I ignore my racing pulse as I send him a message about the videos. He responds and loops in Silas, who very ominously says he'll take care of it. I don't know what that means, but I'm relieved.

Silas has always been good about taking care of those things.

Rock's still with Charlie when I return home at the end of the day, the two lounging on the couch watching TV. She giggles as I drop to my knees and smell her belly, impatient to meet my babies.

Aziel was stupid and accidentally told her everything only one day after she found out she was pregnant, but thankfully, nothing's gone wrong. Her scent is strong, Silas and I seeping out of her every pore.

I love it, and I pepper her belly with soft kisses.

"Why's there blood on your shirt?" she asks.

I frown, glancing down at myself. Sax must have spilled on me earlier. I'm surprised I didn't notice.

"Sax tried to seduce me, and she threatened to send you videos of me in brothels from before we met. I got angry and attacked her. It's okay now, though," I promise, curling my hand around Charlie's and pulling it away from the blood. "Aziel fed me, and I'm feeling much better."

Charlie frowns, and our bond pulls at the mention of the videos, but she doesn't ask any further questions.

"Well, take your shirt off. I don't want you staining my blankets," she eventually decides.

Rock takes that as his cue to leave, and I happily strip before crawling onto the couch to cuddle.

Chapter Twenty-Nine

CHARLOTTE

I MINDLESSLY RUB my stomach as Mom and I make our way to Silas's office. Only he and Aziel are home right now, but I know Aziel will put up a fuss if I tell him our plans. Silas is more understanding, and I'm planning on using that to my benefit.

"Slow down," I huff, trailing after Mom.

I'm in the beginning of my second trimester, and I've been showing for a few weeks now. The twins are huge, and they're slowing me considerably. My males are obsessed with it, Gray especially, and I stick out my belly for pity points as I push open Silas's office door and step inside.

As I hoped, his eyes naturally fall to my stomach before traveling to my face.

Mom greets him. "Hello."

He narrows his eyes. "Afternoon, Patty."

His tone indicates he knows we're about to say something he doesn't like.

"Mom and I are going to the nymph lands to meet with Echo," I say, jutting out my belly some more. It makes it harder for Silas be angry with me. "She wants to show us the rehabilitation facility they're building."

The shifters have been finding and rescuing more females than originally anticipated, especially now that unaccounted-for females are coming out of hiding and requesting to be put in the facilities. News has spread about the trade programs the shifters are launching, and many wish to take advantage of it.

Due to the sudden influx of women, additional facilities are needed. There was a lot of back and forth on where to place them, but eventually, Chev and the other shifter leaders decided to build them in the nymph realm.

The place has been desolate since the nymphs fell, which means there's plenty of suitable land for the shifters to build on.

It's also isolated enough that the shifters don't have to worry about males trying to break in. Only teleporting species can enter the realm, but it's crawling with shifters. They wouldn't make it two steps into a facility before being killed.

"The nymph lands?" Silas repeats.

I nod.

My males have been banned from there, the shifters exiling them after they got everything up and running, and I'm eager to look around. Echo finally got permission from Chev for Mom and me to get a tour of the offices and the in-progress facility, and I'm beyond ecstatic.

A sharp knock on the door behind me draws my attention, and I spin just as Aziel steps inside and leans on the doorframe. He smiles as we lock eyes, but it turns strained when it lands on my mom.

She's been helping me plan for the baby nursery, and I can tell Aziel is missing having me to himself. He's going to have to get used to it, though, because two babies is going to take up a lot of my attention.

"Can I come?" he asks.

I shake my head. "You weren't invited. And I don't think Echo would be happy if you came with us."

My males tend to have a lot of opinions on how they think things should be handled, and neither the shifters nor the elves want to hear any of it. They reach out when they need Aziel's assistance, but other than that, he's expected to stay out of it.

I understand why, even if my males aren't pleased.

"We'll be gone for about an hour," I continue, shifting my weight from foot to foot.

Silas and Aziel aren't going to be pleased with this, but even they've admitted that the nymph lands are safe for me to visit. The place is full of shifters, and I'll be with Echo the entire time.

Aziel crosses his arms over his chest. "No."

I clear my throat, exchanging a sideways glance with my mom. She smiles and nods, silently encouraging me to speak up.

"I'm not asking permission," I say. "I'm telling you where I'm going and when I'll be back. Unless you have a genuine concern for my safety, you have no right to tell me I can't leave."

Aziel grinds his teeth, and I straighten my spine before continuing.

"I'm not a prisoner, Aziel."

"I know that."

"Good. Do you have any safety concerns with me going to the nymph lands with Echo and my mom?" I ask.

Aziel furrows his brow, his face and neck turning red. "No, I don't."

Great. I turn back to Silas, and he presses his lips together to hide his laughter as his eyes flicker between me and Aziel. He continues until Aziel huffs and leaves the room, the Wrath clearly upset.

I'm sure he'll get over it shortly.

"Have a good time, and tug our bond if you need my help,"

Silas says, giving our bond a gentle tug as an example.

"Of course!" I chirp before leaving.

Silas has already added the nymph portal to the approved list—he claims in case of emergencies—and I fiddle with the settings until the black doorway is filled with a blue haze.

Mom grabs my hand, her palms clammy as she presses it against mine. She's not a fan of the portals, despite her always using them to travel back and forth between here and the elven lands.

I step through the blue haze, instinctively holding my breath until I emerge on the other side. My mom is quick to follow, and I shake my head to orient myself before looking around for Echo. She said she'd meet us by the portal, and my pulse races when I don't immediately see her.

We're in the middle of some sort of office building, and I glance at the floor-to-ceiling windows before sliding my attention to the shifters bustling around the open space. There are dozens of them, but their giant frames make the large building feel small. They pay my mom and me little attention as they hurry around, but a few occasionally look over with friendly smiles. I don't recognize these men, and quick glances at their thighs show they're a variety of animals.

"Charlie!"

Echo rounds the long hallway to the right of us, her footsteps quick as she makes her way over. She's wearing her leathers, but her usually flowy hair has been pulled out of her face into a loose braid.

"I'm so sorry I'm late. Chev wouldn't stop talking," she says, rolling her eyes at the mention of her brother. "I'm so excited to show you around."

Mom laughs and welcomes the tight hug Echo pulls her into. I'm next, and I chuckle as the shifter female gives my stomach a quick pat. Echo bounces on her toes, glancing between Mom and me before she spins around and gestures to the room.

"I've pretty much been living here for the past few months," she explains, grabbing both my mom's and my hands.

Her grip is tight as she shows us around the first floor, and I can't help but beam as I take everything in. This is a dream come true, and I subtly wipe at my damp eyes as we make our way to the upper levels.

The building is only three floors, and the top two are full of conference rooms. Chev is inside one of them, and I wave at him through the glass wall before being pulled away by Echo. She doesn't linger for long, and I can tell she's eager to get through this building before showing us the new facility outside.

I'm impatient for that, too, and I can barely contain my excitement when we make our way outside and pile into an open car. Mom and Echo take the two seats in the front, and I hesitate before climbing in.

This vehicle is unlike anything I've ever seen before, with no walls or windows and four poles sticking up from each corner with a hard plastic covering on top. My heart races as I climb into the back, and I nervously plant one hand over my stomach and the other around the pole as it jerks to life.

Echo lets out a loud squeal as she drives us over a large rock, and I fight the urge to duck and roll. What the fuck kind of monstrosity is this? Mom peers back at me over her shoulder, a loud laugh bubbling up out of her throat as she sees the terror in my eyes.

"This is a golf cart of sorts," she explains. "They used to be popular among humans before the decline."

A golf cart? I've never heard of that, and I clamp my lips together as Echo flings us down a gravel path.

The nature here is beyond beautiful, with deep-green grass

and large, sprawling trees. They're flowering in a stunning purple and blue, and we even pass a few tiny creeks along the way. I'd enjoy it more if I weren't in a plastic cube being barreled toward certain death.

I'll never again complain about Gray's rocky teleportation again. It's nothing compared to this.

A few minutes later, Echo veers to the left and begins heading toward what I assume is the rehabilitation facility. It's in the early stages, only the framing completed, and dozens of shifters are currently working on it.

There are a few children among them, the young shifters wearing bright-yellow hard hats as they rush around with axes and planks of wood. I've only ever seen bear shifter children before, and I can't help but smile as I realize this here is a variety.

"Morning!" A shifter greets us as we slow to a stop. He's wearing his leathers, but strapped around his legs are thick kneepads. Two children are standing on either side of him, both wearing matching attire. "He'll be here in an hour," the man continues, warning Echo.

Who?

Echo purses her lips, looking mildly annoyed, before she makes a noncommittal noise in the back of her throat and waves the man away. She doesn't offer an explanation, and I don't pry.

Even if I really want to.

"There isn't much to show you just yet," Echo says, stepping out of the golf cart. Mom and I are quick to follow. "We've got the framing completed, and we're working on electrical and plumbing now."

Echo leads us through the front doors of the building, and I clasp my hands together as I peer around the spacious lobby. It's giant, and sunlight pours in through the window cutouts. I love it, and I do a spin as I take it all in.

The building is only one story, but the tall, vaulted ceilings make it feel huge.

I'm in love.

"We plan to turn this into a visiting room," Echo explains, stepping farther inside. "We'll fill it with couches and comfortable seating areas, and we'll have a portal over here to the left."

"That'll be beautiful," Mom says.

I agree.

Echo leads us through the room and down a hallway to our right. She shows us where the two cafeterias and lounge rooms are going to be, her excitement visibly growing as she continues forward and shows us where the rescued women will sleep.

They'll all have their own rooms with locks, private bathrooms, and even a window. It sounds too good to be true, and I can't wait to go home and tell my males all about it.

I thought the Wrath facility was nice, but it pales in comparison to this.

The women are going to love it.

We continue wandering around for another forty or so minutes, but when Echo begins to anxiously check her watch, I can tell it's time to wrap it up. She's clearly trying to avoid the mystery person she was warned about.

"This has really been amazing, Echo," I say, smiling as she grabs my hand once more. "I appreciate you giving us a tour."

She winks at me over her shoulder before turning back around and groaning. Chev is standing in the lobby, his arms crossed over his chest, and he doesn't look pleased.

"Give me a minute." Echo huffs, stomping away.

The two step aside to talk, and Mom and I exchange glances. Chev and Echo are always arguing, and I take this opportunity to get one more good look at the facility. I can't wait to see it when it's all completed.

The shifters are making quick progress, and hopefully, it will be done within the next couple of months.

"How are things going with you and Niven?" I ask Mom, eager to fill the silence.

I'm making a pointed effort to show interest in her relationship, and I mindlessly pick at my hangnails as I wait for Mom to answer. She moved into the elven lands a few months ago, apparently into the spare bedroom Niven had set up for her while she was still in the human facility.

I think it's a bit peculiar that, as his mate, he put her in a spare room, but I'm not questioning it. The elves have odd customs, especially when it comes to intimacy.

He probably thinks he'll catch on fire if he shares a bedroom with my mom.

"Things are good," Mom says, a dazed look taking over her features. "We've recently gotten into the habit of taking long morning walks together, and I've been teaching him how to cook my favorite human dishes."

That sounds nice. It was never safe for Mom to leave the house when I was growing up, and I'm sure she's loving being able to walk through Niven's lands. My heart tugs as I recall how she and my dad used to take tiny strolls around our background garden.

"You know I'll always love your father, don't you?" Mom asks, seemingly sensing where my thoughts have strayed. "My relationship with Niven doesn't erase my long history with Dave, and your father will always have a place in my heart."

I press my lips together, willing myself not to cry.

"I know that." My voice cracks, and I shake my head before continuing. "I just really miss him."

Mom pulls me into a tight hug, and I mold myself around her as she wraps me in her arms. Her touch is comforting, and I sniffle as she runs her hands down my back.

"I do, too," she admits.

My dad was the best man I've ever known, and accepting that he's gone still feels impossible. It was easy to ignore when there were a million other things going on and I was in a perpetual state of survival, but now that things have calmed and I feel safe, the emotions I've been pushing down since my capture are bubbling up.

My males have been beyond understanding when I wake up crying in the middle of the night because I had a dream about him, and things are gradually getting better, but I can't lie and say I'm not having a hard time accepting Niven.

"I just want you to be happy," I say, pulling out of Mom's arms.

She chews at her bottom lip and pushes a strand of gray hair out of her face.

"Sorry about that!" Echo says, storming into the room. Mom and I step apart, and Echo's steps slow as she glances between the two of us.

"Is everything okay? Do you two need a minute?" she asks.

I shake my head, and out of the corner of my eye, I see Mom doing the same. Echo doesn't look like she believes us, but she doesn't push the subject as she leads us out of the building and back to her golf cart.

My pulse races as I eye the death machine, and I debate calling for Silas as I climb into the back. He'd be here in a heartbeat, but I don't want to get him all worked up over nothing.

Besides, I'm sure Chev wouldn't be pleased to learn one of my males came here. They aren't allowed, and I don't want to get them in trouble. Chev can be petty when he wants to be, and I wouldn't put it past him to find a way to torture Aziel in punishment.

I'm exhausted by the time we arrive at the portal, and Mom asks a shifter to program it to take her to Niven's.

"Goodbye, my baby," she says, stealing the phrase Kato frequently uses with his children. "I'll see you in a few days."

I smile, and she disappears into the blue haze a moment later. The shifter operating the portal then adjusts the settings to take me home, and I give Echo a hug before stepping through.

Aziel's on me the moment I emerge, and he turns off our end of the portal before carrying me into his office. I can't help but chuckle at his crazy antics, and I break out into full-blown laughter when he locks his office door so Silas and Gray can't come in and steal me away.

"Are you feeling a bit possessive today?" I tease.

Aziel huffs, his non-answer all the answer I need.

Chapter Thirty

SILAS

IS THIS WHAT nesting is?

These past few months have been a whirlwind, but it all seems to be coming to a head now.

I lean against the kitchen doorframe, watching Charlie pull everything out of the fridge with surprising haste. The shadows clean it out once or twice a month, but it appears our human is not satisfied with their work. Her belly bumps against the counter as she moves around, the poor female hardly able to do anything without it getting in the way.

She spent all of yesterday rearranging the nursery room, and she's purchased doubles of almost every item we own. She was frantic when we tried to assure her we have everything we need, our female refusing to listen to reason. Her panic got Gray and Aziel all worked up, too, and now the Wrath has ordered our babies new beds while Gray insists on cleaning the floors.

Again.

It's only a matter of weeks before she goes into labor, and with a grin, I approach and hug her from behind. She relaxes into my touch and sighs when I reach underneath her to lift her belly.

She used to hate when Aziel did this, but now she's big and finds comfort in having the weight removed.

"Is everything okay?" I ask, kissing her ear.

Charlie nods, patting my hands that hold her belly.

"Yes. I'm just cleaning," she says, shooting me a small smile.

She knows she's acting crazy, and I find her attempts to hide it cute. She's been wild this entire pregnancy, and there's no use trying to hide it now.

"Silas!"

Aziel's shout travels into the room from his office, but I ignore it. He's impatient.

Charlie leans against my chest, relaxing while I hold the babies inside her. I can't imagine how exhausting it must be to carry that weight around all day, and I understand why she's so eager to give birth. I would be, too, if I were in her position.

"How are you feeling today?" I ask.

She began having contractions last night, but they've been far apart and she says they aren't too terribly painful. She had some false labor pains last week, and I think this is more of the same. I want to feel between her legs to see if she's dilated, but she won't let me.

"I'm feeling like I'm about to explode." Charlie huffs.

She grabs my hand and slides it to the side, and I smirk into the back of her head as I feel one of our babies kick. They hurt her when they do it, and sometimes they make her pee a little, but I can't lie and say I don't find pleasure in seeing and feeling their little feet and fists emerge behind her skin.

Aziel likes it, too, and he somehow convinced Charlie to wear only sports bras as tops around the house so we can always be watching.

It's the best thing he's ever done.

I don't have a crazy amount to do today, my assistants stealing all my work. Gray and Aziel convinced me to hire somebody to help me before the baby comes, and the shadow I chose has been surprisingly helpful. I wanted Rock, but he decided to remain with Gray.

Still, I have more free time now than I ever have before.

"Silas!" Aziel shouts again. "I've got the files you asked for."

I doubt Charlie can hear him, and I sigh quietly before slowly releasing her belly.

"I need to go," I say, pouting. "You can come and sit in my office with me if you want," I offer, fully aware I sound desperate.

Charlie shakes her head. "Maybe. I've got to finish the fridge, and then I'm reorganizing our closet."

Our closet is already organized, but she won't appreciate me telling her that. Instead, I give our bond a playful tug before making my way to Aziel's office. He's tapping away on his computer, but he turns to give me his attention as I enter.

"Have you spoken to her doctor?" I ask.

Aziel nods, pulling out a pile of papers and dropping them on his desk. It's a thick stack, which I wanted, and I happily snatch it up. These papers are filled with documents on human births, and I'm eager to read through them.

Aziel laughs as I spin on my heel and leave his office. Gray passes me in the hallway, the man reeking of Aziel, and he shoots me a toothy grin as he spots the items in my arms.

"You're always so full of worry," he says.

His lips are on mine a second later, catching me off guard, and I return the kiss before pulling away.

"Aren't you supposed to be in Lust?" I ask.

Gray shrugs and glances toward the kitchen, where Charlie clatters around. She curses as something drops to the floor, the noise followed by a loud groan as she bends to pick it up. I can imagine her now, the female taking a wide stance and grabbing her knees as she reaches for the floor.

She's helpless with her belly.

"I've decided to work from home for the next few months," Gray says. "I don't want to miss Charlie going into labor, and I want to be here to help with the babies. Rock's got everything covered in Lust."

That's nice. Rock's been a great help, the demon eager to fill the responsibilities Gray's unable to complete due to his bonds with us. After the incident with Sax, Aziel made Gray limit who and when people could enter his office.

It's no longer a free-for-all, and when it comes to approving performances or anything that requires him to watch sex, Rock is now the one to step in.

The demon seems to love it, and I constantly overhear him and Charlie whispering to one another about his work. She loves the drama, and Rock's more than happy to go into detail about his sexual exploits with her.

He was even in a performance himself last month, and we had to practically drag Charlie away from the portal when we caught wind of her grand plans to sneak to Lust and watch. She claims it was to show her support, and my lips twitch at the memory of Gray taking it upon himself to seek out the demon and demand a photo of his penis for Charlie.

Rock refused, naturally, and Charlie was so mad, she didn't speak to Gray for two days.

She'd been honest when she'd said humans show support by attending events, and she hadn't been sneaking away so she could see Rock's intimate parts.

Aziel was so angry, he popped a blood vessel in his eye.

"What have you…" I trail off as the portal in the hallway lights up, and I turn just in time to see Chev storm inside. He just barely avoids running into the wall, the shifter always dramatic in his entrances. He barely glances at Gray and me as he makes his way to Aziel's office.

I still don't like him, even if my mates do, and I glare at the back of his head. Gray pinches my elbow, but I don't care.

Chev's been coming here weekly to speak with Aziel and provide updates on the females. Readjusting my papers, I spin and follow him into Aziel's office. I want to know what's happening, and Aziel is terrible at remembering and sharing all the details.

He also doesn't ask enough follow-up questions, and I usually have to reach out to Chev for clarity.

Gray follows me into Aziel's office, seemingly feeling the same way.

"It seems we've got an audience today," Chev says, sitting in the chair opposite Aziel's desk.

Aziel chuckles as Gray and I make ourselves comfortable on his couch. This isn't the first time we've interrupted his meetings with Chev, but it's become less common since things with the females began to improve. Most women have been captured and placed in our rehabilitation facilities, and things there look promising.

"We've had six thousand applications for our new facilities liaison positions," Chev blurts out, eager to share the good news. "We have about three hundred females graduating from trade programs this month, and about four hundred have requested to be moved from the facilities into secure housing."

That's amazing.

Chev was adamant we dedicate land for secure housing units, giving the females more freedom while ensuring their safety. We have two in Wrath, but most are in the shifter and elven lands.

Males, including me, aren't allowed on them, but Chev has sent photos. They're small, isolated, female-only communities, complete with everything a person could need. It's not an ideal situation, but it will work to provide females more freedom until the worlds outside the pockets we make for them are safe.

It took Wrath almost four years to reach a point where it was safe for women to be out on the streets among men, and we're hoping we see something similar among the other realms. It'll take the more violent species, like the ogres and dragons, longer, but most others are adjusting well to the new regulations we've put in place.

It also doesn't hurt that they're too terrified of Aziel to go against his law.

Most will obey out of fear, which is better than nothing.

"Is there an update on the women who were rescued from the ogres?" Aziel asks.

Chev grimaces and shakes his head.

"Rehabilitation for them has been challenging," he admits. "Most still don't speak or look males in the eye, and about eighty percent have asked for sterilization."

The room falls silent.

The facilities they reside in are filled with the best therapists and doctors, but most of the women are shells of their former selves. The women rescued from the violent realms hardly leave their rooms, even when we replaced all the male guards with women.

Having a building full of only women is a considerable risk, but it's all we can think to do.

It's starting to look like the ogre-owned females will never leave the facilities, choosing to remain there until they grow old and die. The ogres were into weaker species, so most of those females have short life spans, but it'll still be a long sixty or so years for them.

Aziel clears his throat and flicks a piece of paper on his desk. "What about relationships? Pregnancies?"

Chev snorts. "What about them?" He shakes his head with a humorless laugh. "These women want nothing to do with males, especially on a physical level. A few females have agreed to donate their eggs, and we've been working with the elves on the way to create females in artificial wombs. Now that we know the cause of the decline, they're confident they can figure it out."

Chev straightens in his chair before reaching into the waistband of his leathers, and I turn away as the action exposes himself to the room. Aziel clears his throat, uncomfortable, and Gray cranes his head to get a better look.

I grab the back of Gray's neck and force his head down, refusing to let him see. He's already touched the man with his hand once, and if he grows curious, he can return to those memories. It'll be over my cold dead body that he makes new ones.

Chev hands Aziel a damp, folded piece of paper, and Aziel glares at it before unfolding and reading the contents.

"What's this?" Aziel asks.

"It's not for you, stupid," Chev says. "It's for your scientists. The elves said to share it with them."

I bite my cheeks to stop from grinning, loving when Chev pisses off Aziel. I may not like the shifter very much, but he's an excellent friend to Aziel. They're equally matched, and Chev doesn't give in to Aziel's demands like most people do.

It's good for Aziel to have somebody he can talk to with whom he doesn't share a bed at night. That used to be me, and maybe even Gray, but I'm happy to let Chev step in. Being Aziel's friend can be exhausting, and I prefer being his mate.

Gray wiggles, pushing at my arm until I release the back of his neck. He huffs, poorly hiding his disappointment that he missed the show. I don't understand his recent obsession with Chev, and I have a feeling he's only doing it to try to get a rise out of Aziel.

The incubus is jealous of the friendship.

"And you didn't think to send this digitally?" I ask, gesturing to the note.

Chev's shoulders drop, and he turns to peer at me before returning his gaze to Aziel.

"I can't figure out how to use the photocopy machine," he admits.

Aziel sighs, shaking the paper to air it out.

Is Chev usually this sweaty? Wrath is warmer than the shifter lands Chev is used to, but the man practically *doused* the paper. The rest of his body is bone dry, so maybe only his waistband is bad. The leather they wear is thick.

Shifters don't have much odor when they sweat, but it's still gross.

Aziel drops the subject and begins hammering Chev with questions about the females. Chev answers with ease, surprising even me. For a long time, I assumed the shifters were a dumb species, good for fighting but not much else, but it seems they actually have brains in their large heads.

They've done good work, and their plans are solid.

I wish they'd let me review them. They still refuse to give Aziel and me a complete view of things, and I know Charlie and Gray are keeping secrets. Echo tells Charlie everything, and Gray is kept informed because Lust is paying for the new facilities.

Even Charlie's mom is kept informed through Niven.

The elf is patient with his mate, and Patty lives with him now. I'm not complaining.

"Do you have an update on Mammon and Valentine?" Chev asks, drawing my attention.

Aziel nods. "We've heard reports that Valentine's now living on the coast of Lust, but she hasn't ben causing any issues, so we've left her alone. Mammon's now trying to wage war against the King of Envy, Levia, over some ancient relics, so I assume that's going to be keeping her busy for a while."

Mammon's lost her mind since the death of Vont, and there are reports of her trying to start a fight with a new kingdom what feels like every other week. It's only a matter of time before she turns her attention back to us, but her reputation is so tarnished there's not much worry of her gathering any support.

Something crashes in the kitchen, halting our conversation.

"How's Charlie?" Chev asks, pinpointing the sound.

I blink, my eyes narrowing. I wouldn't say I *like* it when Chev asks about Charlie. Echo comes over weekly to watch movies in our living room with our mate, and if he's so desperate for a health update, he can ask his sister for one.

"Silas?" Charlie calls for me.

She says nothing else, and I push off the couch and head toward the door. Yesterday, she sat on the floor and couldn't get back up, and it's become common for her to summon us multiple times a day.

This whole nesting thing isn't helping, either, the female constantly getting herself into situations and positions she's unable to get out of. I'd like her to stay in bed, but she snaps at me whenever I suggest it. She's as moody as Aziel nowadays.

I quicken my steps as I hear her suck in a shaky breath, faintly aware of the three men at my heels.

Her voice is hushed, cracking. "I think my water just broke."

Chapter Thirty-One

CHARLOTTE

THIS ROOM IS too crowded.

Somebody pushes my hair out of my face, and I blink through my tears as I try to make sense of all the people surrounding me. There are too many, and I lean against Aziel's side as another contraction hits. It feels like my back and lower abdomen are on fire, and I grab at Silas's hand as my body urges me to start pushing.

I knew labor would hurt, but I didn't anticipate this. It feels like these damn babies are trying to rip their way out of me.

Aziel rubs my upper back and kisses my head, his silent support welcome. The poor man barely fits in the small hospital bed I've forced him to join me in, but he voices no complaints as his hips dig into the railing and his feet dangle off the side.

He knows better than to whine.

All three of my males are present, but surrounding them are Chev, Echo, Mom, Rock, and a male nurse I've never met before. A loud groan slips from my lips as the doctor steps into the room, the demon large and imposing.

He makes the space feel smaller than it already does, and

Aziel slides off the bed so I can lie on my back and stick my feet in the stupid stirrups. The doctor has to fight through everybody to reach me, and he almost takes a fist from Aziel as he shoves the Wrath out of the way and places himself between my legs.

I don't like that so many people are looking at my vagina, and I push down the front of my gown to hide it.

The doctor pulls it right back up, and when he shoves some fingers in me to check how dilated I am, I turn to Silas for help. He nods, the man always understanding, and turns toward the crowd at my feet.

"Out," he orders, his tone leaving no room for questioning.

Chev rushes out of the room, the man looking pained. I have a feeling he didn't really want to be here but felt it would be rude to leave. Rock cocks his head to the side, grimacing as he takes one last look at my vagina before disappearing.

That was rude.

Echo pouts, her warm hand landing on my knee before she gives it a gentle rub.

"I'll be just outside," she says, making her exit.

My mom remains, not realizing Silas's order was also for her. I love my mom with my entire heart, I really do, but I need this room to be as empty as possible right now. Having three mates means the room is already crowded, and I can't mentally tolerate the extra bodies.

"You too," Silas says.

Mom frowns, her eyes darting between Silas and me. She opens her mouth, looking like she wants to argue, before snapping it shut when Gray's crackly voice fills the room.

"Get out, Patricia," he hisses.

Things aren't better between them, and he already looks on the verge of tears. He doesn't handle stress well.

Mom lifts her hands in surrender before walking to the head

of the bed. I'm sweaty and gross, and I hold back a sob as she pushes my damp hair out of my face and plants a kiss on my forehead.

"I love you so much, my baby, and I'm so proud of you. Your father would be, too," she whispers. "I'll be outside with Echo."

The mention of my father has my cheeks growing wet, and Mom wipes the tears away before exiting. Gray brings my knuckles to his lips and kisses them as he sits on the edge of the bed, stealing the spot where Aziel was lying just a minute ago.

I groan, another contraction working through me as Silas shuts the door to the room. Despite my pain, I feel like I can finally breathe.

My doctor turns and talks to the nurse, his eyes continuously darting toward a glaring Silas. Silas wanted to deliver our babies himself, insisting he read all about it and is confident in his abilities, but I'm much more comfortable with the professional.

Still, Silas peers between my knees and watches the doctor's every move as if he's the one who knows best. Aziel joins him, listening intently until the doctor says I'm ready to push.

"Are you sure?" I ask, squeezing Gray's hand.

They tried to give me pain medication, but it turns out my good-for-nothing bonds make it so my body works through medicine almost immediately. This would have been good to know before I went into labor, and I let out a low cry when another contraction hits.

Am I going to shit myself? It's been a while since I last used the bathroom.

"Yes, I'm sure, Charlotte," the doctor says, gently urging me off the bed.

I wait for Gray to get on his stool before squatting between his legs. He hooks both his arms underneath my armpits, keeping me upright while Aziel and Silas crouch on either side of me. The doctor wanted me to do this on the bed, but I'd rather do it in a squatting position.

It's supposed to help open my pelvis and allow me to bear down more efficiently, and I need all the help I can get. Demon babies are fucking huge, and I'm going to need all the push power I can get.

Aziel hates when I say *push power*, and I crack a smile as he curls his fingers around my wrist. I can't believe there was ever a time I found his scent unnerving, and I lean into his side and breathe it in as Gray kisses the back of my head.

Another contraction hits, and I clench my jaw and squeeze Silas's hand as the doctor urges me to push.

No baby emerges, and I can't help but let out a disappointed huff.

"Patience, my love." Aziel chuckles, moving my sweaty hair out of my face.

That's easy to say when he's not the one trying to push two oversized babies out of his body.

The nurse rushes around, ensuring everything is prepped and I'm not going into shock. There haven't been many cases of human women delivering demon babies, and they've hooked me up to a million monitoring machines that make it near impossible to move around.

It stresses me out, but my males assure me it's only a precaution. They don't think anything terrible is going to happen.

They'd say that even if they did, though.

We work through three more contractions before my knees turn to jelly and Gray takes over supporting most, if not all, of my weight.

"How much longer?" I cry.

I'm covered in sweat, and Gray helps me wiggle out of my gown to feel some cool air on my skin. It helps, and I lean against his chest as Silas slides a damp rag down my neck.

"A while," the doctor admits.

I groan, and Gray chuckles. *Bastard.*

After what feels like a thousand more painfully useless pushes, there's shouting about a head followed immediately by intense pressure and a cry. My entire lower half is on fire, and I pant as the doctor pulls a baby out from between my thighs and hands it to Aziel.

Oh.

My baby.

It's covered in birth fluids, and its head is shaped a bit like a cone, but fuck if it isn't my most precious treasure. I blink away tears, struggling to clear my vision as Aziel brings my baby to my chest.

I stare down at the red, splotchy baby with a weak smile.

I made that.

"It's a girl," he whispers, turning to show me her front.

I glance between her legs before slowly looking over every inch of her body, imprinting her into memory. She's slightly bigger than a human baby, but she still seems so tiny in Aziel's arms. I take in her stubby toes and rounded belly before landing on her face and freezing.

A loud laugh bubbles up out of my throat before I can stop myself.

Wide, pure black eyes stare up at me.

"She's terrifying," I whisper, cupping her head with a shaky hand.

A few tufty, black hairs spurt out of the top of her head, and I run my fingers through them as I take in her scrunched nose and unblinking, still slightly terrifying, eyes. I love her, evil-looking baby and all, and I watch as Aziel brings her to the nurse.

Gray kisses the back of my sweaty head, and Silas intently

surveils the doctor settling between my legs and preparing for the second baby.

Everybody says this one should be quick, and I sure hope that's true.

I find the sound of my screaming baby comforting, and I glance excitedly at Aziel as he watches over the nurse. He checks the baby's vitals and gives her a quick wipe-down before handing her back to Aziel.

I wanted the gender of our babies to be a surprise, and I can feel through the bond just how happy my males are that it's a girl. Aziel brings her over while we wait for the second to arrive, but he's careful to pull her away whenever I need to push.

Gray and Silas take turns holding her, both smelling her head.

"Is she a fate or a succubus?" I ask, grinning as she's returned to my chest.

It's Silas who answers. "She's a fate."

I knock my knee against his before groaning and doubling over. The doctor urges Aziel to take her away, and I squeeze Gray's hand for dear life as I push.

This delivery is *not* any faster than the first, and I'm about ready to collapse when I finally hear a second high-pitched cry. Gray continues to support my weight, and he removed his shirt at some point so his bare chest is pressing against my back.

Our second baby is pulled from between my thighs and handed to Silas. They're all scrunched up, and Silas smiles down at them before bringing the tiny being to my chest. I spot the penis before anybody says anything, and I beam as I scan my son just as I did my daughter.

I giggle, probably a bit hysterical.

Our son has big, hazel human eyes, and the few strands of hair that sprout out of his head are more brown than black.

"He looks like me," I say.

Gray's chest vibrates against my back, and I stare into my baby's unblinking eyes as he screams in my face. I didn't think our children could have human traits, and I press my quivering lips together to stop from crying as I bring my clammy palm to his belly and feel his heartbeat.

It's beating so fast, and I sob as his chest expands under my fingertips.

"One more big push, Charlotte," the doctor urges. "You're doing so well, and we need to get your afterbirth before you lie down."

He's kind, and he talks me through my final few pushes.

I can feel the second it's out, relief as I've never known it filling me.

Gray carries me to the bed as Silas takes our baby to the nurse. I watch them, blinking back tears as Gray takes it upon himself to clean me. The poor doctor almost gets another fist as he shoves my incubus aside and begins to stitch up my tears, and I focus on my babies to try to distract myself from the pain.

Aziel stands in a corner holding our girl, the Wrath now shirtless so he can feel her bare skin against his. Demon babies don't need the medical care most humans do after birth, and Aziel takes full advantage of that as he hogs our daughter to himself.

"Aziel," I say, holding out my arm.

He frowns, glancing between our daughter and me. "I'm bonding," he pouts.

Still, he steps forward and places her on my chest, finally letting me hold her all on my own.

"What do you want to name her?" Silas asks, approaching with our baby incubus.

Silas puts him in the crevice of my arm, but Aziel quickly snatches him up. Gray continues to focus on me, wiping my sweaty skin with a soft washcloth.

I hum, exhaustion hitting me now that the adrenaline and pain are leaving my system. My entire vagina feels like it's been ripped in half, but I feel better now that the doctor's no longer sticking a needle through me.

Gray pauses to look between my legs, spreading my knees for a better view. I knock my knee against his forehead until he stops.

I gave my males strict orders not to look at my vulva during or after birth. I know they already have, none of them slick in their numerous peeks, but now I plan to enforce it. I know I'm a mess down there, and my males will only panic when they see the bloody, torn-apart skin.

Silas sits on the edge of my bed and touches our daughter, his eyes growing misty as he bends and kisses the middle of her back.

"Her name?" he repeats, turning to me. "Have you thought of one?"

I nod, hoping he likes what I've done. "What do you think of Valeria?"

The room falls silent.

Silas refuses to speak about the fates he knew before most of them were killed, and Rock and I spent months and months digging for information on his birth family. We didn't find anything useful, but it seems all we needed to do was ask Aziel. It turns out he knew Silas's family before they were hunted down and slaughtered, and he's assured us that Silas had a good relationship with his mom.

I'd love to name our daughter after her.

Silas licks his lips, our bond twisting with disbelief. "I'd be honored," he whispers, his voice thick.

His lips are on mine a second later, and I can't help but smile when he pulls away and looks down at our girl.

"I like it," Aziel says, finally taking the initiative to join us.

He sits in a chair before jumping back to his feet, the man too worked up to settle. He begins to pace the room with our son, his fingers lightly prodding at the soft spot on top of his head.

We all watch, and I can tell it's taking everything in Silas and Gray not to tease Aziel for his weird behavior. Especially when he tilts our son's head back and looks up his nose and throat, scanning it for who knows what.

"What about our son?" Gray eventually asks, joining me on the bed.

I shrug, glancing at my males. Do they not want to name him? We've discussed hundreds of names, but Gray and Silas couldn't find ones to agree on. I was open to Ephraim, but Gray is insistent that that's the name of the baby we lost so it can't be used.

"Don't you want to decide?" I ask. "I picked Valeria."

Gray chuckles, feeling our daughter's back before standing and approaching Aziel. My lips twitch as I watch the two, and I let out a small chuckle when Aziel notices Gray's approach and not-so-nonchalantly walks farther away.

"You vomited fifty-seven times in the past eight months. You have more than earned the right to name our children," Gray says, gently stealing our male from Aziel.

Aziel frowns, his fists clenching and unclenching by his sides before he does one of his breathing exercises and follows Gray back to my bed.

Gray sets our boy on my chest before placing a hand on both babies, ensuring they don't roll. My arms are weak right now, the muscles shaking.

"What about David? After my dad," I ask, frowning as Valeria begins to cry.

Aziel swoops her up before turning his back to us and returning to his corner. She settles in his arms as he bounces and whispers to her. The man hasn't given me an ounce of attention since our first baby emerged, and I couldn't be happier.

He loves them despite not being their biological father, and all my fears are squashed as he kisses the tufty hair on the top of Valeria's head. She's still dirty, and his chest is smeared with birth fluids, but he hardly seems to care.

"I love it," Silas says.

Gray agrees, and Aziel is too lost in his own world to give an opinion.

It takes Aziel another ten minutes to calm down enough to join us, his expression full of apologies as he takes in my sleepy face. I don't blame him for getting so distracted, and I shoot him and Silas grateful smiles as they help position the babies for feeding.

Valeria latches on to my nipple almost immediately, but David makes a bit of a fuss. I zone out a few times, exhaustion making it hard to focus, but our boy is latched when I wake back up.

I love how their throats move as they swallow, and I curl my arms around them with a contented grin.

"I did it," I whisper, turning to Gray.

He pauses, removing his cloth from Aziel's now-clean chest as he turns to face me.

"Of course you did," he says. "And soon I'll put another one in you and we can start our hoard."

Aziel raises a brow but doesn't speak up. He's made it more than clear he intends to put the next baby in me, but I have a feeling we all know Gray won't react well to that reminder right now. Emotions are high, and Gray's just excited.

We all are.

Chapter Thirty-Two

GRAY

VAL SCREAMS, HER ear-piercing cries unbearably loud. She kicks at Aziel as he tries to change her diaper, the tiny being unhappy with her dad's actions.

My baby fate is proving to be quite a handful, even at three weeks old, and I watch her and Aziel before sliding my gaze to David. He lies on the floor with a happy grin, staring at the ceiling fan.

Incubus babies are always well-behaved, and I grin as I swoop him up for feeding. He lets out a little whine as he's moved away from the fan, but his happy mood returns as I plop down on the couch and bring the warmed bottle to his lips.

Charlie fed him some breastmilk earlier, but her body's unable to keep up with the needs of two rapidly growing demon infants.

David latches on to the bottle, his nose scrunching as he gets to work sucking down his formula. He eats significantly more than Val, and I squeeze his chunky thighs before glancing back at Aziel. He's finally changed Val's diaper, and he zips up her onesie before joining me on the couch.

Val wiggles in his arms, finally starting to calm her screaming, but she starts up again when Silas steps into the room.

The poor fate looks startled, pausing mid-step. That shock quickly turns to guilt, and our bond pulls as he watches Aziel try and fail to settle Val. It's painful to watch, but my babies gravitate toward their biological fathers. Everything is scent and instinct to them right now, and unfortunately, that often leaves Aziel as the odd man out.

Things will improve as my children grow and no longer rely so heavily upon their senses, but it could be months before we see any change.

I'd be a wreck if I were Aziel, and I'm impressed by how well he's handling the disinterest of my babies.

Silas spins on his heel and tries to leave, but when that only furthers Val's screaming, he carefully approaches and takes her out of Aziel's arms. Aziel kisses Val's head as she's removed, and a second later, he's staring up at the ceiling.

Charlie's upstairs trying to nap, but I can tell through our bond that she's not yet asleep. I'll give her fifteen more minutes before going up and assisting.

Our bonds allowed her body to heal relatively quickly, and even though she's not mentally ready for sex, she still lets me rub her clit whenever she's struggling to relax. The orgasm helps her sleep, and I love the intimacy.

Silas sits in the oversized chair opposite us, his lips forming soundless words to Val as he gets comfortable. A second later, he shuts his eyes and goes still, his body growing stiff at the exact moment Val's does.

Her eyes glaze over, the female trusting her father entirely as she lets him take her to the fated world. Aziel lunges forward to gently shut her eyelids for her, the Wrath always concerned about her eyes drying out.

Silas says it's good for Val to grow acquainted with the fates from an early age. I don't think it would kill him to at least wait until she can support her own damn neck, but both he and Aziel refuse to listen to me when I tell him that.

"Can I help you?" I ask, turning toward the man currently trying to take my baby out of my arms.

Aziel frowns, glancing between David and me before doubling down and snatching the young incubus. David wiggles, clearly annoyed with the interruption to his feeding, before returning to his bottle. I only let him hold David because Val just so brutally rejected him.

"Do you think they'll grow to love me as much as they do you guys?" Aziel asks, gazing at the hand David's placed on my thigh.

His tiny fingers curl around my leg hairs before yanking, the little bastard pulling a good few out. It stings, and I hiss and grab his hand before he can return for more.

"Of course they will," I say, shocked Aziel even needs to ask this. "They're just operating off of smell right now." Cupping David's head, I lean over him to kiss Aziel.

The Wrath doesn't fight it, letting me slip my tongue between his lips in a silent claim. I hate hearing him question himself and the love of our children, and I refuse to release him until he's relaxing and the bond between us is soft again.

David also settles, the tiny demon able to sense the negative emotions in the air.

He's pretty alert, and he can sense whenever one of us is worked up. I'm thrilled by it, and I can already tell he'll be a strong demon. I was a bit frightened when he first arrived, his brown eyes and hair making me worry he'd take on Charlie's human strength, but so far, that doesn't seem to be an issue.

"Charlie told me she's excited to carry your baby next," I whisper, knowing that will cheer Aziel up.

It works, and I grin as Aziel laughs and leans back against the couch.

"I was there when she said it," he says, smelling the top of David's head.

David continues to drink from his bottle, and I watch the two for a moment longer before heading to my office. Charlie was kind enough to give me mine back, my female having stolen it while I was working out of Lust.

I can't imagine going back there like I used to.

I've learned to tune out the noises of the home when I need to, and Rock's doing a great job holding down the fort in my absence.

Well, when he's actually doing work.

The demon is lingering around Charlie and my babies more often than not. He doesn't interact much with David and Val, the man quite awkward with them, but he does seem to enjoy watching them from a distance.

That's much better than Chev, though.

The shifter is constantly up our ass, insisting he hold and play with my babies. He always leaves them smelling of him, too, which I don't enjoy. I like when they smell like my mates, and I especially like when they smell of only me.

Charlie's end of the bond softens as she falls asleep, but I'm sure she won't be out for long. I love how much she loves my babies, but she also needs to care for herself.

That means getting food and sleep, and I make a mental note to have a shadow bring her lunch when she wakes up.

Sometimes I think this entire house would fall apart without me.

I only make it through four emails before Aziel wanders in. His arms are empty, and I stare at them before meeting his gaze.

"Where are my babies?" I ask.

He raises a brow. "*Our* babies, Gray. *Our*."

Whatever. I stare at him, waiting for him to answer my

question. After a few tense seconds, he jerks his head toward the nursery, and I shut my eyes as I listen for the sound of *my* babies' hearts. They're faint from this distance, but I can still make them out. One is sleeping, and the other is on the verge, but it's hard to know which is which.

Val's a good sleeper, and she's usually exhausted whenever Silas takes her to the fated world, so I have a feeling it's she who's out cold. David isn't necessarily a bad sleeper, but he spends more time staring at fans than he does sleeping. The whirling calms him.

"Do you have a lot to do today?" Aziel asks, walking around my desk to see what I'm working on.

I swat him away, not wanting him to see my screen. There's nothing secretive there, but I don't like the nosiness. He and Silas are always in my business, but I'm a grown man who deserves privacy.

Aziel laughs, raising his hands in surrender as he turns and sits on my couch instead.

"Echo's coming over tonight to spend time with Charlie and the babies," he continues, kicking at my rug.

Oh, that's nice.

Charlie's been hesitant to welcome guests since the birth, our female limiting her visitors to her mother and Rock. It'll be good for her to spend some time with Echo. I like the female shifter, even if she always tries to roughhouse with my human.

Aziel clears his throat, drawing my attention. "Charlie has recommended that me, you, and Silas go out tonight."

What? No.

I shake my head, not bothering to hide my annoyance with Charlie's request. I know damn well she only wants us to leave so she can talk trash, and she's got another think coming if she thinks I'll make that easier for her.

If she wants to speak poorly about us, she will do it while I eavesdrop.

I know she has no problems doing that, and I frown at the memory of her telling Echo I was being suffocating. She was seven months pregnant, and I don't think I was wrong to want to take her temperature and feel her belly a few times a day.

"I thought we could go to your bar," Aziel says, ignoring my pointed rejection. "We haven't been in a while, and I bet I can still beat you at pool."

Why's he going along with this? Aziel should be angry Charlie's trying to kick him out of the house. Somehow and someway, I'm being played.

"What are you doing?" I ask, suspicious.

Aziel grins, refusing to answer as he walks farther into my office. He looks good, all tousled hair and big arms, and I lean back in my chair as he sits on the edge of my desk. I wonder if he'll let me fuck him again. As much as he pretends otherwise, he liked surrendering to me. I'm sure we can work out a position that allows him to keep his control.

I can think of plenty off the top of my head, but Aziel can be picky.

"Come on, Gray," Aziel urges, his smile falling when I shake my head again. He scratches the back of his neck, looking awkward before clearing his throat. "Gray, you haven't left the house since the babies were born."

I scoff.

I know I haven't. Why would I leave my babies alone? Just because my mates have found it within themselves to leave for an afternoon or two doesn't mean I need to. While Aziel's whisking Charlie away for a date or Silas is who-knows-where doing fate shit, they should be happy I'm here ensuring our future is safe.

Silas may have worked with the witches to enchant our house when Charlie first fell pregnant, limiting the number of people who could teleport here to only us, but I'd still like to be cautious. It's better to be safe than sorry. That's a human expression Charlie taught me, and I'm taking it to heart.

Aziel sighs. "We're getting worried about you."

I stand, refusing to sit around and listen to him try to make me feel guilty for protecting our children. My apologies for being a family man who loves his babies.

Aziel follows me as I storm out of my office, but I ignore him as I head to the living room. He's never more than a few steps behind me, and it takes everything in me not to spin and shove at him as he quickens his pace to match mine.

I want to relax, but when it becomes clear Aziel plans to join me, I head upstairs instead.

"It's hard to run away from me when you refuse to leave the house." Aziel is mocking me.

I'm going to punch him in the fucking nose.

Aziel continues to taunt me as I hurry into my old bedroom. He doesn't like coming here, claiming the room is forever tainted with my past.

Still, he follows me inside.

"Leave me alone," I snap, spinning and shoving at his chest the second he's through the door.

Aziel ignores me, choosing instead to step closer and crowd me in. I don't appreciate it, and I shove him harder. This time, he jerks, his back hitting the wall. It doesn't make me feel as good as I thought it would, and I make my way to my dresser with a frown.

There are some random trinkets here that didn't make the cut during the move into the wing we all share, and I pretend to take interest in them as I actively avoid Aziel.

He sucks in a slow breath, probably trying to calm himself down, and I watch to ensure he's not about to try to lunge at me before turning my back to him. I'm ready to scream when I hear his footfalls a second later, the man not taking the thousand hints I've thrown in his direction as he wraps his arms around my waist.

The touch feels good, and I can't resist leaning against his chest.

"Nothing bad is going to happen, Gray," Aziel whispers. "We're worried because we care. You've always been so independent, and we don't want to see you lose that." His lips meet the back of my neck as he speaks. "Come out with Silas and me tonight. It's been so long since we did something together, and I miss it. We don't have to go to the bar. We can go to one of the Lust shows you pretend not to like."

He trails a hand down my body, but I push it away.

"I've already spoken to Charlie about this, and she's more than happy with whatever you decide," he promises, misunderstanding my apprehension.

"I'm just not ready to leave home yet," I admit.

Aziel kisses the back of my neck.

I know what he's doing, and I'm determined not to give in when he prods me through our bond. I'm hesitant to let him in, unsure how much of my thoughts I want him to see, but after another few nudges, I give in. Aziel never used to ask, the Wrath often choosing to force his way into our heads whenever he wanted to know what we were thinking and feeling, and I should reward him for actually asking.

We probably never would've gotten him to change if it weren't for Charlie and her scary pregnancy anger.

There's intense pressure as he worms around in my head, and after a moment, he pulls out and squeezes me. I know what he saw, and I swallow past the lump in my throat as I tinker with the items on my dresser.

I've tried leaving the house, but every time I start to teleport, I'm overcome with panic and have to stop.

It feels like my heart is trying to burst out of my chest, and I can't seem to suck enough oxygen into my lungs. I'm scared of what will happen when I'm gone, and the more I've been getting in my head about it, the harder it is for me to leave.

"What if we start with something small?" Aziel suggests. "Charlie is insisting we purchase outdoor playsets for the children. You haven't gone outside yet, have you? What if we walked through the back yard and picked a spot to put them?"

I'm grateful Aziel isn't teasing me for my fear, and I press my lips together before giving a curt nod.

I can handle going into the back yard. It's not too far away, and the connection to the baby monitors should still reach.

"No monitors." Aziel interrupts my thoughts. "Charlie is a capable mother, and she'll kill you if she learns of your spying."

I don't like that, but I choose not to argue as I give another nod. I'm sure I can get Rock and Chev to come over during my absence. They're strong, and I'll assign each one to a baby.

That'll work.

Aziel chuckles, the man probably still in my head, before he pulls me onto my old bed. The frame groans under our weight, the screws loose, but that's easy to ignore when Aziel's crawling over top of me like a bitch in heat.

Chapter Thirty-Three

SILAS

FUCK.

It takes me a moment to understand what's happening, my mind groggy from sleep, but as the warmth covers my mouth again, I reach up and curl my arms around the thighs on either side of my head.

Charlie's legs are smooth, and I slide my hands up the sides of them as I blink open my eyes and stare up at her.

The room is dark, and Charlie gently curls her fingers into my hair before guiding my mouth to her sex. I'm more than happy to please, and I lick at her sensitive skin with a low moan. She tastes good, always does, and I savor every second of this as I fuck her with my tongue.

Gray and Aziel sleep quietly on either side of me, but it's only a matter of time before they wake. I hope they're jealous when they see how good I'm making our female feel. She could have gone to any of us, but tonight, she chose me.

Aziel finally convinced Gray to leave Wrath for the first time tonight, and I can only imagine how much Gray's anxiety and Aziel's forced patience wore them both out. They were only gone for a few hours, but I'm sure it was exhausting.

Who knew all it would take to get Gray to leave was the promise of Aziel buying him things, and I'm eager to see what the incubus picked out at the elven shopping center. I saw a bag from one of their tech stores, and I hope whatever he bought is for me.

He knows I like that stuff.

I dig my fingers into Charlie's hips before sliding them around her waist and down her ass. She didn't tell me not to touch her, and I'm going to take advantage of that.

The plug I put in her last night is still there, and I give it a few gentle pushes as I flick my tongue over her clit. She's wearing one of the bigger ones, and I fucking love it. I'm desperate to be inside her, ideally with my cock, but I'd settle for my fingers and tongue.

"Charlie, let him breathe," Gray scolds, unsurprisingly the first to wake.

He rolls onto his side to better watch us, and a moment later, his fingers join mine at her ass.

He wants in there, but it's mine.

An accidental whine slips from my throat as Charlie listens to Gray and rises, but she's sitting back down at my complaint. I don't need to breathe anything that isn't her pussy.

She's fucking soaked, and I tighten my hold as she rocks forward with a low moan. When I told her I enjoyed being used, I wasn't anticipating her waking me up in the middle of the night riding my face, but I'm sure not complaining.

This is all I've ever wanted.

Charlie tugs at my hair as Gray slides down the bed and pulls off my underwear. I'm already hard, and my hips twitch as he takes me in his hand. He gives me a few slow strokes, and I groan as another calloused hand soon joins in.

Aziel's touch is rougher, probably on purpose, and I squeeze my eyes shut and try to shove my tongue deeper into Charlie's pussy.

I want to live inside her.

I continue working my tongue over her, my licking sloppy as I savor every second. Her thighs tense around my head, the first sign she's about to cum, and I bring my attention to her clit in the way she loves.

My female is going to finish all over my face.

Gray takes me into his mouth, no doubt trying to distract me as he swirls his tongue around the head of my cock and licks up the side of my shaft. He likes getting me in trouble with Charlie, and I refuse to let him win as I bring my focus back to her.

She's so close.

My hips jerk as Gray grazes his teeth over Aziel's mark, and the infuriating incubus giggles as I lose my rhythm with Charlie for a brief moment. He'll see how funny it is when she's turning her need to punish on him.

Aziel sits up, his black eyes on Charlie before he reaches forward and pulls her off my mouth.

She screeches as she's abruptly moved around, but the second she notices it's Aziel's doing, she settles and waits. He's got her wrapped around his finger, and I watch with wide eyes as he nudges Gray aside and sits her over my cock.

He kneels behind her, and Charlie gasps as he reaches for her plug and pulls it out.

"Aziel," I warn him.

My words go ignored, naturally.

"I think you're ready for his cock, baby," Aziel says.

Gray flops onto his back and begins to touch himself. I gaze at Charlie, ensuring she isn't uncomfortable. She's nervous about taking me in her ass, and I don't want her to do something she isn't sure about.

The plugs I've been putting in her are large, but I'm bigger.

"Do you think you're ready, baby?" Aziel asks, kissing Charlie's shoulder.

His lips trail over the mark I left on her, and he makes eye contact with me as he sinks his teeth into it. Gray is possessive of his mark, but I don't mind watching Aziel put his mouth on mine.

The column of Charlie's throat bobs as she gulps.

"Yes," she whispers. "I want it."

My pulse races, and I run my hands up her thighs as Aziel reaches over us both in search of lube. Gray always keeps some lying around, and a second later, the Wrath grabs my hand and covers my fingers with it. I'm happy he isn't doing this himself, and I slide my hand between Charlie's legs and ease two fingers into her ass. This isn't the first time I've fingered her there, but it will be the first time it's done with the intent to go further.

She's nicely stretched from the toy, just as I thought, but she still wiggles as I rock my digits into her.

"Does that feel good?" I ask.

She gasps, her cheeks flushed as she lets out a pretty little moan and nods.

"Do you want my cock?" I continue, grunting when Aziel takes hold of me.

He rubs lube all over my shaft, and I carefully pull my fingers out so he can line me up. He's gentle with Charlie, teasing her with my tip before urging her to sit. She drops down a few inches before tensing, and I grab Aziel's thigh in a silent gesture for him to slow.

He does, and he strokes the length of me that isn't inside her while we wait for her to adjust.

"I'm going to lie on my back once you're comfortable, and you're going to get on top of me," Aziel tells Charlie, his voice low. "Silas is going to fuck your ass from behind, and I want you to take me in your pussy at the same time."

Charlie loves it when he tells her his plans, and she audibly gulps as she clenches around me.

"Will you both fit?" she asks.

Aziel glances at Gray.

I smile, enjoying how he turns to the incubus for help. Gray props himself up on his elbow, one hand still curled around his shaft. He loves when Aziel's inexperience comes out, and he makes no attempts to hide it as he moans and twists his fist around his length.

"Of course they will, baby," Gray tells Charlie. "They're going to be very careful, though, and they're going to fuck you slowly." He shoots both of us a sharp look, the silent message clear.

He'll be stepping in if we're too rough with her—not that I would ever be.

Aziel doesn't look pleased, but he understands Gray knows best.

Charlie lowers another inch, and she pauses to adjust again before sliding down some more. I'm aching, and I tighten my grip on her hips as I fight the urge to thrust up into her. It feels so fucking good, and her ass is so tight.

Aziel rubs her back and whispers quiet compliments until she's seated entirely on me.

Charlie carefully rocks her hips, testing me out, before planting her hands on my chest and lifting a few inches. I force myself to remain still as she eases her way back down. Aziel cups her breasts from behind, his fingers finding and playing with her nipples, while Gray continues to pleasure himself on the side.

I give her a few minutes to get used to the feel of me before sitting up and pulling out. I wait for Aziel to lie down before guiding Charlie on him. Aziel's already hard, and he moans as she grabs his length and guides it to her entrance.

I lick my lips, watching with Gray as she sinks onto Aziel.

"Fuck." Gray moans.

That's exactly how I feel, and I pour some more lube on my cock before crawling over the top of Charlie and bringing my tip to her ass. She gasps as I slowly ease myself inside, and I make brief eye contact with Aziel as she clenches around me.

She's nervous, that much is obvious, and I run my hands down her back until she gives us the go-ahead to begin fucking.

"Okay," she gasps, her voice hoarse.

Her body feels so tight as it stretches to accommodate Aziel and me, and I lick the salty skin of her shoulder as I rock into her. Aziel copies me, quickly finding a rhythm where he thrusts up whenever I pull out. Charlie seems to love it, our female crying loudly into Aziel's chest.

"Do you like this, baby?" Aziel grunts, cupping her chin to hold her head still. "Do you like taking two of your males at once?"

I lean back to watch her stretch around me. She takes us so well, and the feeling of Aziel's cock rubbing against mine through her thin walls is fucking fantastic.

"I've been dreaming of this since I first met you," I admit, reaching around and rubbing her clit. "You've got such a beautiful ass, and…" I pause, grunting as I rock into her a bit harder.

"It's—"

I thrust in again.

"—all—"

Aziel curls his hand around her neck and pushes until her back meets my chest.

"—mine."

Charlie's back arches, our poor female speechless as she takes her males. Gray takes advantage of her position as he kneels and brings his cock to her mouth, rubbing himself against her lips until she opens up and takes him.

She gags almost immediately, and Gray only gives her a second to catch her breath before he's fucking her throat. Her arousal is practically suffocating, and Gray feeds as we all find pleasure in her.

Her hands slide from Gray's thighs to Aziel's chest, and I can tell she's close to cumming as she begins crying around Gray's length. Her ass squeezes me, the muscle so fucking tight as I push in deep and find my release. Charlie screams as I fill her, her entire body shivering as she cums.

"Open your mouth," Gray orders, pulling out and fisting himself.

Charlie quickly obeys, and she stares at him wide-eyed as he strokes his length and cums on her tongue. Aziel watches, holding my thighs so I can't pull out as he thrusts inside her.

He grabs Charlie's face and brings it to his a second later, ignoring the cum covering her as he smashes their lips together. Gray moans as Aziel shoves his tongue into Charlie's mouth, the Wrath tasting the incubus as he jerks up against me and cums.

Aziel twitches as he finds his release, the thin wall separating him and me leaving little hidden.

Charlie shivers as I pull out, and I smile as I grab her plug and slip it back inside her. I want her to remain full of me, and maybe if I'm lucky, she'll find herself wandering around the shifter lands with it in.

I want them to know what I've done.

"That was fun," Gray says, kissing me.

He's moving on to Charlie and Aziel next, and I chuckle as he forces his mouth on both. Charlie sits up as Aziel pulls out of her, and I wrap an arm around her waist to hold her still as my lips graze her ear.

"Did you enjoy that?" I ask, reaching down to feel her swollen holes.

She spreads her legs, letting me prod.

I push Aziel's hand away when he tries to join, but that only causes him to yank Charlie out of my arms. She giggles as Aziel tosses her on her back and rolls over the top of her. Gray is busy searching for towels with which to clean us, and I flop onto my back as I wait for him to return. He gets pissed when I try to take care of myself, and if wiping my dick off is what brings him joy, all the power to him.

I make eye contact with Gray as he returns to the room, but I can't stop a loud laugh from bubbling up out of my throat when he hears a muffled, infant cry and drops the wet towels. They land on the floor with a splat, and he scrambles to put on some underwear before rushing to the nursery.

Charlie looks confused, her ears not picking up on the cry, and I happily take over cleaning while Aziel explains that Val is fussing.

I listen in as Gray soothes her, half my focus on the nursery while I kneel on the bed and wipe Charlie down. I clean Gray's cum off her cheeks and neck before swiping the towel between her thighs, getting her clean enough that she won't drip everywhere on her way to the bathroom.

"Is everything okay?" Charlie asks, our female just as neurotic as our incubus.

I hum, my head cocking to the side as I listen for Gray. He's walking back toward our room, but his hurried pace tells me he's returning empty-handed. He moves slowly while carrying our children, the man afraid of tripping and dropping them.

He's never tripped in the entire time I've known him, demons not prone to those kinds of issues, but he still worries.

"They're fine," I say, spinning and searching for my shirt. "Val let out one little squeak before settling herself. Gray's being dramatic."

Charlie grins as I find the shirt I wore today and pull it over her head, happy to have her surrounded by my scent. It's my turn to pick out what she wears to sleep, and I'll be damned if I lose a night because of some late-night fun.

"I am not dramatic." Gray huffs, storming into our room.

"No, you aren't," I say, hoping to prevent the defensive argument he launches into whenever we comment on his need to monitor our children obsessively.

We thought Aziel would be the one who went crazy, especially after how intense he became toward Charlie during her pregnancy, but surprisingly, he's better than Gray. He's still a bit extreme, constantly checking in on Val and David, but I'm no better, so I keep quiet.

Epilogue

Two Years Later
AZIEL

CHARLIE SHUFFLES INTO my office with a huff, my mate on the verge of tears as she readjusts the wiggly, crying baby in her arms. The tiny thing screams bloody murder before craning her neck and sinking her teeth into Charlie's bicep, and I jump up to help.

The toddlers hanging off her legs latch on to me as I near, Val and David planting their butts on my feet while they tightly wrap their arms and legs around my ankles. They giggle as if they've just gotten away with some grand heist, and Charlie rolls her eyes before rising to her tiptoes and kissing my chin.

"I'm late for lunch with Mom and Niven, and Gray and Silas are nowhere to be found," she says, grimacing as she pulls her thoroughly gnawed-on arm out of Cassia's mouth.

Our baby Wrath is a menace, and now that she's beginning to teethe, she's sinking her tiny teeth into anything she can reach.

I grin, obsessed even when she uses me as a chew toy. I heal fast, and I've gotten used to the dull pain of her pointy baby teeth.

We thought Val was bad, but Cassia is significantly worse. If she's not screaming, she's biting, and in the rare instances she isn't doing either of those two items, it's only because she's feeding.

More than once, I've caught Gray crying as he tries to soothe her, the poor incubus unable to comprehend why his baby won't settle. He's taking Cassia's sour attitude harder than anybody, and I instinctively reach out to stroke him through the bond.

He's never been good with stress.

"Go on. I'll take the monsters outside to play," I say, pulling Cassia into my arms.

Charlie shoots me a relieved smile as she hands our baby over, and I chuckle before patting Charlie on the butt.

"Goodbye, my little loves," Charlie says, crouching to talk to the children sitting on my feet.

They press sloppy kisses to Charlie's cheeks before returning to my ankles, their attention spans short. Charlie doesn't seem to mind, and she tousles their hair before bouncing back to her feet and rushing out of the room.

I glance at the two demons on my feet. This is a new activity they've gotten into, one I'm sure Charlie regrets teaching them. It's a game human children play, but now it's all Val and David want to do.

The pair fight as they hang on to my legs, neither bothered by the baby screaming in my arms. I bounce Cassia as I make my way to the back yard, walking slowly so the toddlers don't fall off my feet. They screech and readjust their grip on my ankles with each step.

Gray typically watches them over lunch, but he's been busy this week.

Besides, I don't mind the excuse to take a break.

I was beginning to miss my little gremlins.

They release my legs and rush to their playset as I approach the back door, the two racing toward the large, wooden structure. I sit on the grass with the still-crying Cassia. She's already been fed, and her diaper is clean, but I still lift her butt to my nose just in case.

Nope. Definitely clean.

She curls her tiny fingers around my hair as I sniff her butt, and I wince as she yanks on the strands the moment I try to lower her. It hurts, and I do my best to be gentle as I pry her fingers loose. I'm not very good at this, always unsure how much force is too much, and I let out a sigh of relief when Gray pushes open the back door and rushes toward me.

He chuckles as he opens Cassia's hands.

"She really hates your hair," he says, sitting beside me.

I nod, more than aware of this. If she keeps it up, I might have to shave my head. I'd rather have that than be forced to endure her tearing it out piece by piece. While I might heal quickly, my hair grows slower, and I don't want to look patchy.

It's not a good look for the King of Wrath to be bullied by a six-month-old child, although maybe my people would like that. They're pleased I now have a claimed heir, and they've been obsessed with her since birth.

I set Cassia on the ground so she can crawl and explore. She wiggles back and forth, pawing at the grass before making herself busy with some weeds.

"My meeting with the council ran long, but Rock's got everything handled for the rest of the day," Gray says, leaning his head against my shoulder. "Did Charlie seem mad when she left?"

I grin, shaking my head before reaching out to grab Cassia as she tries to shove a weed into her mouth. She seems to take that as a personal offense, and her face grows red as her bottom lip wobbles. Gray swoops her into his arms and tips her upside down before she begins to cry.

One of her rare giggles emerges as Gray plays with her, and I turn to Val and David. They'll be out here for hours if we let them, the two loving the outdoors.

I enjoy listening to their laughs and screams as they make up little games and challenges with one another, and even though there's a ridiculous amount of work I need to get done today, I'm in no hurry to get up.

I'm afraid I'll blink and my babies will be adults.

Charlie's content with our three right now, and even though she's made it more than clear she's open to having more in the future, it won't be until our current babies are grown. Our bonds grant her the liberty of time, a benefit she's eager to use. Her body now ages as ours do, and she'll have hundreds, if not thousands, of childbearing years.

Gray went practically feral when Charlie declared her desire to wait, the incubus seemingly having gotten it in his head that our female would continue popping out children until the house was overrun with them, but he hasn't said anything to her face. Instead, he rants to Silas and me like the scared little male he is.

Charlie won't hear it, and I secretly hope he slips up and demands more to her face. I'd quite enjoy seeing her put him in his place. She's better at it than Silas and I are, and it's always entertaining.

"Did Silas tell you Val went into the fated world by herself for the first time yesterday?" Gray asks.

I frown. No, he did not tell me that.

I don't like the idea of her traveling there without Silas. He claims the fates will keep her safe and it's good she feels comfortable there, but I don't trust one word that comes out of his slimy mouth.

Val can barely wash her hands, let alone travel through some secret, exclusive dimension alone.

Gray snorts, reading my poorly concealed anger. "Calm down, Wrath."

I clench my jaw and spin around as Silas's scent fills the air.

He's sitting on the other side of me a second later, his knee pressing against mine as he pats Cassia's butt and squeezes her arm. She stills at the touch, evaluating Silas before losing interest and returning to her game with Gray.

"I don't think it's safe for Val to go to the fated world by herself," I say, picking up the weed Cassia was trying to eat earlier.

It's covered in her spit, and I grimace before dropping it back on the ground.

"I was going there by myself at her age." Silas grabs my shoulder. "It's normal and healthy."

I don't believe it, but I don't have much of an argument. I'm not a fate, and I don't understand her needs as much as Silas. I probably won't understand David's needs when he hits puberty, either, and I shiver at the thought of him seeking the type of nourishment Gray does.

I want all my children to remain virgins as I did, waiting until they find the person—or people—they want to bond with, but I know that's not reasonable. Especially not when Gray and Charlie are so insistent we let them explore when they're ready.

I've lost all control over my fucking household.

"Daddy!" Val and David scream from the playset.

Gray hands Cassia to me, laughing as she immediately sinks her teeth into my arm. She's only got two tiny teeth sticking out of her gums, but she's sure learning how to use them. I pull my arm from her mouth before sticking my fingers into her armpits, loving how she screams and wiggles.

Demons aren't ticklish, and I have to say this is my favorite trait of Charlie's our children have picked up. Each of them has a spot or two that makes them go wild, and I can't stop a cheesy grin from spreading over my face as Cassia grabs my wrists and pushes my hands away.

Gray makes his way toward the playset, but he halts when David pops his head out from behind the small, wooden house and holds out his palm.

"No! Daddy Silas!" he explains, rejecting Gray.

Silas is up a second later, more than happy to be summoned.

Gray was brought to tears the first time he was rejected, but now he takes it in stride as he raises his hands in surrender and returns to me.

He pauses to glance behind me, and I spin just in time to watch Charlie step through the back door. Her pants are unbuttoned, a clear sign she just ate a giant meal. I debate telling her she's forgotten to button her pants, but I decide against it as she moves to the spot Silas once occupied and sits down.

"Echo invited me to hunt an Ucka with her and Chev tomorrow," she says.

What? I haven't heard one word of this, and I was just speaking with Chev earlier this morning. Why didn't he tell me? I'm a better hunter than most, if not all, of the shifters. Charlie touches my lips, forcing the corners of them up into a smile.

"You should take it as a compliment they didn't invite you," she says, pulling a freshly picked weed out of Cassia's mouth. Cassia snaps at Charlie, visibly angry by the thievery, but she quickly forgets and moves on "You're very big and strong, and you're able to kill the Ucka too easily. They want a challenge."

Gray chuckles, patting my back.

They're making fun of me.

"Besides, we all know you'll be lurking in the woods stalking Charlie anyway," Gray adds.

I push his hand off me. It was one time, and I was careful to keep my distance so I didn't interrupt. Charlie wouldn't have known I was there if Chev hadn't opened his big mouth and pointed me out.

Besides, I enjoy seeing Charlie hunt, and my mate loves how I fuck her into the forest floor afterward.

"Plus, Echo still doesn't like you," Charlie continues, finally sharing the real reason I wasn't invited.

You hit a female in the throat once, and suddenly, she's got a lifelong grudge against you. I still believe it was her fault for running through the portal like that, and if Chev could get over it, then she should, too.

Silas yells, throwing himself on the ground as Val lunges for him. David holds a plastic sword to his throat, keeping him in place so Val can steal his shoes. It's a fake game Gray taught them when he saw Silas wearing his favorite boots one day, and it seems to have stuck.

The two toddlers successfully steal Silas's shoes before sprinting toward Gray. They're so proud of themselves, and Silas props himself up on his elbows to watch them hand their treasures to Gray. Gray levels his stare with Silas as he accepts them, the silent threat loud and clear. He's not above using the children to get what he wants, especially regarding his clothing.

"Mom and Niven also agreed to babysit next weekend," Charlie continues. "So we can go to the wedding."

Gray shoots me a sideways glance, but I ignore it. He struggles leaving our children with anybody, even Patty and Niven, but Charlie's beyond excited for the wedding. Many rehabilitated females are finally beginning to acclimate into society within the safer lands, and this is the first wedding of one.

We were invited, and Charlie's made it clear she intends for us to attend. I'm not particularly looking forward to attending the ceremony of a couple I've never met before, but I'm not going to be the one to ruin Charlie's mood.

This is a big deal.

Many women have decided to undergo artificial insemination with the help of the elves, and several females have already been born, but very few women have entered relationships. They want little to do with men, and this wedding is a step in the right direction.

"I can't wait," I say, pulling Charlie into my chest.

Gray gnaws at his bottom lip before shifting his attention back to Silas, David, and Val. This will be good for him. He can't hover around our children forever.

"I love you." Charlie sighs.

I smile and curl my arm around her back for a better cuddle. Her pulse races, and our bond warms in response to my touch. I love her reaction to me, even after all this time.

"What about me?" Gray asks, lying on the ground next to Cassia.

Our baby crawls on his chest, her tiny hands struggling to grab hold of Gray and pull herself up. Charlie reaches forward to help, placing a hand on Cassia's bottom and giving her a boost.

"Yes, I love you too." Charlie laughs.

Gray relaxes, content, as Silas carries our two toddlers over, one tucked under each arm. They swat at one another across the fate's torso, their tiny nails digging into the other's arm. For being an incubus and a fate, they're quite violent with one another.

I love it.

They sprint back to their swing set the second Silas sets them on the ground, the two not ready to stop playing. I don't know where they find the energy, but I hope all this playing means they won't make too much fuss at bedtime.

Val's recently decided she's never tired, and David insists we read him at least two books before he even considers getting into bed.

Gray shuffles so he's resting his head on my lap, and Silas kisses Charlie before taking a seat on the other side of her.

I slip my fingers into Gray's hair, mindlessly brushing out the strands as I watch my family. Never in a million years did I think I'd find myself this content, and if I'd been told when I first met Charlie that this was where we'd end up, I wouldn't have believed it.

Charlie and Silas continue to kiss until David voices his disgust, prompting the two to break apart. Charlie has something planned for Silas tonight, and I'm eager to watch it play out. It's been a few days, and Gray's getting hungry. I can feel it through the bond, a slow pulsating in my lower abdomen that urges me to feed my incubus.

"I've been thinking a lot about this, and I'm ready to put another baby in you," Gray blurts out, turning to Charlie.

I perk up, interested in watching this interaction.

Charlie rolls her eyes, nudging Gray with her toe.

"Nice try," she laughs, taking it in stride.

Gray shrugs, not looking surprised, before reaching over and patting Charlie's belly.

It prompts her to look down, and I take great pleasure in seeing her eyes grow comically wide as she realizes she's been walking around with her pants unbuttoned. She scrambles to fix it, her cheeks a bright shade of red, and I lie back on the grass and stare at the sky.

It's clear today, but I only get a second to enjoy it before the shadow of a wobbly toddler blocks my view.

Cassia falls on my face, her knee digging into my neck.

I hiss. "Fuck!"

I pick Cassia up, and Charlie kicks my foot.

"Aziel," she scolds. "Watch your language!"

I personally think Cassia should watch where she's burying her knees, but I'm going to keep that particular thought to myself.

I kick Charlie right back and plop Cassia on my chest so I can try to remove the dandelion stem hanging out of the corner of her mouth.

I love them.

* * *

END OF BOOK 3